He tightened his grip in her hair until Nisha winced and gave a little cry. With his other hand, he reached down and seized her thigh, curling his fingers and digging his nails into her flesh.

"No!" she cried. She struggled in his grip.

Suddenly he released her. "Not this time," he said quietly. "Maybe not next time. But it will be some-time soon." He studied her for a moment, like a man examining the beauty of a flower before squeezing it in his fist. Then he grunted and turned away.

Nisha forced herself to take slow, even breaths. *Not this time*, she thought, imagining herself impaling the warrior on a spear or crushing his face with a rock. And then, just as suddenly, her husband's face flashed in her mind, his gentle smile, his loving eyes, the shape of his lips. She remembered him looking down at the shape of her body, her brown-tanned skin peeking out between the panels of deer hide. They had been together for three years, but it had always been easy for him to arouse her—and for her to excite him. He had always wanted her. He was with her still. . . .

CHILDREN OF THE SUN

CHILDREN OF THE SUN

Charlotte Prentiss

AN ONYX BOOK

ONYX
Published by the Penguin Group
Penguin Books USA Inc., 375 Hudson Street,
New York, New York 10014, U.S.A.
Penguin Books Ltd, 27 Wrights Lane,
London W8 5TZ, England
Penguin Books Australia Ltd, Ringwood,
Victoria, Australia
Penguin Books Canada Ltd, 10 Alcorn Avenue,
Toronto, Ontario, Canada M4V 3B2
Penguin Books (N.Z.) Ltd, 182–190 Wairau Road,
Auckland 10, New Zealand

Penguin Books Ltd, Registered Offices:
Harmondsworth, Middlesex, England

First published by Onyx, an imprint of Dutton Signet,
a division of Penguin Books USA Inc.

First Printing, November, 1995
10 9 8 7 6 5 4 3 2 1

To Andrew, Bonnie, John,
Moira, and Wendy.
For all of us,
the best is yet to come.

PART ONE

Abduction

Chapter One

Nisha woke suddenly in the night, and she felt afraid. Her eyes sprang open and she found herself taking quick, urgent breaths, fighting a tightness in her chest and throat. Her skin was prickling and her pulse was beating fast.

She clutched her rabbit-pelt blanket and peered into the darkness, trying to understand what had happened. She could see nothing. She strained her ears, but she heard only silence.

She sensed the warm, heavy form of her husband, Jorlor, sleeping beside her on their bed of bison hide. Her boy-child made a tiny noise as he shifted in his sleep where he lay on his mat on the floor. There was no sound from outside her little home. Even the wind was still.

She reached out to her son and touched his face very gently, feeling the warmth of his breath on her fingertips. If he had cried out, surely he would still be crying now. He wouldn't have fallen back into quiet slumber at exactly the same moment she opened her eyes. So, what had woken her?

She lay for a long time, calming herself. Faint gray dawn light started creeping around the edges of the panel of woven beargrass that covered the window in the wall opposite her bed. Soon, everyone in her village would be awake, and Winnor, the shaman, would be coming for her child to prepare him for the naming ceremony. This was supposed to be a special day, a day of gladness and celebration. There was no reason in the world why she should be afraid.

Nisha swung her legs down to the cold stone floor. She groped in the dimness, found her deerskin robe, and pulled it over her head. Then she bent down and picked up each of her moccasins, turning them over and shaking them before she put them on in case a scorpion had taken refuge in one of them overnight. Finally she crept to the doorway, ducked around the flap, and emerged into the chill morning air.

There was a sandy path outside her door, with little box-shaped homes clustered close either side, their walls fashioned from rough-hewn sandstone blocks. A wooden ladder stood close by. Nisha took hold of it and climbed to the top of her home. Her moccasins made a faint scuffing noise as she moved up over the domed roof of hard-baked mud supported by ironwood branches beneath.

Her village had been built atop a mesa—a wide pillar of red rock that stood alone overlooking a vast expanse of desert. From her roof she could see in all directions across a shadow-land whose stillness was so complete, the only sound she could hear was her own breathing.

The sky above was still totally black, but there was a jagged line of light along the mountains far to the east. As she watched, a sliver of brilliant gold appeared.

Faintly, in the distance, she heard a gentle cooing sound. It was a white-winged dove, she realized. She smiled with sudden pleasure. The doves had finally arrived from the south. There would be no more spring rains now.

The bird cried again, and this time there was an answering call from its mate. Then other birds woke and started to sing as the sun lit up the land.

Somewhere in the village, a baby squalled. A dog barked. Nisha heard someone walking to the cistern and splashing water on his face.

"Nisha?"

The voice came from directly below. It was Winnor, standing outside her home. He was a tall man, slender and graceful, like a deer. He possessed great magic, though, which made him seem stronger in his way than the most physically powerful hunter.

Today he looked especially intimidating, wrapped in his ceremonial lion skin, with his face painted brown and black and his hair matted with sand so it stood out like a huge mane that trailed down to his waist.

Nisha hurried down the ladder, stopped in front of him, and inclined her head respectfully. "Greetings, Winnor."

He eyed her a moment, and for some reason she felt the same anxiety that had gripped her when she woke. But that made no sense; Winnor was a good man, a healer who cared for his people. And even though he would have her son with him for the rest of this day, there was no danger in that. The child had already survived his initiations. He had been shown to the Sun Spirit last year at the summer solstice, and he had been offered to the Winter Spirits six months later. Both of the spirits had smiled upon him. He was a strong, healthy child.

"Something troubles you," said Winnor.

It embarrassed her that he could sense her thoughts so easily. "Just a dream that woke me this morning," she said, "nothing more. Let me fetch my boy for you."

Nisha ducked back into her home. She could see the room clearly, now, with the infant lying on his mat. She noticed with surprise that he had opened his eyes but was completely silent, looking up at her solemnly as if he understood everything that was about to happen. Even when she picked him up and swaddled him in his deerskin pouch, he said nothing.

She carried the boy outside. "May the Cat Spirit speak clearly," she said to Winnor. It was common knowledge that he gained most of his power from the spirit of Mountain Cat; it spoke through him whenever an important decision needed to be made.

The shaman took the child and studied him for a moment. "You've raised him well," he said, and beneath the shaman's face paint, his lean face widened in a smile.

"Thank you, Winnor."

Her boy finally decided to speak. He let out a little cry, and he squirmed and turned his head toward Nisha. She put her palm on his forehead. "Be still, little one. Mountain Cat is going to speak for you. There's nothing to fear." Although—was it his fears or her own that she was really trying to calm?

"You are fortunate, Nisha," said Winnor, as he shifted the child's pouch to the crook of his arm. And she knew that this was so. Only one infant in three lived to his first birthday; the others might die of childhood illnesses, or they would be claimed by Sun Spirit or the Winter Spirits as unfit for the tribe. Nisha knew some women who had mothered as many as six children, and had lost them all. But this boy was her first, and tonight, he would be acclaimed as a member of the tribe.

"He'll be well cared for," said Winnor, turning away with the boy in his arms. "I will see you tonight, Nisha, at the ceremony." He walked away, then, among the clutter of little stone buildings.

People were emerging into the brightening day. They saw Nisha and called out greetings, and she saw how they smiled at her. A naming ceremony was a special source of happiness for everyone in the tribe. So why did she feel that a little pit of darkness was still gnawing inside her? She waved to her neighbors, then went back into her home.

"Nisha?" Jorlor called. She found him sitting on the edge of the bed, pulling his robe on. He was a dozen summers older than she was, but still he looked young. As far as she was concerned, the tiny lines around his eyes made him seem wiser, not older. He was broad shouldered and well muscled, a swift runner and a good hunter—yet he wasn't the kind of man who ever felt a need to show off his strength. In fact, she had chosen him because he was so calm, slow to anger, and quick to forgive. She needed that kind of stability to balance her own impulsive nature. So many times, she would run to him full of excitement or distress—and he always listened patiently, then said a few words, and she found her powerful emotions evaporating, leaving her wondering what she had been so worked up about in the first place.

"Winnor has taken the boy?" Jorlor asked.

"Yes. Just now."

"So we can enjoy our day of rest."

She nodded quickly. She felt a sudden, urgent need to be outside, away from the village. Perhaps that would help her to escape her strange mood. "The weather's clear, and the rains have gone," she said. "Will you walk with me?"

He rubbed his jaw. "There won't be much hunting. The game is still thin from the winter."

"But I wasn't thinking about hunting." She fingered the thongs tying her robe, and she gave him a certain smile. She saw him looking down at the shape of her body, her brown-tanned skin peeking out between the panels of deer hide. She and Jorlor had been paired for three years, but it was just as easy to arouse him now as it had been when she had first chosen him as her mate. And this was another reason why he was the right man for her: He always wanted her.

He reached for his spear and his hunting knife. "I'll bring these anyway," he said, with his eyes still on her body, "so it'll look as if there's some purpose to our journey."

"You're afraid of what people may think of us?" She laughed. "I think it's too late to worry about that."

The only way from the top of the mesa to the desert was down a vertical cleft in the rock. Nisha knew it so well, she could find her way even in total darkness. Her fingers moved instinctively to the little handholds that had been cut into the sandstone, and she didn't even think about what she was doing as she braced herself between the faces of the cleft and half slid, half lowered herself to the desert floor.

She stood there and squinted up. Jorlor was passing a

bottle down to her on the end of a leather rope. The bottle
was woven from agave fibers and lined with mesquite
glue to make it watertight. She caught it and slung it over
her shoulder on its carry-handle fashioned from deer hide.
The bottle was empty now, but before they returned to the
mesa, they would fill it from the river that flowed in a little canyon close by. No one in her tribe would ever think
of returning home without bringing water to add to the
communal supply in the cistern.

Jorlor threw her his spear and a little pouch full of
pemmican and corn bread. Then he climbed down to join
her.

She caught hold of him and hugged him tight, enjoying
the warmth and strength in his body against hers. "I'm
glad you're coming with me," she said softly. Her hand
dropped down, and she found herself running her fingers
around his flank, slipping them in between the panels of
his robe. She was surprised by her own boldness, so close
to the mesa where her tribe made its home. Yet here she
was, touching him intimately, feeling him grow hard
against her palm. He grunted with surprise, then quickly
drew in his breath.

She drew back and giggled, covering her mouth with
her hand. Her cheeks flushed red as she saw the look in
his eyes. "Later," he said, "we will finish what you've
started here." For a moment he seemed fierce, but then he
slid his hand around behind her neck and up into her
braided hair, and he pressed his mouth against hers. When
he drew back, he was grinning.

She smiled to herself as she started walking beside
him. Sometimes she wondered if there was something
wrong with her for needing sex so often. But whenever
she talked about it to the other women of her tribe, they
just told her to count her blessings. Many of them con-
fided in her that they had gradually lost interest in their
husbands, and saw nothing especially wrong with that.

Together, Nisha and Jorlor walked out from the shadow
of the mesa, into the morning sun. The rough, red, sandy

soil was dotted with scrub grass, but on this spring morning it was mottled with color, too. Fed by the rains and
woken by the warmth of the spring sun, thousands of
flowers were opening. Nisha saw white primroses, orange
poppies, yellow desert sunflowers, little red ocotillo
blossoms—the desert had literally bloomed overnight.

High in the brightening sky, two hawks circled in an
updraft, scanning the land for ground squirrels that had
woken from their long winter sleep. From the top of the
mesa came distant sounds of village life, as women did
chores and men sharpened their knives for the hunting in
months to come.

A hundred paces from the mesa, Nisha and Jorlor came
upon a thin figure squatting alone on the sand with his
spear resting across his knees. Nisha recognized him as
Helchar, an elder who had been a fine hunter before his
eyesight had begun to fail.

She saw a small hole in the ground just in front of him.
"Rattlesnake, Helchar?"

He glanced up at her and grinned without humor. "Yes,
Nisha. Almost struck me yesterday. We'll dine on him tonight. Fine gift for you and your boy on Naming Day."

"Thank you," she said.

Helchar looked from Nisha to Jorlor. "Good hunting,"
he said, with a sly smile.

"To you, too," Jorlor said gruffly.

The old man was still grinning at them as they walked
away toward the west.

They climbed a tumble of rocks that looked as if they
had been thrown by some huge spirit hand. A shallow,
narrow canyon lay just beyond, cradling a river that was
swollen with spring melt from distant mountains. Insects
were humming busily, and on a smooth, flat slope that ran
down to the river's edge, women were pushing pointed
sticks into the soil, planting a score of corn seeds in each
hole that they made. An elder in ceremonial dress walked

among them, and in the cool, dry desert air, Nisha heard
him muttering prayers to the Sun Spirit.

She and Jorlor detoured around the scene of the planting, not wanting to disturb the sacred ritual. They crossed
the river downstream, wading waist deep. Nisha splashed
her face and drank from her cupped palms. This bounty
was rare indeed; for most of the year, the river was a
sluggish, shallow creek.

They moved on across the plain, walking slowly, pausing often to look at the carpet of blossoms. Finally they
came to a low hill. There was lush grass growing here,
just as Nisha remembered it. The grass was especially
thick and tall where there was a narrow gully in the land.

They were far from the mesa, now, and hidden from
view. She cast down her bottle and threw herself into the
grass. She sprawled on her back and looked boldly at
Jorlor while she loosened the thongs that tied her robe.
Slowly she peeled the edges of her robe apart, till she was
completely naked before him.

Jorlor watched her steadily as he set down his spear. His
movements were slow and deliberate, and she watched the
muscles moving in his arms and shoulders. She felt a tingling warmth growing inside her. This was the feeling she
loved most, to be desired by him and to feel her own need
growing in return. She felt like one of the blossoms out on
the desert, opening its petals to the sun. The world seemed
to shrink around her till she was aware of nothing but Jorlor and the sensations in her own body—the warmth of her
skin, the heaviness of her breasts (as if they were literally
swelling with desire), and a moistness gathering between
her thighs.

Jorlor cast his robe aside and stood naked in front of
her. Slowly, deliberately, he kneeled down, placing one
knee either side of her waist. The tall grass waved around
them in a breath of wind, and from high above, Nisha
heard the high-pitched whistling cry of a red-tailed hawk.
She glimpsed it, a speck circling against the bowl of blue,
and she wondered if it was watching them. Then she

wriggled lower between Jorlor's thighs, till she could tease and rouse him with her mouth.

She closed her eyes and the world turned warm red. His skin was hot under her touch, and she felt the tension grow in him. She reached around behind his hips and pulled him toward her, taking him in deeper. She heard him make a little groan.

Then let him go. She wriggled up and opened herself to him, lying on her back with the cool grass stalks against her shoulders and buttocks. He fell on her and entered her, and she clenched her fists, seizing handfulls of the grass. She gave a cry as he started thrusting, and she pushed against him vigorously, making their bodies slap together.

He leaned forward, pinning her to the ground, and she felt totally possessed by him. She cried out again as the sensations surged and crested and her body clenched on him, as if she wanted, somehow, to keep him there and never release him.

His hands gripped her shoulders almost painfully, in a little spasm, and then he, too, reached his climax. He gave a long, deep sigh as he gradually relaxed, and then he slumped down into the grass beside her, breathing heavily.

For a long time, neither of them spoke.

"Maybe this year you'll bear me another boy-child," Jorlor said softly.

Nisha opened her eyes and saw him staring up at the sky. His face seemed totally at peace.

"If Mother Moon wishes it," she said. The Moon Spirit, after all, controlled all the changes in a woman's body.

Jorlor was silent for a while longer. "Sometimes," he said, "I feel this is more than I should have."

She rolled over and pressed against him. "It's not right for you to say things like that."

He shrugged. "Life can be unkind," he said.

She made a little irritable sound. Jorlor had lost his first wife to the coughing sickness less than a year after the two of them had been paired. He had spent several years alone, doubting that he would ever have another woman, till she had chosen him as her mate. Even now, he still seemed unable to trust his good fortune.

"I'm here, and I will always be here with you," she told him. "You'll have many years of happiness. Why can't you believe in that?"

"You've never known real misfortune, Nisha," he told her. "You've been lucky so far, but luck comes and goes."

She was beginning to feel impatient. This was the side of him she liked least. His calm, accepting nature made him easy to be with—but sometimes it made him too fatalistic about his life. She was not like that herself; she believed that a person gained nothing without reaching out for it. "Sometimes we make our own luck," she said. "Like when I chose you. I wanted you, and I got what I wanted."

He smiled faintly. "You are still young."

She shook her head angrily. "Nineteen years isn't young. And you're not so old, either. At least, you don't have to be if you choose not to. It's all a matter of how you feel inside."

He opened his mouth to speak, then froze. His eyes narrowed. He was listening for something, she realized.

"What is it?" she whispered to him. Then she heard it herself: a faint rustling that was different from the background noise of the wind wafting through the grass. Jorlor started to sit up, but she pressed her palm against his chest. She straightened her leg till her toes touched his spear. Cautiously, quietly, she dragged it up to him.

Still lying in the grass, he turned the spear till he held it across his chest. He waited a moment, still listening.

The rustling sounds stopped. Whatever animal it was, it might have heard them move.

Jorlor waited for a long time. Nisha felt tension growing inside her. She lacked his patience. If she had been here on her own, she would have leaped out of cover almost immediately.

But like any wise hunter, Jorlor never exposed himself if he had a choice. Like old Helchar, he could wait by an animal's burrow for a whole day if he had to.

When he finally sprang up onto his feet, he moved with no warning at all, making her flinch in surprise. He crouched forward and turned quickly, first one way, then the other, his eyes darting to and fro, peering just above the level of the grass. His spear was up on his shoulder where he could cast it immediately.

He grunted. Slowly, he stood up straight, so that his chest was above the grass. He strode forward, letting the spear drop to the level of his hip.

Cautiously, Nisha followed him. She saw what he had seen: a place a score of paces away where the grass was bent and broken. A large animal had been there.

"Mule deer?" she whispered.

"Perhaps." He nodded toward a path that had been trampled, leading away from the area. The bent blades clearly showed that someone, or something, had run away from them.

Jorlor glanced around one last time, then squatted down, studying the ground. It was so rough and stony, she doubted he would find any tracks.

He pointed. "Look."

There was a sandy patch that was still a little damp from the rains. When she examined it closely, Nisha saw the faint, shallow imprint of a moccasin. She eyed it for a long moment, feeling confused and uneasy. "It seems someone followed us out here," she said. "Old Helchar seemed to guess where we were going. Maybe someone else—one of the young hunters—"

He shook his head. "The moccasin is not from our tribe."

Nisha felt cold inside. She shook her head, angry with the way that her anxious emotions threatened to spoil the warm, bright spring day. "How can you be sure?"

"Stitching, there." He ran the tip of his finger around

the depression in the soil. Tiny dents were barely visible where thongs had pressed into the sand.

Nisha wished she could argue with Jorlor, but now she saw the imprint of the stitching, she realized that he was right.

He stood up and dusted specks of sand from his fingers. "Maybe one of the Gray Mountain people."

"But why should they come here to our land? We mean them no harm."

Jorlor shrugged. "Of course not. And they mean no harm to us, either. Why do you say that?"

"Because—" She broke off, not knowing how to explain the coldness that was still gnawing inside her. Her tribe lived in peace with its neighbors. In the Old Times, men had turned against one another, but that was so far in the past, it was beyond living memory. The Gray Mountain people to the west, the Deer Hunter tribe to the east, the Silver River people—all their neighbors lived in harmony with one another and with the land, trading once or twice a year, sometimes marrying into one another's clans.

"Maybe a young hunter strayed farther than he intended," said Jorlor. "We're not far from Gray Mountain territory. Perhaps he saw something, or heard something." He smiled faintly at Nisha. "He came to look, and he saw what he shouldn't have seen, and then he got scared of being discovered, so he fled." He planted his spear in the ground, then bent and picked up his robe.

She watched him putting it on. The sun was warm, the birds were singing, and the land was laden with spring's bounty. Truly, she told herself, this was a fine day to be alive. She went to Jorlor and once more she hugged him, pressing her cheek against his chest, listening to the steady beat of his heart. This time, though, his strength wasn't quite enough to overcome the foreboding that nagged inside her.

Chapter Two

At sunset, the people gathered in a space on top of the mesa just beyond their cluster of little homes. There was a great slab of white limestone here, and as the sun-streaked sky slowly faded and the land was plunged into shadows, the table of rock seemed to glow alone in the growing light of the moon.

A small fire burned, roasting rabbits and ground squirrels on hardwood sticks. The fire was small because wood was scarce in the desert lands and the People of the Mesa had long since learned to make do by burning dried animal droppings. Still, the orange light touched people's faces, and in the dancing radiance they looked eager to enjoy this special night.

Nisha greeted her mother, Taenar, and hugged her tightly. "Thank you, child," Taenar said, stroking Nisha's thick black hair, "for giving me such a strong grandson." She smiled fondly at Nisha and then kissed her on each cheek. "I pray to Sun Spirit that he will live long."

"This is good," said Rargnor, Nisha's father. He patted her shoulder once, twice. For him, this was a significant gesture—an unusual display of emotion. He tended to be a stern, silent man, and she always felt it had been a disappointment to him that she had flourished while his two boy-children had both died before their first year. Still, that was the will of Sun Spirit, who had claimed them both. In the face of Sun Spirit, what good did it do a man to nurse his anger?

She looked up into his face, hoping for something—a

smile, perhaps. But he just patted her shoulder again, then turned away.

She felt a pang, but she had long since learned to armor herself against her father. Jorlor was standing close by, and his presence was all she really needed to restore herself.

She had returned to the mesa with him late in the afternoon, and they had not arrived empty handed. Jorlor had surprised three ground squirrels hiding at the base of an ocotillo bush, feasting on its little red flowers. Two of the squirrels were roasting, now, at the fire. And Nisha had brought back a double handful of fruits that she had gathered from a cluster of prickly-pear cactus. She passed the fruits among the villagers around the fire and kept one for herself. She held it out to Jorlor between her finger and thumb, so that he could score the spiny red skin with his flint knife. Then she peeled the skin back and gorged herself on the sweet flesh inside. She turned to Jorlor and kissed him, sharing the fruit between their mouths. Around them, their neighbors whooped and laughed and clapped.

A basket was passed from person to person, full of fire-baked patties made from ground corn and acorn paste. Then there were strips of dried venison that someone had hoarded through all the winter months. And someone else handed around a roasted agave shoot. Each villager took a turn peeling away a layer and chewing the molasses-colored skin.

"People!" It was their chieftain, Ilu, calling to them. He clapped his hands three times, and gradually their happy chattering died down. They turned expectantly.

He stood with his two sons and his wife squatting on the rock behind him, and he looked carefully at each of his people in turn. There were almost fifty of them, altogether: men, women, and children sitting in a semicircle under the nurturing face of Mother Moon.

"The Rain Spirit has refreshed the land," said Ilu. "The Sun Spirit has blessed it with life. We give thanks." He picked up a handful of dried ears of corn, each one the size of a man's thumb, and cast them into the fire. The villagers murmured their approval.

"We praise the spirits for feeding us and protecting us," Ilu went on. "And we praise the Old Ones, our forefathers who built our homes here on the mesa." His voice was frail and his old eyes seemed to have trouble seeing in the moonlight, but his people loved him no less for that, and everyone listened respectfully, even though his words were familiar from a hundred other feast nights.

"In the Old Times," Ilu went on, "men ran wild across the land. From my grandfather I learned what his grandfather had told him: the story of What Used to Be."

Everyone knew this story and could recite it word for word, just as easily as Ilu. But hearing it was part of the ritual. It reaffirmed the way things were. The villagers listened with expectant faces.

Ilu cleared his throat and clasped his bony hands. "In the beginning, the land was heavy with game. Bison grazed as far as the eye could see. The grass grew green, and even the summer days were cool. The spirits were generous with their gifts."

Everyone sighed and nodded.

"The first men were fools," Ilu went on. "They didn't listen to the wisdom of the spirits. They killed without reason. They even turned their spears against one another, till Sun Spirit became angry with their foolishness. He punished them by parching the land till there was no grass left for the game to eat. Is this not so?"

There was a murmuring of agreement.

"Then Sun Spirit chose a man named Grom who was wiser than the rest," Ilu went on. "He gave to him a sacred thing. A black knife, an enchanted blade that would kill all his enemies. Sun Spirit told Grom to make peace instead of war, and live in harmony with his fellow men. Sun Spirit said that if Grom was truly wise, he would never need to use the enchanted blade. And so long as the blade never tasted any blood of man or beast, Sun Spirit said he would give Grom a special, sacred place to live, safe from all enemies, here on this mesa." Ilu nodded slowly. "And so it was." He reached up and took hold of something that hung on a thong around his neck. It was a slim black triangle that gleamed in the moonlight. He pulled the thong up and over his crown of white hair, and held the triangle high.

"From Grom, through all the generations, this knife has never been used against man or beast. Always, we have honored our bargain with Sun Spirit. And always, he has let us live in peace with our land and our neighbors."

The people sighed happily now. They clapped their hands, once, twice, and a third time. The ritual was complete.

"All right, now." Ilu looped the thong back around his neck. "There is a boy-child who is ready for naming." He blinked and frowned for a moment. "Nisha's child." He nodded to himself, pleased that he had remembered her without having to be prompted. "Winnor! Is the boy ready?"

The shaman had been waiting in the shadows. He moved forward, still clad in the skin of a mountain lion but also wearing many ceremonial necklaces of painstakingly colored porcupine quills woven together with agave fiber. His sanded mane of hair was decked with white feathers.

Nisha leaned forward quickly as she heard her child cry. She saw the boy then, still swaddled in his deerskin pouch, in Winnor's arms.

The infant squalled louder as Winnor handed him to Ilu, and Ilu held him high for everyone to see.

"When was this child born?" Ilu called out.

"One year before this day," Winnor answered.

"And at the summer solstice, did you place him before Sun Spirit?"

"I did," the shaman said.

"And did Sun Spirit take this child?"

"No. Sun Spirit tested him, but at the end of the day, the child was still alive and strong."

Ilu nodded solemnly. "And in the winter solstice, you offered him again?"

"For one day," said Winnor, "he was placed where the Winter Spirits could speak to him."

"And did they take him?"

"They, too, spared him," said Winnor. "It was a harsh winter. Five children were offered, but this was the only one who lived."

"Good," said Ilu. "His strength has been proved by the spirits. He is worthy of our people. And so, now, you have named him?"

"I sat with him and the women elders," said Winnor. "We fed him and praised him, and I ate blood root and listened to the words of Cat Spirit. And Cat Spirit told me his name shall be Orc."

"Orc!" the people shouted out, while the infant struggled and cried.

"Does he have a guardian spirit?" Ilu asked.

"His guardian spirit will be the spirit of the deer," said Winnor. "I spoke with the Lion Spirit, and he told me so."

The people shouted happily. Many men who were blessed by Deer Spirit became good hunters. Nisha blinked, feeling surprised and moved. She reached for Jorlor's hand and gripped it tightly.

"Good!" cried Ilu. "Orc, son of Nisha, has joined our tribe. I say it, and it is so." He fumbled with the deerskin pouch, opened it, and pulled the struggling child free. Little Orc bellowed louder and waved his arms and legs, while Ilu held him high, and the people cheered.

Nisha was crying now. She felt Jorlor urging her to stand up. Clumsily, she got to her feet and stepped forward. She reached out, took her child from Ilu, and hugged him to her.

Much later, while Jorlor still sat with the rest of the people and sang songs around the fire, Nisha went to her home and placed her child on her own bed of bison hide. Orc would share it with them now, from this night on. No more would he sleep on the pad on the floor.

The people of her tribe had left little gifts of food for her. She tried to tempt Orc with some warm corn paste, and he swallowed just a little before he turned to her breast. Well, there was no harm in letting him have her milk tonight. There were still many days left to wean him.

She heard a footstep at the doorway. Nisha looked up with surprise and saw Winnor standing there. He had shed his robe, combed the sand from his hair, and washed the red dirt from his cheeks. He was just another man now, not much older than Jorlor, yet still with a sternness in his face that spoke of his special powers.

He squatted beside Nisha and pulled out a little pouch. "Deerskin," he told her. He tied it on a thong around little Orc's neck. "Deer Spirit will watch over him, now."

"Thank you, Winnor," Nisha said. She hesitated. There were questions in her mind, but there was something about the shaman that always made her reluctant to ask him anything.

"Speak, Nisha," he said.

She was surprised by the gentleness of his voice. She gave him a quick, cautious look, and found that his sternness had softened slightly. He genuinely seemed to want to hear what she had to say. "I was wondering," she began. "You know, I have always tended to ask too many questions, and the elders get impatient with me—"

He smiled faintly. "I know. But I will not be impatient, Nisha. Certainly not on this night."

She flashed him an awkward smile. "Thank you," she said. She tried to compose her thoughts. "When I listen to Ilu's stories, even though I've heard them so many times, sometimes I seem to hear them in a new way, and I wonder about the Old Times. I wonder if—if it was *really* so. When you speak with Sun Spirit or Cat Spirit, do they ever tell you—"

Winnor placed a hand on her arm. Nisha jumped from the contact, then smiled with embarrassment. "Some things are not meant to be spoken of," he said softly.

"I don't mean to be disrespectful," Nisha went on in a low voice. "I just want to know. Was this tribe really chosen by Sun Spirit? Was there ever a man name Grom, and did he really found this tribe? And is it really his knife that Ilu wears?"

Winnor grunted. He shook his head, then sighed. "There are many stories," he said in a low voice. "And every tribe has a different tale to tell. One thing I have learned, though, is that all the stories speak of a time before the beginning, when people lived in another place, which they left to come into these lands."

Nisha nodded.

"As for the knife," Winnor went on, "the elder women have a tale that they tell only among themselves, which says that Sun Spirit gave the knife to a woman who ruled our tribe, not a man."

Nisha felt shocked. This was far more than she had expected to hear. "Can it be true?"

"Of course not." Winnor gave her a strange smile. "Ilu is our chieftain. He has already told you what is true."

Nisha studied the shaman's face. She didn't know what to say.

"It would be a strange idea, wouldn't it," Winnor went on, "for a woman to rule our tribe."

"Strange indeed," said Nisha. "Men are stronger, after all."

"But still women have their own strength," Winnor went on. "Look at you, Nisha. You chose Jorlor. You claimed him even though there were elders who disapproved because he was so much older than you. But now you have the son you wanted, and the life you wanted. Who gave you these things?"

His eyes were unblinking, almost ghostly in the faint moonlight that shone in through the window.

Nisha moved uneasily. "I—no one. I took them for my-self."

"So are you more powerful than the male elders of our tribe?" He didn't wait for her to answer. He stood up and brushed dust from his robe where it had trailed on the floor. "Women have power, Nisha, even though it may not seem to be so. The Moon Spirit is strong in you. Moon Spirit enchanted Jorlor, so he serves you now. Do you understand?" He turned toward the door. "It's good you asked me questions," he said. "Perhaps we will talk more, you and I." Then he frowned at her, and she felt the full weight of his stern gaze. "But we will only speak more if you agree not tell anyone. Not your father, your mother, your husband, or your child. Understand?"

She nodded quickly, feeling dizzy and bemused by what had happened. "Yes. Yes, of course."

He gave her a curt nod. He turned and walked out of the room without another word.

Later, when Jorlor had joined her and was lying on the bed with Nisha and their child, she still found the sha-man's words echoing in her head. Why had he chosen to speak so frankly to her? What game had he really been playing? And why had he told her that they would speak again?

"Is there something wrong?" Jorlor asked, frowning at her.

"Nothing." She shook her head quickly.

Jorlor looked down at little Orc, lying on the bed be-tween them. "He seems happy now."

Orc was sleeping quietly. Nisha looked down at him—and for some reason, she found herself remembering what she and her husband had found in the tall grass. "Jorlor," she said. "Do you think we should have told anyone about the footprint?"

He grunted. "Not tonight. This was a feast night. In any case, it doesn't matter. Someone strayed onto our land, then ran away." He shrugged.

She nodded silently. Still, she wished she had mentioned it to Winnor.

"Are you happy, Nisha?" Jorlor asked softly.

She dragged her attention back to him. "Of course!" she cried. She smiled and kissed him quickly on the cheek. "I'm very happy. I have everything that I always wanted."

"Good." He nodded, then lay back on the bed. "So do I."

Chapter Three

Nisha dreamed of Moon Spirit. She saw a face like a mask, round and radiant, so silver-bright that it hurt her eyes to look upon it. The features seemed to shift and shimmer, like ripples in a pool. "Wake, Nisha," Moon Spirit told her. "Wake. It is time."

Nisha didn't understand. She felt warm and happy, sleeping with her husband and her child, and she knew it wasn't yet morning. "Later," she muttered in her sleep.

"Nisha, wake up!" Moon Spirit's voice grew louder, and it was edged with urgency.

Nisha tried to murmur another protest—but there was something over her mouth. Warm skin, roughened by wind and sun and hard physical labor. Suddenly sleep fell away from Nisha's mind and she found herself in her home with Jorlor pressing close behind her, his hand covering her lips. "Wake up!" he was whispering urgently, his lips touching her ear.

She reached up to pull his hand away. "What is it?" she whispered, turning to face him. She felt confused, and the dark feeling of fear was leaping up inside her again.

"Listen."

She froze, straining her ears. There was a faint rasping sound—a footstep on rock. Nisha drew in her breath.

"Someone has climbed the mesa," Jorlor whispered. "Maybe more than one person." He sat up and fumbled for his spears. She heard a rustling noise as he pulled on his robe. "I should have listened to you," he said, "when we found that footprint yesterday."

She blinked and pushed aside the rabbit-pelt blanket and found her own robe. "Why would people come here at night?"

His hand suddenly gripped her shoulder and squeezed hard. Once again, she listened. This time she heard someone breathing heavily—someone who wasn't used to the climb from the desert below. There were more stealthy footsteps.

"Who was on watch tonight?" Nisha asked. "Why doesn't he sound the alarm?"

"Embar," Jorlor muttered. "He probably fell asleep." He seized Nisha's wrist. "Listen to me. Take our child and run to the Sacred Tree. Hide on the ledge there, and you'll be safe."

Only one tree grew on the mesa. According to legend, it had been there for all of time. Just beyond it, there was a short drop to a ledge that would be barely big enough for her to crouch on.

"You think these people mean us harm?" she whispered. She found the idea almost inconceivable. Travelers rarely passed this way, and they were always friendly, always willing to trade.

He grunted. "It's best to be cautious."

Jorlor was always cautious, she reminded herself. He lacked her faith in the goodness of life. She shouldn't be so alarmed by him. Still, the idea of strangers up on the mesa frightened her. "What about you?" she asked.

"As soon as you go, I'll sound the alarm. Quickly, now! Through the window." He helped her up, and she dropped through the window, behind the house. She turned and reached up, and Jorlor passed her boy-child out to her.

"Quickly!" Jorlor hissed to her again.

She glanced around in the darkness, feeling confused. The moon had set. There was only starlight to guide her, and she couldn't tell if anyone might be lurking amid the rocky outcroppings on top of the mesa.

Cautiously, she started walking. She still felt confused.

Her people had always lived here and always would live here. Ilu possessed the sacred knife, and it had never spilled blood. Sun Spirit watched over his people. The thoughts chattered in her head as she stumbled over the mesa to the meeting place where the fire had been built. She strained her eyes in the darkness and finally saw the Sacred Tree, its spidery branches silhouetted against the night sky. She hurried to it, seized its trunk, and tried to draw strength from it. Orc was awake now, squirming and protesting. "Hush!" she urged him, gripping him tighter as she edged forward.

"Awake!" It was Jorlor's voice back among the houses, shouting so loud, it made her flinch. "People! Wake up!"

Nisha dropped down onto her knees, slipped off her moccasin, and felt with her bare foot for the edge of the mesa. She found it and dropped her legs down. The ledge was just below. She had to be careful. Beyond it, there was a sheer cliff. She set little Orc on it first, still wrapped in his pouch. Then she lowered herself. A root of the Scared Tree looped out from a crack in the sandstone; she grabbed it and held it as tightly as she could.

Nisha heard people calling out sleepily, wanting to know what was going on. Then there were other voices—men yelling to each other in an accent that she had never heard before. Suddenly there was a war cry, a gutteral yell so terrible and full of blood lust, it chilled her. And then there was an agonized scream.

Nisha peered out from her hiding place. She could see across the mesa to the cluster of houses, but the light was so dim, she couldn't tell what was happening. She heard people stumbling out, shouting to each other. Someone cursed, then there was a thud, the sounds of a struggle, followed by women screaming and running feet.

She felt a terrible pang. She shouldn't be hiding like this. She should be by Jorlor's side—and yet, she had to protect her child. The screams and shouts were a cacophony now. She heard a clink of flint against stone, cries of pain, curses and moaning.

Someone scrambled up onto the roof of a house, and she saw his silhouette briefly against the stars. Someone else went up after him, but was thrown backward. She heard his body hit the rocks below. Nisha sobbed at the thought that the victim might have been Jorlor.

Someone was begging for mercy. The attackers voiced their war cry once more. Nisha couldn't stand it any longer. She ripped one of the thongs from her robe, tied it around little Orc's wrist, then lifted him, set him beside the tree, and tied the other end of the thong around its trunk. "Stay there, and be quiet!" she whispered to him, even though he had no idea what the words meant.

She could barely see his face, a pale shape staring up at her in the night. He made a little whimpering noise. She pressed her fingers to his lips. "Shhhh!" she told him.

Before she could allow herself any second thoughts, she turned and ran lightly across the limestone slab. She grabbed a dry bramble branch, thrust it into the embers of the fire, and waited impatiently for it to light. Then she ran on, holding the branch high. The flames sizzled and crackled, shedding a sudden dazzling radiance.

The battle seemed to be going on in the main path between the houses. She went around behind them, scrambled up onto a boulder, then managed to climb onto someone's roof. She held her torch out—and its light revealed a terrible scene. There was a mob of people hemmed in by the rows of houses. Men were flailing at each other. More of the intruders were climbing up to the top of the mesa from the ground below. She saw one of them stare up at her, point at her, and shout a command.

A warrior was hauling a bundle of spears up over the edge of the mesa. These men had hoped to gather and arm themselves before anyone discovered them, she realized. Jorlor had spoiled that plan.

One of the invaders seized a spear, took aim, and hurled it at her. She cried out in surprise and dropped down to her knees. She felt the shaft hiss past her.

"Nisha!" It was Jorlor's voice. He still lived!

She peered over the edge and saw his face turned up toward her.

"Get away!" he shouted. "Do as I told you!"

She opened her mouth to answer—but the invaders suddenly rushed forward, holding their spears in both hands and stabbing them into the confused mob of villagers. There were terrible screams. Nisha watched in horror as she saw the people of her tribe falling and bleeding, clutching themselves as their blood spurted from under their hands.

Jorlor turned to face the aggressors. He raised his own spear—but a shaft came hurtling over the heads of the men in front of him. It struck him in the throat with such force, its flint head emerged from the back of his neck. He gave a terrible gargling scream and fell backward.

"Jorlor!" Nisha screamed. She dropped the flaming branch. It fell down into the melee, showering sparks. She threw herself off the roof onto the attacker who had speared Jorlor. Nisha felt the sudden shock of physical contact with the man as she landed on his back, curled her fingers around his face, and tore at him in a frenzy, trying to take out his eyes.

He threw her off him and she fell down among the crush of people, and her ears were filled with screams. The man she had scratched reared up, touching the scratches on his face and cursing. Nisha got up onto her hands and knees and butted her way through the mob till she found Jorlor. Quickly she reached inside his robe for his knife. But it had gone. Then someone caught her by the neck in a fierce grip. She was lifted and thrown against the wall. Her head smacked against the sandstone and she screamed with shock and pain.

There was chaos all around her. The people of the mesa were trying to retreat, but the invaders had placed themselves all around the cluster of homes. The villagers were hunters, not warriors; they knew nothing of hand-to-hand fighting. They had no room to aim and throw their spears out of the melee—but the invaders could easily throw their spears in.

Nisha tried to turn around, but someone grabbed her by the neck and slammed her against the wall again. She glimpsed his face. He had a broken nose and an ugly, crooked smile. "Give me a thong!" he shouted to a man nearby.

Nisha found herself suddenly facing the wall while the man tied her wrists tightly behind her. She moaned in distress, wishing she had done as Jorlor told her. She should have stayed in hiding with her child. She had been crazy to think that she could do anything without a weapon of her own. She felt wetness on her face and wondered for a moment if it was blood. No, she realized; it was tears.

Strong hands gripped her by the upper arms and turned her back to face the crowded path. She looked up at the man with the crooked mouth and smelled his heavy, acrid scent. Suddenly she felt his hand grabbing her breast. She screamed in shock and rage. She drew up her knee and kicked out.

The man grunted and fell back. Nisha seized her opportunity, doubled forward, and butted her way between the attackers.

"Stop her!" one of them shouted.

"Leave her," someone else said. "There's nowhere she can go."

With her hands tied, she couldn't climb down from the mesa to the ground. But her child was her main concern. She butted her way out among the grunting, thrashing bodies. Something wet and hot and sticky splashed across her forearm, and she realized with horror that it was blood from one of her kinfolk. "Jorlor!" she cried, knowing that she was abandoning him, but knowing that she had no choice, and in any case, he was dead.

She ran back across the meeting place and glimpsed other figures running from the slaughter. She bumped into someone—she didn't know who it was—and almost fell. But then she saw the Sacred Tree, and no one was near it.

Gasping for breath, she dropped to her knees. Orc was still where she had left him. He was bawling, although his voice was barely audible above the din.

Quickly, Nisha glanced behind her. No one seemed to be coming after her—at least, not yet. How could she cut through the thong binding her wrists? The sandstone rocks were too soft. She found herself weeping in misery and frustration. She squatted down, arched her back, stretched her arms as low as she could, and tried to work her bound wrists around and under her buttocks. She moaned as the thongs cut deep into her skin. But finally she managed it. She pulled her knees up to her chin and grunted with pain as she dragged her wrists around, over her heels, and finally up in front of her.

They were still bound, of course, but now she could use her fingers. She fumbled with the thong that she had used to tie Orc to the tree. Her fingers were trembling so much, she had trouble untying the knots. Finally, though, they came loose. She scooped Orc up in her arms—

"Hey!" The voice was so close, it made her flinch in terror. But then she ran. Somehow, maybe she could hold Orc against her while she eased herself down the cleft in the rock to the ground.

A hand grabbed her by the hair and whirled her around. Even in the darkness, she was sure it was the same man who'd thrown her against the wall; the same man who'd killed Jorlor. She recognized the shape and scent of him. She tried to move away—but if she took more than a step backward, she would be off the edge of the mesa.

Unexpectedly, he grabbed hold of her son. "No!" she cried, as Orc was pulled out of her arms. For a moment she glimpsed the boy in the man's hands, and she remembered how Ilu had held him, while everyone in the tribe shouted their approval. And then, while Nisha watched in horror, the invader tossed Orc aside.

The child flew out through the air, yelling in terror. He disappeared into the darkness, falling freely through the air, out over the edge of the mesa, to his death.

At first Nisha couldn't believe what she had seen. It was too monstrous; too terrible. Then an inarticulate rage rose up inside her. She threw herself forward, screaming and raking at the man's face.

He threw her back. For a moment she thought that she, too, was going to fall to her death. But she reached out and managed to seize his robe, and she held onto him to keep her balance.

He took hold of her wrists, raised them, then hit her hard in the belly. She gasped and collapsed onto the ground, unable to breathe.

The man stepped back, rubbed his face with his palm, then peered at it. There was a dark smeer of blood. He muttered something, looked at Nisha, and kicked her.

She was crying silently now, still unable to draw a breath. Everything that mattered to her had been taken from her. Why hadn't she let the man throw her over the edge to join her child on the desert floor? Why had she bothered to save herself?

Someone was throwing fresh fuel on the fire. Suddenly the flames leaped up, making everything visible. Nisha watched numbly as she saw the invaders dragging men, women, and children out from among the houses. Most of the men were badly wounded, and many more were dead. The invaders forced everyone who still lived to get down on the ground, then speared them quickly and methodically. For a moment the air was full of cries for mercy and shouts of pain; and then there was an even more terrible silence.

Methodically, the invaders moved among the bodies, grabbing each person's head in turn and tilting it up. At first Nisha thought that the warriors were just checking to see that all the victims were dead. But then she saw that the men were using knives, cutting hanks of hair from each dead person's head.

Finally, each of her kinfolk was dragged to the edge of the mesa, and one by one, they were rolled off it. Faintly, from far below, Nisha heard the bodies thumping into the desert sand.

She saw her father with a spear in his chest, lying limp on the ground. A man kicked him off the mesa, and he was gone. She saw her mother, likewise, gone.

Old Ilu had had his throat cut. His head was lolling back, and his eyes were staring wide. His mouth was open in a silent scream as he was dragged to the edge of the mesa by one of the invaders—the man with the crooked mouth who had tied Nisha's wrists. He picked up Ilu to toss him over the edge, then noticed the ceremonial knife hanging around Ilu's neck. The man lifted the thong over Ilu's head and held the knife in one hand while he tossed Ilu away with the other.

Finally, Nisha saw Winnor. The shaman was still alive as two of the invaders dragged him down from one of the rooftops where he had hidden himself. At first he seemed to lose all courage and let himself hang limply between them. But then, when they braced themselves to support his dead weight, he suddenly twisted free. A spear was lying on the ground close by. He seized it, whirled around, and plunged it into the chest of the man closest to him.

For a moment, Nisha felt hope leap inside her. But Winnor had made a brave, futile gesture, nothing more. The invaders yelled in rage, gathered around him, and jerked the spear out of his hands.

One of the men leveled a spear at Winnor's chest. Winnor stepped backward. He seemed strangely calm, and there was a light of righteousness in his eyes. He looked from one attacker to the next, and he smiled.

It was a strange, crazy smile. Nisha felt something twist inside her as she looked on Winnor's face. Was it Cat Spirit that had made him so proud and brave? Bit by bit, he backed away from his adversaries, while they advanced on him. He took a step backward, then another—and then he screamed as he fell over the edge of the mesa, and she heard his cry echoing down below.

Nisha moaned. He had chosen to die by his own will. He had kept his pride to the last moment but still, he was gone.

The men with the spears glanced at each other, then started dealing with the handful of young women who had been allowed to live. Two men marched over to Nisha, where she was lying on the ground. One of the men, she saw, was the same one who had tied her wrists and had killed Ilu. He stopped in front of Nisha, reached down, grabbed her hair, and forced her to stand up. She found herself looking into a face that had been broken and scarred by countless battles. One side of his mouth turned down in a habitual scowl; the other pulled back from his teeth as he eyed her and gave her a hideous imitation of a grin.

He glanced at his partner, then back at Nisha. "Pretty woman," he said. Then he lifted her tribe's sacred knife and weighed it in his hand, pointing it at her. "Shall I kill you, pretty woman?" he said.

Nisha trembled with emotion, wishing there were some way to strike out at him and spill his blood. Never before had she wanted to kill anyone but now, as she looked at this warrior in front of her, and all the other warriors on the mesa, the desire totally possessed her. Nothing would satisfy her so much as seeing their blood.

Well, she thought, it didn't matter what she wanted. These men had killed the people she lived for and cared for, and there was no way to undo that. So maybe it would be best for her to die. If so, she vowed to follow Winnor's example. She would be defiant to the end. Bravely, even though her knees were shaking, she tilted her head up and spat into the ugly face opposite her.

The man growled at her. He let go of the knife around his neck and pulled back his fist.

"Stop that, Kron." Another man came striding over. He had scratches on the side of his face—and Nisha realized with dismay that he was the one who had killed her husband and child.

The one named Kron turned to him. "Just playing with her," he said. "That's all."

So he hadn't really planned to kill her at all. Nisha felt another wave of despair. Should she leap off the mesa and end her own life? Why did she deserve to live, if so many of her kinfolk had died?

The man with the scratched face pushed the man named Kron casually aside, and he paused in front of Nisha. In the light from the fire, his skin looked sallow. He had high cheekbones and a wide, thin mouth. His eyes, though, were the most memorable feature of his face. They were dark and mean, showing an implacable savagery. "This one we will take with us," he said. "There's few enough women as it is. And this one is the finest." His voice was casual, as if the matter of Nisha's life and death was of hardly any interest to him. He turned to Kron. "What's that you have there?" He gestured at the flint knife.

"I took it off an old man."

"Give it to me." He held out his hand.

Reluctantly, Kron complied.

Nisha couldn't bear to be silent any longer. "You killed my husband," she said. "You killed my child!"

The man with the scratched face turned and eyed her. "Yes," he said, "I did." He frowned as if he was seeing her clearly for the first time. Unexpectedly, he reached out and grabbed Nisha's face in his hand, turning it first one way, then the other. Then he ran his hand over her body, and he reached up under her robe. She cried out in shock and pain as his bloodstained fingers probed her, treating her like an animal that he had captured.

"You disgust me!" she screamed at him. "You should die! All of you should die!"

The man watched her face. "Maybe in a while I will have a chance to break your spirit," he said softly. "I hope so."

Suddenly Nisha knew that she couldn't kill herself—at least, not while this man lived. She felt her rage churning in her, overwhelming her fear. She let out a tormented scream and threw herself forward, reaching up with her bound hands, trying to seize hold of him.

He stepped backward quickly, and she found herself stumbling and falling painfully onto her knees.

She heard him laugh. She looked up at him through her tears, just in time to see him weighing the flint knife in his hand and then tying it around his own neck. "Bring her and the four others," he said. Then he walked away.

Chapter Four

At daybreak, the men tied a thick leather rope around Nisha's body, looped it under her arms, then lowered her over the edge of the mesa. She hung helplessly, turning slowly, bumping against the face of rock as the rope was paid out.

She felt exhausted and overwhelmed by what she had seen. She had no way to comprehend the horror of it. Her mind felt empty and blank.

Her feet touched the sandy soil, and a man who had climbed down ahead of her untied the rope. He ordered her to sit down with her back to the rock, and he jabbed her with the point of his spear when she didn't move quickly enough to please him.

One by one, all the women were lowered from the top of the mesa. After Nisha came Rilla, a thin, awkward girl who hadn't yet been paired with a man, and had only just come of age. Her eyes were wide and fearful in the faint dawn light. When she slumped down beside Nisha, Nisha felt the girl trembling.

Somehow, Rilla's fear helped Nisha to cope with her own emotions. It was easier, she realized, to worry about someone else than to think about herself, and it gave her an opportunity to feel useful. "Be calm," she said softly. "See, they are going to let us live. That much you can depend on. You will survive, Rilla."

Rilla sniffed back her tears. "I don't want to live."

"I felt the same way," said Nisha. "But we have a duty

to all our kinfolk, Rilla. If there is any way, we must avenge their deaths."

Rilla didn't answer. She stared blankly at the ground in front of her.

The next one down was Jerl, a woman four years older than Nisha who had had a husband and two children. Jerl was generous and hard working, a big, strong woman who had always been a source of comfort and inspiration to the villagers. But as she joined Nisha and Rilla, she seemed lost, cut off in her own private world. She didn't respond when Nisha spoke to her. She sat down hard on the ground, and her face showed nothing.

The last two women were Orlu and Lazonah, two sisters, both of them younger than Nisha. Both of them were sobbing and wailing. They tried to turn to Jerl for comfort when they joined her at the foot of the mesa. But Jerl wouldn't even look at them. It was Nisha who spoke up. "We will live," she told them, as forcefully as she knew how. "Listen to me! The men have chosen to let us live. We are the fortunate ones. Think of that."

Privately, Nisha wondered whether what she said was true. Could she really feel fortunate to be captured and abducted by these warriors? There had been times in her life when she'd felt lost, wanting her father to care for her more, and wishing that her mother had more strength to stand up to him. There had been times, too, when Nisha had had to fight for what she wanted—especially when she had chosen Jorlor, and the elders had disapproved. But even when she clashed with her tribe, the tribe had still given her comfort, just by the fact that it existed. There had always been people who cared for her, there had always been food and shelter, and she had assumed that there always would be.

No more. In a few brief moments, she had learned how little she knew about the world. Jorlor had been right: She had been lulled by her own good fortune. Her tribe had endured for centuries, yet it had been decimated overnight.

She thought of Winnor, and her last conversation with him, when he had told her that she possessed more power than she knew. Where was her power now? And what good did it do her to reach out for what she wanted, if it could all be taken away so easily?

She thought of Jorlor and felt the terrible pain of his loss. But the pain just reaffirmed her feeling of duty. Even if the other women were unable to help her, she must still find a way somehow to avenge the memory of her husband, her son, her parents, and her tribe. She must kill the men who had taken everything from her and destroyed her people. Nothing else would settle the debt that she owed to the people who had died.

The men began lowering heavy leather sacks from the top of the mesa. Nisha smelled corn and pemmican, jerky and ground acorns, and she realized that all of her tribe's stores were being looted.

Finally the men themselves came climbing down, and she heard them shouting to one another, grinning like hunters who had brought back a rich harvest of game. But they weren't talking about deer or rabbits; they were bragging about the number of her people that they had killed. The women around Nisha started wailing, and she found herself crying silently as she sat against the mesa with her wrists still bound in front of her.

Just a few paces away she heard Kron talking about what he had done. He described how he had trapped old Ilu like a crippled rabbit and had toyed with him a little before slitting his throat and tossing him off the edge of the mesa. And then he laughed.

Nisha imagined herself seizing a spear and thrusting it into Kron—stabbing him again and again, then lifting a rock and bringing it down upon his skull. She groaned at the awfulness of the vision. She was a gentle person, a kind person. She had fought, sometimes, with other children when she was young, but she'd never truly hurt anyone. She'd never even enjoyed hunting very much. Could she really spill a man's blood? She honestly didn't know. Yet her vow of vengeance burned in her, and she knew beyond doubt that any man who had tormented and killed the leader of her people deserved to die.

The man whose face she had scratched stepped out in front of the rest of the men. He was the leader, she realized. His name seemed to be Grep; she'd heard a couple of the other warriors hailing him and asking him for instructions while the supplies were being lowered to the ground.

"This is not a time for talk," Grep said. His voice wasn't loud, but the other men instantly fell silent. "We must travel east and hide ourselves," he went on.

There were some murmurs of agreement.

"What about the women?" That was Kron speaking. "I killed ten men. I have a right—"

"You killed five men, four women, and one child," said Grep. "But yes, you should choose. After I make my own choice."

Nisha saw Grep looming over her. "This one," Grep said, looking down at her, "is the finest of them. She'll be mine."

Nisha felt a wave of anguish. To be chosen by the man who had killed her husband and child—how could she endure that?

"But I was the one who found her," said Kron.

Grep turned swiftly. "What do you want, to punish her for spitting at you?"

There was some muffled laughter from the other men.

"That's not what I meant," Kron said, but Grep cut him off.

"Choose one of the others," Grep said. The softness was gone from his voice. The words were as sudden as a slap.

Kron grunted. He didn't attempt to argue. He bent down and peered at first one woman, then the next, turning their faces up to the faint light. "Her," he said finally, gesturing to Orlu.

"Good." Grep turned to another of the men. "Plorngah, how many did you kill on the mesa?"

"Eight." The voice was deep and slow. He was a huge brute of a man.

"You're a strong warrior, Plorngah. So now, you choose."

Plorngah picked Rilla, the youngest, and Nisha closed her eyes and shuddered at the idea of him violating her. Plorngah, too, deserved to die, and Nisha tried to console herself by vowing that it would be so.

Grep called on two more men name Yahonn and Irm and praised them for their fighting courage before telling them to claim Lazonah and Jerl, the last two women. Then Grep organized the party for their journey out across the desert. Each man was given a pack or a sack to carry across his shoulders, loaded with food from the village stores. The women were pulled up onto their feet, and they, too, were given heavy burdens. Even though Nisha had managed to pull her bound wrists around in front of her, she still found it difficult to keep her balance. Young Rilla, with her wrists tied behind her, stumbled under the load of her pack and she fell down on the stony ground.

Plorngah grunted in anger and Nisha glimpsed the huge man's silhouette from the corner of her eye as he kicked Rilla, then dragged her up by her hair, ignoring her cries of pain. "You fall again, you'll be beaten," he told her. She yelped as he smacked her face, hard. Then he jabbed her with his spear. "You'll walk in front of me now."

Nisha turned away from the terrible sight—and found herself face to face with Grep, her own captor. She gave a little start.

He reached out, twined his fingers into her hair, and tugged gently, tilting her head back. "I chose well," he said softly, turning her to face the dim dawn light. "You have a special beauty. Very special." He gave her a thin, nasty smile as he reached up and fingered the scratches that she had inflicted on his cheek. "You have spirit, too—although I'll deal with that soon enough." His eyes narrowed. "What did your tribe call you?"

"Nisha." It was hard for her to speak even one word to him, she loathed and distrusted him so deeply.

"Nisha," he repeated. "I hope you don't think I'll treat you like that." He nodded toward Plorngah. "There are much better ways to train a woman to obey."

She pulled her face free of his hand. "I will never obey you," she said.

He laughed softly, then traced his forefinger across her cheek. "If you disobey me," he said, moving a little closer, "you will suffer for it, Nisha. If you please me, you'll be rewarded. Now, which would you prefer, eh?"

She glared at him. She said nothing.

He stepped back, reached for something, and brought it up toward her face. She flinched—then realized it was just the leather rope that the men had used to lower the women and the sacks of food from the mesa. Swiftly, he tied the end of it around her neck. "This will remind you to follow me," he said. He coiled the rest of the rope around his waist. "Come, now," he called to the rest of the men, as he turned away from Nisha. He started walking east across the desert, away from the mesa, dragging her behind him.

Grep set a fast pace, and Nisha found herself struggling to keep up. Her moccasins had been lost somewhere up on the mesa, and her bare feet were soon scratched by brambles and abraded by the stony ground. She winced at every step, but vowed not to complain. She refused to show any weakness to her captors.

Behind her, she heard one of the women sobbing and one of the men swearing at her. Plorngah and Rilla, she guessed. The girl was thin and weak, and the burden that she was carrying was far too heavy for her. Suddenly she cried out, and Nisha heard her falling down on the ground.

Grep stopped, and Nisha turned her head. She saw

Rilla lying on her back, still with her hands tied behind her. She was crying hysterically and trying to wriggle away from Plorngah.

"Get up!" he shouted at her. He jabbed her flank with the point of his spear, drawing blood. "Get up, you!" He jabbed her again.

Grep muttered something. He strode back to Plorngah. "The pack's too heavy," he said. "Empty out half of it and leave it here or add it to your own."

Plorngah turned slowly, frowning. "She should learn—"

"Do as I say, Plorngah."

The big man's face changed. His belligerence faded. He became apologetic. "Right away," he said.

"The day grows brighter," said Grep. He nodded toward the sun that had risen ahead of them. "We have no time to waste here."

Plorngah set down his own pack, then opened the bag that Rilla had been carrying and transferred some of the burden. He worked quickly while Grep and the other men stood watching. Nisha hesitated. She saw that Grep wasn't paying attention to her, and the rope that linked her to him had fallen slack. She felt a little pang of fear at the idea of doing something that might anger him, but then, once again, she felt defiant anger erasing her anxiety.

She stepped over to Rilla where the girl lay on the ground weeping. With difficulty, under the load of her own pack, Nisha got down on her knees beside the girl and placed her hands on Rilla's shoulder. "Courage, young one," she murmured.

Rilla looked up quickly. She sniffed back her tears, then glanced anxiously at Plorngah. The big man had turned around and was glowering at Nisha. The other men in the party were watching without speaking.

The rope suddenly jerked tight around Nisha's neck. She winced and found Grep staring down at her. There was a tension in his face that she hadn't seen before. His thin lips pulled back in a vicious, humorless grin. "She is

Plorngah's woman," Grep said. "You have no right to touch her. Do you understand?"

"She is one of my people!" Nisha blurted out.

Grep dropped down beside her. He seized the rope around her neck and twisted his hand suddenly, tightening the leather cord. Nisha found herself choking. She raised her bound hands and started prying helplessly at the noose that was strangling her.

"You have no people," Grep told her calmly. "There is only me. I am your people."

She told herself that he wouldn't kill her. He would have done that before, if he'd intended to. But he had killed Jorlor, and he had killed Orc, and when she looked into his face, it was frightening in its bland indifference to her life. She could die here on the desert, and he would calmly walk away.

Her face felt as if it was swelling. Her mouth was gaping wide. There was ringing in her ears. And still he held the rope tight.

Her vision started to darken. She felt her legs thrashing on the ground, and they hardly seemed to belong to her. She suddenly lost all control, twisting and flailing. Grep's face, cruel in its indifference, seemed to rise up above her into the dark sky. She felt her back arching, her tongue swelling, all her muscles straining—

She found herself choking and gasping, with her cheek pressing against the soil. She was sweating and trembling. The breath rasped in and out of her lungs. There was a terrible throbbing pain around her neck where the rope had dug into her skin.

Something touched her head. It was Grep, turning her to face him. "That was your first lesson," he said quietly. His face loomed over her, filling her view. "When I have more time, I will teach you more."

Nisha wanted to cry. It would be so much easier to break down like Rilla and vent all the misery welling up inside her. But even now, she wouldn't allow it. She bit her lip and closed her eyes, fighting back the tears.

"Get up, now," said Grep. "If you give me more trouble, I will kill you."

He meant it; she no longer felt any doubt of that.

She squirmed around and got up onto her knees. She noticed his spear lying on the ground nearby, and she realized that he had dropped it when he was choking her. For a moment she imagined herself seizing the spear. Her wrists were bound, but they were in front of her body. She could grab the shaft and leap up, thrusting the point into Grep's chest. The other men would kill her, of course—but wouldn't that be the best way? She could die as Winnor had died, ending her suffering while taking vengeance on the man who had organized the massacre of her tribe.

For a moment, she almost did it. But then she thought of Kron, and of Plorngah, and of all the other men who should pay for what they had done. If she was going to honor the vow that she had made to her husband, her parents, and her child, she could not throw her life away so cheaply.

Reluctantly, she struggled up onto her feet.

"You will do nothing unless I permit it," Grep told her.

Weakly, Nisha nodded.

"Do you understand?" he snapped at her.

"Yes." Her throat hurt when she tried to speak. She winced.

He smiled faintly. "Good." He turned back to Plorngah. "Are you ready?"

"Yes." He nodded quickly.

Once again, Grep led the way forward.

Chapter Five

When the sun was halfway to the zenith, they came to a gully where a small spring flowed and a pool of water reflected the sky. Nisha knew this place well. Her people had often paused here when they were on their way home after hunting small game and gathering berries on the slopes farther east.

The gully was choked with boulders, making it impossible for anyone to lie down to rest. But there were caves in the limestone walls of the little canyon, and that was where Grep led his people now.

"Kron," he said, "you'll keep watch till noon. Irm, you'll watch till dusk."

The two men nodded wordlessly. Everyone was setting down their packs, flexing their shoulders, and finding places to sit on the stony ground.

Nisha turned to Grep. "There's no need to post a guard," she said cautiously. "There are no people in these parts. This land used to belong to—my people."

Grep gave her an appraising look. "A woman must learn to hold her tongue," he said, "unless a man asks her to speak. Do you understand?" He sat down and leaned against the rough wall of the cave. "Reebowa! Fetch water."

A young man stood up quickly—then hesitated. "I have a cactus spine in my foot, Grep," he said, speaking in a halting, high-pitched voice. "It pierced my moccasin. I wonder if someone—"

"Fetch the water!" Grep snapped at him.

Reebowa ducked his head and backed away. He seized a leather bottle and limped down among the boulders to the pool while the other men watched him. Nisha heard some of them chuckling as the scrawny young man made his way back, wincing each time he stepped on his afflicted foot. He held the bottle out to Grep but stared at the floor, not meeting the older man's eyes.

"Good boy, Reebowa," said Grep. He slapped his shoulder.

"My foot—"

"Later, my friend." Grep raised the bottle and drank out of it while the other men waited. Finally, when he had drunk his fill, he passed the bottle around. Each time it became empty, Reebowa was sent to fill it again, and the men laughed louder every time, watching their servant limp and yelp with pain.

None of the men even thought of offering water to their captives. The women huddled together at one side, looking miserable and saying nothing.

Grep turned back to Nisha. "Have you ever seen other raiding parties on the plain?"

She shook her head.

"No," he said thoughtfully. "If there had been others, your tribe would have defended themselves properly." He looked at his men. His high cheekbones caught the light as he gave them his dangerous, thin-lipped grin. "We did well, eh? We spilled their blood. We stole their food and their women, and we killed anyone who stood in our way."

Nisha looked at the men and saw them nodding, looking proud of their conquest. She despised them all, even Reebowa, who was too young or too stupid to know any better.

"We lost Timor," someone said.

"We did." Grep nodded slowly.

So that was the man whom Winnor had killed.

"Timor was always careless," said Grep, with a shrug. "I warned him many times." He reached in the pack that he'd been carrying and pulled out a handful of pemmican. "Eat now."

Nisha realized that the men had been waiting for his permission. She marveled at the way they obeyed him. He wasn't stronger than they were, and he seemed younger than some of them, yet he spoke as if it was unthinkable for anyone to defy him. Perhaps he was more cunning than the rest of them; she sensed that his mind was sharp. Still, that didn't explain his power over them.

The men started gorging themselves, eating like animals. The sounds of their lip-smacking and belching filled the cave. But still, the women were offered nothing. Nisha gazed sadly at Rilla, at Jerl, and at the two sisters, Orlu and Lazonah. A couple of them gazed dully back at her, but no one dared to speak.

Finally, when the men were sated, they threw some leftovers onto a wide, flat rock and poured some water onto another rock that had a concave, dish-shaped surface. Plorngah turned to Rilla, grabbed her by the hair, and pushed her forward till her face was inches from the scraps of food.

The other men grunted in amusement as Rilla crouched with her hands still tied behind her and seized the scraps in her lips and teeth, then did her best to chew them.

Kron, Irm, and Yahonn urged their women forward and forced them to dine beside Rilla. Nisha watched in dismay as the women humiliated themselves and the men laughed at them.

"You too," Grep said quietly.

"No," Nisha said, avoiding his eyes.

Grep grunted. "Understand," he said, "a woman who loses her strength will be of no use to me."

She looked up at him. Once again, she saw how casually he would dispose of her if she didn't meet his needs. And if that happened—or if she weakened herself by not eating—she would be defeating her own purpose. To fulfill her dream of vengeance, she would need to be strong.

She joined the other women at the stone slab and licked

up every last morsel. And then, when the slab was bare, she turned back to Grep. "May I have some more?" she asked.

He threw his head back and laughed, and the sound echoed in the cave. Then he reached into his pack, scooped up a handful of pemmican, and held it out to her on his open palm.

She bowed her head and licked the powdery food from the skin that was stained with the blood of her kin. A couple of the men jeered at her, but it no longer mattered. If each mouthful made her stronger, that was reason enough to endure any humiliation.

She finished the last of the food from Grep's palm, then turned quickly as she heard a cry of surprise from behind her. Plorngah was gripping Rilla and bending her over a boulder. The huge man lifted her robe with a casual sweep of his hand, then kneeled behind her and entered her. She gave a loud, fearful scream and Nisha cried out in dismay, knowing that the girl had never been taken by a man before. Plorngah held her down and thrust into her, a couple of the men cheered him on, but it as a desultory business. Most of them seemed indifferent and were settling down to sleep.

Yahonn turned to Lazonah and pulled her robe open, exposing her body. Lazonah bit her lip and looked away from him. He was a stupid-looking man with broken teeth and terrible scars disfiguring the left side of his face. Within moments, he was following Plorngah's example, taking Lazonah from behind.

Irm eyed Jerl, then grunted with disinterest and turned away. Jerl, meanwhile, ignored him. She was still as silent as she had been before, and her eyes were empty as she stared at the opposite wall of the cave, paying no attention to anything around her.

Kron reached for Orlu, but Grep caught his arm. "This is not the time," he said softly.

Kron grunted in annoyance. "I have a right—"

"Last year, you fell asleep on your watch." Grep

grinned and shook his head. "Sex is like wine for you, Kron. It makes you stupid."

There were some snickers from the other men. Kron shook Grep's hand off his arm and turned away, looking deeply angry. But he didn't argue. He seized his spear, stood up, and walked to the mouth of the cave. He sat on a boulder and rested the spear across his knees with his back to the rest of the nomads.

Grep leaned back against the wall of the cave and watched Nisha through half-closed eyes. "Stand," he said quietly.

She had been dreading this moment. She was afraid that if he even laid his hand on her, she'd turn into a mad creature.

She stood up and waited.

"Open your robe," he said.

With her hands tied in front of her, she could just manage to loosen the thongs. She looked around at the rest of the men, but most of them seemed to have been sedated by the food, and many were already asleep.

With her elbows, Nisha managed to open her robe. She eyed him defiantly as she exposed her body to him.

His eyes narrowed as he surveyed her. She saw his jaw clench. She sensed him thinking of something he would like to do, or something he was planning to do—but he showed no intention of moving from where he lay.

Nisha felt a wave of relief. But then she thought of Jorlor and his kindness, and the way he had touched her with respect, rousing so much love and passion, and an overwhelming sadness welled up inside her. It had been hard for her to accept that he was really, truly gone, and she would never see him or touch him again. Now, though, it was starting to seem real—and the sense of loss was almost more than she could bear.

Savagely she suppressed the feeling, reminding herself of her vow. *I will kill him for you, Jorlor,* she said in her head. *He'll pay for what his people have done. I promise.*

"Go and lie down," Grep said, waving her away.

"Maybe tomorrow I'll have you. Maybe the day after that."

Maybe he wanted to keep her in a state of uncertainty. Maybe he enjoyed playing that kind of game. Well, it made no difference. It was a small thing compared to everything else that had already happened.

She moved a short distance away, sat down, and watched Grep as he closed his eyes and lay with his head pillowed on his arm. It was strange to see him like that, so defenseless. She could seize a rock and attack him with it—but of course, the other men would kill her instantly, and Kron was on guard, so there was no way for her to escape.

She looked at the other women. The men had already finished molesting them, leaving them slumped down, pale and exhausted. Nisha exchanged glances with Orlu but decided she still didn't dare try to talk to her.

Should she try to sleep? She was weary, yet she couldn't rest. She noticed Reebowa sitting on a rock on his own, near the mouth of the cave, with one leg crossed over the other. He had taken off his moccasin and was squinting at the sole of his bare foot. He was farsighted, she realized. He couldn't focus well enough to see the cactus spine and remove it.

Her first impulse was to let him suffer. But then she had a better idea. She went to him and sat close by. "Can I help?" she murmured.

He turned quickly, then gave her a suspicious look.

She glanced at his foot. "I can see the spine," she told him. "It will only take me a moment to pull it out."

He eyed her doubtfully, then shrugged. "All right."

She kneeled, raised her hands, and ran one fingertip across his heel. The spine had been broken off, but there was still enough of it for her to grasp. She took hold of it carefully, drew it out, then showed it to him. "It's done," she said.

He blinked, looking confused. He put his moccasin

back on, then rested his weight on his foot. He gave her a slow, stupid smile. "Thank you," he said.

"Nisha," she said. "My name is Nisha."

"Nisha." He grinned and nodded. But then his grin faded and he glanced around nervously.

"No one noticed," she told him. She forced a smile, then turned away from him.

She looked around to see if there was anything else that she could or should do. All the men were asleep now, except for Reebowa. And the women were lying with their eyes closed.

Nisha decided that she needed to think. She picked her way to a boulder near the mouth of the cave, not far from Kron. She sat there and stared out at the gully as the sun grew brighter, and she started trying to come to terms with the enormity of everything that had happened. That was surely the first step. Only after she had calmed herself could she hope to make plans for the days that lay ahead.

For a long while, she stared at the land and sky and listened to the insects humming and the birds calling. Some of her anger and fear subsided, and some of the tension left her body. But as she became calmer, she started seeing her situation more clearly, and she began to wonder if she had been fooling herself. There were twenty-three of the warriors, and any one of them would overwhelm her in a physical fight. Grep had already made it clear that if she disobeyed him, he would kill her. And if the men were taking her back to their own village, there would be even more of them there.

Nor did it seem that she'd get any support from the other four women. They seemed full of despair, and apparently, she wasn't even allowed to talk to them without permission.

So it was easy to vow revenge—but how could she ever hope to make such a vow come true? Instead of nursing her defiance, she might do better to swallow her pride and learn, instead, how to please them.

The thought of that was unbearable. No, she told herself: Even if it seemed impractical or impossible, she had made a solemn vow. She would rather die than break it now.

She looked across at Kron. There he was, the man who had killed the chieftain of her tribe, sitting with the spear across his knees—perhaps the same spear that had sliced poor Ilu's throat. It was the most terrible injustice that he should be allowed to live. But how could she ever kill him?

He shifted his position, and she saw the sun gleaming on the muscles in his naked forearm as he moved. He was no bigger than Jorlor had been, but Nisha saw that he was a lot more powerful. Then he seemed to sense her watching him, and he turned to look at her. "What do you want, woman?" he growled at her. "You should be back there with the others."

He sounded angry—probably because she'd spat at him, and he had not been allowed to take her as his own or punish her. But she also saw that he wanted her. With her wrists tied together, she hadn't been able to fasten her robe properly after showing herself to Grep. It hung half open, and she saw Kron's eyes glancing down, peering at the curves of her body.

So here it was, so clear that she couldn't avoid seeing the situation. Kron wanted her. Perhaps he had never had a woman so beautiful. But he had been prevented from having her when Grep had claimed her. He was frustrated, and he was angry.

It seemed obvious what she should do. But could she bring herself to do it?

"I came out to talk to you," she whispered to Kron, looking at him squarely, trying to suppress the disgust that she felt.

"Talk?" He glanced at her body again, then made an irritable sound. "There's nothing to talk about with you."

"It was disrespectful," she said, "for me to spit in your face."

He shrugged. "Grep will teach you your place. No doubt of that." He gestured impatiently. "Get back there with the other women. I don't want you here."

"Why?" She tried to be bold, even though it scared her. "Don't you like looking at me?"

He glanced at her again, and the muscles in his face tightened.

Nisha seized the moment. She fumbled with her robe, and let it fall wide open.

She saw Kron's hands tighten on his spear. His chest swelled as he took a deep breath and held it, staring at her body. Then his eyes narrowed suspiciously. "What do you want? You're Grep's woman. You better remember that."

"I can do things for you," she said, forcing the words out through the tightness in her chest. "If I can do favors for you, perhaps you'll help me in some way."

"What do you mean—let you escape?" He snickered.

"Of course not," she said. "You'd be punished if you let that happen." She looked at him frankly. "I'm a slave of your people now, Kron. I must beg for favors. Maybe if I please you, you can give me extra food, or help me in other ways."

Actually she thought there was little chance of him doing that. But she wanted him to think that he could take advantage of her.

Kron's smirk faded from his face. He eyed her carefully. "You do something for me, I do you some favors, eh?"

She nodded. She felt so nervous, she was almost trembling. Still, she reminded herself of her vow.

Kron glanced over his shoulder and she saw him checking carefully that Grep and the other men were asleep. Then he jerked his bead, beckoning her closer.

Nisha stood up. She felt unsteady on her feet, but she forced herself to walk over to him, still with the front of her body exposed. Suddenly she imagined seizing his spear, skewering him with it, then fleeing from these terrible people, back across the desert. But no, she told herself: He might cry out and rouse the others, and even if she killed him silently and ran for her life, that still wouldn't fulfill her vow.

She thrust aside the fantasies of violence and stood before him with her head meekly bowed.

He bared crooked yellow teeth. He lowered his voice. "What are you offering me, woman?"

Nisha felt so repulsed by him, it was awful to have to stand so close to him. Still, she forced herself to speak enticingly. "You can touch me if you want," she whispered.

Keeping one hand on his spear, he reached out and grabbed her. She flinched from the sudden contact, but she didn't pull away.

Kron rubbed his hand down her flank, then stole another glance behind him. He was breathing heavily now. Nisha saw that she didn't need to fear him. She was his slave—but now that she saw how he wanted her, he was her slave too, in his own way.

She told herself to be bold. "I can give you pleasure, Kron. I've always been good at pleasing a man."

He glanced back into the cave again, and this time, she saw that he was looking at Orlu, the woman he had taken as his own.

"She's only fifteen summers old," Nisha said quickly. "She hasn't yet learned the things that a woman can do."

Kron turned back to her. He opened his mouth to speak.

"Wait!" she whispered. "I think I heard someone move."

"Cover yourself." His voice sounded urgent. "Get away from me."

Nisha turned her back and quickly fastened her robe, as well as she could. Her fingers were trembling, but she found herself feeling well satisfied. Kron was powerful and he had killed her loved ones without remorse yet here he was now, in fear of his life.

"Get back there with the others," he hissed at her.

She inclined her head respectfully. "I will do you as you say, Kron." She turned and went back into the cave. She didn't need to look at him to know that he was watching her as she walked away.

Chapter Six

Nisha lay close to the other women, and she managed to sleep fitfully for a while. Then she started dreaming of the massacre at the mesa. She woke with a little cry and lay on the rough floor of the cave blinking, trying to understand where she was.

Gradually she remembered everything, and she slumped down under the weight of the pain and loss.

The nomads and the other women in the cave were still asleep. Then she saw Jerl lying close by, and the woman's eyes were open.

Nisha edged closer to her. "Do you think it's past noon?" she whispered.

Jerl's expression never changed. Slowly, she nodded.

Nisha reached out and placed her hands on Jerl's shoulder. "Are you all right? I've never seen you this way."

Jerl said nothing.

"You were always the one that people turned to," Nisha went on. "I remember just last winter, when little Tara slipped and broke her leg so far from the mesa—you were the one who carried her all the way home and took her to Winnor, and stayed up all night watching over her . . ." Nisha trailed off. "You were always so strong."

Jerl's face still showed nothing. She lay without moving. Finally, she sighed. "I did everything for the tribe, Nisha," she said. "The tribe was what I lived for."

Nisha blinked, wondering how to respond. "You still have us," she said. "We can help each other, Jerl. Maybe one day we can begin again."

"No." The word was heavy and final. "The tribe is gone, Nisha. There is nothing to live for anymore."

Nisha found herself growing impatient in just the same way that she used to get irritated by Jorlor when he became grim and fatalistic. "Jerl—"

"No." She rolled over, moving awkwardly with her hands still tied behind her. "There is nothing to say, Nisha."

Nisha slept some more. She jerked awake suddenly when she felt something nudging her shoulder. Once again, she was disoriented. This time, when she opened her eyes, she saw Rilla bending over her.

"I want to talk to you," the girl whispered.

Nisha glanced toward the cave mouth. Kron was no longer on guard; another man had replaced him. The afternoon light was starting to fade. She guessed that the warriors would be rousing themselves soon, to march through the night. She pulled Rilla close, so their cheeks were touching and they could speak directly into each others' ears. "What is it, Rilla?" she whispered.

"I want to know what we're going to do." Rilla's voice was uneven. She sounded desperate, and Nisha guessed that the girl had been lying and fretting for a while, working herself up to a desperate pitch. "I can't stand it, Nisha. To be treated like this, after what happened to our people—"

"What do you expect of me?" Nisha interrupted her.

Rilla fell silent. She pulled back a fraction. "I don't know. You seem calmer than the rest of us. You seem as if you know what to do."

Nisha made a little impatient sound. "When Grep almost killed me, out on the desert, did it seem then that I knew what to do?"

Rilla made a plaintive sound. "Please don't mock me. Please. I can't stand—"

"All right. Be calm." She paused for a long moment, trying to order her thoughts. It would be too dangerous to

confide in Rilla; the girl wasn't brave enough or stable
enough. "There may come a time," Nisha said carefully,
"when there's something we can do. Especially if we can
work together. Do you understand? We have to wait till
we find out where we're being taken, and what will be
done with us. You must wait, Rilla. Can you do that?"

"I don't know." She sounded tearful.

"Do you want to give up?" Nisha made her voice
sound severe.

Quickly, Rilla shook her head.

"Then you have to be patient."

"I'll try." She sniffed back tears. "Thanks for talking to
me. You make me feel better." She hesitated. "I tried to
talk to Orlu and Lazonah, but they won't speak. They've
just—stopped being themselves. And Jerl, too. I feel so
alone."

Nisha nodded. "I know." She glanced at the other
women, then back at Rilla. Maybe she'd been too hard on
the girl. Rilla was the youngest and physically the weak-
est, but still she was showing more spirit than the others.
"We'll talk again when we can," Nisha told her.

The girl nodded. She opened her mouth to answer, but
Nisha gave her a warning look. One of the men was stirring nearby. "Later," Nisha whispered.

Rilla edged away.

It was strange, Nisha thought, to find herself being the
strongest in the group. But then, as she thought back, she
realized that she had always tended to enjoy solitude
more than the other villagers. They had depended on the
community, while she had depended on herself. Now that
their community was gone, they were lost.

She lay on her side with one shoulder propped against
a rock, watching the warriors as they woke one by one.
They stood up, yawning, scratching themselves. They
picked their way out of the cave. She heard them urinat-
ing and smelled the thick, foul odor of their excrement.

Grep stood up. He looked around, and she saw how
carefully his eyes moved. She reminded herself never,

ever to underestimate him. "Nisha!" he called to her. "Take food to the men." He nudged a big bag of pemmican with his toe. "Everyone must eat. We have a long march tonight."

Obediently, she did as he said. It was a humiliating task, because each time she stopped in front of one of the warriors he would take his time, leering at her, studying her face and body before he rummaged in the bag. Nisha realized that Grep must have known this would happen, and it was part of his game: to humiliate her, and to show her off to the other men. Well, she thought, sooner or later he would pay for this, too.

Finally Nisha reached Kron. At first he looked at her boldly, as the others had done. But then, as she shifted slightly and he glimpsed her flesh inside her robe, something changed in him. He scowled, grabbed his handful of pemmican, and forced it down in two huge mouthfuls. Then he glanced around and saw Orlu. He jumped up, strode over to her, and grabbed her. He bent her over and entered her violently, making her scream. He climaxed within moments, then stepped back, breathing hard. Some of the men cheered him, but Kron looked as if he still wasn't satisfied.

Nisha watched with dismay. It seemed obvious to her that he had taken Orlu so violently because he was frustrated by the way that Nisha had tantalized him. Did that mean it was all her fault? She shook her head helplessly. She had made her decision, and she had to live with the possibility that it was a mistake. She wanted Kron to be interested in her—obsessed with her, even. That was the only way she knew to gain some influence over him.

When the men had finished eating, the women were allowed to consume some scraps, and once again Nisha asked Grep for more food. She looked up at him hopefully and saw his eyes narrow as he looked back at her. He scooped pemmican out of his bag and extended his hand toward her—but when she went to eat from it, he closed his fingers into a fist and rapped it against her forehead, just hard enough to make her wince and pull back.

Several of the men were watching, and they laughed.

Now Grep opened his hand again—but each time she moved forward, he closed it again, and the laughter grew louder.

She looked at his face. His thin lips were parted slightly, showing some faint pleasure in her humiliation but his eyes were as cold as ever. Power, she realized—power was his greatest pleasure, perhaps even greater than the pleasure he got from sex. Very well, she would cater to his needs. "Please," she said to him, making her voice as pathetic as she knew how. "Please, I am so hungry."

He studied her for a moment, and Nisha was afraid that he could see through her pretense. "Open your mouth," he told her.

Obediently, she opened it wide.

He leaned forward, grabbed her hair with one hand, and jammed his other hand against her lips, forcing the powdery pemmican in.

The men laughed louder while Nisha choked and struggled to swallow the food. She looked up at Grep and saw him laughing, too. She felt a twist of fury—but then, just as quickly, she pushed it aside. It didn't matter if he chose to humiliate her. Nothing mattered, so long as she got what she needed. "Thank you," she said, when she had finally managed to chew and swallow. She bowed her head.

He stood up, stepped over to her, and jerked her up onto her feet. Suddenly she felt his hand on her body, grabbing her so roughly, it hurt. His other hand twined in her long hair, twisting and tugging till tears came to her eyes. "Shall I have you now, eh?" he said.

His face was very close to hers. Really, he was not so bad looking, especially compared to the scarred, filthy men who followed him. But there was a prurient cruelty in the curve of his mouth, and when she looked into his eyes, all she could think of was the amount of blood and death and suffering they had seen. It was like food to him, she thought to herself. He fed off other people's pain.

"Do you want it now?" he said, giving her a little shake. He was frowning as if she had displeased him in some way. Then, suddenly, she understood. He had warned her, originally, that she should obey him—but that wasn't what he really wanted. He wanted her to cry out and struggle like some helpless animal in a snare, so that he could toy with her and punish her and *force* her to obey. If she was docile from the start, she would be no challenge for him, and he would get bored with her. This was why he had chosen her in the first place: She had dared to scratch his face, and he savored the challenge of her rebellious spirit.

Nisha tried to think how she should act. "Let go," she told him. "It hurts."

His frown disappeared. He smiled. He tightened his grip in her hair till she winced and gave a little cry. Then he reached down with his other hand and seized her thigh, curling his fingers and digging his nails into her flesh.

"No!" she cried. She struggled in his grip.

Suddenly he released her. "Not this time," he said quietly. "Maybe not next time. But it will be sometime soon." He studied her for a moment, like a man examining the beauty of a flower before squeezing it in his fist. Then he grunted and turned away.

Nisha forced herself to take slow, even breaths. *Not this time,* she thought, imagining herself impaling Grep on a spear or crushing his face with a rock. *Maybe not even next time. And maybe not sometime soon. But sometime.*

As the sun set outside the cave, everyone was made ready for the journey ahead. Grep saw to it that each person's pack was properly tied so that its straps wouldn't chafe and its contents wouldn't shift, and he surprised Nisha by taking as much trouble over the women as the men. He also saw that scraps of deerskin were wrapped around the feet of women who had left the mesa without moccasins. This didn't indicate any kindness on his part, Nisha realized; it was a purely practical matter. There was a long trek ahead, and if anyone became incapacitated it would hold the whole party back.

Finally, he cut the thongs binding the women's wrists. "We will be climbing some rocky slopes," he said quietly. "You will need to steady yourselves. But understand this: If any of you tries to escape or moves against me or my men, you will be killed. And if you talk among yourselves, you will be punished." He took his long leather rope and tied it around Nisha's neck, then looped and knotted it around each of the other women's necks till they were all linked together. "We will leave now," he said.

It was good to be out in the cool night air. Far behind her to the west, Nisha thought she could just make out the shape of the mesa, a tiny finger against the last colors of the sunset. Even now, it was hard to believe that her people weren't still there, safe in their houses, pursuing their daily lives.

But Grep led the way father east, and she had to turn away from the home of her people. Perhaps, she thought, this was the last time she would ever see it. The thought filled her with a terrible melancholy.

They settled into a steady rhythm, marching across the desert floor. Before long, they approached a ridge that marked the edge of Nisha's people's territory. The Deer Hunter tribe lived on the land just beyond, but Grep turned away from their land and started north.

After a while longer, he took them up a steep slope strewn with boulders. Nisha was surprised, because she knew of no tribes who dwelled here. The terrain was so rugged and so bare, there was no game and very little water. Farther on, she knew, the slopes became still steeper, leading to mountains that no one in her tribe had ever felt willing or able to climb.

Was this where Grep's people had come from originally? There was something purposeful about the way that Grep was traveling. Surely, there had to be more women somewhere, in a camp of some kind, waiting for the men to return.

Hardly anyone spoke as they followed Grep up the rocky hillside. Everyone was moving cautiously, because the surface was so treacherous underfoot. Several times, one of the women lost her footing and the leather rope jerked painfully tight around Nisha's neck.

In the middle of the night they all paused to rest and shared some food. Some of the men grumbled briefly about the punishing journey, but Grep silenced them with a few sharp words, and none of the women dared to say anything.

Then the journey continued, taking them across bare, rounded outcroppings of rock that had been scoured with grooves as if a giant had scraped them with his fingernails. The grooves provided secure footholds, but still the surfaces were so steep, everyone had to use hands as well as feet to keep a secure grip.

Finally, Grep led them on an arduous zigzag climb up a sheet of rock crisscrossed with cracks where tiny, stunted bushes grew. They reached the summit—and suddenly Nisha found herself in a sparse, dry forest of pinyon pines and eucalyptus trees. She looked around in amazement, never having seen vegetation growing in such density and profusion. She breathed deeply, and the smell of pine needles and eucalyptus sap was almost overwhelming.

Grep was searching for something in the shadows. Finally he grunted with satisfaction. "Here," he called to them.

The men moved forward, dragging the women with them. Everyone's feet crunched over dry pinecones and dead leaves. A thick, black wall of foliage loomed up ahead—but Grep had found a tiny gap in it, and in single file, his people followed him through.

Nisha found herself in an area where the underbrush

had been cleared and the charred remains of a fire lay
amid a circle of stones in the center. There was open sky
above. All around the edges of the clearing, bushes and
saplings and small trees had been stacked to form a wall
that was so dense, it would hide the firelight and discour-
age any wanderers from finding this place by chance.

"Reebowa, fetch water," Grep said, dumping his pack.
"Goljer, build a fire. We will rest here." He turned, then,
to the women and started untying the rope that linked
them.

"Is this your home?" Nisha asked him tentatively.

He grunted disdainfully and didn't bother to answer as
he loosened the knot in the leather cord around her neck.

Chapter Seven

While the men ate around the fire, Grep reached into his bag and brought out a leather bottle that Nisha hadn't seen before. The neck was tightly tied with two thongs, and Grep had to use his teeth to loosen the knots. Then he drank from it briefly, pausing and pressing his lips together, savoring the flavor before passing it to the man on his right. Nisha caught a whiff of the aroma, and it was sharp and sweet. Corn wine, she realized. Her own people had used it sometimes, usually in midsummer and midwinter, to mark the solstices. The wine took away pain and made people shout and laugh, but if they drank too much of it, it plunged them into a stupor.

She watched the men as the bottle was passed around, and she saw the eager way they reached for it. Finally, it came back to Grep. He held it for a moment and eyed Nisha speculatively. "Drink," he told her, pushing it into her hands.

Cautiously, she raised it to her lips. The liquid was thick and sweet, but at the same time, it burned her mouth and throat. She coughed and gasped.

She heard the men chuckling as she blinked and wiped tears from her eyes. This was far stronger than anything her tribe had ever brewed.

"More," Grep told her. His eyes were intent.

She shook her head and handed the bottle back to him.

His eyes grew fierce. "Drink more," he told her. She heard the edge in his voice.

She hesitated. She didn't want to anger him, but—

He gestured to two men sitting near her. "Rorq! Farg! Hold her!"

Before she had time to react, each man seized her arm. She gave a little cry of surprise as she saw Grep standing up and stepping over to her. He held her by the hair and jerked her head back till she was facing the sky. She cried out, and he seized the opportunity to jam the neck of the bottle into her open mouth. The sweet, searing liquid splashed over her lips and cheeks and down her throat. She gulped convulsively; it was the only way she could avoid choking. Her stomach itself seemed to catch fire.

"Good," said Grep. He gestured for the men to let go of her. He tied the neck of the bottle and sat down again. He seemed to have no further interest in Nisha now that she had been forced to obey him.

Nisha glanced around and saw Rilla watching her. The girl was looking distraught, as if she wanted to help in some way. The other women were close by, but none of them was paying any attention. They were huddling together on the ground, trying to ignore the scene by the camp fire.

Some of the men started singing. Their voices were quiet at first, but as more of them joined in, the noise became raucous. Nisha frowned, trying to catch the words, and she realized that it was a warrior song.

> We spilled the blood of every man we found
> Stole their food and burned their houses down
> Raped their women naked on the ground
> For we are fearless warriors of renown
> Fearless warriors, fearless warriors
> Fearless warriors of renown

There were more verses, each more bloodthirsty than the one before. She looked at the men's grimy faces in the flickering firelight, and she saw the lust in their eyes. It was not the lust that she had seen so often in Jorlor, when she tempted or tantalized him; it was a lust to conquer and destroy. There was something terribly wrong here, she thought. The evil of the men was as tangible as their sweat, as pungent as their body smell. Looking at them, she felt they must have been possessed, somehow, by a dark spirit. This must be how the world had been in the Old Times, before Sun Spirit had forced people to live in peace.

But where was Sun Spirit now, and why had he not spoken to these savages? And why, after so many generations, had Sun Spirit abandoned her people and sacrificed them? She was sure that her tribe had done nothing wrong—certainly nothing to deserve the terrible punishment they had received. It was wrong; it was all wrong.

She found her thoughts moving sluggishly. There was a fuzzy feeling in her head as the wine did its work. She was finding it hard to concentrate, hard to focus.

Grep stood up and grabbed her hand, hauling her onto her feet. "Dance," he told her.

She blinked at him. For a moment she almost lost her balance. "Why?" she asked.

He jumped up and smacked her face. "Dance!" he shouted at her. She saw him balling his fists, and she guessed that he would start hitting her more seriously if she didn't obey.

Nisha looked down at the ground. Tentatively, she moved her feet.

Grep started clapping his hands, and the other men picked up the rhythm. They were all watching her, now. Everywhere she looked she saw faces flushed from the wine and filmed with sweat. She felt frightened. Was he going to offer her to them? Were they all going to rape her?

"Dance!" Grep commanded her again.

Clumsily, she started moving around the fire. Her robe was hanging half open, but she hardly noticed it. Vaguely, she knew she was acting foolishly, without self-respect. But the corn wine made her feel that it didn't matter. None of it mattered. There was a warmth inside her that comforted her and told her not to worry. Her skin was glowing. Her body felt langorous. The men clapped and she found herself stepping to their rhythm, even though she knew that still, it was wrong. They were evil people, they deserved to die, and she shouldn't be displaying herself.

She stopped suddenly and blinked in the firelight. She swayed and almost fell. With difficulty, she focused on the man directly in front of her. It was Kron, she realized. His eyes were wide, full of that awful killing lust that all the men seemed to share. But there was more than that. He had lust for her as well. She met Kron's eyes. Emotions welled up in her. She would do anything to conquer this man, subjugate him, humiliate him—

He saw the fierceness in her eyes and it triggered something in him. Slowly, he stood up.

The clapping stopped.

Kron didn't seem to notice. He took a slow step forward, like a cat stalking its prey. His lips parted, showing his teeth. *Yes, touch me. Touch me, and Grep will kill you.* She tilted her head back, challenging him, and she let her robe open wide.

"Do you want to fight me for her, Kron?"

It was Grep's voice. He walked over, smiling faintly, and stopped less than an arm's length away from the man.

The trancelike mood was suddenly broken. Kron blinked and turned.

Grep seized a spear from a man sitting nearby. He feinted with it. "You want to fight, Kron? Eh?"

Kron stepped backward. His face was turning red with anger. He glanced around at the other men as they started laughing and mocking him. He growled something at Grep, then turned and lunged into the shadows, away from Nisha and the scene by the fire.

As Nisha watched him go, she felt herself tremble with a confusion of emotions. She glanced at Grep, and the world seemed to tilt under her. She flung out her arms to steady herself, but she found herself falling, even though she could have sworn she was still standing upright. Distantly, she realized she was lying on the ground, with grass blades against her cheek and the fire scorching her shoulders. She tried to say something, but the world was turning, receding, and her vision went black.

Later, she felt someone behind her. "Jorlor?" she muttered, before she realized that she was with the nomads in their camp.

"Quiet," a voice told her in an urgent undertone. Two hands seized her robe and started dragging it up, over her buttocks.

Nisha rolled over, turning away from the man till she faced him. The fire had burned down, and the darkness was almost complete. Nisha was still dizzy from the corn wine, but she was sober enough to know that the man behind her was Kron.

He lunged forward and pushed her over onto her back. His hand clamped over her mouth while his weight pinned her under him. She felt his breath on her face and found herself enveloped by his odor. "Quiet, now," he murmured. He glanced quickly left and right. The other men were all sleeping, Nisha realized. "Quiet or I'll kill you," Kron went on. He fumbled with her robe and she felt his rough palm rasping over her smooth skin, groping for her breast.

She opened her mouth wide, then bit down on his hand. He made a muffled protest, swore, and jerked his hand away. He reared up and made a fist to strike her.

"I'll scream, and you'll die," she hissed at him.

He hesitated. His face twitched. "You've been playing with me," he murmured. "You're going to pay for it now. I swear."

"Lie down," she told him, trying to calm herself so that her calmness might infect him, too. "I'll give you what you want."

His shoulders hunched. He glared at her suspiciously.

"Lie beside me," she whispered.

Reluctantly, he obeyed.

Nisha glanced quickly either side of her. The men were scattered here and there, some lying on their backs, some lying on their sides. Most were snoring loudly. She saw Grep next to the fire. That was where she remembered passing out; and yet she was over here in the shadows now. Someone had evidently dragged her here. Well, she was glad of that. It suited her purposes.

She studied Grep till she was sure that he was asleep. His head was facing in the opposite direction, and he was breathing regularly.

Was anyone else watching her? Most of the men close by were snoring. She drew in her breath quickly as she saw the firelight gleaming on someone's eyes. Reebowa, she realized. The boy who had been used as a flunky by the other men was only a few paces away, and his eyes were open.

Or were they? She blinked in the dim light and saw that the boy had quickly turned his head away. Whatever might happen between her and Kron, he didn't want to see it. He was timid; he didn't want to be involved in any trouble.

So, Nisha thought, she could decide freely what to do with Kron. Maybe she should submit to him—then scream for Grep and hope that Grep would kill him for her. On the other hand, it might not work out that way. Kron might blame her for tempting him, and Grep might believe it. Also, she had a suspicion that if she allowed Kron to have sex with her, it might make her worthless to Grep. The warriors seemed totally possessive of their women. If she was defiled by Kron, Grep might simply . . . dispose of her.

There was a middle path, though. A way to satisfy

Kron without being defiled, and at the same time, tantalize him even more. She had considered this when she had talked to him back at the cave. Even now, she wasn't sure that she could go through with it. But the corn wine was still working to soften her perceptions. If she could stop herself from thinking about what she was doing—

She reached down and slipped her hand inside Kron's robe. Her fingers brushed across his belly and moved lower.

He seized her wrist. "Stop that!"

She eyed him challengingly. "Don't you want me to touch you?"

He glowered at her. His broken face was full of suspicion. "What do you mean?"

She felt a moment of pure wonder. These men were ignorant, more ignorant than she could have imagined. The way that they'd used the women in the cave had been the only way they knew. They were like prairie dogs. Suddenly, Nisha saw a whole new spectrum of possibilities.

"I want to give you pleasure," she whispered to Kron. "Are you afraid of that?"

His grip on her wrist slackened a little. "No woman—"

"No woman ever touches you this way?" She told herself to be bold. "In my tribe, it's considered an art for a woman to please a man by touching him. I feel sorry for you if you've never known such pleasure."

He hesitated. Then he drew a flint knife from inside his robe and raised it to her throat. "I can kill you," he told her. "Remember that."

She tried not to think about the knife. She summoned her courage and started fondling him.

Kron drew in his breath sharply. She felt a little tremor in his hand where he held the blade against her skin.

She closed her eyes so that she wouldn't have to look at his face. She told herself to forget who he was and where she was. She touched him as skillfully as she knew how. He responded swiftly—far more swiftly than she'd hoped. He started breathing noisily through his mouth. The knife fell away from her throat. In just a few moments, her touch had seduced him. He groaned as he reached his climax. Then he shuddered and slumped down.

. She took her hand away and opened her eyes. She saw his face, wide eyed and shaken.

"I told you," she said, "that it was a special pleasure."

Gradually, he regained control of himself. He licked his lips and drew back, eying her suspiciously. "How did you ever learn—"

"I told you. In my tribe, pleasing men is an art that all women learn." She smiled faintly. "It's a pity that you chose Orlu. She's so young, she only had a man for the first time this year. I doubt she's had much experience yet."

Kron grunted irritably. He got up on one elbow. She saw his eyes moving furtively, checking that no one was watching. Then he looked back at her. "You'll say nothing about this," he told her. "Do you understand?"

"Of course." Privately, she felt intense satisfaction as she saw his nervousness. He had taken a risk, she realized. He was worried by what might happen to him if Grep found out. That alone was a measure of how much he wanted her—and how much power she had over him now.

He slid the knife back inside his robe. "I should have been allowed to choose you from the start," he muttered. "I earned the right."

"Maybe you still can," she whispered.

He gave her a hard look. "What are you saying?"

"You're a strong man, a fierce man, and a clever man, isn't that so? Grep is strong and clever, too. But maybe not as strong as you."

He looked at her a moment more, then turned toward the fire. He was eyeing Grep, she realized. He brooded for a moment, squinting into the night, then swore under his breath. "You'll say nothing," he told her again.

"Of course not."

He stood up, straightened his robe, and crept away among the sleeping men.

Chapter Eight

They woke at dawn. It was cold at this altitude, and Nisha shivered, hugging herself in her thin deerskin robe. In the desert, she had never known this kind of dampness that seemed to seep through her skin. Even during the spring rains or the thunderstorms that came at the end of summer, it had never felt quite like this.

Her head was aching, and there was a bad taste in her mouth from the corn wine. She went to a big leather trough that Reebowa had filled with water that he had brought from a spring nearby. She splashed her face and stood for a moment rubbing her throbbing forehead.

"Are you all right?" It was Rilla's voice from beside her. "When you collapsed last night, I was worried."

Nisha glanced cautiously around to make sure they weren't being watched. "It was too much wine, that's all."

Rilla was silent for a moment. "Plorngah took me again last night," she muttered. "I can't bear it, Nisha. It hurts so badly—" She broke off, looking down at her reflection in the water. "I have to try to kill him."

"Rilla! They'll execute you!"

A hand gripped her shoulder and turned her around. It was Grep. He had come up on her without her noticing him. She flinched, fearing that he had heard them talking.

"Eat," he said. "You'll have to climb farther today. Hold out your hands."

Obediently, she did so. He dumped a ration of pemmican and ground corn into her wet palms, then moved on.

Nisha turned back to Rilla—but the girl had gone.

The women were roped together as they had been the previous day, with Nisha taking the lead and Jerl at the rear. Most of the men walked ahead, with only a couple of them following the women to make sure they didn't dawdle.

They followed a winding path through the forest of juniper and pinyon pine. A little family of wrens darted from branch to branch overhead, keeping pace with the warriors for a little way. Then a couple of crows suddenly burst out of a nest high in a white oak tree and shouted down at the intruders.

It was a bright, clear day, and despite the grim circumstances, Nisha found herself fascinated by the changing scenery. Her people had always behaved as if their territory was the center of everything. Sometimes they had foraged on some gentle slopes far to the south, but no one had ever even tried to climb the mountains, because it seemed as if there would be little game there. She realized, now, the beauty that they had missed.

After a long while, Grep led them out of the forest onto a dry, flat, gravelly plateau dotted with scrub grass, sagebrush, and stunted hackberry trees. Nisha saw some yucca plants and grabbed some of their pale yellow flowers as she passed by. As she chewed on them, the fragrant taste reminded her of all the times she had walked out with Jorlor in the springtime, and she felt a sudden wave of sadness. It was still hard for her to convince herself that she would never, ever see him again.

When they reached the end of the plateau, another forest began. This one covered a slope far steeper than anything they had climbed so far, and the trees were much taller. Pines and maples towered ten or twenty times the height of a man. Nisha stared up at them in amazement. In the desert, the only trees were poor stunted things, starved of water and barely bigger than sagebrush bushes. She had never imagined that anything so grand and imposing could exist.

She picked her way carefully up the steep, rocky slope, pushing between dense scrub. Small animals leaped away, rustling through the undergrowth, and squirrels ran from branch to branch overhead.

Finally they reached the top of the long, hard slope and found something even more daunting. They were on a rocky ridge that marked a line between steep forested slopes that fell away either side. The ridge curved around and ended in a huge, flat face of limestone pockmarked with holes and crevices. The rock slanted so steeply, it looked almost vertical. Nisha couldn't imagine scaling it yet that was where Grep was leading them. She watched as he repositioned his pack on his shoulders, then started up the rockface, reaching for handholds and footholds that she could barely see from where she stood.

One by one, the men followed him. Clearly, they had tackled it many times before; they moved with the same confidence that she used to feel when she was ascending from the desert to the village at the top of their mesa. But there had been a cleft in the mesa that provided a sense of security as she braced herself between its faces. Here, she would be exposed like a fly on a wall.

When it was Nisha's turn to begin the climb, she told herself to look only at the rock in front of her. She concentrated on placing her hands and feet exactly where the man in front of her had placed his. Behind her, she heard one of the women complaining; but then one of the men—Plorngah, she thought—uttered a brief threat, and the complaints subsided into grim silence. Nisha glanced back and saw Rilla right behind her, then Orlu and Lazonah and Jerl, all of them clinging to the rock with grim intensity. After that, Nisha refused to look down.

She was almost at the top when she heard the scream from behind her.

She froze. Her immediate fear was that one of the

women had slipped, and at any moment, the rope around her neck would jerk tight, dragging her down. She dug her fingers into a deep crevice, flattened herself against the rock, closed her eyes, and held on with all her strength.

Moments passed, and nothing happened. Bit by bit, she dared to let herself hope that she would live.

She heard one of the women sobbing, and one of the men cursing. Nisha allowed herself a quick glance over her shoulder. She saw Rilla immediately behind her, and Orlu and Lazonah clinging to the rock father down. But behind them, where Jerl should have been, the rope dangled freely.

At the foot of the slope, far below, lay a tiny crumpled form with a bright red stain growing around it.

"Go on!" one of the men shouted from below. "You can't turn back. Climb!"

Nisha turned and faced the rock. For a moment she rested her forehead against its rough, cool surface. If Jerl had fallen by accident, she would have been still roped with the rest of them. The fact that she had managed to loosen the rope and separate herself could only mean that she had chosen to end her life.

"Shouldn't we try to go to her?" It was Rilla's voice.

"We can't help her," said Nisha, "and even if we could, she wouldn't want it."

Grep was waiting for them when they finally dragged themselves up to a long, wide ledge at the top of the rock face. He seized the end of the rope, examined it, then threw it to the ground. He turned to Plorngah, who'd been the last man in the line. "She untied herself," he snapped. "And you didn't even notice."

The big man shifted uneasily. "It's a hard climb," he said in a low voice. "I was watching the rock."

Grep turned to the other two men who had followed the women up the face. He glared at them in silence. Neither one of them would meet his eyes. "You'll all suffer for this," he said. "Because of your carelessness, we have only four women. Four!"

"But it wasn't our fault." Plorngah frowned, and his round, fleshy face suddenly looked like the features of a small boy. "There was nothing—"

The protest seemed to release Grep's anger. He stepped forward, scythed his arm, and slapped the big man's fat face, hard. "Quiet," Grep snapped.

Plorngah took a step backward, looking surprised. And then something happened so quickly, Nisha could barely follow it. Plorngah cried out. He was suddenly toppling, waving his arms. His left leg shot out from under him. He smashed down on the ledge where he'd been standing and yelled in pain. Both his legs flipped over the edge of the ledge. Rilla had been squatting right beside him. She reared backward, avoiding his flailing arms for fear of him dragging her with him.

Grep moved quickly. He grabbed Plorngah by the hair. The big man yelled again. He kept on sliding forward and out, into empty space, and Grep wasn't strong enough to hold his great weight.

"Help me!" Grep shouted.

The two nearest men dropped down onto their knees and seized Plorngah by his clothes. There was a ripping sound as one of the seams gave way and the thongs parted—but the other seam held. Plorngah's whole body was dangling, now, over the cliff.

The three men grunted and heaved, struggling with him. Slowly, bit by bit, they managed to haul him back up. Finally one of them grabbed his legs and heaved him onto the ledge.

He lay there gasping. "My knee," he muttered. "Hurt my knee."

"Turn over." Grep showed no emotion.

Plorngah managed to roll onto his back. He yelled with pain as he tried to straighten his leg. His knee was bleeding, and his leg was bent at a bad angle.

Grep squatted down. He made a cursory inspection and

felt the knee briefly, while Plorngah groaned and gasped. "Broken," said Grep, standing up. He brooded for a moment. "We should leave you here."

"No!" He struggled to get up, then screamed as he put his weight on his injured knee.

Grep grunted in irritation. "You two." He nodded to the men who had helped pull Plorngah back to safety. "Let him lean on you. When we get to the top, we'll make him a crutch." He turned to the women and went from one to the next, checking that the rope was still secure around each of their necks. "There will be no more accidents," he said. He looked slowly at each person in his party. "The next man who allows an accident to happen will be killed." He didn't bother to wait for anyone to reply. He returned to the front of the party and continued leading the way forward.

The ledge broadened gradually as it took them upward. Nisha saw that it had been formed in the junction between two great plates of rock. It was a diagonal line ascending directly to the top of the rock formation, which was flat, as if it had been sheared off by a giant axe.

Plorngah limped ahead of her, and the two men had to struggle to support his weight. Up ahead, Nisha saw vegetation at the summit. To her left, there was a panorama so sweeping, she thought she must be able to see all the way back to the mesa of her tribe, if she only knew where to look. How often she had stared out from her home and watched the sun rise above the jagged peaks far to the east. She'd never imagined that she would actually stand on those peaks as she did now.

When they reached the summit, Nisha found herself in yet another kind of woodland. The trees were wiry and small, only about twice the size of desert trees, and spaced relatively close together. Their bark was dry and gray. The ground was hard, and she saw that there was really no soil—just a thin, sandy layer covering a table of limestone that stretched away ahead of her farther than she could see.

In fact, she realized, she was standing on top of a formation like the mesa of her tribe—except that it was vast, a
ragged-edged island of rock. It was a plateau, so large that
it might extend as far as the whole valley she had grown
up in.

Grep went with a couple of the men to one of the taller
trees, tore off a branch, and started trimming it with a
knife to make a crutch for Plorngah, who was sitting on
the ground, clutching his leg and groaning softly.

Nisha saw Rilla standing close by, staring at Plorngah
with a strange expression. Her eyes were bright and her
cheeks were flushed. Nisha squatted down beside her.

"I did it," Rilla whispered to Nisha.

"Did what?"

Rilla turned to her. "On the ledge. I rolled a pebble
under his foot. That's why he fell."

Nisha's eyes widened. She looked in Rilla's face and
saw that it was true.

"You see how much pain he's in?" Rilla whispered.

Nisha reached for the girl and embraced her. She
stroked Rilla's hair and squeezed her shoulders. Skinny,
timid Rilla. "I underestimated you," Nisha whispered.
"I'm sorry."

"There'll be other times when the men can have accidents," Rilla murmured. "Don't you think?"

Nisha nodded slowly. "You may be right. If we are
careful, yes. At least, I hope so."

Chapter Nine

They walked through the forest on the plateau for most of the afternoon before finally emerging in a great area where the trees had been completely cleared away.

Nisha stared with amazement at the hundreds of tree stumps littering the area. She found it hard to imagine the labor that must have been needed to chop so much wood. But what surprised her even more was the structure at the center of the clearing: a long wall of trimmed tree trunks lashed together, twice the height of a man.

As Grep led his party across the clearing, a welcoming shout rang out. There were men on guard at the top of the wooden wall, Nisha realized. She saw their spears silhouetted against the sky.

A narrow, movable section of the wall was dragged aside as Grep approached. His warriors filed in, shepherding the women with them. Nisha discovered that there wasn't just one wall, there were four, joined at the corners, forming a huge rectangular compound where five long, narrow wooden houses had been built parallel to each other. The houses were huge, each of them big enough for fifty people or more, yet they were crude and ugly compared with the homes that her people had lived in, and there was a ruthless practicality about them that she found strangely disturbing. What sort of people would choose to build primitive homes like these? And what sort of people would choose to live in them?

The house at the center was the biggest of all. Nisha saw a door opening at the near end of it, and some men emerged carrying spears. Each of them was decked out in sheepskins with the fur facing out, stained bright red with berry juice. They moved with ceremonial dignity and wore leggings and necklaces embellished with elaborate ornaments of feather and bone. Strange little tufts of animal hair dangled from each man's spear, and the wooden shafts were painted with bold stripes and whorls. Each man's face was painted, too, in broad strokes of red and white.

Grep held up his hand, and his party came to a halt just inside the main gate, facing the houses. Meanwhile, the men in red had lined up each side of the doorway that they'd come out of, and a tall, massive figure was emerging among them. He was clothed in a patchwork of fox, squirrel, rabbit, and badger furs. His robe was fringed with dozens of raccoon tails, and the head of a mountain lion had been mounted on his chest with its jaws gaping wide.

Grep moved forward and extended his arms with their palms upward. "Greetings, Worr," he said.

The big man stepped down from his house, taking his time, moving with elaborate dignity. He had a large, fleshy face and thick lips which turned down in a habitual scowl. He paused to scrutinize Grep, then eyed the warriors and their captives. "One man missing, eh?" he said. His voice was deep and gutteral, resonating in his barrel chest.

"Timor was killed," said Grep. "And Plorngah is injured." His tone was neutral, and Nisha sensed a cautiousness in him that she hadn't seen before. "We bring food for many months," Grep went on. "And four fine women."

Worr slowly grinned, showing irregular yellow teeth. He threw a massive arm around Grep's shoulders. "Good hunting, eh?" He chuckled, then let go of Grep and started inspecting the packs and sacks of looted food that the warriors had slung down on the ground in front of them. He nodded approvingly.

Then he moved toward the women. As he came closer, Nisha saw him more clearly. His black hair hung to his waist. His face was dark tanned and so plump, his eyes were almost lost in the folds of skin.

His fat lips widened appreciatively as he stopped in front of Rilla. He reached out, took her face in his hand, and turned it up toward him. Then he slapped her thigh and chuckled.

He moved on to Orlu, then Lazonah. Finally, he stopped in front of Nisha.

Nisha told herself that if she had managed to cope with Kron and Grep, she shouldn't be cowed by this man. And yet, despite herself, she felt afraid of him. Kron had killed the chieftain of her tribe, and nine others. Grep had killed her husband and child. But at least those two men had shown that to some degree, they valued her.

As she looked into Worr's face, she had the sense that she had no more value to him than a piece of food for his table. His eyes narrowed as he studied her features. "Name?" he said.

She wondered why he hadn't asked the other women for their names. "My name is Nisha," she said, trying to sound calm and neutral, following Grep's example.

"She's not been taken yet." It was Grep's voice. "I saved her for you, Worr."

Nisha felt a chill inside her. She had suspected some sort of ulterior motive in Grep, but not this.

Worr gave her a fat, ugly grin. He reached out and patted Nisha's cheek—except that his touch was so heavy, it was almost a slap. "A fine prize," he said. "But I have five wives. Five is sufficient." He gave Nisha one last, appraising look. "She's yours, Grep. Use her well."

Grep inclined his head respectfully. But standing to one side, Nisha saw Grep's eyes, and there was a watchfulness, a reserve that belied his gesture of respect.

"The other women," Worr said, "they've been taken, eh?"

"Yes." Grep nodded.

"Then we shall have a pairing ceremony. Right away; why wait?" He clapped his hands. "Yik!" he shouted without bothering to look around. "Gather the people."

A thin, nervous-faced man in Worr's honor guard went striding down between the houses, shouting for the tribe to gather. Nisha saw that there were wooden ladders and ramps around the walls of the stockade, where the men on guard had been standing. These guards started climbing down now, heading for Worr's house in the center of the compound. Meanwhile, more men started emerging from the fifth of the long houses.

Nisha frowned. There were no women here. And no children, either.

Worr was taking more time to survey Grep's warriors and the food they had looted. "One man dead, one wounded, not so bad. You killed all your enemies?"

"All except these women."

Worr chuckled. "You'll tell us the tale tonight, Grep." He came to Plorngah, who was leaning on his improvised crutch. "What happened, eh?"

There was a short silence. Nisha glanced at Plorngah and saw his eyes moving uneasily.

Worr frowned at him. "I said, what happened?" There was a sudden sharpness in his voice. Without warning, he kicked Plorngah's bloody knee.

Plorngah shouted with pain. He staggered and almost fell. For a moment, he was unable to speak. "Accident," he muttered. "Out on the cliff path."

Worr spat on the ground at Plorngah's feet. "Accident." He sounded disgusted. "This tribe doesn't need sick men or stupid warriors."

"It'll heal," Plorngah said quickly.

"It will, eh?" Worr paused and scratched himself under his robe. "All right," he said, "one month. Then we'll see, eh?" He turned. "Come." He swept his arm and pointed to the open door of the long house that was his.

* * *

Nisha started following the men, but several of Worr's scarlet-robed guards stepped in front of her. "This way," one of them said. He led her and the other three women from her tribe to another of the houses and banged on its door of rough-hewn poles. The door creaked open on leather hinges and Nisha glimpsed women inside the building cooking and sewing and preparing food. There were still no children, though. And no old people, either: All the women had the look of young wives.

The woman at the door was stern faced, broad shoul-dered, built almost as heavily as Worr. She had hard gray eyes and a time-ravaged face. She took one look at the four women, then shouted something over her shoulder.

A few moments later, two women from the house came to join her. "Wash them for a pairing," said the stern-faced one. "Come." She strode out, and Nisha and her companions found themselves escorted by the other two women toward a corner of the compound that was fenced off by a crude wooden screen. Behind it, they found a shallow pool in a hollow in the rock.

The big woman gave instructions, and her two helpers untied the rope that linked Nisha, Rilla, Orlu, and Lazo-nah. Then their clothes were taken away and they were nudged toward the shallow pool.

Nisha hesitated. "Where are you taking my robe?" she asked. It wasn't her best one, but still, it was the only item of clothing that would remind her of her life on the mesa.

The big woman seized Nisha by the hair, held her head, and slapped her hard. "Wash!" she said. "That robe isn't yours anymore."

There was only room for two of them at a time. Nisha and Rilla squatted down in the water and rubbed it over each other. They looked into each other's eyes, and Nisha saw that Rilla's pleasure at hurting Plorngah had been short lived. The girl was shivering, and not just from the cold. Her face was pale, and she kept glancing toward Worr's house.

Nisha wished she could think of something to say. Unfortunately, she was filled with her own apprehensions. If there was really going to be a pairing ceremony right away, she would have to act far sooner than she'd expected.

One of the tribeswomen helped Nisha out of the pool, and the stern-faced woman stepped forward to examiner her. She told Nisha to open her mouth so that she could look at Nisha's teeth. She felt her body, searched her hair for lice, then probed between her legs. "Healthy enough," she said, and started to turn away.

"Wait," said Nisha. "Please," she added, as she saw the woman's warning look. "Could I ask—what's your name?"

She glared at Nisha for a long moment. "Uwa, sister of Worr," she said.

"Oh." Nisha felt disconcerted. "Well, I just—want to know what will happen in the pairing ceremony."

Uwa folded her arms. "Worr will ask who's claimed you. If a man speaks for you, you'll be paired with him. If no man speaks, Worr chooses."

Nisha tried to think. This was all happening much too fast. "May I ask—one more question?" She tried to make herself sound respectful and polite.

Uwa said nothing. She waited.

Nisha forced a polite, ingratiating smile. "If a man of this tribe—has already coupled with me," she said, "I must be paired with that man, is that right?"

The woman gave her a disparaging look. "Why should any other man want you, if you've been defiled?"

"But back at my tribe," Nisha persisted, "I had a husband. I coupled with him."

Uwa snorted. "You think we care if you chose to couple with a savage out on the plains? That was before you joined this tribe." She turned away. "Jin! Cut her hair!"

Instinctively, Nisha reached up and clutched her head.

"Why?" she whispered, as the woman named Jin came toward her.

"Only men have the right," said Jin. She spoke softly, as if she was afraid to draw attention to herself. She was a slender, graceful women with large, sad eyes. She would have been beautiful, Nisha thought, if she didn't look so beaten down.

"You mean only the men in your tribe may have uncut hair?" Nisha asked.

Jin nodded. "Sit," she said, pointing to a boulder.

Nisha sat on the rock. She closed her eyes, feeling sad. Jorlor had always loved touching and looking at her hair. Jin took a flat piece of wood in one hand, slid it into Nisha's hair, then sawed with a flint knife in her other hand, using the wood as a chopping board. Nisha winced and gave a little cry. The blade was sharp, but still it tugged enough to bring tears to her eyes.

After the haircutting was done, someone brought Nisha a robe of rabbit pelts and she wrapped it around her nakedness. She half-expected some further preparation— perhaps red earth to rouge her cheeks, or ornaments for what was left of her hair. She had spent a whole day preparing herself when she and Jorlor had been paired. But Uwa paid no further attention to her and pushed her brusquely aside as Nisha's companions took their turn under the knife.

Nisha felt a deep, intense sadness. She looked again at the wooden walls of the stockade, and she began to realize that it had been built not just to keep the village safe, but to keep its women from escaping. She looked at Jin's face, and the faces of the other woman taking orders from Uwa, and both of them shared the same look of submissiveness and defeat. They truly were slaves, Nisha thought to herself.

Then another thought came to her. If a man like Plorngah was threatened for being useless to the tribe, what would happen to a woman who was too ugly or too old to be of any interest to the men? Nisha thought she knew the answer—unless, of course, the woman happened to be the chieftain's sister.

When all the women's hair had been cut and they had all been given rabbit-skin robes, they were led back across the compound toward Worr's house. The compound was completely deserted now. A low chanting came from the house, and there was the steady beat of a drum.

As Nisha approached the house once again, the sheer size of it amazed her. Her people had been forced to use space sparingly on top of their mesa, and wood was so scarce, it was treated with reverence. In any case, constructing stone houses was such an arduous task, no one would have considered building a large one under any circumstances. But here, where the land seemed to stretch away forever and there was an unending supply of trees, Worr's tribe had been able to do things as lavishly as they chose.

The door was opened for her, and hands thrust her inside. The air was heavy with the sharp tang of male sweat and wood smoke. Gradually, Nisha's eyes adjusted to the dim light, and she saw that the men were sitting on the ground in rows, all facing the far end where Worr was reclining on a big chair fashioned from logs lashed together with heavy thongs. Either side of him, his honor guard stood in their red robes and painted faces.

The door creaked shut behind Nisha and her three companions. She glanced over her shoulder and saw that none of the women of Worr's tribe had come inside—not even Uwa. She, Rilla, Orlu, and Lazonah were the only women here.

Yik, the timid young man who had been told to gather the tribe, came over to her now. "Walk to the front," he said, gesturing.

Nisha led her companions down a center aisle between the ranks of men. As they chanted, Nisha saw them following her with their eyes, and she shivered with distaste.

At the end of the house she found that a low platform had been made from logs. She stepped up onto it, feeling the rough bark under her bare feet. Yik followed her; he pushed her and Orlu to one side, then Lazonah and Rilla to the other.

Nisha turned to face the crowd of men, and she saw Grep seated in the front row and Kron close by. Kron gave her an ugly, brooding look, and she wondered what she was supposed to make of it. Then she realized: It was a warning.

Worr held up his hand and the chanting stopped. The silence was sudden and disconcerting. The only sound was of the fire splitting and crackling.

The big chair creaked under Worr as he pushed himself out of it and stood facing his people.

"Kneel," Yik hissed at the women. "Show respect!"

Reluctantly, they obeyed him.

"What will become of us?" Orlu whispered. Nisha glimpsed the young girl's face, wide eyed and lost.

"Quiet!" One of Worr's guards poked Orlu with the shaft of his spear. Nisha looked at it—and now that she saw it close up, she realized that the ornamental tufts of hair dangling from it were not from some animal. The hair was human, and each clump was embedded in a square of skin from a victim's scalp.

Nisha remembered seeing Grep's men slicing with their knives, cutting hair from her people before they threw the bodies off the mesa. She closed her eyes for a moment, feeling sickened. How many men did a warrior have to kill to qualify for Worr's honor guard? Was that the custom here?

"Men of the Warrior Tribe," Worr called out, spreading his fat arms to embrace the crowd in front of him. "See what Grep has brought us. Food for our stores, and women for our pleasure. He is a fine man and a brave warrior."

There was a murmur of assent. Nisha glanced at Grep

and expected him to look pleased—yet his face showed nothing. He was staring placidly at Worr, and waiting.

"These women are ready to be paired," Worr went on. He glanced to his right, then to his left. "You." He pointed to Rilla. "Step forward."

She looked terrified, standing there in front of the ranks of brutal warriors in the great wooden house. It was hard for Nisha to remember that Rilla had almost killed a man that afternoon. Perhaps, Nisha thought to herself, that was Rilla's greatest advantage. No one would ever see her as a threat.

"Did any man take this woman?" Worr called out.

In the second row, Plorngah struggled to his feet. "I did," he shouted.

Worr paused a moment, eyeing Plorngah with cruel amusement. Then he glanced at Rilla. "Claim her now," Worr said.

There was a murmur of laughter as Plorngah limped awkwardly to the front. He grabbed Rilla's wrist and pulled her roughly off the platform.

"I pronounce you paired," said Worr.

In Nisha's tribe, a pairing ceremony had taken an entire evening, with many prayers to the spirits for good fortune. This, here, was ugly and wrong; it offended her in every way.

Worr turned to Lazonah. The girl was standing with slumped shoulders, staring at the floor in front of her. Once again, Worr asked if any man had taken this woman and Yahonn stood up to claim her.

Nisha felt her stomach clenching. She was afraid now—because she had already decided, out by the washing pool, that she would have to resolve things as well as she could during the ceremony. She had hoped to wait longer, to learn more about these people and their customs, so she could be more sure of herself. But clearly, she couldn't afford to wait.

Well, she told herself, she had been willing to sacrifice

her life out on the mesa. She should certainly be willing now, with far more at stake.

"You!" Worr's voice rang out. But he was pointing at Orlu, not at Nisha.

Orlu glanced at Nisha and gave her a quick, sad smile. Then she stepped forward.

"Did any man take this woman?"

Kron stood up and stepped forward. "I did." His voice was low, and his face was grim. He grabbed Orlu's wrist and pulled her away to one side. He no longer looked at Nisha.

Finally, Worr turned his attention to Nisha, and his prurient eyes gleamed. "Now," he said, lowering his voice. "You, girl. Step forward."

Strangely, now that the time had come, Nisha's fear drained away and she felt serene. It was all up to her now. She took a step forward toward the rows of men.

"Did any man take this woman?" Worr called out.

There was a long silence. Nisha drew a deep breath. She held it and clenched her fists, waiting.

"All right, then," said Worr. "The choice is mine. I choose Grep—"

"Wait!" Nisha cried. Her voice was so loud, it was almost a scream.

There was a long, stunned silence. "Quiet, you!" shouted the guard behind her. He smacked her shoulder with the shaft of his spear.

"Hear me!" Nisha cried. From the corner of her eye she saw Worr's face creasing into deep lines of suspicion. Ahead of her, she saw Grep's face turning rigid with anger. She only had a few precious moments.

"That man." She turned and pointed to Kron, standing at one side with Orlu. "Last night, he coupled with me."

There was a murmuring that quickly rose in volume. The house was suddenly filled with a roar of men's voices.

For a moment, Kron looked shaken. Then he jumped to

his feet. "Liar!" he shouted. He started forward with a murderous expression.

"Hold him." It was Worr speaking. "Hold him!"

Two of his guards ran forward and seized Kron by his arms. He was so furious, he could barely speak. There was a tic in his face. His eyes were staring wide. He started struggling with the guards.

"Order," said Worr.

"Order!" his guards shouted out. They thumped their spears on the platform where they stood. "Order!"

In all her life, Nisha had never imagined such a spectacle. And now, here, she had provoked it all, with just a few words. She watched it in wonder.

She stole another quick glance at Grep and saw that his expression had changed. He was looking thoughtful now, turning to Kron and examining him. Grep's eyes narrowed and his face started to look the same as when he had seized Nisha and tried to throttle her out in the desert.

The murmuring of the crowd was gradually dying. Nisha took another deep breath. "Kron came to me last night when we camped in the forest," she cried out. "I'd been given corn wine. I was too drunk to stop him."

"Quiet!" the guard behind her yelled again. He sounded outraged.

"It's not your place to speak here," Worr said, glaring at her. "No woman may speak here."

Grep stood up. "Did any man see Kron last night?" he asked. His voice was quiet, but there was a frightening edge to it. He looked slowly around. "Does this woman speak the truth?"

"She lies!" Kron shouted again.

Grep shot him a quick look. "I know you well, Kron. Remember that." He turned back to the men around him. "Well?"

Nisha waited nervously. The long moment dragged on. Finally, she saw she would have to speak again. "There was one who saw me," she shouted out. "Reebowa!"

Worr glowered at her—but then, reluctantly, he turned back to the crowd. "Is that boy here?" he asked.

Nisha held her breath. Slowly, Reebowa stood up.

Grep saw him. "Speak," he told the boy. "You have nothing to fear, Reebowa. Just tell the truth. No man ever needs to fear the truth—so long as he's innocent."

Reebowa bobbed his head. His eyes moved nervously. "I saw—" he began, then swallowed hard and tried again. "I saw Kron go to her," he said, the words tumbling out in a rush.

Grep was only a few feet away from Kron, who was still being held by the guards. Calmly, Grep took hold of the black ceremonial flint knife that he still wore around his neck. He jerked it free from its throng, tossed it into the air, and caught it so that its point faced Kron.

"No!" Kron shouted. But it was already too late. Grep pivoted and thrust his arm, putting all his weight and strength behind the blow. The blade sank deep into the side of Kron's neck.

Grep jerked the knife out and stepped back as a great fountain of blood erupted. The blade had pierced the carotid artery. Nisha could hear the blood hissing as it pulsed in rhythm with Kron's heart.

Kron screamed and clutched his neck, but there was no way he could stem the flow. Everyone in the room was jumping up, shouting. Men started pressing forward.

"Hold him!" Worr pointed at Grep. "Hold her!" He pointed at Nisha.

Nisha didn't resist as the guards seized her arms. Her eyes were on Kron as his knees buckled. He turned his face up to her and she saw the horror in his eyes. She found herself shaking with emotion. She had half-expected to feel regret or remorse, but now that he was dying in front of her, she felt no sympathy for him. "You killed our chieftain!" she screamed at him, amid all the other voices shouting around her. "You killed *ten* of my people!"

Something changed in his eyes. Finally, he understood.

He summoned the last of his strength and pulled free from one of the men holding him. He lunged toward her, waving his hand as if somehow he could grab her and pull her down. But then his mouth fell open and his eyes rolled up, and he crashed forward onto the floor, floundering in his pulsing blood.

"Clear the house!" Worr was shouting. "Only my guards will stay. And you." He pointed at Grep. "And you." He leveled his arm at Nisha.

Chapter Ten

"There must be no violence, no killing in my house." Worr spoke slowly, lolling in his big chair, while Grep and Nisha kneeled before him and Worr's guards stood in a circle around them. Once more the house was silent except for the crackling of the fire. Worr's rage had ebbed into smouldering anger. Kron had been dragged away, although the floor was still thick with his blood, and red streaks showed the path that his lifeless body had taken.

"My honor was at stake," Grep said quietly. "Kron had defiled my woman. This woman, here, who I had brought as a gift to you, Worr."

Worr gestured to acknowledge the point. "You had a right to do as you did." Slowly, he shook his massive head. "But you know well, if I allow violence in this house, my power is threatened." He spread his heavy hands. "It was a transgression. A transgression must be punished."

Grep grunted. "So be it."

Nisha looked from one man to the other. It was impossible for her to judge their feelings toward each other. She sensed a history stretching back over many years, and most of it seemed deeply buried.

"You will be stoned," said Worr.

Grep hesitated for just a moment. His back stiffened. "Why so severe?" he said.

Worr shrugged. "You are the leader of my warriors. If I show you mercy, men won't respect my rule. That's clear enough."

Once again, the two men exchanged a look. Grep's face was as impassive as before, but something changed in his eyes. Nisha almost thought, for a moment, she saw a look of contempt. Then, in a moment, it was gone.

"I have spoken, and it is so," said Worr.

"Yes, it is so." Once again, Grep was impassive.

Worr grunted. "Now, what about this woman?"

He said it so casually, without even glancing at her, Nisha took a moment to realize that he was talking about her.

Grep sighed. "She's been defiled." He sounded like a man who was ready to dispose of a spear because the end of its shaft had split.

Nisha summoned her courage. If she had spoken out before, she could do so again. And once again, she sensed she wouldn't have a second chance. "I have not been defiled," she said.

Both men turned and stared at her. There was a long, frozen moment. "You *lied*?" Worr leaned forward. For a moment she thought he might pull himself up out of his chair and rip her with his fat hands.

Nisha felt fear. If Worr gave a command—if he merely gestured—his warriors would kill her with their spears; she had no doubt of that. But the truth was on her side, she reminded herself. And it seemed that these men had never known a woman like her. She had the element of surprise, if nothing else. "I didn't lie," she said bravely. "May I explain?"

Slowly, Worr sat back in his chair. His fleshy lips pulled back from his teeth. He rubbed the side of his jaw. "What a gift you brought me, eh, Grep?" He made a noise that was halfway between a cough and a laugh. "She behaves like a bitch in heat, and she speaks like a man."

Grep was still studying Nisha, reevaluating her. He said nothing.

"You are insolent," Worr said to Nisha, "speaking in my house a second time without permission." He pointed at her. "You'll be punished for this. What do you think about that, eh?"

"I would like to speak the truth, because it may be useful to you," Nisha said, staring directly back at him.

Worr slowly shook his head. "You've already spoken too much. A man just died because of your chatter." He gave her a long, brooding look. Then he shifted restlessly in his chair as his curiosity got the better of him. "All right! Speak."

She tried to order her thoughts. For some reason, she was more nervous now than when she'd denounced Kron. She felt the same way as when she had followed Grep's men along the narrow, rocky ridge. If she placed her foot carelessly either to the right or to the left, she would probably die.

"I told you that Kron coupled with me," Nisha said. Her voice was unsteady and she paused for a moment, trying to ease the clenching of her stomach. "But," she went on, "there is more than one way to couple with a man."

"Speak plainly, woman!" Worr snapped at her.

"Kron tried to force himself on me," Nisha said. "He said he would kill me if I cried for help. I was afraid of him. I didn't want him to take me. I told him I would please him some other way. So I touched him with my hands, and that was how I satisfied him."

There was another long, frozen moment. Worr looked disbelieving. "What do you mean, you *touched* him?"

Now Nisha felt some confidence. All of these men were the same. They were so ignorant, so brutal, they used women the way they would use animals. They had no idea what a woman could do for them, if they would ever allow it. "In my tribe," she said, "women know many ways to satisfy men. We study the art of love as thoroughly as your tribe has studied war. A woman can use her fingers to give a man extreme pleasure—by touching his genitals."

Worr stared at her hands for a moment, then back at her face. "You say Kron let you do this, eh?"

"At first he was reluctant. But after he experienced it, he became eager." She raised her jaw challengingly. "In fact, he craved more."

Worr turned to Grep. "You knew of this?" He sounded incredulous.

"Of course not." Grep made a slicing motion with his hand. "If I'd know what she did with Kron, I would have dealt with him then."

Worr relaxed back in his chair. He looked at Nisha again and his eyes narrowed thoughtfully. "So you were never penetrated by Kron. Only your hands touched him."

"Yes."

Suddenly Worr chuckled. It was an ugly sound. "Maybe we should chop your hands off," he said. "That way, you'd be cleaned."

Was he serious? Nisha stared back at him, feeling a wave of dismay. But then the dismay was smothered by a bigger wave of anger at the way he was toying with her. "If you take away my hands," she said, "none of you will ever know the pleasure that Kron knew."

This time, Worr laughed out loud. "She growls and she has claws, Grep. She's a mountain cat. Do you still want her?"

Grep glanced at Nisha. He paused for a long moment. "Even a lion can be tamed," he said softly.

"Maybe so, provided a man has enough strength and patience," Worr said.

Grep shrugged. "I want her."

Nisha despised him for the way he spoke, and yet, at the same time, she guessed that she would have been—disposed of, if Grep hadn't accepted her. She felt suddenly weak with relief that her life would be spared. And yet—Grep's greatest pleasure seemed to come from power. She doubted she could tempt and control him as easily as she had Kron. In fact, he might even take pleasure in torturing her to break her spirit.

Well, there was no point in agonizing over it. The decision had been taken.

"Very well," said Worr, "it is so. You and she are paired."

That was it. It was done.

Worr scratched his face reflectively. "Now that she's your wife, I think I'll leave it to you to decide how she should be punished for speaking in my house. Just be sure you do something, Grep, and do it publicly."

Grep nodded.

"All right, there's still your own punishment to deal with," Worr went on. "We'll do it now. Justice should always be swift, eh? In the meantime, we'll put your little she-bitch in the Family House till you're ready for her. I don't want her with the other wives. She could cause trouble."

"Agreed," said Grep.

Worr pulled himself out of his chair and Grep quickly got to his feet.

"Stand!" a guard nudged Nisha.

The big man stepped down and slapped Grep on the shoulder. "You're strong, Grep. The stoning won't be so bad for you." He turned to Nisha. "You listen. You belong to Grep, now. You're his wife, you understand? You won't touch any other man, eh?"

"Yes." Nisha nodded.

Worr reached inside his robe and scratched himself. "Cause any more trouble," he went on, "I will crush you and drink your blood, and Grep will have nothing to say about it."

He gestured impatiently. "Now go," he said

There was a mob of men waiting outside the house. They surged forward as Worr's guards opened the door. Nisha flinched from the press of bodies, and she held back, letting the guards push forward and create a path. "Make way!" the guards shouted.

"What's to be done with him?" a warrior cried out.

"What's the decision?" someone else shouted.

"Stoning," one of the guards said.

Within a moment, the news rippled through the crowd. There was a murmur of surprise—and then Nisha saw something change in the men's faces. Their eyes widened and their nostrils flared. They looked as if they'd picked up the scent of some fresh game.

The mob turned and surged ahead of Grep and the guards, pushing their way between two of the long houses, heading toward an open area at the far end of the compound. No one was interested in Nisha anymore. Worr's guards were focusing all their attention on Grep, holding him at spearpoint as he marched forward, calm and unemotional, staring straight ahead.

Nisha wondered what she should do. Should she look for the Family House, where Worr had decreed that she should stay? There was no sign of Uwa or anyone else to tell her what to do. And she had a terrible curiosity to see what was going to happen to Grep.

She followed the crowd to the open area. Everyone had gathered around a white stone that was shaped like a thick, heavy tree trunk, standing as tall as a man. The guards were stripping off Grep's robe, leaving him naked.

It was difficult for Nisha to see above the heads of the warriors. She glanced around and saw a rock nearby. She climbed up on it. Now she could see Grep stepping toward the stone pillar, with his back to the mob. Two guards seized his wrists, dragged his arms around the pillar so that he was embracing it, and tied his wrists behind it.

Meanwhile, the other guards were telling the crowd to step back, and two men appeared dragging a big basket. The basket was full of small stones—pebbles, flints, and fragments of granite. The crowd swarmed around it, and men started eagerly grabbing the biggest, sharpest rocks.

"Hear me!" Yik had climbed up to the wooden walkway that ran around the inside of the stockade. He looked out over the crowd. "For shedding blood and taking a life in Worr's house, this man, Grep, will be punished. He will be stoned." He licked his lips nervously. He was such a thin, ineffectual male, Nisha wondered why this brutal tribe had allowed him to live. But maybe that was why they tolerated him: He performed a function that was too menial for a warrior, just as Reebowa was useful as a flunky to do chores during a journey.

"Let each man take a stone," Yik shouted out. He looked down and waited till everyone had had a chance to dip into the basket. Then he waved his long, thin arms. "Let the punishment begin!"

The men in the front of the crowd took aim and hurled their missiles into Grep's unprotected flesh. Nisha drew in her breath sharply as she saw Grep twitch and jerk with the pain of the attack. Blood started flowing freely from a dozen wounds.

The men paused for a moment, evaluating the results of their assault. Reluctantly, they stepped aside, and the next row took their place. They threw with all their strength, baring their teeth and taking savage satisfaction in the punishment. Nisha wondered how many of them had been disciplined by Grep at some time in the past. This seemed to be a time for settling old scores.

Another rank of men moved forward and hurled their stones. Nisha saw Plorngah among them, leaning on his crutch, casting a large flint with his free hand. The flint caught Grep on the thigh and tore a deep gash. Plorngah grunted with satisfaction as the blood started oozing out. Then he hobbled away.

Grep was twisting to and fro, trying futilely to evade the missiles that continued to fly at him. Nisha saw his face turned to one side, pressed against the rock. His eyes were tightly closed and his jaw was clenched. His face was covered with sweat.

And this was all her doing, Nisha thought to herself. If she had said nothing, Grep would not have killed Kron, and this punishment would not be taking place. She hated the brutality of it, and the awful satisfaction that the men

were taking in it—yet, at the same time, as she saw Grep
suffer, she felt no remorse. The punishment was trivial
compared with the atrocities he had committed against
her people.

The last few stones were thrown. The crowd had satisfied its blood lust, and the men were turning away. Nisha
saw some of them chuckling, and she heard a few of them
boasting about the amount of damage they'd done. She
remembered how Grep's warriors had talked the same
way as they came down from the mesa after killing her
kinfolk, and she shuddered, feeling overwhelmed by the
awfulness of this tribe and its people. These men were no
better than the rattlesnakes that old Helchar had hunted
with a simple sense of duty. They were venomous creatures who had to be killed, because that was the only way
to protect innocent people from them.

As the crowd dispersed, two of Worr's guards stepped
forward and untied Grep. His back, buttocks, and thighs
were wet with blood, and flies were starting to gather on
it. He seemed too weak to stand, so they lifted him under
his arms. He was breathing in short gasps through his
clenched teeth. Someone threw his robe around him to
cover his nakedness, and he screamed from the touch of
it against his ripped skin.

"You! What are you doing there?"

It was a woman's voice. Nisha turned and saw Uwa
standing and glaring at her. Quickly, Nisha stepped down
from her vantage point. "I was watching—"

"You were told to go to the Family House. You have no
business here." Uwa grabbed Nisha's arm and started hus-
tling her forward—then stopped as Grep was led past
them by the guards. His eyes were closed; he didn't notice Nisha.

"I hope you realize," Uwa said in a low, threatening
tone, "what happened here is your fault."

"I only spoke the truth," Nisha said defensively.

Without warning, Uwa slapped Nisha's face. The blow
was so sudden, it caught Nisha entirely by surprise. She

stumbled and almost fell. "Show some respect!" the woman snapped at her.

Nisha said nothing. She held her cheek. Already it was hot and throbbing.

"Listen to me," Uwa said. She dragged Nisha up till her face was less than a hand's breadth away. "Truth or lies, you spoke where no woman may speak, and now one man is dead and another has been stoned because of it. You'll learn to keep silent. Else you'll suffer. I'll see to that."

Nisha felt a great urge to strike back—to take out all her pent-up anger on this woman and scream and fight and claw her face. But, she reminded herself, this was Worr's sister. Be patient, she told herself. Sooner or later, there might be a time for revenge. This was certainly not that time.

Uwa took Nisha's arm again and walked her beside another of the long houses. "So," she said, in a calmer tone, "my brother says you are paired with Grep now."

"Yes," said Nisha.

Uwa made a disdainful sound. "He's always enjoyed a fight. That's what he wants with you. He'll fight you and drag you down and trample you. That's his way."

Nisha felt a moment of dread. Still, she thought to herself, Grep had been badly hurt by the stoning; he wouldn't be capable of doing anything to her for a while at least. If nothing else, that would give her time to learn more about this place.

"He doesn't even need you," Uwa went on. "A fourth wife? He isn't even interested in the first three."

"He has three other wives?" Nisha asked in surprise.

Uwa gave her an impatient glance. "That's of no importance to you. Not yet, anyway. You'll keep away from the Wives' House. You'll stay in the Family House, I already told you that."

Nisha shook her head. "I don't understand."

Uwa took her around to the front of one of the long houses. She pushed Nisha roughly back against its wall.

The impact jarred Nisha, and she winced as her head hit the rough-hewn wood. "Listen to me!" Uwa snapped. "It's not your place to understand or not understand. You'll learn to do as you're told."

Nisha closed her eyes, forcing herself to remain silent. She waited.

"Grep has been taken to our shaman," said Uwa, "to have his wounds treated. He'll stay there till he's healed. Then, maybe, he'll call for you. Till then, my brother doesn't want you interfering. You'll stay in the Family House, here, and mind your business."

Nisha nodded wearily.

"I hope that's clear enough for you," Uwa said, giving her a little nudge.

"Yes. It's clear." She thought for a moment. "My friends—the women from my tribe—will I see them?"

"No. They'll be in the Wives' House." Uwa turned to a primitive wooden door set in the wall close by. She wrenched the door open. "Now get inside here, and don't cause any more trouble. Otherwise, you'll be the one standing naked at that stone pillar."

Nisha looked up at Uwa's face. She saw no kindness, no mercy. Slowly, Nisha turned and walked through the open door.

As it closed behind her, she found herself suddenly thinking of Jorlor, and missing him more than she had ever missed anyone or anything in her life. And then she remembered what he had said, just the day before the massacre: "You've never known real misfortune, Nisha. You've been lucky so far—but luck comes and goes."

PART TWO

~w~

Revenge

Chapter Eleven

She was pushing her way through a dense mass of bushes and vines. The air was warm and sweet with the smell of pinecones and juniper.

Nisha found herself walking on her hands and knees. She didn't question it; somehow, it seemed right and natural as she threaded a stealthy path through the forest, ducking under brambles and ivy, slipping like a shadow between the trees.

It was good to be here. The forest felt like a home to her. Dry leaves were crisp under her palms. She smelled water just ahead.

She came to a path that others had made before her, and she followed it down a slope, into a glade where a stream fed a dark pool.

She paused for a moment, breathing the odors of the land and straining her ears for any hint of a threat. No; there was nothing here to harm her. She moved out from under some bushes and went to the pool, eager to taste the cool water.

But when she lowered her head to its surface, she saw her face reflected in front of her, and she stopped in confusion. Her face was the face of a cat: a big, golden-eyed mountain lion.

Nisha gave a little cry of fright, and she woke.

She lay blinking in the dimness, trying to understand what she had dreamed. A baby was crying and a woman was trying to soothe it. There was the smell of wood smoke and roasting meat. A crude bed of pine branches was hard under her back, and the chill air had made her muscles ache. She shivered in her furs.

The dream had been so real, she felt as if her mind had been stolen by the lion spirit. Even now, the spirit seemed to be hovering close by, like a shadow just outside her field of view. What could it possibly mean? Was it trying to tell her that she should escape this tribe and wander freely through the forest? But how would she survive with no spear, no bow, no knife, and no way even to make a snare?

Three weeks had passed since she'd denounced Kron and seen him killed by Grep. For three weeks, Nisha had dwelled in this dim, smoky house where children were always complaining, women were always bickering with one another, and babies were always screaming.

A figure stooped over her. A hand shook her shoulder. "Come, Nisha. It's getting late."

A woman was looking down at her—a weary, homely woman named Pawtix who supervised the House. Pawtix had been a warrior's wife eight years ago, but then she'd had children, and after a while her husband had taken a younger woman. At that time, Pawtix had feared she would be cast out, left to die naked on the plateau like many women when they were no longer wanted. But she was a hard worker, always helpful, always obedient, and she loved children. So Worr had put her in charge of the Family House, and she had been here ever since.

"Come on." Pawtix shook Nisha more roughly. "Yowan needs feeding, and Jir soiled himself and needs to be washed."

Wearily, Nisha sat up. She hated the sight of this long, tall house crudely built from logs and mud. The air was always smoky, because the fire that burned at the center wasn't vented properly. The latrine at the rear of the building added its rank odor. Nisha's bed was nothing more than a heap of pine branches on the floor of cold, bare rock. And day and night, there were always children to take care of, and never quite enough food, and never enough women to cope with all the chores. Everyone who lived and worked here was perpetually weary and bad tempered.

"Have you heard any news of my friends?" Nisha asked, as she picked her way among the children and the other women and splashed her face with water from a cistern near the fire. As the days had passed, she had found herself thinking more and more of Rilla, Orlu, and Lazonah. She had never been especially close to them when they had lived together on the mesa, but now she craved their company. They were close by, in the Wives' House, but Nisha was seldom allowed outside, and she had barely glimpsed Rilla a few times. Even then, there had been no opportunity to talk.

Pawtix shook her head and said what she always said: "You shouldn't worry about them, Nisha. I would have heard if anything bad had happened."

"And what of Grep?" Nisha asked, as she dried herself.

"I hear he's much stronger," said Pawtix.

Nisha took a moment to absorb this news. According to tribal gossip, Grep had been hurt much worse by the stoning than anyone had expected. He had lost a lot of blood, and many of the wounds had festered. He had run a high fever and had been unconscious for two days in the shaman's house. Pawtix said that some of the men at the stoning had smeared excrement on the flints that they threw at him, so as to be sure that the wounds would be infected. When Grep led his warriors into battle, they followed him and obeyed him unquestioningly—but only because they feared him. Secretly, it seemed that many of them hated him for the cruel discipline he inflicted. The stoning had been a rare chance for the men to vent their anger.

Even now, according to Pawtix, Grep was still being treated by the shaman. But if he was getting stronger, maybe the time was finally coming when he would send for Nisha. She looked forward to it with a mixture of anticipation and dread. She would do almost anything to escape her servitude here in the Family House—but the idea of serving Grep as his wife was unimaginable, and she hadn't been punished, yet, for speaking out in Wor's house. Her current situation was grim, but her future might be even worse.

The other women in the Family House were starting the morning chores. Eight women worked here, altogether. A few, like Pawtix, had aged to the point where their husbands had lost interest in them. Others were pregnant and would live here till they gave birth. After that, they would surrender their babies and return to the Wives' House to continue serving their husbands.

Pawtix was humming to herself as she cleaned one of the infants. "I wish I could be as cheerful as you," Nisha said, as she turned to the two-year-old named Yowan, picked him up, and tried to quieten his crying.

"Well, it could be worse, couldn't it?"

This was Pawtix's favorite phrase, and it grated on Nisha's nerves. "It could be better, too," Nisha said in a low, intense voice. "Pawtix, the women of this tribe are treated worse than my tribe used to treat its prairie dogs. It doesn't make sense for us to let this happen. There are more of us than the men, and the men are so used to the way things are, they're complacent. If we stood together and raised our voices, they couldn't punish us all. They need us, Pawtix. Don't you see?"

Pawtix's face changed. She was staring at Nisha with mounting horror. "Stop that talk!" she hissed. "Talk like that will get you stoned, or worse." She glanced around quickly, then shook her head to erase her memory of what she had just heard. "There's no place in this tribe for a woman who speaks against a man."

"Yes," Nisha said wearily. "I know."

There was a sudden commotion outside the house. Nisha heard shouts and running feet. "Stop them!" someone cried.

"Get spears!" That was a man's voice.

It was late in the morning and Nisha had been wetting some corn paste before baking it by the fire. She glanced at the other women. All of them had stopped what they were doing.

Nisha felt suddenly anxious. "Is the village being attacked?" she said.

No one answered her. Finally Pawtix went back to the job she was doing, repairing a little fur robe for one of the children. "Whatever it is," she said, "someone will tell us if it needs our attention."

"No," said Nisha. "If there's really an emergency, the men may just forget about us."

Outside, there were more shouts and running footsteps.

Nisha made her decision. "I'm going out to see," she said.

"Nisha, that's not wise." Pawtix gave her a warning look.

But Nisha was already at the door, pushing it open. There was no fixed rule against women straying out of the Family House. Often, they needed to fetch water or food from the stores. But it was generally understood that you had to have a good reason to leave your work and venture into the compound, and if Uwa happened to find a woman who lacked such a reason, that woman would be punished.

Nisha stepped into the daylight. She blinked and shaded her eyes from the brightness of the sun. The main gate had been dragged open, and some of Worr's guards were running out, holding their spears high. A crowd of warriors was gathering at the north wall of the stockade, peering through the narrow gaps between the wooden posts, talking and shouting excitedly.

Everyone seemed too preoccupied to notice her. Impulsively, she ran between two of the long houses and found a spot away from the crowd, where she could peek through the wall without attracting any attention. She saw the scarlet-robed guards running across the open space around the village where all the trees had been cleared away. She heard someone shouting, giving orders.

Nisha changed her position, trying to see where the guards were heading. She drew in her breath with dismay. There were two tiny shapes in the distance, fleeing toward the trees at the edge of the clearing. They were women; she felt sure of it.

There was another barked command. The warriors drew back their arms and cast their spears. A swarm of thin black shafts was briefly silhouetted against the sky.

For a timeless moment, it seemed as if the fleeing women would reach the safety of the trees. But then there was a faint, distant scream, and the running figures fell.

An exultant shout rang out from the red-robed guards, and they ran forward to the figures that had slumped to the ground. Nisha saw the women being lifted up by their heels and dragged back to the village. And as they came closer, she saw their faces. One of them was Orlu; the other was Lazonah.

The guards reentered the compound and the warriors gathered around them. Nisha stood for a moment, clenching her fists, feeling her nails biting into her palms. She leaned one shoulder against the stockade to steady herself. She didn't want to believe what she had seen. She told herself she could have been mistaken. *Be calm,* she told herself. *Be calm!*

She took a step, then another step, and suddenly she found herself running forward, her bare feet thudding across the rough, rocky ground.

She peered over the heads of the men who were crowding around the main gate, and she didn't care whether anyone noticed her or recognized her. She had to see.

The guards came in through the gate and passed close by her, dragging their victims like dead game. And Nisha saw that her initial assessment had been correct: One of the women was Orlu, and the other was Lazonah. Both of them were still alive, moaning and struggling feebly. Lazonah was bleeding from two wounds in her side. A spear was still embedded in Orlu's thigh, and its shaft was scraping on the ground.

The door of Worr's house opened, and the chieftain emerged wrapped in his furs. More of his guards gathered around him. He nodded to the men who had brought the fugitives, and he pointed at a wide, flat slab of rock in front of his house.

Nisha had noticed this slab many times, and because of the dark stains on it, she'd assumed that it was used for butchering game. What puzzled her, though, were the dozens of small boulders scattered around it. The village was maintained with a military concern for neatness and order; it seemed odd that the clutter of loose boulders had never been cleared away.

The two women were lifted up and thrown onto the slab. Orlu was screaming, trying to grab the spear that was stuck in her thigh. Lazonah shouted with pain as she landed on the flat rock, and she clutched her wounds.

The men of the village clustered around. They stooped and grabbed hold of the boulders around the slab. They heaved them up and started piling them on top of the wounded women.

Nisha felt weak with the horror of what she saw. She imagined herself running forward, seizing the men, throwing them aside, and embracing her kinfolk, saving them from this terrible death. But that was the most childish fantasy. If she interfered in any way, Nisha sensed with total certainty that she, too, would be slaughtered.

She felt tears running down her face. She hugged herself, trembling with grief and rage. She turned away, but she still heard Orlu and Lazonah screaming as they were crushed to death.

Finally, blessedly, the screaming stopped. Nisha dared to look again at the scene, and she saw Worr stepping down, swaggering toward the slab. He waved his arm, and the crowd backed away to make room for him. He stood for a moment, surveying his people. "This is what happens," he shouted, "when someone betrays our tribe."

The men murmured their agreement.

Blood was trickling out at one end of the slab. Worr stepped over to it, rubbed his fingertips in it, then licked his hand.

Suddenly Nisha found herself on her knees, vomiting onto the ground while the crowd dispersed and Worr ambled back into his house, followed by his guards.

"Nisha?"

She looked up quickly, fearful of being punished for being out here. She saw a thin figure standing over her. It was Rilla, she realized.

She struggled up onto her feet and seized Rilla's hands, then embraced her, hugging her close. "I'm so glad you're here," she cried. "I thought, perhaps—"

"That I had climbed over the fence like Orlu and Lazonah?" Rilla shook her head. "I tried to persuade them not to. It seemed so clear that they wouldn't survive. But—you know, that was what they wanted."

Nisha stared at Rilla in disbelief. "They wanted to *die*?"

"They knew they wouldn't be able to feed themselves out on the plateau, even if they managed to escape." Rilla sighed. "I think they were hoping to reach the cliffs and jump over the edge."

Nisha felt a conflicting mixture of emotions—sadness that her kinfolk had wanted to end their lives, and anger that they had given up so quickly. She looked into Rilla's face. The girl had always been thin, but now she seemed gaunt. "What about you?" Nisha said. "Do you want to die? Is life so terrible in the Wives' House?"

Rilla glanced quickly around. She took Nisha's arm. "We shouldn't stand here. We'll be noticed."

Feeling like a furtive forest creature, Nisha followed Rilla into the shadow of one of the long houses.

"The men just make use of us, that's all," Rilla said, pitching her voice low. "We do chores, we sit, we prepare food, and when our men summon us, we go to the War-riors' House."

"Yes?" said Nisha. "And what happens?"

Rilla turned her head away. She didn't seem to want to talk about it.

"I need to know," said Nisha. "I'll be joining that house soon enough."

Rilla gestured helplessly. "A man may make his wife stand naked for the other men to see. Or they'll make us beg for scraps of food. Or one of us will be publicly beaten, for the slightest reason—or for no reason at all." Rilla looked back at Nisha. "And then of course the hus-bands have sex with their wives, and it's always harsh and painful."

Nisha felt the weight of Rilla's words. She could see more clearly, now, why Orlu and Lazonah had wanted to end their lives. And yet, even now, there was a part of Nisha that refused to admit defeat. After all, she had turned two men against each other, and one of them had died while the other had been grievously wounded. If she had done that once, couldn't she do something like it again? Sooner or later, surely some opportunity would have to present itself. "We must never give up hope," she said simply, placing her hand on Rilla's shoulder.

"But there is no hope!" Rilla pushed Nisha's hand aside. "We'll be used and abused, we'll bear children for these men, and then we'll be cast out to die on the pla-teau. If it's going to happen anyway, why go through all the years of suffering first? Why not end it now?"

"Well, why not?" Nisha found herself getting angry with Rilla. "If it's all so hopeless, why didn't you run out there with them?"

Rilla's mouth turned down at the corners. Her lip quiv-ered. "Because I was too afraid," she whispered, as tears welled up in her eyes.

Nisha grabbed her by the shoulders and shook her. "Listen to me! Look at me! You saw what happened to

Kron. And how Grep was punished. That was my doing, Rilla!"

"Not so loud, Nisha!" The girl glanced nervously around.

Nisha grunted with irritation. "There are so many women in this tribe. If they would just stand together—"

Rilla jerked free. She laughed sadly. "Their spirits are broken before they even come of age. They're like frightened rabbits, Nisha! Do you really think they can turn into fierce mountain cats like you?"

"I just say that there must be a way," Nisha insisted.

Rilla laughed bitterly. "What are you going to do— seduce them all and make them all fight one another and kill one another so that they can have you?"

"I will do whatever I can," said Nisha. "That's all I know." She suddenly felt weary, and lonelier than before. For the past three weeks she had sustained herself with the idea that when she was reunited with the other women of her tribe, they would be able to act. But now two of them were dead, and the third seemed incapacitated by her own fear.

Nisha sighed. "Just don't do what Orlu and Lazonah did," she said to Rilla. "I'll be with you soon, as soon as Grep is stronger and moves me to the Wives' House. Then we'll see what we can do."

Rilla nodded vaguely. She hardly seemed to be listening.

Nisha thought for a moment. "Do you speak to Worr's wives, in the Wives' House?" she asked.

Rilla shrugged. "Sometimes."

"Have they said anything about—a punishment for me, for speaking in Worr's house? He said he would leave it to Grep, but I was wondering—"

The question seemed to bring Rilla back from her distant contemplation. "They said nothing about that," she told Nisha. "But they did ask me about the ways that women of our tribe give pleasure to a man."

"They asked you that?" Nisha suddenly saw the implication. If Worr's wives had asked Rilla, it must be because Worr had told them to. So, Nisha thought to herself, she had roused the fat man's curiosity. "What did you tell them?" Nisha asked, turning back to Rilla.

Rilla shrugged helplessly. "I told them that I'm young, Nisha. I had not even been paired when—when the warriors came and killed our people. And I'm not a bold person, like you. I told them—"

"You two, what are you doing there?" the voice was stern and commanding.

Nisha looked around and saw Uwa's bulky form looming over her.

"You shouldn't be out here," Uwa said, glaring at them.

"I heard the men running and shouting," Nisha said quickly, "and I was afraid. I had to see what was happening. I thought—I thought perhaps another tribe was attacking us."

Uwa scowled. "Well, you're wanted. Grep has asked for you. He's in the shaman's house." She grabbed Nisha's arm. "I'll take you there." She glanced at Rilla. "As for you, get back to the Wives' House where you belong."

Chapter Twelve

The shaman lived in a small hut of his own, separate from the five long houses that occupied the center of the compound. Nisha entered the little wooden building cautiously. There was the smell of medicinal herbs, and juniper wood smoldering in a fire at the far side of the hut, where faint light penetrated through a smoke hole in the roof.

"Hello?" Nisha called out. Uwa had refused to enter the building and had pushed Nisha inside on her own. It was so shadowy and dark, all she could really see was the smoldering fire, some stones ranged around it, and some beads and fetishes hanging from the roof beams.

Suddenly a figure loomed up in front of her. Nisha gave a little cry. The face was like an apparition, ghostly white with vacant black circles where the eyes should have been. The body, too, was white, crisscrossed with bold black stripes. It was the shaman, Nisha realized. He was naked except for a thin strip of whitened deerskin around his hips. His entire body had been painted, down to his feet. He raised a rattle high over Nisha's head and shook it, and the noise was so sharp, it made her flinch.

The shaman made little birdlike cries and stepped around her. He froze motionless for a long moment, then sidestepped, slowly waving his arms as if he was feeling the contours of the space she inhabited. Finally he stepped back and pointed toward the opposite side of his house.

Nisha's eyes had begun to adapt to the gloom. She saw

a figure stretched out near the fire. It was Grep, she realized.

He was so still, he seemed lifeless. But she saw his eyes gleaming in the faint light, and he was looking at her. "Come here," he said softly, and pointed to the floor beside his bed.

She crept forward. As she did so, the shaman lowered a flap of deer hide across the doorway of the hut, so that now it was almost totally dark.

"Sit," Grep told her. Reluctantly, Nisha sat on the dirt floor.

Grep raised himself on one elbow and studied her for a moment. "They have fed you well in the Family House."

It wasn't what she had expected him to say. "Yes, they feed me well enough," she agreed cautiously.

"You look as fine as I remember," Grep said, "although, of course, looks can be deceptive."

Nisha said nothing.

Grep grunted with discomfort. With difficulty, he sat up. He turned his back toward her. In the light that filtered down from the smoke hole in the roof, she saw that some of the wounds had scabbed over, but others were still leaking pus. The skin was a terrible mess of inflamed sores. Nisha felt a wave of nausea, but she forced herself not to turn away. She told herself to feel glad that this terrible man had been forced to suffer.

Slowly, Grep lowered himself to the bed. "I paid more dearly than I expected," he said, "for killing Kron." He spoke the words in little spasms, and she guessed that movement caused him intense pain.

Nisha had been dreading this line of conversation. "I hope you don't blame me," she said quickly. "I didn't know the customs of your tribe. I only spoke the truth—"

"Quiet!" he snapped at her. He faced her again, and his eyes were watchful and alert. "The only people I blame are those who act against me," he went on. "And that's why I called you here, to find out whether you deliberately set me against Kron." He turned his head. "Rorth! Come here!"

The shaman moved forward. He was still holding the wooden rattle in one hand. In his other hand he had picked up a leathery disc. Nisha had trouble seeing it in the dimness. But then she caught the distinctive aroma and realized that it was a peyote button.

Some of her apprehension abated. Her tribe had traded each year with the Red Valley People for peyote that grew on their land to the south. She had consumed it many times in rituals when her people danced for rain.

"You will eat this," Grep said.

She looked directly into his eyes. "What is it?" she asked, trying to keep her voice neutral and her face expressionless.

He grunted irritably. "Rorth! See she eats it."

The shaman bent over her. He pushed the peyote to her lips. Nisha made a show of reluctance, then finally opened her mouth. She ate as much as the shaman chose to give her—perhaps half of the disc.

"Rorth believes you are possessed," said Grep. "He thinks a Night Spirit controls you, and he will drive it out."

Nisha glanced cautiously at the shaman. He threw up his hands and shook his rattle again, then gave a sudden high-pitched scream. He stepped around Nisha, then started dancing and shouting in a language that she had never heard before.

"Lie down on the floor," Grep told her. "This will take a while."

Nisha lay on her back on the ground, looking straight up at the underside of the roof while the shaman continued dancing, pausing for long moments and lapsing into silence, then leaping and screeching like a bobcat. He bent over her and chanted and shook his rattle in her face. He clenched his fists and went into a trancelike state with his body completely rigid. Then he moaned and let his head loll back, and then he danced again.

Winnor, the shaman of Nisha's people, had never behaved like this. He had chanted softly, speaking kindly to the spirits, begging for their help. He had never shaken his fists and screamed. Instinctively, she distrusted this shaman of the Warrior Tribe. She remembered something that Winnor had once said: "When a man shouts louder, his words mean less."

Gradually, she started to feel the effect of the peyote. Her stomach churned and she doubled over. The shaman thrust a bowl in front of her and she retched into it. Then she lay back and watched the room change around her. Each wooden pole in the roof above her seemed to sprout fresh green shots. The hard earth beneath her softened and grew warm, like the flesh of a giant beast. She looked at her own hands, and they glowed gently in the dimness.

The shaman peered into her eyes and nodded to himself. He spread his arms, contorted his face till his mouth was gaping wide, and let out yet another long, piercing scream. Then he sprang up and started dancing in a frenzy, shaking his fists at the sky. He went to a basket beside Grep's bed, pulled out a handful of gravel, and flung it down on Nisha. Then, without warning, he kneeled astride her. He seized her head between his hands and pried her jaws open.

In her drugged state, his face turned into the face of a beast. She cried out, fearing that he would eat her.

Her cry seemed to satisfy him. He clapped his hands together in front of her face, clenching them as if he held something. Then he threw his palms into the air, releasing it. Quickly, he drew back back from her.

Another face took his place. Distantly, Nisha realized it was Grep, yet in her eyes, the features changed. It was Jorlor staring down at her.

Over the years, she had learned how to keep a piece of her mind untouched by the peyote, even while her senses were full of colors and shapes that seemed more real and powerful than the world itself. What was it that Grep wanted, anyway? She remembered that he doubted her. He wanted to know if she had acted against him.

The image of Jorlor comforted her, so she clung to it. She told herself that his spirit had come here to help her in this test. "Thank you," she murmured to him.

Someone was saying something. Asking her something. Jorlor was asking if she wanted to hurt him. "I would never hurt you," she said, and Jorlor's eyes seemed to glow and expand until she saw through them into a landscape of wildflowers.

Would she do anything Jorlor asked her to do? Of course she would. She found herself smiling, lying in tall grass, with the sky so blue, she felt as if it would drown her. And there was the white disc of the moon looking down on her, with two black holes where the eyes should have been. The disc grew larger till it shattered the blue sky into dark fragments. But she didn't mind; Mother Moon was her friend.

"Did Kron defile you?" The words came from somewhere outside of this wonderland of colors. She found herself laughing, and her voice was the voice of a red-tailed hawk. She was circling up into the sky, laughing at the idea that she would give herself to any man other than Jorlor. "No," she cried, and laughed again. "Kron disgusted me. I would never let him abuse me."

And the rational segment of her mind that stood to one side also laughed, seeing how very simple these questions were, and how easy it was to please the people who were asking them.

For a while, she drifted. Then there was an acrid smell. Something was burning. The shaman had lit some herbs and was wafting them toward her with a black feather from a turkey vulture. The fumes stung her nostrils. "Sleep," a voice said. She didn't want to sleep, because the colors were so beautiful, and she wanted to run across the desert and gather the wildflowers. But there was something about the burning smell that was making her drowsy.

"Not yet," she said. But it was too late. The colors faded into darkness.

When she woke, she sensed that a long time had passed. The light filtering into the shaman's house had changed subtly, and she guessed it was now late afternoon. Only a trace of color till clung to the dark wooden roof above her; the rest had been washed away as the drug had left her mind.

She was still lying on the floor, but the shaman had gone. Grep was sitting up, resting his elbows on his knees. He was watching her.

For a moment, Nisha wondered if he might have touched her body while she was unconscious. But no; if he took her, he would surely want to see her yield. It would be too easy for him to take advantage of her while she was asleep.

Slowly, she sat up. She raised her hands to her head. "I had such a strange dream," she said.

He grunted. "The disc you ate is powerful magic."

"Oh." She frowned. "The shaman—did he drive out the Night Spirit?"

"Perhaps he did." Grep made a disparaging sound. "I am only interested in things I can see and touch." He stood up and went to the door of the hut. He beckoned for her to follow.

Nisha scrambled onto her feet and followed him warily. She was surprised to see him moving like this; she'd thought he was too weak. Had he pretended to be, just to see how she would react?

He drew the door flap aside. "The house, there," he said, pointing to the long building close by. "That is the Warriors' House. You know that, don't you?"

She nodded.

"I rule that house."

"Yes," she said, waiting beside him, not sure what to expect.

"And I will return to it tonight," he said. "My back still gives me pain, but I'm strong enough." He let the flap fall, shutting out the light. He turned to her, a shadowy, ominous figure in the semidarkness. "I want you to understand something. You saw me stoned by the people in the meeting place. But I'm stronger than any man in that house. Not just in my body, but my mind. And they respect that strength—even while they hate it, because it means they must serve me." He paused for a long moment. "Do you understand?"

"Yes," she said. She understood that in his world men struggled for power, which only one of them could ultimately possess. It seemed to her a terribly small pleasure and ambition, yet that was the way of this tribe.

He reached out. He was so fast, his fingers were gripping the back of her neck before she even saw him move. His grip tightened till she gave a little cry.

"Are you stronger than I am?" he asked. His face was close to hers. She could feel his breath on her cheeks. Part of her cringed from his touch and wanted to struggle, scream, and run from him.

She held herself in check. "I am weaker than you," she said, for that was what he wanted to hear.

He nodded slowly. "You are weaker. So, you will serve me, too." He let go of her. "Otherwise, you will be punished, and if you still resist, you will die."

She averted her eyes. Inside herself, she raged at him. But she showed none of that. "May I ask a question?" she said tentatively.

He nodded.

She phrased it carefully in her head. She had to be careful with him, especially now that he seemed cautiously ready to trust her. "You talk of the strong ruling the weak," she said. "But you seem stronger than Worr."

She saw sudden tension in the muscles of his face—the same terrible tension that had seized him when he had half strangled her out in the desert. She flinched away from him. She hadn't expected this.

But this time, his anger wasn't directed at her. He stood for a moment, flexing his fingers. "Worr is a powerful man," he said. "And he is our chieftain. He must always be shown respect."

The words were spoken simply, yet there were emotions locked behind them that were not simple at all. She heard an underlying anger, and the same contempt she had glimpsed in his face for just an instant when Grep had faced Worr in Worr's house.

The thought that Grep despised Worr excited her, because it meant there was an uneasy balance of power between them, just as there had been between Grep and Kron. But this time, the balance was far more crucial. If it tipped, it could alter the fate of the entire tribe.

Nisha summoned her courage to go on. "When I spoke to Worr about—my ways of pleasing a man," she said, "I saw a certain interest in his eyes."

"When was this?" His eyes were alert. He was frighteningly fierce, and instinctively, she stepped back.

"After Kron died," she said. "When I kneeled beside you in front of Worr. I could tell from the way he looked at me, he wanted to know what I had done that had tempted Kron so easily."

Grep grunted. He bowed his head, deep in thought. "Your two friends, today," he said, "I understand they tried to flee our village, and they were caught and crushed."

"Yes." For a moment, she remembered the heap of boulders outside, and once again, in her imagination, she saw Worr licking blood from his fingers. Quickly, she banished the thought.

Grep raised his hand and looked at her. "But Rilla still lives."

Now Nisha understood his line of questioning. "Rilla is very young," she said. "She is not yet—experienced."

Grep smiled faintly. "So you are the only one, now, who has the knowledge of the women of your tribe."

"Yes," Nisha whispered.

"And I own you," he went on.

Nisha bowed her head. She said nothing.

"I think it is time," he said, "for you to show me this knowledge of yours." He reached for her fur robe, loosened the thongs, and pulled it open. Instinctively, she almost raised her hands to stop him. She had to force herself to stand passively in front of him while he stood staring at her body. Then, with a sweep of his arm, he pulled the robe completely off her and tossed it aside.

He pointed to the bed beside the fire. "Lie there," said. "I will have you now."

Chapter Thirteen

She felt afraid as she lay down on the bed of straw. She was far less sure of herself with Grep than she had been with Kron. Yes, Grep wanted her; but he was much more shrewd, and there was much more violence in him. He showed such a need for power, she felt as if she was surrendering herself to one of the wild thunderstorms that used to lash her home on the mesa in late summer each year. The lightning that had seared the desert had been just as frightening as Grep was now.

"Lie with your hands by your sides," he told her.

"But—" She hesitated. "If I am going to show you—"

"Obey me!" His voice was like a smack across her face. Mutely, she complied.

He shed his own clothes, then squatted down beside the bed. She saw something hanging around his neck and with a little start of recognition, she realized it was the black flint knife. For a moment Nisha was overwhelmed with a sense of outrage. It was wrong for her to be naked, here, with this man who had slaughtered her kin and debased everything that she cared for.

But if she truly wanted revenge, she would have to bide her time. With difficulty, she managed to look away. She told herself to be calm as Grep reached out and touched her. She flinched, fearing that he would be rough, but he slid his hand lightly across her skin, learning the curves of her body.

"I will test you now," he said.

She felt a new leap of fear. What did he mean?

"I must be certain that you have surrendered to me," he said. He turned toward the fire, and she saw his sharp, thin profile outlined in the red glow of its embers. He reached for a pair of sticks, dug them into the ashes of the fire, and dragged out a small fragment of wood, only half the size of her little fingernail. He raised it to his lips and blew on it, so that it glowed as a single spark in the darkness. Then he turned to Nisha.

"No!" she gasped, as she saw that he was going to place it on her skin.

"Don't move," he warned her. And he dropped the ember.

It fell on her belly. For an instant she felt nothing—and then it was a speck of burning pain. It was not quite as bad as she had feared. No worse than stubbing her toe when she was climbing over rocks or striking her finger when she was using a hammerstone to shape a flint. But now he was pulling another little ember from the fire, and the anticipation of the pain was worse than the pain itself. Once again he held the ember above her skin, and he watched her face as he let it fall.

Nisha cried out. In the dim red light, she saw Grep smile. He wanted her to suffer. Maybe he even wanted to mar her beauty. She felt her eyes growing wet with tears of rage. She looked up at his face and imagined herself lashing out like a cat, scratching his face as she had when she'd seen him throw his spear at Jorlor. But those scratches had long since healed. She would do far worse now, if she had the chance. She would gouge the skin deeply until his face was red with blood.

But that was a helpless fantasy, nothing more. Once again, she told herself to be patient. She clung to that thought as he placed another, larger ember on her skin, this time on her thigh.

"Please," she whispered, "it hurts—"

"Quiet," he told her. At the same time, though, she saw that he liked hearing her whimper. His face showed his pleasure. His nostrils were flaring. He was breathing deeply. She moaned and she saw the satisfaction that it gave him. "Just lie still," he warned her again, as he placed an ember between her breasts. "I own you, woman. I can do anything I want. Do you understand that?"

Yes, she understood it perfectly. She moaned again as he set yet another little ember on her. The little dots of pain were really not so terrible; they were like the bites of stinging ants. But it would be best if she gave him the idea that it was a terrible torment. "Please," she gasped, "please stop."

He reached out and grabbed her by the hair, holding tightly, so she couldn't move her head. Carefully, he placed an ember in the center of her forehead.

This was worse than anything that had gone before. He was marking her where everyone would see it. Despite herself, she started crying.

He watched the tears run down her cheeks and he nodded slowly. He set down the two sticks and sat back on his haunches. "Make room for me there," he said. "Move to the side."

Reluctantly, she obeyed him.

He placed himself beside her. His body was very muscular, gleaming in the dim red firelight. For a moment, he actually looked a little like Jorlor. "Now you will show me," he said, "what made Kron act like such a fool. You will do it now, or I will punish you more."

Could she do it? She was filled with emotional turmoil. If she refused, she was sure he would make good on his threat. And once again, she reminded herself that it was a means to an end. She should not think of herself betraying Jorlor by lying with the man who had killed him. She should think of it as her *duty* to Jorlor. There really was no choice.

She ran her hand across Grep's chest, touching the muscles, and she half-closed her eyes, and she started fondling him lightly. He was very hard, very large, and she heard him grunt with surprise as her fingers caressed him.

Nisha felt Grep's breath on her cheek. She was obviously arousing him. She looked at his face and felt buoyed up by the knowledge that the power was not all his, after all. She was controlling *him* now—his lust, his emotions. No other woman had done this to him. And so, despite all his anger and cruelty, there was still something inside him that was vulnerable to her, because he wanted her. No, more than that, he *needed* her. That was why he had chosen to be paired with her. He was far more cautious and guarded than Kron had been, but on the inside, he was not so different: he wanted to possess that special, elusive quality that he sensed inside her.

Then she had another thought. Grep could beat her or punish her and make her obey him in fear of losing her life. But the part of her that he craved—the special, secret inner self—was the one part he could never really touch. If she followed his orders, it would always be out of fear, nothing more than that. It would be a charade. She would never care for him any more than his warriors did. She would never want him, as he wanted her.

Suddenly she felt contempt for him and soaring new confidence in herself, because in a way his need for her made him weaker than she was. She told herself that she could manipulate that weakness, calmly and coldly, if she was careful enough.

The pain from the burning embers suddenly seemed trivial to Nisha. She had endured it, and she could endure much more if she had to, and the more she endured, the more it would prove her strength.

Impulsively, she squirmed down and kissed his chest and stomach. It was her decision, now, whether he would enjoy pleasure. She started toying with him, tantalizing him, making him want her. Her hands roved over his body, and she felt tension ripple through him. Finally, she used her mouth on him.

He hadn't expected it. He cried out in surprise and

reached out as if he wanted to stop her. But his hands never touched her. Gradually, he let them fall by his sides.

She used her mouth till she sensed he was almost at his climax. Then she pulled back and held him in her fist. Slowly, she moved her hand, watching his face intently. His lips were parted. He was panting. It was up to her, now, whether he achieved fulfilment or frustration.

She moved her hand in sudden fast strokes. Quickly, with savage pleasure, she used her hand to bring him to a shouting, quivering climax.

For a long time afterward he lay staring at her. He seemed confused at first, then thoughtful.

Finally, he stood up. Without a word, he picked up his robe, put it on, and stepped outside the hut. Faintly, she heard a trickling sound as he urinated onto the ground.

When he returned, he sat down and threw some more wood on the fire. "You spoke truly," he said. "Your people have mastered the art of pleasure, just as my people have mastered the art of war."

"Yes," she said simply.

He gave her a warning look. "You will never do that for any other man." His voice was harsh. "Never, do you understand me?"

She nodded without speaking, telling herself not to be frightened by his fierceness. She had just seen him lying and gasping, staring at her, eager for her. His anger couldn't make her forget that.

He seized her by the hair. "If I ever find you've disobeyed me, I will punish you as you have never been punished before. And I'll kill any man you give yourself to."

She winced as he tugged at her hair. "I have no reason to betray you."

He nodded slowly. "That is true. I doubt any other man in the tribe would want you, after what they saw you do in Worr's house." His anger gradually ebbed, and he smiled faintly. "Worr was right: you're dangerous as a mountain cat."

She blinked. It was strange to hear him say that, after her dream that morning. But perhaps it was just a coincidence.

"So it's the custom of your tribe," she said, "that a man can kill any other man who touches his woman?"

"Of course. That's why it was right for me to kill Kron." He didn't bother to look at her. "No one would respect me if my wife was defiled and I allowed the other man to live."

"But what if the other man tried to kill you first?"

He gave her a scornful look. "Only a weak fool would try to steal a woman from her rightful owner. A fool like Kron." He reached up to the knife hanging from his neck and ran his thumb around the blade. He turned the blade in his hand and gazed at the reflection of the firelight on its polished surface.

"But suppose the other man was lucky," she said softly. "He might be weaker than you, but he could still slay you with his spear."

Grep grunted dismissively. "Then I would deserve to die, and he would deserve to take you."

She nodded slowly. A plan had already formed in her mind, although the danger of it terrified her. She sat up and combed her fingers through her hair. Then she reached for her rabbit-pelt robe and dragged it around her shoulders. "There is something you should know," she said, trying to make her tone sound matter of fact.

He didn't answer. He sat staring into the fire.

"I told you," she went on, "that Worr looked at me in a certain way."

He gave her a quick, careful look. His eyes narrowed. Then he quickly shook his head. "Worr would never dare touch a wife of mine." He smiled faintly. "Let the old man wonder what he's missing."

"I'm sure you're right," she said. "But I need to know what I should do, if he ever tries to make me submit to him. It would be hard for me to resist. After all, he is our chieftain."

Grep seized a thick stick of wood. "If Worr ever touches you, I will kill him," he said. With a quick, rippling movement he snapped the thick piece of wood and threw the pieces into the flames, raising a shower of sparks.

"You would kill him?" She tried to make herself sound surprised and fearful. "Even though he's the chieftain?"

He turned toward her, and there was a righteous look in his eyes. "If Worr breaks the law of this tribe by forcing himself on my wife, then he deserves the same justice as any other man. No one would condemn me for killing him. They would respect me for it." He paused, becoming more thoughtful. He was silent for a while. "I suppose some of his guards might defend him," he went on, "but—our people are more loyal to our laws than to any one man, even if he is the chieftain." He nodded. "That is how it would be." But then he gestured dismissively. "This is foolish talk. Worr is getting old and slow. He respects the laws we live by, and he would never take the risk."

There was a long silence. Fragile yellow flames sprang up, licking the new wood that Grep had added. Sap hissed and spat.

Finally, Nisha gave a nervous laugh. "Well," she said, "I'm sure you're right. But—if he seems to desire me, I'll be sure to tell you."

"Of course." He gave a curt nod.

"You wouldn't—punish me for that?"

Grep shook his head. "I would punish you only if you tempt another man. Now, enough of this talk." Abruptly, he stood up. "You will go to the Wives' House, and I must go to the Warriors' House." He tossed his long hair behind his shoulders and straightened his robe. He winced for a moment as his back pained him.

She rose to her feet, moving slowly, and she saw him

watching her body as she closed her furs across her breasts. "I did please you, didn't I?" she said.

He gave a curt nod. "And you will please me again."

As they stepped out of the shaman's hut, Nisha found that the light of the day had almost gone. Grep strode ahead and she hurried to catch up, though she took care to stay a step behind him, since this seemed to be the custom of his tribe.

She noticed a number of men filing into the village through the main gate, leading a score of young boys who had been out refining their hunting skills. Such lessons could be brutal; she had spent a lot of time at the Family House washing wounds and pressing herbal remedies on bruises and swellings. Not that the boys seemed to care; to them, a wound was something to be proud of.

The party coming in through the gate was dragging something. Nisha saw that two poles had been lashed together to form a crude sled, and a figure was lying on it. "Is that a man there?" she asked.

Grep frowned. "Yes." He marched directly to the sled, and the warriors made way for him as he approached.

Cautiously, Nisha followed. She saw that the man on the sled had had his robe torn open, and there were deep, ragged gouges down his chest. His throat had been severed, and his head was lolling to one side. From his bluish pallor, it looked as if he had been dead for a day or more.

"What happened?" Grep demanded.

"Mountain lion," one of the men said.

For a moment, Nisha felt disoriented. She found herself reliving her dream of the forest, seeing her cat-face reflected in the pool of water.

The strange feeling gripped her more tightly as she remembered that only three days ago, Pawtix had mentioned that some other warrior had been savaged by a lion. Had she had her dream because of that? Was her spirit linked in some way with the spirit of a great mountain cat that was roaming the land?

"We will find the beast that did this, and kill it," said Grep. "Till then, there shall be no more scouts going out alone. They must travel in pairs."

He glanced again at the dead man, then turned away. He saw Nisha standing close by, and gesturing impatiently. "I told you to go to the Wives' House," he said. "You have no business out here."

The strange feeling fell away from Nisha's mind. Suddenly she was back in the real world with the stony ground cold and hard under her feet and the warrior on the sled lying dead before her.

"Go!" Grep told her.

Quickly, she obeyed.

Chapter Fourteen

Inside the Wives' House, all the women were hard at work. Some were weaving baskets from beargrass or painting them in ornamental patterns using berry juice. A couple were grinding dried ants and grasshoppers, mixing them with seeds to make flour. Several women were mending men's clothes that had been torn during their hunting and fighting outside the village. A few others were tidying the house, sweeping the stone floor with grass brooms. Nisha paused for a moment. At first the scene seemed pleasant enough, and much quieter than life had been in the Family House. But there was something wrong. People in her own tribe had always smiled and sung while they worked, but no one was smiling here, and no one was singing. At first she couldn't understand why. Then she saw an older woman walking among the ones who were working, and she realized that it was Uwa.

This house was not a place where people worked because they felt a common purpose and desire; it was a place where Uwa told people what to do and punished them if they failed or disobeyed.

Uwa saw Nisha and marched over to her. "So, finally you join us," she said.

Nisha looked at the woman's face. There were deep lines around her mouth, and her gray eyes were as hard as little stones.

"Yes," said Nisha. "My husband—"

"Come." She hustled Nisha down the length of the house, past a fire where water was simmering in a big clay pot that stood on a circle of stones. A few of the women glanced up at Nisha as she passed, but no one spoke.

"Here." Uwa pointed to three women who were squatting together on a thin straw mattress in the far corner of the house. They were stretching a deer skin that had been cleaned but not yet cured. "These are Reive, Ellel, and Innaw. They are Grep's other wives. You will eat with them and work with them." She gestured to the mattress. "You'll sleep here with them. And if you need anything, you'll ask me." She turned to go.

"May I ask one thing?" Nisha said.

Uwa's lips pinched together. She waited without speaking.

"Is Rilla here? My kinfolk. Plorngah's wife."

"She's not here. She's with him now." Uwa turned away. She made a tut-tutting sound. "Warla!" she shouted to another of the women. "What are you doing? Do you want me to tell your husband how lazy you are? Don't you remember how he beat you last time, eh? Or are you so stupid, you've forgotten?"

Nisha tried not to hear the woman's hateful voice. She squatted down in front of the three women. "Greetings," she said.

At first, none of them said anything. They stared at her with large, doubting eyes, like deer that found themselves confronted with a bobcat and were wondering if it would harm them.

"My name is Nisha," she went on.

"We already know your name," one of them said.

Were they naturally timid, or had they been scared by what they'd heard about her? Probably they blamed her for what had happened to Grep.

"Your name is Reive?" Nisha said to the first woman.

She was graceful and slender, but she seemed high strung and tense, as if she would flinch if Nisha reached out to touch her. Still, Reive held herself with more pride than the other two. Perhaps she was the leader, in which case, Nisha should try to befriend her first. If Reive decided to accept Nisha, the others would probably follow her.

"Let me help," said Nisha, gesturing to the wooden frame where the skin was being stretched. "There are four sides to the frame. And now there are four of us."

Reive seemed to think about the suggestion carefully. "All right," she said, "but remember, you are the junior here. We will tell you what needs to be done, and how you're supposed to do it."

Nisha nodded in silence. Why did it have to be this way? Why were all the women so fearful and so grudging, even toward one another? Because the men had trained them that way, of course. Well, Nisha told herself to make the best of it. There was no way of knowing how long she would have to live in this house and share her days with these women. And if she gained their trust, there might be a chance—just a chance—that they might help her.

"I'll do whatever you say," Nisha said with an agreeable smile and a little shrug.

Reive nodded and seemed to relax a little. "Good. Tighten those thongs there." She pointed to the edge of the skin nearest Nisha, where it had not yet been stretched to the frame.

For a while, they worked in silence. After the hide had been stretched it was placed aside, to be smoked tomorrow outside the house. Nisha mentioned that she needed moccasins, and Reive gave her the materials and tools to make new ones. She set to work, happy to have something useful to do, and eager to prove how well she could do it.

Bit by bit, Reive began to talk. She seemed to feel a need to display her authority and her knowledge. That was useful, because there were many things that Nisha still needed to know. The women in the Family House had been so sad and weary, mired in the drudgery of their lives, they hadn't shown any interest in the workings of the tribe.

"Why is it that the tribe grows no corn?" Nisha asked, as she used a stick of charcoal to trace the shape of her foot on one of the pieces of hide that she'd been given. "There's so much land outside the walls, and there seems to be more than enough water. It should be possible to grow two crops a year, maybe even three."

Reive was mending a seam in her robe. She sucked on a leather thong to soften it, then used a wooden awl to poke the thong through holes in the deerskin. "No women are allowed outside the village walls," she said.

"I know that," Nisha said patiently. "But still there should be a way—"

"If we have less food than we need, the warriors take it from other tribes," said Reive. "What do they care about planting corn?"

Nisha was silent for a moment, thinking. Then she went back to work. The job was hard, because women weren't allowed to own or even touch knives. The flint blade she had been given was squared off at both ends and was no longer than her thumb.

"It seems to me," she said cautiously, "it must be dangerous for the men to live by stealing from other people. One day, won't they find a tribe as fierce as theirs? Wouldn't it be safer for this tribe to learn to feed itself?"

The women glanced uneasily at each other. "Our men are so fierce, no tribe has ever beaten them," Reive said flatly. "Besides, it's a matter of honor for them to fight and kill their enemies. How much honor do you think there would be in growing corn?"

Nisha looked at Reive's face, trying to see if she approved or disapproved of the situation she described. But it was impossible to tell. Nisha thought she sensed something buried in Reive—a hint of rebellion, wrapped under layers of caution and habitual obedience. But she couldn't be sure.

"Tell me the history of this tribe," Nisha said. That should be an easier topic to discuss.

"Long ago," Reive said, "there was a man named Yov who lived among the Cave People, to the east of here. Yov was the chieftain's son, and he was stronger than all the other men, including the chieftain himself. So the chieftain feared Yov, and he made it seem that Yov had committed a crime against his tribe, so they cast him out."

"There are people who live in caves near here?" asked Nisha.

"Three days from here," said Reive. "They are brave, terrible warriors. But Yov was the bravest of all. So he was sent out into the wilderness, where the chieftain thought he would die. But Yov took three women with him, and he was such a fine warrior, he fed them all by hunting game on the plateau."

Nisha nodded. She listened patiently.

"Yov gave his wives four boy-children and many girl-children," Reive went on. "Together, they built this fine village here. Then Yov slipped and fell from the cliffs one day while he was out hunting, so his four sons ruled the tribe. These were the elders of our tribe. They lacked the courage of their father, and they were poor hunters, so the village was soon short of food. But one of them had a son named Worr, and the spirit of Yov found new life in Worr. He was the greatest hunter and warrior there had ever been."

Nisha nodded slowly. "And what happened to the elders?"

Reive eyed Nisha for a long moment. Her face was impassive. She said nothing.

"Are they dead?" Nisha asked softly.

"Some died in battle," said Reive. "Some had accidents."

"And this was the way that Worr came to power?"

Reive smiled faintly. "This was the way."

We understand each other, Nisha thought to herself.

She realized she could learn a lot from Reive's way of telling only the facts, yet somehow communicating much more. Nisha always tended to blurt out the truth. But that was not always the best policy.

"Worr had a vision," Reive went on. "He saw that the Warrior Tribe are the chosen tribe, destined to rule the whole plateau. He decided that he would do almost anything to fulfill that vision. The people admired him. His junior warriors worshipped him. They are his guards now." Reive's eyes narrowed as she watched Nisha carefully. "You will not say anything disrespectful of Worr," she said.

"Of course not," said Nisha. "He is our leader."

"Yes." Reive nodded. "He is our leader."

She despises him, Nisha thought to herself. *She knows that he killed the elders who were his uncles—and maybe even his father, too. She sees that Worr has filled his people with fear, and he trained the men to live by preying on others and spilling their blood. And now everyone pays the price, because the men care only about power and death and glory. And Reive cannot speak of these things, for fear of being crushed or stoned or tortured.*

"Thank you for talking to me," Nisha said. She turned to the other two women, Ellel and Innaw, and found them looking nervously from her to Reive, as if the conversation had panicked them. Nisha tried to give them a reassuring smile. "I hope we can all become friends," she said.

"You four!" Uwa came striding down the length of the house. "Why are you just sitting there?"

"It's my fault," Nisha spoke up quickly. "I was asking them questions, so that I can learn to be a better member of this tribe, and a better wife."

Uwa eyed her with disgust. "If you cause trouble, I'll see that Grep hears of it." She turned away.

Later, five women came into the Wives' House. Nisha was startled by the sight of their clothes, which were per-

fect, pure white deerskin, richly ornamented with stitching and designs that had been etched into the hide. "Who
are they?" she whispered to Reive.

"Worr's wives," Reive said. "It was their turn, tonight,
to cook and serve the meal in the meeting place where
the men eat. Now they've brought the leftovers for us."
She got up quickly from where she had been sitting on
the floor.

Everyone was gathering around, eager to eat whatever
scraps remained from the men's feast. For a while the
only sounds were of women gnawing on rabbit bones,
drinking soup, chewing jerky, and tearing at flat patties of
corn bread.

Nisha thought that the food had been better in the Family House, where she and the other women had cooked for
themselves and the children. She felt humiliated, now, to
be scavenging the men's leftovers. But even Worr's own
wives were forced to eat this way, and if she was too
proud to join them, she would starve.

One of the women in white came over to Nisha as she
was scouring the last scraps of corn paste from the basket
it had been baked in. "You are Nisha," the woman said.

Nisha looked up at her. She was young, perhaps only
fourteen, and strikingly beautiful, though she had the
same meek, cautious look that all the wives seemed to
share. Nisha nodded respectfully. "Yes, I'm Nisha."

The other woman smiled faintly. "We've heard everything about you."

Nisha shrugged. "I suppose you have. Gossip always
travels fast." She glanced around. A couple of the other
wives were nearby, and she felt sure they were listening.
"I would like to talk to you," she said. "Can we go—"

"Over here, if you like," said the woman. She led the
way to a large mattress at the back of the hut. This was
where Worr's wives slept, Nisha realized.

She sat down on the mattress, noticing that its skins
were softer and its filling was thicker than the one that
she was supposed to share with Grep's wives. "What's

your name?" she asked, as the other woman sat down with her.

"My name is Yan," she said. She eyed Nisha some more. "Some of the things that we've heard—"

"From Uwa?" Nisha asked.

"Yes, partly from Uwa." Yan's voice was neutral and her face showed nothing, but there was a look in her eyes that said she trusted Uwa no more than Nisha did.

"So you know that I turn men against each other, and they die because of me," said Nisha.

Now Yan allowed herself to smile. "It seems far fetched," she said. "Of course, you are very pretty, Nisha, but even so—"

"There's a little truth in it, though," said Nisha, making herself sound sober and sincere.

Yan paused. She waited.

"The women of my tribe studied the art of pleasing men," Nisha went on. "It seems that this art is unknown here. That was why Kron behaved—so foolishly. And that's why Grep accepted me as his wife, even after everything that happened in Worr's house."

"I heard something about this," said Yan. She was eyeing Nisha cautiously, now. "In fact—well, my husband wanted me to learn this art of yours." Her cheeks turned slightly pink, and she looked away in embarrassment. "I spoke to your friend Rilla, but—"

"Rilla is young," said Nisha.

"Yes," Yan agreed, "Rilla is young."

"And as for me," Nisha said calmly, "my husband has told me not to speak of these things to any other women."

Yan looked up quickly. "He did?"

Nisha nodded. She waited while Yan absorbed this new fact. "Of course," Nisha went on, "I suppose if Worr asked me himself, I could hardly refuse. I mean, he is our chieftain."

"I see." Yan gave Nisha a shrewd look.

"I would certainly like to help you if I could," Nisha

went on. "After all, if we make our men happy, our own lives are happier, isn't that so?"

"You, there!" It was Uwa's voice. "Nisha, you should be back at your work. Yan, Worr wants you." Uwa strode past and started calling out the names of other women whose husbands had called for them. One by one, wives hurried out of the house, and Nisha watched them go.

Grep had not called for any of his wives, so Nisha sat back down with Reive and the other two women, and she continued working on the moccasin that she was making. She felt nervous and excited by the idea that she had managed to set something in motion, although she wasn't exactly sure, even now, where it would lead. It was like throwing a large stone onto a slope of loose boulders. The stone might roll a little way and then stop, or it might hit another stone, which would hit still other stones in turn, until there was an avalanche.

"You do good work."

Nisha looked up quickly. It was Reive who had spoken. She was leaning forward, inspecting the thong-stitching that Nisha had laboriously completed. "Thank you," said Nisha.

"We were afraid you'd be a trouble maker," said Reive.

"Of course not," said Nisha. She looked directly into Reive's eyes. "I acted foolishly in Worr's house three weeks ago, but that was because I didn't know the customs of this tribe. It would be foolish for me to think of making trouble deliberately. It would hurt us all."

After a while, the fire was allowed to burn low and the women who hadn't been called out of the Wives' House started settling down to sleep. There was barely enough room for Nisha to lie with Grep's other three wives on the one mattress, but they tried to make room for her. Even if the bed had been comfortable, though, Nisha would have had trouble dropping off. Her mind was buzzing with everything that had happened to her, and everything she had done.

Through half-closed eyes she watched Uwa make a final inspection of the women in the house. She walked slowly up and down, then retreated to a bed beside the door. After that, the only sound was of sleepy breathing.

The straw in the mattress was poking into Nisha's side, and she was uncomfortably aware of Reive, beside her, snoring gently. The night wore on, and Nisha found herself thinking back to her times with Jorlor—snuggling with him on winter nights, running with him when they went hunting together, or clutching his hands while she was birthing her son. They were sad memories, yet in some strange way they comforted her, because they gave her life meaning. And gradually, they lulled her to sleep.

Nisha felt a hand on her shoulder. She opened her eyes and looked up. A shadowy face was peering down at her. "Shhh!" A finger was pressed against Nisha's lips.

Nisha saw that the woman bending over her was Yan. She felt a pulse of excitement. Could it be happening so soon? Well, why not? She had planted the idea, after all. It wouldn't take long to take root.

Yan glanced nervously around, then beckoned. Nisha moved off the mattress, taking elaborate care not to disturb the other wives.

Yan pulled Nisha close and whispered directly into her ear. "Worr wishes to see you. I told him that you are willing to talk to him about—what we discussed. You will wear this robe." She shrugged off her white deerskin and threw it around Nisha's shoulders. "If the guards on the stockade see you, they'll think you're one of us. Pull the hood up, now, around your head. There are two guards at the main door of Worr's house. I told them I would be back there in a moment. It's very dark in there. If you keep your head covered, they'll think you're me."

"All right," said Nisha.

"Walk all the way to the far end of the house, through the door behind his chair," Yan went on. "That's where Worr sleeps. And he's expecting you."

Nisha nodded. "Thank you." She turned and started to

creep down the length of the house, toward the door. Uwa was still in her place, guarding the exit, but she had her back turned.

Nisha opened the door and stepped out of the house, into the darkness.

Chapter Fifteen

The night was cold and clear. The stars looked so bright, Nisha imagined that if they touched her, they would burn her skin like the glowing embers that Grep had taken from the fire.

Beneath her white robe the spots where the embers had touched her still throbbed a little, reminding her of her hatred for Grep. With renewed determination, she crept forward.

Up on the stockade around the compound she saw a guard silhouetted against the moonlit sky. He turned in her direction and Nisha sensed that he was looking down at her. But he did nothing, and he shouted no challenge. It must be common enough for him to see wives moving in and out of their house, and it would be no cause for concern—so long as none of them tried to leave the compound, of course.

Nisha approached Worr's house. She pushed the door open and found two of Worr's guards standing just inside, as Yan had said they would be. Quickly, she bowed her head. But the house had only a couple of windows in its wooden walls, and the interior was in almost total darkness.

Nisha moved quickly toward the platform made of logs at the far end. It was the first time she'd been here since the pairing ceremony, when Grep had killed Kron. She looked down at the floor of packed earth, expecting to see his blood still staining it. But if a stain was there, it was hidden in the shadows.

Nisha stepped up and moved around behind the big chair. She pulled aside a door flap and found herself in a smaller room lit by several flames in stone bowls of melted animal fat. On one wall, deer antlers had been mounted either side of a huge black bearskin, with its head facing the doorway and its jaws gaping in a silent snarl. Deerskins covered the floor. Spears stood in each corner, and wood had been stacked beside a fire in a stone hearth.

Dominating the room was a high platform built from logs and covered with a thick straw mattress upholstered in goat skins. And on the platform was Worr, lying back amid a heap of leather pillows.

Nisha stood facing him, feeling nervous. He eyed her and said nothing. Then, with a casual movement, he pointed to the floor beside him. "Come here," he said.

Quickly, she obeyed. She stood where he had pointed, then dropped to her knees. It was strange to be alone with him like this, and she would have felt scared if Grep hadn't been so certain that Worr wouldn't dare to touch her. The chieftain's fat body disgusted her, and when she looked at his thick lips, she couldn't help remembering, once again, the way he had licked blood off his fingers—the blood of the women of her tribe.

Worr watched her silently for a long moment, like a predator waiting to see if its prey was going to fight or flee. Finally, he grunted. "You know why I told you to come here," he said.

"I think so, yes."

He reached inside his robe and scratched his chest. "This is my tribe, eh? There are no secrets from me in my tribe. I have a right to know what happens here."

She lowered her eyes respectfully. "Of course."

"So," he said, "there are things you know, which I want to know. But you won't tell Yan. Is that so?"

"My husband—" Nisha began.

"What of him?" Worr reached for a basket of pine nuts beside his bed, scooped up a handful, and chewed them noisily, showing his yellowed teeth. He was like a great sleepy bear, lying here in his lair. He was easily twice her size.

"Grep told me not to share my knowledge with any other woman," said Nisha. "But you are my chieftain," she went on. "As you say, it would be wrong for me to hide anything from you."

Worr gave her a hard look. Slowly, he frowned. The heavy wrinkles of his face looked deeper in the flickering yellow light, and his eyes were almost lost in shadow. He poked his finger into his mouth, reaching for a piece of pine nut wedged between his teeth. He extracted it with his fingernail, looked at it, and flicked it away. "Did you tell anyone you were coming here?" His voice was much quieter, now. It wasn't challenging her anymore.

"Only your wife, Yan," said Nisha.

"You didn't tell your husband?" His little eyes watched her carefully.

Mutely, she shook her head.

"Maybe he'd punish you for coming here without telling him," he said. "What do you think about that?"

"I'm a stranger in your tribe," she said. "I don't know the customs here. If my chieftain summons me, surely I should obey."

Worr grunted. He smiled slowly. "So," he said, "tell me what I want to know."

Nisha paused, thinking carefully. "In my tribe, women were treated equally with men. They didn't fear men."

"I've heard of tribes like that." Worr made a disparaging gesture. "The men are weak. They're easy to kill."

Nisha felt an urge to defend her people—but she suppressed it. There was no point in arguing here. "The women felt free," she went on. "So they had confidence, and they took an active part in lovemaking. Also, they truly cared for their men, because the men were good and kind to them. So the women wanted to please their husbands."

Worr grunted. He watched her silently.

"When I was with my husband," Nisha went on, "we were often playful together. It was joyful for us to please each other." For a moment she had to fight back a wave of intense sadness. But she reminded herself again of her purpose, and she forced herself on. "I used to try different things to give my husband pleasure," she said, "and so I learned the things that men enjoy. I learned how to caress my husband, how to use my hands on him, and my mouth as well, to excite him. I satisfied my husband in many different ways."

"He let you do these things to him, eh?" Worr was studying her with prurient interest.

"He let me, just as Kron let me," said Nisha, "because they gave him the most intense pleasure he had ever known." She watched Worr for a moment, and saw that there was still doubt in his face. "Earlier today," Nisha went on, "I showed Grep some of the secrets of my people."

Worr grunted. He levered himself up, digging his elbows into the pillows around him and leaning forward. "And what happened?" he demanded.

She shrugged. "He said that I had spoken truly about my talents. He said that my people had mastered the art of pleasure, just as your people have mastered the art of war."

Worr gave her a long, brooding look. Then he grabbed another handful of pine nuts. "You'll teach these secrets to my wives," he said, with an air of finality.

She felt afraid of defying him. Clearly, he was used to having his way in everything. But everything depended on her refusing to do what he wanted.

"I don't think I *can* teach your wives," she said in a low voice.

He pointed his finger at her. "You'll do as I say. It doesn't matter what Grep tells you. You won't say anything about it to him, and he won't know the difference. Understand me?"

Quickly, Nisha shook her head. "It's not Grep. The

problem is—your women are scared of you. They would be afraid to touch you. They're probably afraid even to look at you. And a woman must be bold, to do the things that I know how to do."

Worr clamped his lips into a scowl. He glowered at her. Then, abruptly, he rolled off the bed. His bare feet thumped down onto the floor. He went to the fire and threw a log on it, then walked toward her. He was less than an arm's length away, and she found herself craning her neck to see his face. "Grep offered you to me," he said, pointing down at her. "When he brought you into this village. You remember that?"

"Yes." Nisha felt her stomach grow tense as she mustered her courage for what she had to say. "And—I was disappointed when you refused to take me."

His eyes narrowed. He sat heavily on the side of the bed. "What's that?"

Nisha shrugged. "Any woman would prefer to be paired with the chieftain of a tribe," she said, "if she had the choice."

Worr stared at her a moment. He breathed deeply, and his nostrils flared. "You're an insolent woman." His voice was low, almost a growl. "If you were my wife, I'd have you beaten till your spirit was broken. What do you say to that?"

"I would try to persuade you not to," she said. "I would give you so much pleasure, you would be grateful for my spirit."

Worr scowled. Nisha noticed him flexing his fingers, as if he wanted to seize hold of her. She found herself tensing up as she prepared herself to be grabbed by him.

But then he turned away. He moved back to his original position on his bed, and fell against the pillows. His hand groped down between his legs, and he rubbed his crotch. He seemed hardly aware of what he was doing.

He turned his eyes back to her again. "Stand up," he said.

Obediently, she did so. And then, without being asked,

she shrugged off the fine white robe that Yan had put around her shoulders. Under it, she was wearing just a simple deerskin. Her arms and her lower legs were bare.

He stared at her for a long moment. "It's a serious matter," he said, "to touch another man's wife. You saw what happened to Kron. So you can't pretend you don't know now. If I thought you had ideas about that with me, you'd be on the slab out there, like those two women this afternoon. Those friends of yours."

"I understand." She looked down, avoiding his eyes. "I would never try to defy my own chieftain. That would be foolish indeed."

There was a long pause. The new log of wood has hissing in the fireplace. The little dishes of fat were still sputtering and flickering, shedding their fitful light. Somewhere outside, an owl screeched.

Worr studied her body for another long moment, then shook his head. "Go back to the Wives' House," he said.

Nisha felt disconcerted. She looked up at him, wondering if she had misunderstood. "I thought—I hoped you might—"

He laughed, showing his teeth. "You're Grep's wife, woman. This tribe has its laws. And Grep has his warriors. They hate him, but they obey him."

Nisha tried to decide what to say. She hadn't expected this. "What if Grep dies?" she blurted out.

Worr sat up. He rested his elbows on his knees, letting his fat hands dangle between his legs. "What are you saying, woman?" His tone sounded dangerous.

She sensed she had overstepped a boundary. "One day, all men must grow old and die," she said, trying to recover herself. "It is the natural way of things."

Grep still stared at her. He said nothing.

"Grep's life is full of danger," Nisha went on. "He leads his warriors to attack other tribes. Anything might happen."

"You respect Grep?" Worr asked her sharply.

That was a dangerous question. Nisha said nothing.

"You respect me?" Worr went on.

"Of course." She looked up directly into his eyes, praying that he wouldn't be able to tell how deeply she was lying.

There was another long pause. "You'll leave now," Worr said. "And you'll not say anything about this, eh?"

Nisha inclined her head. "Naturally." She hesitated. "Your wife Yan can be trusted—?"

"She can be trusted, because she knows she'd be beaten and tortured if she ever spoke out of turn."

Something quivered inside Nisha. Silently, she made a vow: that after she dealt with Grep, she would deal with Worr.

"It might have been better," Worr went on, "if Grep had had you killed instead of thinking he could tame you." He glowered for a moment, then waved his arm. "I'll think on this. You go back to the Wives' House."

Nisha nodded. "Thank you," she said, "for the honor of being in your company." She picked up the white robe and wrapped it around herself again, taking her time, knowing that he was watching her as she moved. She took care to conceal her face under the hood, then turned and ducked through the door flap, leaving Worr alone in his room.

Outside, the night seemed colder than before. Nisha paused for a moment, breathing deeply and feeling some of the tension drain out of her. She suddenly felt very alone. There was no one to turn to, no one to confide in, and no one to give her confidence as she played this dangerous game. For a moment she wondered if she could really see it through. She was one young woman in a tribe of the cruelest, most ruthless warriors. How did she dare to plot against them?

But then she thought of Jorlor, and her vow to avenge his death and all the deaths of her people, and that renewed her strength.

She clutched the white robe around her and picked her

way across the compound. She wondered what Worr would do next. She'd seen the lust in him, and she was sure he wanted her. Was he secretly afraid of Grep? Was that why he'd held back? No, she decided—he was just a habitually cautious man, and he probably suspected some kind of trap.

She stopped, feeling suddenly dizzy. A torrent of sensations swept through her mind like a great gust of wind making leaves tremble on trees in a forest. The moonlight seemed to flare brighter, and everything around her caught its radiance and glowed in the darkness. When she looked at her own hand, it seemed alive with light.

She closed her eyes for a moment. Sometimes she had experienced this, after using peyote. The drug seemed to wear off—and then, unexpectedly, it would return like a brief flicker of flame in the dying embers of a fire.

She opened her eyes again. The strange fluorescence had gone. But now, a new vision was superimposed on her view of the compound. Trees and scrub seemed to shimmer into life where the bare ground had been. Her viewpoint shifted and she seemed to be on her hands and knees, as she had been in her dream. Suddenly she realized she was seeing the outside of the stockade at the same time as she saw it from the inside.

Nisha clutched her head. How could she be dreaming while she was awake?

A voice sounded in her head. It called her name, and instinctively she knew it was the voice of the mountain cat.

"Cat Spirit," she whispered. "What do you want from me?"

It called to her again. She found herself stumbling forward across the compound, heading toward the wall of logs. She felt intuitively certain that the mountain lion was out there.

She pressed her palms against the rough wood of the stockade. "Here I am," she whispered. "Tell me why you are speaking to me."

She saw a shadow flitting across the clearing. Her scalp tingled. Her body felt light, as if a breath of air could blow it up and away. "Come, Nisha," the spirit called in her head. "Leave the village."

There was a sudden shout from somewhere above. Footsteps thumped on the wooden ramp above her head. A man swore. She heard him grunt with the effort of throwing something—a spear.

The shadow dodged to one side and there was the sound of flint striking stony ground. The shadow raced away, inhumanly fast, and then it was gone.

"What's happening there?" Another man's voice.

"Mountain cat. Right down there. Big one."

The two guards were silent for a moment. Then one of them made a dismissive sound. "Lion wouldn't come this close to the village."

And that was true, Nisha thought, as she crept away to the Wives' House. Big cats always avoided the scent of men. Still, it had been there; she was sure of it. Why had it risked its life? And why had it called to her?

Chapter Sixteen

Nisha felt a hand shaking her roughly awake. "Get up and go outside," a voice snapped at her. "The others are waiting for you."

For a moment, she thought she was back in the Family House. She blinked and looked around in confusion, then saw Uwa glaring down at her and realized she had overslept. Reive, Ellel, and Innaw had gone.

Nisha rolled over and groaned. She was deeply weary. It was an effort to move. She dimly remembered creeping in during the night. She had shed her white robe beside Worr's wives where they slept.

"Nisha, get up!" Uwa was glaring at her.

Nisha struggled onto her feet. "What needs to be done?"

"Your turn to prepare food for the men. Hunters brought in two mule deer early this morning. Reive, Ellel, and Innaw are already out there. Go and help."

Nisha nodded. She gathered her rabbit-pelt robe around herself and walked to the door of the long house.

She stepped out and paused, looking around the compound, remembering her glimpse of the mountain lion outside the fence. For a moment she could almost imagine that it had been just another dream.

"Nisha!"

Reive and the other two wives were squatting on the ground beside half a dozen hunters who were wielding knives, skinning deer carcasses.

Nisha told herself not to think about the previous night.

It would be good, perhaps, to tackle a simple task where there were no questions and no uncertainties.

Together, they stretched the deerskins across frames fashioned from tree branches tied with thongs. Then they used blunt-ended flints to scrape all the fat and flesh away from the undersides of the skins. It was hard work, kneeling on the ground, holding the scraper in both hands and dragging it to and fro.

Nisha turned to Reive, who was kneeling beside her. "In my tribe," Nisha said, "we used to take hides out into the desert and put them near ant hills. The insects did all the work for us, stripping the flesh away."

Reive paused for a moment. "The men let you do that?"

"The men did it *with* us," said Nisha. "When any task needed to be done, our people did it side by side."

Reive smiled faintly. "But you're not in your tribe anymore. You're in our tribe now. And here, the men know what's best for us."

Did Nisha hear a note of bitterness again? She looked closely at the young woman's face, but it was as expressionless as it had been the day before.

"Which way do you think is better?" Nisha asked, while Ellel and Innaw watched nervously. "To work side by side, or to follow orders?

Reive's eyes narrowed a fraction. "It makes no difference what I think," she said.

"Why not?"

Reive grunted. "Because I am a woman." Quickly, she went back to work with her scraper.

When the skins had been cleaned, they took them to a shallow pool of water and used stones to weight them beneath the surface.

"How long do you soak them?" Nisha asked.

Reive shrugged. "Three days, perhaps four."

"The same in my tribe," Nisha said, half to herself, remembering the many times she had done this with Jorlor.

After the skins were soaked, it would be time to rub a mixture of fat and brains into them, working relentlessly for an afternoon or more. Then the skins would be smoked over a fire of rotten wood to make them supple and waterproof, fit to serve as a robe, a door flap, or a mattress cover.

Now that today's part of the chore was done, Nisha went with the women to wash herself. They squatted together in the same pool where Nisha had bathed before the pairing ceremony in Worr's house.

The women sang a simple song as they rinsed the animal blood from their skin. "In this village I was born," they sang. "In this village I was wed. In this village I eat the food my husband gives me. In this village, I work. In this village, I will die."

Nisha watched the women as they sang, and she marveled that they were so resigned to their fate. They were scared, of course. But that wasn't the real answer. They had never known any other way of life. It must seem inconceivable to them that things could be different. In which case, how could she rouse them to fight back?

At the center of the compound, the hunters had finished butchering the animals, and the blood had been collected in big leather bowls. The entrails had been slit and emptied and set aside to be dried and cured. The necks had been severed with stone axes, and the carcasses were ready to be roasted.

The rest of the chores were strictly women's work. Uwa came out to supervise as the women built a fire, skewered the animals on poles, then lifted them up onto wooden supports. "There'll be extra for us tonight," Uwa said, as the flames started leaping and the venison began to pop and sizzle. "Worr's sending out a hunting party. He wants the lion that's been killing our scouts." She turned and nodded toward the far end of the compound. "Grep and a dozen men will be gone before sunset." She turned and walked away.

Nisha looked toward the Warriors' House. She saw that

men were bringing their packs outside, checking them, and repacking them. Then Grep emerged and started moving among his men, giving orders.

"He's not well enough to go," said Ellel.

"No, he's strong," said Innaw.

Was there just a hint of admiration in her voice? Certainly, her face showed respect. Even though Innaw must have been beaten by Grep many times, she seemed to look up to him. And in a way there was some sense to that, because there was definitely some status attached to being one of Grep's wives.

Nisha noticed Reive frowning. "What's the matter?" she said.

"I hope he's strong enough," Reive said quietly. "It would be unfortunate if anything happened to him out there."

"Unfortunate?" Nisha gave her a questioning look.

Reive looked at her frankly. "If he dies, Nisha, we will be given to a lesser man, or cast out to starve. Didn't you think of that?"

"Oh. Of course." Nisha averted her eyes. "You're right." Then a sudden thought occurred to her. "Who decided that the men should go out and hunt this mountain cat?" she asked.

Reive shrugged. "Worr, of course."

"And was he the one who ordered Grep to lead the party?"

Reive gave her an odd look. "He didn't need to give an order. It's Grep's duty."

Quickly, Nisha stood up. She wondered if there were a way to speak privately with Grep. No; that would be taboo. The men were all gathering together, shouldering their packs, making ready to leave the compound.

She didn't have much time. Nisha hesitated—then noticed a tall, thin figure striding past with a bag slung over his arm. It was Reebowa. She ran after him and touched his arm. "I must speak to you," she said in a low, urgent voice.

He saw her and took a pace backward, looking afraid of her. "What about?" He glanced around quickly. She sensed he might turn and run from her at any moment.

"Keep on walking," she murmured. "Between the houses, here." She guided him into the narrow pathway, where they were partially hidden.

"I can't—" he said.

"I have a message for Grep," she interrupted him. "It's important to him. Do you understand? Do this for him, not for me."

Reebowa shifted uneasily. "A message?"

"Yes. You must tell him privately, when no one else can hear. Do you understand? You must do this."

Reebowa looked doubtful.

"Tell him," Nisha said, "if he returns to the village late tonight, he must go to Worr's house." She seized his arm. "Even if it's the middle of the night. Do you understand?"

"But the warriors will be away till tomorrow or the next day," Reebowa said.

Nisha gave a curt nod. "Maybe so. But tell Grep what I told you. Tell him!"

"Why?" Reebowa asked.

She felt exasperated. "It's best if you don't know. You saw what happened the last time, when you knew something that you shouldn't have known. You had to stand up in front of all the tribe."

She waited a moment, watching him relive the anxiety of being compelled to testify against Kron.

"Now," she said, "repeat what I've told you. Grep will be furious if he ever finds that I gave this message to you, and you didn't pass it on."

Reebowa shuffled his feet. "I have to tell Grep that he should go to Worr's house, if he comes back tonight."

"Yes. And tell him that this message is from me. And make sure no one else hears it." She squeezed his arm tighter. "I think Grep will reward you if you do this thing for me."

Reebowa nodded, avoiding her eyes.

Reluctantly, she released him. Could he be trusted? She had no way of knowing. He seemed less tainted by the ways of the warriors than any of the other men, but she had no idea what his private thoughts were like. She stood and watched as he continued on toward the warriors assembling their kits. Then she turned away. She should be back with the other wives, she told herself, doing what women were supposed to do.

When Grep led his men out of the compound, Nisha deliberately didn't watch them go. She tried to pretend that this day was no different from any other day. She sat with the three women, turning the spits, catching the fat that dripped from the carcasses, and pouring it back over them. Smoke from the fires drove away most of the flies, and the sun was warm. Once in a while, she fetched more wood for the fire. She told herself not to think about the night that lay ahead.

She pretended to listen while Reive chatted with Ellel and Innaw, talking about friends and relatives and children, women who were pregnant in the Family House, people who were suffering ailments, warriors who might be growing tired of their wives, warriors who had been injured while raiding other tribes—the gossip flowed on. Some of it helped Nisha to understand the Warrior Tribe, but the conversation always had an underlying level of tension. Once in a while it would stray to a topic that was taboo—and the women would quickly change the subject. Instinctively, they said nothing critical about the men, nothing bad about their lives in the village, and nothing about women who had been punished or cast out.

Even the talk about children sounded wrong to Nisha's ears, since the little ones were reared almost entirely in the Family House. Reive had given birth twice, but she hardly ever saw her children. It was the way of the tribe for a young wife to please her husband, not waste herself caring for offspring. Older women could deal with that chore. If the child was a girl, it needed little attention anyway. If it was a boy, then it was the father's job to teach the youngster how to kill and fight.

Nisha was distracted from the conversation when she noticed a woman emerging from the Warriors' House and making her way toward the Wives' House. The woman was limping and she kept pausing to rest. It was Rilla, Nisha saw with dismay. "I have to help my friend," she told the other wives sitting around the fire. She jumped up without waiting for them to reply.

Rilla was sobbing. Her thin face was crisscrossed with welts and cuts. One of her feet was swollen and marred with dark purple bruises. Nisha ran and put her arm around the girl's shoulders, but Rilla screamed and jerked away. "Don't touch me!" she cried. Then she looked up and saw it was Nisha, and she slumped into Nisha's arms.

With difficulty, Nisha helped the girl to the Wives' House. She pushed open the door and guided Rilla through it. Uwa was sitting at her place just inside, and she stood up, scowling. "Your place is by the fire!" she snapped at Nisha.

"But this girl is badly hurt," Nisha protested.

Uwa made an impatient sound. "I'll deal with her."

"No!" Nisha cried. She spoke instinctively; there was no way to hold herself back.

Uwa glared at her for a long moment. "No woman speaks to me that way," she said. Her voice was no longer fierce. It was calm and cold. Abruptly, she strode out of the house.

"Now you'll be hurt, too," Rilla said. "Leave me, Nisha, please. I'll be all right."

"No," Nisha said again, more gently this time. She walked Rilla along to her place in the house, and the other women paused in their chores and stared at them uneasily. No one stood up or moved to help. They were reluctant to show sympathy for Rilla in case it might suggest that they sympathized with the crime that she must have committed to deserve such a beating.

Nisha sat Rilla down on the mattress that she shared with Plorngah's other wife, Jees.

"She's still with Plorngah," Rilla said, as she saw Nisha glancing around. "He's beating her now."

Gently, Nisha removed Rilla's robe. The girl's back was scarlet and purple. "Why?" Nisha asked helplessly. "What happened?"

"We did nothing wrong." Rilla's voice was low and shaky. "Tonight is the night of the full moon. You remember what Worr said, about the tribe having no place for a crippled man? Plorngah's leg still isn't healed, and he wasn't taken on the lion hunt. When they return, they may cast him out or kill him." She shook her head. "He was so angry and full of hate, he turned it on me and Jees. And if he's cast out or killed, it seems there'll be no place for her anymore. No one will want her. She's much older than I am, and not good looking."

Nisha stood and went to the cistern, filled a leather bowl, and carried it back to Rilla. Tenderly, she washed the girl's wounds. "We will take our revenge on these terrible men, Rilla," she murmured.

Rilla shook her head. "It can never happen. You're the only one, Nisha. No one else even thinks of such a thing."

"Not now," said Nisha. "But one day, if I rouse their anger—"

"They have no anger," said Rilla. "It was beaten out of them long ago. Don't you see, Nisha? Don't you see?"

A little later, Nisha rejoined Reive, Ellel, and Innaw by the fire. They gave her furtive, doubtful looks as she sat down with them.

"Plorngah hurt my friend," Nisha explained.

The women looked at each other. No one said anything.

"I had to help her," Nisha went on.

"If Plorngah thinks you are sympathizing with his wife," said Ellel, "it will anger him. I hope you understand, Nisha. You should never interfere."

Nisha stared at her for a moment. "This is wrong," she

said. She knew she shouldn't say the words, but the emotions were too strong inside her. "You know it's wrong. I see it in you. You know!"

There was a long silence. Finally, Reive spoke. "You're a fool to talk like this," she said, so softly that Nisha could hardly hear her. "Do you think we need to hear you lecture us?"

Nisha glanced quickly at Ellel and Innaw. They were both watching her carefully. Could they be hiding a secret streak of rebellion? Had she been deceived by their smokescreen of trivial chatter?

Slowly, Nisha turned back to Reive. "If there are women who dream of rebellion," she whispered, "I must know—"

Reive gave a quick little shake of her head. She was looking beyond Nisha, at something behind her.

Nisha turned. She saw Uwa striding out from Worr's house, looking even grimmer than before. Nisha froze, fearing the worst.

But Uwa didn't even glance in her direction. She marched across the compound staring straight ahead, and disappeared back into the Wives' House. The door banged shut behind her.

There was a lot of extra food that evening, as Uwa had predicted. The women in the Wives' House gorged themselves, and many of them seemed happy in the knowledge that their husbands were out on the hunt and wouldn't be calling for them tonight.

After the feasting was done, the women sat together and sang songs while they worked at their chores. Uwa made no attempt to impose discipline; she retreated to her place by the door and ignored everyone.

Nisha went to Rilla after a while. The girl was sleeping quietly beside Jees, who had been just as badly beaten. Nisha looked down at the pair of them, and she felt a deep sadness. To herself, she moved Plorngah higher on the list of men who deserved to die.

Later, she worked on her moccasins. When the fire finally died down and the singing and the chores were done, Nisha joined Reive and Ellel and Innaw on their straw mattress, and this night, she was so exhausted, she slept almost immediately.

Chapter Seventeen

"Nisha." The voice was a whisper, and it seemed to come from inside her own head. Nisha struggled awake, thinking at first that Cat Spirit was calling to her. But no; it was Yan.

Nisha turned her head, and Yan reached out quickly to restrain her. "Careful," she hissed. "Don't disturb the others."

Slowly, Nisha moved off the mattress. She looked down in the darkness and saw that Reive had been sleeping close beside her. The woman muttered in her sleep, then tugged at the bison hide she had been sleeping under, and grew quiet once more.

Nisha stood for a moment, listening, checking that none of the other women in the house had woken.

"Here," Yan whispered. She shrugged off her white robe and held it out. She gave Nisha a meaningful look in the dim firelight. "Worr wants to speak to you again."

"You'll say nothing of this," Nisha hissed to her as she took the robe and wrapped it around herself.

"No," said Yan, "and neither will you, unless you want us both to suffer." She drew herself up reprovingly. "I don't know what you're doing, Nisha—but I know I should have listened to other people when they told me not to get entangled with you." She turned her back, then, and picked her way to join Worr's other wives.

So be it, Nisha thought to herself. She shrugged on the white robe and crept through the long house, past Uwa, and out into the night.

This time, she didn't stop to savor the cool darkness. There was a fluttery feeling in her stomach. She felt herself trembling as she ran quickly across the open space to Worr's house.

The two guards were standing just inside the door in the semidarkness, exactly as they had been the night before. She ducked her head as she passed between them, and she wished, in a way, that they were more alert. She might need their strength and their spears before the night was over. But of course, there was no way she could tell them that. She hurried down to the big chair at the opposite end of the room, slid behind it, and ducked through the door flap.

Worr was waiting for her. In fact, he looked as if he hadn't moved from his place on his bed since the night before. But then she saw his face more clearly, and she realized he was in a very different mood. His dark eyes were gleaming, and there was a tension in his neck and shoulders that hadn't been there before. He levered himself up, moving with surprising speed for such a big man. His robe fell open as he moved, and she glimpsed his chest and his groin. With a little start, she realized that he was sexually aroused.

He stepped to one side, seized one of the spears that stood in the corner, and turned swiftly, bringing the point of the spear around till it was only a hands' breadth from her face. "Get on the bed," he told her.

Instinctively, she gave a little cry.

"Quiet, you." He didn't bother to raise his voice. He didn't need to. His authority, here, was absolute.

Nisha backed away and scrambled up onto the mattress on the platform of logs. The straw rustled and yielded under her weight.

Worr moved forward, still pointing the spear at her face, forcing her to wriggle away from him across the bed till her shoulders were against the wall. He stepped around the bed and stood over her, and he nudged the point of the spear against her throat.

Nisha flinched, but she forced herself not to cry out. She told herself that he was testing her, just proving to her that he was in control. He had not called her here to kill her. But her pulse still raced, and she found herself having trouble breathing.

"Uwa tells me you should be punished," Worr said. Slowly, still holding the spear, he sat on the edge of the bed. He traced the spear point down from her throat to her chest, using it to part her robe. She feared that he was breaking her skin, but she didn't dare look. The point came to rest just below her left breast, near her heart.

Nisha tried to clear her throat. It was so dry, she could barely swallow. "I helped a woman who had been beaten by her husband," she said. Her voice sounded frail and scared in her own ears—but maybe that was not such a bad thing. Worr probably wanted to see her scared, just to reassure himself that he controlled her.

"You must learn," said Worr, "not to interfere." He gradually pushed harder on the spear, and Nisha felt the point break her skin. There was a tiny trickle of wetness.

She whimpered and flinched from the hurt. "I will learn," she said, looking up into Worr's face. It was almost hidden in shadow, but she saw the blood lust, and she felt his breath warm on her cheeks. The smell of him was strong, and it stank like a fox's lair.

He grunted. "You'll learn, yes." He released his pressure on the spear. "Otherwise, I'll have you killed. There'll be no women making trouble in my tribe."

Abruptly, he threw the spear aside. It clattered loudly against the wall.

Nisha realized she had been holding her breath. She let it out with a gasp.

Slowly, Worr grinned. He reached out and grabbed her by her hair. He jerked her face up, then turned it from side to side. "You're strong, for a woman. But I'm stronger. You understand that, don't you? Eh?" He twisted his hand suddenly, pulling hard on her hair, forcing tears to Nisha's eyes.

She had a sudden vision of herself lashing out with her foot, kicking him in the groin, then wriggling free and grabbing the spear that he had cast aside. She would plunge it into him and make him fall and bleed and die right here in front of her, while she stood on his throat to stop him from screaming. Then she would walk calmly out of his house, past his guards. She would run to the main gate and open it before the guards out there realized what was happening. She would race across the clearing outside the stockade, like the cat that she had seen the previous night. She would vanish into the forest—

With a struggle, she brought herself back to reality. She was a young woman, not a mountain lion. The guards would come after her and kill her, just as they had speared Orlu and Lazonah. They would drag her back and crush her to death. Grep would still live, while she would be dead. And even Worr might survive a spear thrust from her. Her sacrifice would have been for nothing.

"You are far stronger than I can ever be," she whispered to Worr. "You are the strongest of any men in this tribe. That's why I'm here now."

He grunted with satisfaction and released his grip on her, though she could see in his eyes that he still didn't trust her.

He shrugged off his robe with a quick motion and let it fall onto the floor. His rounded body stood before her, with his male organ sticking out hard beneath his belly. "Take your robe off," he ordered her, as he climbed up onto the bed.

She did as he said, taking the opportunity to glance down at the wound he had inflicted on her chest. It was just a tiny cut, and it had hardly bled at all. He had been careful not to mark her, she realized. His only purpose had been to scare her.

She made herself naked. Part of her was recoiling in disgust from the idea of coupling with this man, but she refused to let herself think about it. If it would serve her purposes, it would be no worse than what she had done with Grep. She arched her back as she tossed her robe aside, and she saw him looking down at her breasts. He reached out and grabbed her casually, squeezing hard, till she grunted with pain. He chuckled, then. "Lie down," he told her.

Obediently, she lay on her back. He stretched out beside her and studied her for a moment, as if he could eat her with his eyes. At the same time, he was fondling himself. "So," he said, "now you'll show me this secret of yours. But you won't ever say anything, eh? Because you know what would happen to you if you did."

"Of course," Nisha said. She hesitated. All the time she'd been in his room, she had tried to remain aware of any small noise from outside the house. And now, she imagined there was the faint sound of a footstep. "Worr—" she began.

"You'll do it now," he said.

"Yes—yes, I will. But I want you to bring your spear up onto the bed with us. Just in case. I'm scared, in case Grep should—"

He made an impatient gesture. "Grep is out under the stars with his men. I saw to that."

"Yes, I know." She paused again. She was sure, this time, that she'd heard something—yet still it could have been her nerves.

She turned back to Worr. "What if Grep suspected something? Yan could have told someone about my visiting you last night. If Grep comes here, I want you to be prepared. Please."

"Quiet, woman!" He was getting angry. "Even if your husband came here, my guards—"

"Your guards didn't even glance at me when I came in," Nisha protested.

"Because they were told a woman would be coming here. And they were told not to interfere. Do you think I'm a fool?"

She averted her eyes. "I'm sorry," she whispered. "I just want us to be—safe."

He was still glowering at her, as if she had insulted his pride. "Turn on your stomach," he told her in a low, mean voice.

"Why?" She looked up at him uncertainly.

Quickly—far more quickly than she would have thought possible—he slapped her. His fat hand smacked her cheek, snapping her head to one side. "No more talk from you."

Nisha felt a wave of frustration. This was wrong; it was not the way she'd wanted it to happen. But there was no point in defying him. Mutely, she turned over onto her stomach.

She heard him moving behind her. His hands closed around one of her ankles. She felt him tying a thong. Her leg was dragged out toward the corner of the bed. He tied her other ankle the same way, to the opposite corner.

"How can I pleasure you like this?" Nisha cried out.

"First, I teach you your lesson. Then, you pleasure me."

She managed to raise herself on her elbows. She turned her head, craning her neck. She managed to see him getting up onto the bed. Then his fat hands seized her by the shoulders and pushed her down. She felt his breath on the back of her neck as he edged forward, kneeling between her parted legs.

"Please!" she cried. "Untie me!"

He didn't answer. He slumped forward, and his great bulk pinned her. He took hold of the back of her neck with one hand.

Nisha felt moisture on her face. She was crying, she realized. They were tears of frustration, tears of anger—at him, and at herself, because she hadn't dealt with him cleverly enough. She never should have allowed this to happen. She had thought she could get him under her control, the way Grep had been. And now—

His bulk was squeezing the breath out of her. But then, as he was poised to penetrate her, she felt a change in him. He stiffened. One moment, he was on her; the next, he was pulling away.

"Hold him!"

A shout, a scuffling sound. Nisha's heart suddenly seemed to explode in her throat. She heard quick footsteps, a grunt, another shout.

Nisha managed to squirm around. Two of Worr's guards were in the room. She saw their scarlet robes. And Grep was right behind them. Worr was scrambling across his bed, reaching for the spear he had thrown aside. She glimpsed his face. He looked startled. He even showed some fear.

"Hold him!" Grep shouted again. But the guards seemed too stunned to react. Worr was fumbling, grabbing his spear, scrambling up onto his knees—

"Kill him!" The words escaped from Nisha before she had time to think. She squirmed and struggled, incapacitated by her bonds. With all the force of her mind, she willed Worr to cast his spear. More than anything, she wanted to see Grep fall. Worr had abused her, and in time, she would take revenge on him for that. But Grep had slaughtered her husband and child. "Kill him!" she screamed again.

Worr was up on his feet, now. He paused for an instant, confronting the three men. His eyes darted quickly from one to the next. Grep had already leveled his own spear, but the two guards were reacting slowly, looking nervous and confused.

Worr gave a great bellow of rage. He feinted, then lunged, skewering one of the guards in the belly. The man screamed, dropped his own spear, and clutched Worr's shaft where it had penetrated him. He fell down on his knees with a look of horror.

There was still a chance, Nisha told herself. If Worr could kill all three men, there would be no witnesses.

Worr planted his foot on the fallen guard and wrenched his spear out of the man. But the other guard was moving quickly to one side, flanking the chieftain.

Worr yelled and sliced his spear at Grep, but Grep evaded the thrust easily. He jumped up onto the bed. Nisha felt the straw mattress sag under the weight of his feet where he stood right beside her naked body. Worr was cornered, now, with the guard on one side of him and Grep on the other.

"Put down your spear, Worr!" Grep shouted.

Worr snarled, turned suddenly, and swung his spear in an arc. The tip of it sliced across the guard's face, and he shouted in pain. His cheeks were suddenly covered in blood. He dropped his own spear—but somehow he managed to seize hold of Worr's.

Worr bellowed. His muscles flexed and bulged as he tried to pull his spear free. The guard was slumping down on the floor, his blood was running freely from his face and across his chest, but he wouldn't let go.

Grep stepped forward. He leveled his own weapon and thrust it toward Worr's forehead. "Let go of your spear!" he shouted.

Worr snarled at him. He kicked the guard in the chest—but still the wounded man held on.

There was the sound of hurrying footsteps. More guards were suddenly pushing their way into the little room.

"Help me!" Worr shouted to them. "Kill these traitors!"

"This woman is my wife." It was Grep's voice, sounding above the confused voices of the guards. "Do you hear me? This is my wife. Worr was raping my wife."

Worr looked up at Grep, and his face contorted. Suddenly he dropped his own spear, seized Grep's, and pulled forward on it with all his strength. Grep was unprepared. Nisha saw him stumbling forward, falling from the bed, turning, and slamming down on his back on the floor. His head landed just inches from the stones around the fireplace. His hands lost their grip on his spear. Worr wrenched it free, turned it, pulled it up, then thrust it down with an exultant shout.

Grep squirmed on the floor and the spear slashed his

robe, barely missing his body. The shaft dug into the packed earth, pinning Grep by the furs he wore. He jerked at them futilely, but they were stuck fast. In desperation, he reached for one of the heavy stones from beside the fire, lifted it, and hurled it with all his strength.

His aim was true. The stone struck Worr squarely in the middle of his forehead.

Worr stood for a long moment with his mouth gaping wide. He raised his arms as if he were a sleepwalker trying to fend off an imaginary enemy. Then his eyes rolled up, his knees buckled under him, and he fell.

There was a long moment of silence. Down on the floor, Grep wrestled with the spear that pinned him. Finally, he managed to pull it free. He stood up, looked at Worr, then turned quickly to the guards. "You saw," he shouted. He pointed to Nisha, on the bed. "He brought my wife here—"

"I saw." The guard who had been slashed by Worr was getting up onto his feet, trying to staunch the blood from his wounded face. "Worr was on her when we came in. We told him to stop, but—" He sounded confused. Nisha imagined the man trying to come to terms with the situation. He had been attacked by the very man he had pledged to guard with his life. His own chieftain had betrayed him. "He speared Toron, there." He turned and pointed to the other guard, lying in a great pool of blood, still clutching his stomach. His face was pale and his eyes were closed.

Grep kneeled beside the man. "Dead," he said.

The other guards were murmuring uneasily among themselves. "Why are you here?" one of them asked Grep. "You were sent out—"

"I suspected him," said Grep. His voice had been shrill before, but he spoke with calm assurance now. "That's why I came here. I told Toron my suspicions, and we looked through the gap at the edge of the door flap—"

"It's true," Toron said. "We saw him tie her and then get up on the bed."

"This is a serious business, Grep," one of the guards said. "A very serious business."

"Yes," said Grep. "I realize that."

Worr groaned. He rolled over on the floor.

"Tie his wrists!" Grep shouted. "Quickly, now. Before he kills another man."

The guards hesitated. Two of them glanced at each other, then at Toron's face. Finally, they went to obey.

Grep bent down, picked up Nisha's deerskin robe, and threw it over her, covering her nakedness. Then she felt his fingers loosening her bonds.

With a cry of relief, she rolled over onto her back. "Thank you!" she cried, staring up at Grep. "Thank you for saving me!"

He gave her a long, steady stare, and said nothing.

Chapter Eighteen

The guards gathered around her. Their faces were angry and accusatory, even though she had clearly been the victim. Several of them demanded to know what had happened, and when she turned to Grep, she found him looking at her with the same grim expression.

Haltingly at first, she told them that Worr had sent for her, and she hadn't dared to refuse him. He was the chieftain, and she was afraid to disobey him. She had entered his room, and almost immediately he had thrown her on the bed and tied her down. And then—well, she was thankful that the men had come in and found her here. If they had arrived just a few moments later, Worr would have raped her.

The guards still looked unsure. They saw Worr, semiconscious, groaning, propped up against the wall with his hands lashed behind him. They turned to Grep. Why had he come here? Had he known what was going to happen? Why hadn't he stayed out with his men?

"I brought him back here," Nisha said, before Grep could answer. "I'd seen the way Worr looked at me, ever since I came to this village. I knew what was in his mind, and I was scared of him. I told my husband that I was afraid of what might happen if he ever left the compound. And I was right!" She stared at each man in turn, challenging them to disagree with her.

Worr made a growling sound at the back of his throat. "The woman lies," he grunted. He coughed and spat, then glared up at Nisha with a hatred so pure, she found herself flinching from the sight of him. "She tempted Kron," said Worr, "and he died for it. She tempted me the same way." He turned his face toward Grep. "And you, you fool, you think you can control her. You're wrong. She's poisonous. She's filth. We should have executed her."

Grep stepped over to Worr. He stood looking down at the man. "I know the truth of what I saw, Worr," he said quietly. "You tied my wife down, and you were forcing yourself on her." Grep gestured to Toron. "He saw, too, through the crack of the door flap. We were watching you, Worr. And Nelik, before you killed him." Grep nudged the body of the fallen man. "He saw, too."

Worr was panting for breath. His face was flushed bright red. "I never told her to come here!" he shouted.

"Liar!" Nisha screamed back at him. "How do you think I could have come here on my own, if you hadn't arranged it for me?"

"Enough." Grep held up his hand. He turned to the guards. "Worr has violated my marriage. He shall face me in front of the tribe." He eyed the guards. Some of them still looked uncomfortable, but none of them spoke against him.

"Take care of Toron," Grep said quietly. He gestured to Worr. "And hold him here till tomorrow, at noon." He turned to Nisha. "Come," he said.

Outside, the sky was still black but the first trace of dawn was touching the horizon. Nisha followed Grep, her thoughts buzzing in her head. Was he as calm as he seemed? Would he hold her responsible in some way? After all, she had hinted that this might happen. But she said nothing as he led the way to the Warriors' House.

Inside, the building was almost empty. "Where are the rest of your men?" she whispered.

"Still camped in the woods. They would have made noise if I brought them back here. I had to enter the village quietly." He shot her a quick glance. "When I received your message, I didn't know whether you could be trusted. I didn't want anyone else to know till I found out for myself whether what you said was true."

"I was loyal to you!" she blurted.

He gave her another look, and said nothing. He led her past rows of beds, only a couple of them occupied. One of the sleeping figures was Plorngah, Nisha realized. She hesitated for a second, fighting a sudden urge to go to him and kick him, rip at him, do anything to hurt him for what he had done to Rilla and Jees.

But now was not the time, and in any case, if Plorngah's leg was really not going to heal, he might soon be killed anyway.

"Come here," said Grep. There was a wall at the end of the house with a doorway in the center. He pulled the flap aside and waited for her to walk through.

She found herself in a room like Worr's, but smaller. Instead of a big bed built of logs, there was a simple mattress on the floor.

A fire was smoldering amid some stones in one corner. Grep went to it, picked up some tinder, lit it, and took the flame to a piece of fat on a stone that served as a lamp. When the fat started sputtering, he set the lamp on a piece of log that jutted out from the wall, then turned to face her. "So now," he said softly, "you will tell me the truth."

She stared at him in the flickering yellow light. His face was impassive, but there was a hardness in his eyes that made her feel cold inside. She had been scared of Worr, but Grep had always been a more dangerous adversary. Worr was a big, brutal thug, yet she felt she understood him. He wanted to hold onto this power, he wanted to enjoy his pleasures, and there was not much more in him than that. But Grep was meaner and more cunning, and he took a more active pleasure in his cruelties. She had seen for herself how much he enjoyed other people's suffering.

"What I said to the guards was basically true," Nisha

said in a low voice. "You saw yourself, Worr tied me down—"

Suddenly she found herself reeling backward, unable to breathe. He had punched her in the stomach, so quickly she hadn't even seen him move. She slammed against the wall and slumped down onto her knees, clutching herself and grasping.

Casually, Grep seized her by the hair and dragged her to his bed. He kicked her onto it, then sat down beside her. "The truth," he said. His voice was still as quiet and calm as ever. "Otherwise, Nisha, I will hurt you."

Nisha squinted up at him. Gradually, she managed to breathe again. She used the moment to play for time. How much could he possibly know? What should she say? What would convince him?

"All right," she whispered. "All right, I will tell you everything."

He waited in silence.

"Worr summoned me the previous night," she went on. "He told Yan—one of his wives—to ask me my ways of pleasing a man. I refused to say. So Yan went and told Worr, and then Worr sent her back to me and commanded me to visit him in person. I went to his room, and—I told him, it isn't possible to give my skills to his women, because they fear him too much. They will never have the confidence to touch him."

"Go on." Grep's voice was toneless. He was watching her, and waiting. She couldn't tell, yet, if he believed anything she had said.

"I could see he wanted me himself," Nisha said. "But he was scared of you finding out, so he sent me back to the Wives' House. But then, during the day, when he told you to take your men out of the village, I suspected that he wanted you out of the way. And that could only mean one thing. That was why I sent my message to you."

"All right." He gave a curt nod. "And why did he tie you down?"

Nisha shrugged helplessly. "I—angered him. By talking too much. He said he would punish me, and after that he would force me to pleasure him."

Slowly, Grep leaned back against the wall. She saw the tension flow out of him—tension that she hadn't even realized was there. He had been like a snake, coiled to strike at her. "It's good that you have told me the truth," he said. His voice had been calm before, but she realized that he had achieved that by willpower. Now, he sounded relaxed. He was no longer suppressing his pent-up anger. The anger had gone—for the time being, at least.

He smiled faintly. "I never went far from the compound. I sent my men on without me, and as soon as it was dark, I climbed a rope at the rear of the stockade. The warrior on duty there was one of my own men; I had seen to that. I told him to say nothing. So, I was hiding near Worr's house, watching Yan come and go. And I watched you when you went there." He paused, enjoying her look of surprise. "There are thin gaps between the logs in the wall of Worr's house," he went on. "One of the gaps is easily wide enough to see through, if you know where to look. So I watched you with Worr. When I saw him throw you down, that was when I went to his guards. I knew I would need witnesses."

"Ah." Nisha looked down, feeling her pulse tapping fast inside her chest. He was even more clever than she had feared. But how much had he been able to hear, when he'd been watching her from outside? If he had heard her telling Worr how much she wanted him, or warning him to arm himself against Grep, surely Grep would kill her for that. On the other hand, if Grep had heard her, she would already be dead. She shivered again. She had taken a far bigger risk than she'd realized.

"What's the matter?" His eyes were alert. He missed nothing.

"I'm scared," she said.

He grunted. "You should be scared." Quickly, he seized

her by the neck and gave her a little shake. "I think there was some truth in what Worr said. You tempt men. First Kron, then him. How many others, eh?"

"It's not my fault," she gasped. She looked at him imploringly. "I warned you, didn't I?" She tried to make herself sound plaintive. "First, I told you that I'd seen the way Worr looked at me, as if he wanted me. Then I sent the message to you. I wanted you to know. And when you found me with Worr—didn't I shout to you to kill him?"

Grudgingly, he nodded.

"You *should* have killed him!" she cried. "You had him at your mercy, with a spear pointed at his face."

"It wasn't—wise." Grep released his hold on her and sat back, flexing his fingers. "His guards are loyal to him—or they were. If some of them had burst in while I had my spear in Worr's body and his blood on my hands, I think they might have executed me before I had a chance to speak."

She nodded slowly. He was probably right. She had seen in the guards' faces, how hard it was for them to accept what had happened.

"Today, he will die," Grep went on. "In front of everyone." He said it calmly, without a hint of emotion. Once again, Nisha felt cold inside.

"After you kill him," she said, "then, will you be the new chieftain?"

"Yes," he said. "Worr has no boy-children. I am the next in line."

She forced a smile. She reached out and touched his shoulder. "Then this is good. You should thank me for what happened."

He didn't answer. He reached out, opened her robe, and ran his hand over her body. She forced herself to sit passively without flinching.

"Lie on your stomach," he told her.

Obediently, she did so. What was he going to do now? She hoped he wouldn't force himself on her. She was so exhausted, she wasn't sure how much more she could take. And even though she had managed to seem as if she worshipped Grep, she still feared and hated him as much as ever.

He ran his hand down her naked back. "He was going to force himself on you," Grep murmured.

"Yes," she whispered.

"I wonder if he would have made you scream."

"Perhaps."

"My men can't understand why I have you as my wife," he murmured, half to himself. "They agree with Worr. They think you're dangerous. And now that you've brought down our chieftain, they'll be even more convinced."

She could hear his breathing growing deeper. She could feel the tension rising in him. So why did he keep her, if all the village feared her? Suddenly she remembered what Uwa had said. *He's always enjoyed a fight. That's what he wants with you. He'll fight you and drag you down and trample you. That's his way.*

Grep loved power, and he loved conquest. The bigger the conquest, the more powerful it made him feel. If he could control her and subdue her and show his people that she obeyed him, he would seem more powerful not only in his own eyes, but in theirs, as well. He would be the man who tamed a woman who was as dangerous as a mountain cat.

"Give me the pleasure, now, that you gave me before," he told her. He took her hand and guided it to his flesh.

She told herself that she was glad to do it. Here was the proof that all Grep's cruelties, all his pretensions of power were just a facade. He might be stronger than she was, and he might still kill her if she faltered on the dangerous path that she was treading. But so long as she lived, and so long as he needed her this way, he didn't control her. She controlled him.

Expertly, she touched him, while she watched his face.

He clenched his jaw. His eyes half closed. His chest heaved. He made a groaning sound at the back of his throat. He arched his back, and within moments, he reached his climax.

So where is your power now, she thought to herself, as she watched him slump against the wall, breathing deeply. Her anxiety suddenly disappeared. She felt calm as she wiped her hand clean. Once again she had gambled, and she had survived. One brutal, evil man would die tomorrow—not the one she had chosen, but perhaps that was for the best. If Worr had killed Grep and had taken Nisha as a new wife, she wasn't sure she would have had so much influence over him as she had over Grep now. Worr was not so much in love with power, and he might care just as much for eating as he cared for sex. Yes, it was best this way. And certainly Worr deserved to die, after what he had done to Orlu and Lazonah after they tried to escape from the village.

Grep stirred. "I must rest," he said. His voice sounded thick and weary. He gestured to the mattress beside him. "You will rest here with me."

Obediently, she lay down.

He fumbled with something, then reached behind her. "What are you doing?" she asked, as she felt him wrapping a thong around her left wrist.

"I believe you told me the truth tonight," he said. He dragged her other arm behind her and tied her two wrists together. "But I'd be foolish to trust such a woman." He found another thong and looped it loosely around her neck, then tied it to a branch that protruded from one of the logs that formed the wall of the house. "Now," he said, "we can sleep." He went to the lamp and blew it out.

Nisha squirmed uncomfortably. She felt a spasm of anger. Certainly, she could sleep like this, but it was humiliating to be trussed up like an animal.

Then, just as quickly, her calmness returned. He was

afraid of her, she realized. That was why he had to tie her before he dared to sleep beside her.

Lying in the semidarkness, Nisha smiled to herself as she drifted off to sleep.

Chapter Nineteen

It was a bright, clear day as the villagers gathered at the end of the compound. The warriors had failed to find and kill the mountain lion, but they had come back with a couple of deer. They joined the rest of their people in the meeting place, and this time everyone was present, even the wives and small children.

Worr had been tied to the pillar where Grep had been stoned just three weeks ago. He was almost naked, wearing nothing but a dirty loin cloth. A big round pebble had been forced into his mouth, and a strip of leather had been wrapped around his jaw so that he couldn't speak. Another strip of hide had been tied around his head as a blindfold.

The villagers barely spoke as they sat in a semicircle around their disgraced chieftain. Nisha saw many of them avoiding looking at Worr. Their lives were normally governed by strict, unchanging rules. Suddenly, the order in their world had been destroyed, and it seemed to disturb them deeply.

She, of course, was to blame. Whenever someone glanced in her direction, it was with a look of hate. She was sitting with Grep's other wives, but they acted as if she didn't exist.

Nisha saw Rilla sitting close by. Here, at least, was a friend. Nisha stood up, stepped among the people, and squatted beside her. She seized her hands and clasped them tightly. "I'm happy to see you," she said. It sounded inadequate, but what else could she say, with all the people of the tribe around her? She bent her head closer to Rilla. "How are your wounds? Are they starting to heal?"

Rilla nodded uneasily. She didn't speak.

"What's wrong?" Nisha murmured.

"I'm afraid." Rilla's voice was almost inaudible. Suddenly she reached for Nisha and whispered to her urgently. "Nisha, I can't believe that—that you did this thing. They'll kill you. You can't go on—"

"Grep will protect me from them," Nisha said.

Rilla stared at her in amazement. "You trust him?" She shook her head violently. "He massacred our people. He kills for the pleasure of it. He'll kill you, too."

Nisha stroked the woman's cheek. "I am more secure, now, than I was before. And if either of us dies, it will be Grep, not me."

"You!" The voice was loud and commanding. A hand grabbed Nisha's shoulder.

Nisha turned and found herself facing Uwa. For a moment, the two of them stared at each other. Uwa seemed as grim and fierce as ever—and yet, as she looked into Nisha's face, the big, ugly woman's confidence seemed to waver. "Go to your place," she said, more quietly.

Today, your brother Worr will die, Nisha thought to herself as she looked at Uwa. *And I'm to blame.*

Nisha turned back to Rilla. "Be strong!" she said to her. Then she made her way back to join the other wives.

A few moments later, Grep stepped out in front of the people. The crowd had been murmuring quietly before; now, everyone lapsed into total silence. Somewhere in the distance, a bird cried out—a shrike, calling to its mate. The wind blew, stirring dust and whispering around the long wooden houses. A young child complained, and there was a slap as a woman disciplined it.

Grep stood and surveyed the people. He was wearing the clothes of a warrior: heavy moccasins with calfskin wrapped around his lower legs, a bearskin robe belted tightly, and more calfskin wrapped around his lower arms. He held a spear that Nisha had seen before—the same spear that had been in Worr's room. It was highly ornamented with dozens of fetishes and scalps.

Grep's face was painted with bands of black and green. His hair was pulled back and braided. He looked fierce and proud as he stood out in the open space in the sun, and he let the moment of silence drag on, while Worr stood helpless behind him, unable to see or speak.

Finally, Grep extended his arm. He pointed to a man standing to one side. "Come," he called.

Toron stepped out. His face was horribly swollen, and there was still an ugly gash where Worr's spear had cut him. He was barefoot, he had daubed his hair with mud, and he had sliced his red sheepskin into broad ribbons that flapped around him in the wind. This was how he showed his anguish over what had happened.

He turned his wounded face toward the crowd, and people murmured uneasily.

"Tell them," said Grep.

Haltingly, Toron described what had happened. Grep had demanded access to Worr's house. Grep, Toron, and Nelik had peered through the door flap and seen Worr forcing himself on Nisha. They had confronted him. Worr had fought back. Worr's spear had killed Nelik and slashed Toron's face.

Toron was not a good speaker, and he still seemed shaken and confused by what he had witnessed. He hesitated and stumbled as he told his story, but this just made his story more powerful, more convincing to the crowd.

"Were you loyal to Worr?" Grep asked him quietly.

Toron nodded. "Yes." He nodded again. "Always."

"Do you feel betrayed?" Grep said.

Toron grimaced. "He is my chieftain. But he broke our code. He turned against us. He killed Nelik." He touched his own face and winced.

Grep turned back to the crowd. "Does any man doubt what Toron says?" He stood holding his spear, surveying them. "Step forward, anyone who challenges Toron. Step forward now!" He pointed to the ground in front of him. "Come before us all!"

There was a long silence. Finally, one man stood up and started picking his way through the crowd. It was Plorngah, limping on his injured leg, leaning on a spear to steady himself.

Grep frowned at the man. "You have nothing to tell us. You were sleeping when this happened."

Plorngah ignored Grep. He turned toward the crowd and searched their faces. Then he saw Nisha, and he pointed at her. "This woman is the cause," he shouted. "Listen here: I have been crippled." He gestured to his leg. "Kron was tempted, and he was killed. And now Worr." He bared his teeth. "I say the woman should die."

Nisha wondered if she should respond. Probably not; as a woman, she wouldn't be expected to speak. But it was hard for her to sit in silence as Plorngah glared at her.

"You are speaking of my wife, Plorngah," Grep said quietly.

Plorngah turned and looked him up and down. "You're a fool for letting her live. You'll suffer for it, just like me, and just like Kron."

There was a long, ugly silence. "You insult me in front of our people, and you insult my wife." Grep slowly shook his head. "Step back, now, while I allow you that choice."

"I choose not to," Plorngah shouted. "I choose to tell you what you should already know. Your wife has brought chaos and death to this tribe. She should be cast out or killed."

Grep's face was stony. "You are provoking me, Plorngah."

Plorngah tossed his spear aside. He lurched unsteadily on his bad leg as he threw his arms wide. "Kill me!" he shouted. "My life is over anyway. My leg will never heal. I may as well die. But be warned, you'll die too, if you let that woman live!"

Grep weighed his spear for a moment, then cast it with

a swift, effortless sweep of his arm. The shaft flew straight from his hand to Plorngah's heart, and it was hurled with such force, Nisha saw the point emerge from Plorngah's back in a spray of blood.

The crippled man staggered, clutched himself, then fell in the dirt. He made a choking, coughing sound, and then he gasped as his lungs deflated. A liquid red circle started spreading out around him on the ground. His eyelids closed, fluttered, and were still.

Calmly, Grep walked to the fallen man. He took hold of his spear and methodically worked it out of Plorngah's body. He took a fragment of sheepskin from inside his robe, wiped the blood from his spear, and then examined it carefully to make sure that the shaft hadn't been damaged and the flint hadn't been chipped.

Nisha watched him with terrible fascination. Grep moved unhurriedly, as if he was alone in his room, building a fire or lighting a lamp. He completely ignored the warriors, guards, women, and children gathered around. From his face, no one would guess that he had just killed a man whom he had known all his life. She wondered how it must feel to have so much confidence, so much indifference to other people.

Finally, Grep set down his spear. He pulled a flint knife from his belt, bent over Plorngah, and seized the dead man's hair in his free hand. Grep's right arm moved swiftly, using the flint to mark a square in the skin at the crown of Plorngah's head. There was a ripping sound as Grep tore the section of scalp away. He tucked the hank of hair in his belt, leaving the bloody skin dangling. He wiped his knife, put it away, then turned to a couple of Worr's guards. He gestured.

The men moved forward. They seized Plorngah's legs and dragged him out of the meeting place.

Grep turned back to the crowd. "Rilla," he called out. "Jees. Step forward now."

Nisha tensed. With dismay, she saw Rilla standing up, looking terrified. Nisha clenched her fists, digging her nails painfully into her palms, as Rilla stumbled toward Grep, with Jees following behind her.

"Face our people," Grep told them.

The women glanced at each other. Rilla was so scared, she could barely stand. Jees seemed calmer; her face showed nothing as she turned toward her tribe. But there was a look of despair in her eyes.

"These wives have no husband now," Grep called out. He turned to Jees and tilted her face up. "Does anyone speak for this woman?"

There was a long silence. No one spoke.

"She shall be cast out," Grep said, matter of factly. He gave her a little push, and Jees stumbled out of the meeting place, holding her face in her hands. Nisha saw a guard grab her arm and march her away, and she was gone.

Grep turned to Rilla. He eyed her for a long moment. "This woman," he said, "I take as my own."

There was a murmur of surprise. Rilla stared at Grep, looking stunned. Then her eyes widened in fear. "No," she whispered.

Grep made a little sound of irritation. "This is not your place to speak. Go, join my other wives. You are one of them, now."

Rilla shook her head. "No," she said again.

"Go!" Grep shouted at her.

The word was like a slap. Rilla stepped backward, then turned and ran into the crowd. Somehow, she found Nisha. She slumped down beside her, and Nisha felt the girl trembling.

Out in the meeting place, Grep had turned back to Toron, who was still standing out in the sun. "Now," said Grep. "We will continue this business here. Plorngah said what he wanted to say. Does anyone else wish to speak?"

The silence, now, was fearful. Nisha looked at the faces of the men around her, and she saw that they resented that Grep was already acting as if he was the new chieftain. At the same time, though, he had cowed them. He was so methodical, so cold, he truly was the most formidable of all the warriors. Three weeks ago, they had stoned him and tried to kill him, but he had returned here as if his power had never wavered.

Grep waited. The moment dragged on.

"Very well," he said finally. He turned to face Worr, stepped over to him, and cut the thongs binding the chieftain to the stone pillar. Grep ripped the blindfold away, and Worr shook his head, squinting and blinking in the bright sun. The big man flexed his hands and arms, then reached up, pulled the gag out of his own mouth, and hurled it aside. He glowered at Grep.

"Give him your spear," Grep said to Toron.

Toron hesitated.

"Give it to him!" Grep snapped.

Hastily, Toron stepped forward. He held out his spear to Worr. The fat, ugly chieftain snatched it out of the guard's hands.

"You sent me out of our village so that you could defile my wife," Grep said. And now, finally, he showed some emotion. The contempt that he had masked for so long was obvious in the way he watched his adversary. "You were our chieftain, but you broke one of our most sacred laws. What do you have to say, Worr?"

The chieftain licked his fat lips, then wiped his mouth on the back of his hand. He stood for a moment with his shoulders hunched and his arms dangling, and Nisha saw him shift his grip on his spear. He squinted at Grep and bared his teeth. It seemed as if he was going to speak— but then, without warning, he charged forward. His bulk moved with the force of a bison. He made as if to throw his spear, and Grep dodged to one side, started to bring up his own spear, then saw that there wasn't time. Grep stepped backward, sidestepped again—but Worr anticipated him. The chieftain ducked down and rammed his head into Grep's stomach.

The force of the blow sent Grep flying backward. He thumped down on his back on the ground and Nisha saw pale dust billow up around him in the sun. The people around her let out a gasp of surprise, and they jumped to their feet.

Worr raised his spear as he advanced on Grep. The big man was panting with the exertion of his quick dash. A sheen of sweat had broken out across his naked shoulders.

Grep scrambled backward on the ground. So long as he was lying in the dirt, there was no way he could defend himself with his spear. The shaft was too long; its end would dig in if he tried to bring the point up toward Worr.

Worr made a strange sound. It was a rasping, gutteral chuckle. He stood over Grep and slowly lowered the point of his spear till it was just an arm's length from Grep's stomach. "You could have killed me when I was tied to the pillar," the big man said. "It was your right, eh? But you've always been proud. Too proud. And now you pay for that."

Grep quickly rolled over—but Worr sidestepped along with him, and when Grep faced Worr again, the chieftain's spear was still aimed directly at Grep's abdomen, and there was still nothing that Grep could do to strike back. Worr's face showed a horrible pleasure in the helplessness of his enemy.

Grep reached up, trying to grab the spear that was pointing at him. But it was just out of reach. Grep's shoulders thumped back down on the ground.

Worr stared down at Grep with the same hatred that Nisha had seen the previous night when the chieftain had glared at her. The muscles clenched in Worr's throwing arm. He braced himself to plunge his spear into Grep's belly.

Grep squirmed around. He was still holding his own spear, even though it seemed useless to him. He swung it, now, like a long club, parallel to the ground. The shaft smacked against Worr's shin.

The big man grunted more in anger than in pain. He shifted his weight instinctively to his other leg. Grep was ready for him; he kicked out with all his strength. His heel thudded into Worr's knee.

Worr was knocked off balance. He shouted in fury and plunged his spear down. But he was falling sideways, and he had missed his opportunity. His spear went wide; it dug harmlessly into the dirt.

Grep kicked out again. This time, Worr's leg shot out from under him and the big man toppled forward. Grep was already pulling out his knife—the same knife he had used to scalp Plorngah just moments ago. As Worr toppled down, Grep brought up the blade.

Worr slumped onto Grep, impaling himself. The big man yelled and clawed frantically at the knife buried deep in the right side of his chest. Blood surged across his skin. He bellowed in fury.

Grep rolled over and up onto his feet in one swift motion. Now the two men's roles were reversed; but Nisha knew immediately that Grep wouldn't make the same mistake that Worr had made. Grep paused only for a moment to take careful aim, then plunged his spear into Worr's bloated body.

The man shouted in agony. Grep worked the shaft savagely, and bloody pulsed out around it. He pulled it free, then stabbed again, and again, and still again, till Worr's cries finally lapsed into silence.

Grep stood for a moment, breathing heavily. He stooped, seized his knife, and wrenched it out of Worr. He walked slowly around the fallen chieftain, staring at him as if he half expected Worr somehow to come back to life. But the big man was no longer breathing. He lay motionless, covered in his own blood. His eyes were wide and unblinking. His mouth was gaping.

Grep wiped sweat out of his eyes. The encounter had shaken his composure, at least a little. A tic worked at the side of his face. He turned suddenly to Worr's guards standing close by, watching in silence. "Get me an axe," he snapped at them.

They stared at him.

"An axe!" he shouted.

A young man turned and ran into one of the houses. No one else moved. The villagers were still on their feet, standing transfixed, staring at their fallen chieftain. They must have known that Grep was likely to kill him, but still they seemed stunned by the sight of it.

The young man came running back. He pressed the stone axe into Grep's hand.

Grep kneeled down, took a firm grip on the axe with both hands, raised it high above his right shoulder, then brought it down with all his strength where Worr's arm was stretched out on the ground. The axe severed the wrist in a single blow.

Grep stood up. He walked around Worr, kneeled down again, and smashed the axe into the chieftain's other wrist.

Having cut off the hands, Grep moved down and chopped off both feet. Finally, with three massive blows of the axe, he severed Worr's neck.

He stood up, breathing heavily. He kicked Worr's head, sending it rolling away. Then he turned and surveyed the crowd. He glowered at them for a long moment, almost as if he wanted to kill and dismember them as well.

He turned to Worr's guards. "Strip him naked and hang his body by the gate," he said. "Let the vultures pick him clean. Give the rest of him to the shaman."

Grep turned away without waiting for a response. He retrieved his spear, straightened his robe, and walked out of the meeting place.

Chapter Twenty

"I don't understand," Rilla whispered, as she lay with Nisha in the Wives' House. "Why did Grep want me as his wife?"

The house was dark. The fire had burned low, and all the other women were outside with their husbands. Earlier, in the Warriors' House, the men had officially made Grep their new chieftain. Now that the sun had set, it was a time for feasting and celebration, but Grep had told Nisha and Rilla that he didn't want them with the rest of the tribe, and they should stay in the Wives' House until further notice.

"I told Grep that I could never teach the women of this tribe how to touch and please a man, because they're too fearful," Nisha said. "And I think Grep saw the truth of that." She stroked Rilla's hair, where the girl lay beside her. "You're the only woman from our tribe who still lives," Nisha went on, "other than me. So, you're the only one who might learn to please a man the way I do. For that reason, I'm sure Grep wouldn't want any other man to have you."

Rilla looked at Nisha doubtfully. "You speak as if you know these things for a fact."

Nisha shrugged. "I've learned how Grep thinks. He wants other men to envy him, fear him, and hate him for everything he has—his strength, his power, and his women."

"But why?" Rilla said again. "Why does he need to be that way?"

Nisha sighed. "You've seen how the young boys are trained in this tribe."

"Yes," said Rilla. "They go out with the men, and they come back beaten and bruised. Sometimes they're badly injured. Sometimes they even die out there."

"So perhaps pain is like a sickness that spreads from one person to the next," said Nisha. "A child receives it from a man, and then that child grows older, and he passes it on—to anyone, or everyone."

Rilla wrapped her arms around Nisha and pressed her head between Nisha's breasts. "I miss our people so much," she said. She started crying, and her thin body shook as she sobbed. "I don't understand how you can be so strong. I don't know how you can bear to be in this terrible place, and speak like this, and not be afraid."

Nisha felt deeply weary. "I do feel fear," she said. "But I feel anger, too. And the anger is stronger. I've vowed that these men will pay for what they did, Rilla. My vow gives me the strength to continue."

Rilla suddenly pulled free. She rubbed the tears off her cheeks with some angry swipes of her arm. "But look what your vow has done!" she cried. "Worr is dead, and Grep is even more powerful than before, and now he's claimed me as his wife—"

"Shhh." Nisha pressed her finger to Rilla's lips. "Be calm, Rilla." She pulled the girl back down onto the straw mattress. Even though they were alone in the house, she was afraid of being overheard. "This was not what I planned," she whispered. "I warned Worr to defend himself when I was in his room. I expected that Grep would be the one to die."

"You're crazy." Rilla looked at Nisha as if she was a stranger. "All this killing—" She shuddered and closed her eyes.

Outside, there was the sound of cheering. Nisha sat cradling Rilla's head and she listened, trying to guess what was happening. She was puzzled that Grep had told her and Rilla to stay here, while all the other women were with their husbands in the celebration. Perhaps Grep was afraid that she would make people feel uneasy if she was seen among them. Many of them—perhaps most of them—probably wanted her dead by now.

But so long as Grep believed that he could control her power and use it for his own ends, he would let her live. It didn't even matter to him if she had caused the death of Kron or Worr. He had no love or respect for his kinfolk; she'd seen it in his face after he'd hacked off Worr's head and turned to confront the crowd. He was so full of hate, he despised them all.

Nisha shook her head in wonder. Rilla was right; it was strange that Nisha could feel so calm about being in the middle of this situation. But so long as she saw that Grep needed her—as a plaything, or as a way to tantalize other men and prove his power to them—she felt secure.

There was another burst of cheering from outside, and then the villagers all started singing. They actually sounded happy. Grep must be managing them skillfully, feeding them generously, smiling over them, persuading them that life would continue the same way that it always had before. Yes, that was why he wanted Nisha and Rilla out of sight. He needed to reassure his people. He needed them to fear him, too—but not so much that they would run from the village in terror. After all, his power would be meaningless if there were no people to use it on.

Rilla's crying had gradually subsided. The girl seemed to have fallen into a fitful sleep. Well, Nisha thought, that might be a good example to follow. She lay down and let her weariness wash over her. While the people of the tribe celebrated and honored their new chieftain, Nisha surrendered herself to slumber.

Once again, Cat Spirit called her.

Nisha woke with a start. She had been outside in the forest, padding through the undergrowth—and now she heard Cat Spirit's voice inside her head.

"Nisha!"

She jumped. She felt her heart flutter and she peered quickly around, blinking in the dimness. "Cat Spirit," she whispered. "What do you want from me?"

She sat for a long moment, waiting for an answer, trying to understand. But there was no sound, now, except for the breathing of women sleeping in the house.

The celebration must have ended. The wives had returned here. But they weren't sleeping in their usual places. Figures were scattered everywhere, as if they had just passed out wherever they happened to find themselves. Nisha sniffed the air and noticed a faint, sweet smell. Corn wine, she realized. She remembered how Grep had passed it around when his warriors had rested in the hiding place in the forest. So, that's why the villagers had sounded so happy while they were singing around the fire.

"Nisha!"

She jumped again. It was so strange to hear the spirit speak in her head. It frightened her.

"Come, Nisha."

Once again she glimpsed the land outside the stockade. Then she found herself looking at the same spot where she had seen the cat before. Should she try to ignore it, or should she obey?

She stood up. There was no need to move quietly; everyone was deeply asleep, drugged by the wine. Nisha picked her way among them, and she crept out of the house.

A fire still glowed where the feast had taken place. People were stretched out around it, snoring under the stars. She paused, staring in wonder at the warriors on the ground. Were any guards on duty? Maybe not. She felt a little surge of excitement. Many of the men were sleeping with their spears beside them. She could seize a weapon. She could kill a dozen warriors—maybe a score—and she could escape.

The idea was so intoxicating, her heart started fluttering again, and she felt herself trembling. She had to steady herself against the wall of the Wives' House as she tried to calm herself. She had to be careful. She couldn't be sure that all the guards were unconscious.

"Nisha!"

She shook her head impatiently. Why wouldn't Cat Spirit leave her alone? But maybe it had led her out here for a purpose. Maybe it had known that she would find all the men in a drunken stupor. That was an exciting thought.

Nisha crept quickly across the compound, toward the stockade. She went to the place where she had seen the cat, and she peered between the logs. At first, she saw nothing. Then she jumped back with a muffled cry as a shadow seemed to materialize in front of her, just the other side of the wooden barrier.

"Nisha!"

This time, the voice didn't speak in her mind. It was a man's voice, a hoarse whisper, calling her name.

Nisha froze. She was transfixed. Were her senses deceiving her?

"Nisha, can you hear me?"

The voice was eerily familiar. With a terrible mixture of excitement and fear, she moved close to the logs again and peered between them. Now that she had time to look more carefully, she saw that the shadow wasn't an animal at all. It was a man.

"Winnor," she whispered. "Winnor, can it be you?"

"Yes, Nisha."

Her knees trembled. She found herself slumping against the wooden wall. "But I saw you jump to your death," she gasped. "Over the edge of our mesa. Is this your dead spirit now?"

He laughed softly. "I jumped where there was a ledge to land on," he told her. "By the tree. Do you remember that spot?"

She closed her eyes. He had saved himself by hiding where she should have left her child. She remembered watching Winnor backing away from the men with spears. He had jumped backward off the mesa—and the ledge had been there to catch him.

Excitement leaped up inside her. "You outwitted them, Winnor! Did anyone else—"

"No." His tone was grim. "I was the only one who survived."

She felt a pang of sadness. But she should be glad that even one of her tribe's menfolk still lived. "Was it you who called to me?" she whispered.

"Yes. The spirit of Mountain Cat is strong in me. You know that, Nisha."

She knew. She remembered the lionskin that he had often worn, and the way it helped him to use the strength of the animal spirits.

"Was it you out in the forest, for the last few weeks?" she asked him. "Have you been killing the warriors, making it seem that a mountain lion attacked them?"

He chuckled softly. "Yes, Nisha."

"But how have you survived out there?"

"I have my spear, and some thongs for snares. But tell me, Nisha. Why were they celebrating tonight? I try to watch the village, but there are things I can't see, and my spirit vision is like light through dark water. I sense only blurred images."

"I've been turning the men against each other," she told him, feeling quiet pride in what she had achieved. "Because of me, their chieftain is dead, and the man who killed Ilu is dead, too. But—the man who led the attack on our tribe is the new chieftain now. He has the sacred black knife of our people. He wears it like an ornament!"

"Calm, Nisha," Winnor whispered to her.

She took a moment to calm herself. "Somehow," she went on, "I will kill him too, and I will reclaim that knife from him. Maybe I will even use it to end his life. They shall all die, Winnor. I have made a vow." She pressed her palms against the rough logs, wishing she could reach between them and touch him. "They are all asleep,

Winnor, drunk on corn wine. In fact—you can come inside! Winnor, together we can kill them all!"

There was a long silence. "No," he whispered.

She clenched her fingers, digging them into the bark on the logs. "Winnor, this may be our only chance!"

"I sense the life spirit is strong in some of them," he whispered back to her. "A small sound could wake two or three men. They would rouse the rest. We would die, Nisha."

She wanted to argue with him, but reluctantly, she saw that he was right. In a village full of the most ruthless, brutal warriors, it would be foolish to think that she and Winnor could run wild without being caught. Her excitement faded as quickly as it had come. "Then what shall we do?" she asked him.

"It's difficult," he said. "They've started sending out their scouts in pairs. And they sent a hunting party to look for me."

She nodded. "I know."

"I've done what I can, Nisha." His voice suddenly sounded weary. "They will probably find me if I stay out here for many more days. And it seems that you, too, have done what you can. Perhaps we should leave this place tonight, while the guards are asleep."

She could hardly believe what she heard. "You mean, give up?"

"There's a tribe in the flatlands, far to the south. I visited them once. The people of Green Canyon. They are gentle and wise, Nisha. They would accept us as their own."

"But—I can't!" She shook her head. To run away, now, like a mole-rat diving into its burrow, while Grep still lived . . . it was inconceivable.

"Be sensible, Nisha." He no longer sounded strong and cunning. The hardship of living half starved in the forest for so many days had worn him down. "If you have killed even two of them—"

"Three!" she hissed at him.

"Three?" He sighed. "Then surely you see, this can't go on. You must leave now."

She felt as if she was being torn apart. She thought of Winnor, wise and kind, and she was almost overcome by the desire to join with him and escape this terrible place. But still, she had made her vow. "I can't go with you," she said. "I promised the spirit of Jorlor, and my child, that I would avenge them."

There was a long, sad silence. "I fear you'll die before your vengeance is done," he said. "And truly, I don't think the spirits would want you to shed still more blood."

She didn't want to hear those words. She shook her head angrily. "I made a vow."

He seemed to realize, finally, that he couldn't persuade her. "Who else from our tribe still lives?" he asked.

"Only Rilla. All the other women are dead."

"Rilla." He sighed. "Send her out to me, Nisha. At least let her escape."

She nodded slowly. He was right; Rilla should be free. The girl was too timid to help Nisha in her struggle; there was no point in keeping her here.

Nisha heard a faint sound from behind her. She turned quickly, with all her senses alert. A man lying on the ground near her was muttering something. She watched him roll over; but then he fell back into his stupor.

"There's no time to waste," Winnor whispered to her.

"I know." She hesitated. "But Winnor—can you guide me? After you go away from this place tonight, I'll be completely alone. Can you tell me what I should do to honor the vow that I've made?"

"You mean, how can you kill every single man in this tribe?" His voice was gently mocking. At first it angered her, but then she realized, he was still trying to persuade her to give up on a plan that seemed hopeless to him. He was trying to save her from herself.

"Yes," she said stubbornly, "I want vengeance on every single man."

There was the sound of an owl from the end of the compound, near the main gate. Of course; she should have guessed that he would be waiting there. Nisha ran as fast as she could, leaping over the sleeping men in her path. She reached the gate and fumbled with the stout leather bands and the wooden crosspiece that held it closed. Finally she managed to drag the gate open a little way. Winnor was crouching in the shadows. She flung herself forward.

He jumped up, just in time to catch her. He held her as she clutched him.

"Where is she?" he was whispering to her. "What happened, Nisha? Where's Rilla?"

Her tears were running freely. Finally, she managed to catch her breath. "She killed herself," she gasped. "And it's my fault. She was so scared of Grep, she couldn't bear the thought of being his wife. It's all my fault!"

He stared at her uncomprehendingly. "She's dead?"

Nisha sniffed back her tears. She suddenly despised her own weakness. "He'll pay," she muttered. "For this, and everything else."

"You still won't come with me?" He gripped her hand.

"No." She dragged herself free. "You go, Winnor. I have work to do here. Especially now."

She heard something—a man groaning. She spun around. In the moonlight, she saw one of the warriors sitting up and rubbing his face with his hands. Clumsily, he got to his feet. He staggered over to the cistern where the tribe maintained its water supply. He dipped his hands into the water and drank noisily.

"I must go, Nisha." Winnor was slipping away into the night. "I can't force you to leave this place. But I'll send Cat Spirit to you, to give you strength."

She wanted to beg him to stay. But if he joined her in the compound, he would be killed. If he stayed outside in the woods, Grep's men would find him sooner or later, or he'd starve to death. There was no sense in him staying here. It was her own fault that she was being left alone. He was being wise; she was being foolish.

"Hey." The voice came from behind her.

She turned and saw the man by the water cistern peering at her in the darkness. He staggered forward, still half drunk. "What's happening out there?"

"I thought I heard the cat outside," she said, trying to pitch her voice low so that she wouldn't wake all the other men. Quickly, she stepped back in and secured the gate.

The warrior shambled over to her. As he came close enough to recognize her, he stopped short. "Grep's woman," he muttered.

"Yes," she said.

"You should be in the Wives' House." He circled around her like an animal avoiding a piece of tainted food. "Go on," he said. "Back to your house."

He was afraid of her, she realized. Normally, the knowledge would have given her some satisfaction. At this moment, though, it seemed irrelevant.

She turned away from him and walked among the other sleeping men. She felt numb, detached from her surroundings, like a spirit drifting through the night. *Goodbye, Winnor,* she said inside her head.

For a moment, her vision shifted. She seemed to be walking among trees. But then the vision faded, and she no longer shared Winnor's view of the world. He was gone—completely gone—and she was alone.

She reached the Wives' House, paused, and turned to look back. The man who had spoken to her was already slumping down on the ground again to sleep some more. He was so drunk, when he woke up the next morning he might not even remember seeing her. And if he did, she would just deny it.

Nisha paused. There was still time, she realized. She could run back to the gate, open it again, and dash out into the wilderness, calling to Winnor. He would hear her, or sense her, and he would wait for her, and then they could be safe together. By the time the warriors understood that she had gone, she and Winnor would be far away.

But there was no point in thinking about that. She had already made her decision.

She opened the door of the Wives' House. She walked inside, and she closed the door behind her.

PART THREE

—ᙏ—

Liberation

Chapter Twenty-One

In the days after Rilla's death, Nisha participated in the daily life of the village because she had no choice. But the fierce flame of her spirit burned low, and her vow of revenge seemed to recede from her the longer she spent among the Warrior Tribe. She wondered again and again if she should have left with Winnor, but every time she came back to the simple fact of her sense of duty. She refused to allow herself the luxury of regret. And so, for the time being, she endured life as well as she could.

It had been a frightening, difficult day when the villagers first learned of Rilla's suicide. In the gray light of dawn, Nisha fetched Uwa and showed her the girl's body hanging from the braided rope.

Uwa was silent for a long, slow moment. And then, without a word, she walked out of the house looking even grimmer than she normally did.

The women, meanwhile, were waking up. One by one, they saw what had happened, and there were wails of dismay. But when Uwa returned to the house with Grep, everyone fell silent. The women huddled together looking wide eyed and frightened while Grep surveyed the scene, then climbed up and used his knife to cut the rope. Rilla's body fell to the ground with a heavy thud.

Grep turned and looked around. "When did this happen?" he demanded.

"I think while everyone was celebrating," Nisha said. "Rilla was beside me when I fell asleep. The people outside were still singing songs. When I woke up—"

"Why did she kill herself?" Grep reached down to the crumpled figure and cut the rope from around her neck. He coiled it, watching Nisha, waiting for her to answer.

"Plorngah had beaten her," Nisha said. "She feared him, and she was terribly unhappy. But after Plorngah—died, you took her as your new wife, and—she feared you even more."

Grep grunted. There was a tension in him that made Nisha nervous. The tendons of his neck were tight and his jaw was clenched. She could almost smell his anger, and the reason for it was easy enough to see. A woman had defied him in a way that made it impossible for him to punish her. Rilla had escaped more surely than if she had run out of the village into the woods. There was no way, now, that Grep could catch her, torment her, and watch her suffer.

He turned and glared at Uwa. "You are responsible for the women in this house."

She looked startled. Then she drew herself up. "You told all of us to join the celebration. And you decided that these two," she jerked her head toward Nisha and the body of Rilla lying on the floor, "should stay in here alone."

Nisha was surprised to hear the woman speak so sharply to him. She half expected Grep to lash out at her. But instead, he seemed to lose his fearful tension. "So be it," he said softly. He nodded to Uwa, then walked calmly out of the house.

A few moments later, four men came in. They had been Worr's guards; now they were Grep's. They strode straight to Uwa, seized her by her arms, and marched her out of the house, ignoring her protests.

Nisha had joined Grep's other three wives in their usual place on the mattress on the floor. She turned to Reive. "Why is Uwa being blamed for this?" she asked.

Reive raised her eyebrows a fraction. "It should be clear enough."

Nisha shook her head. It was still hard for her even to

think after the death of her friend. "It wasn't Uwa's fault. If anything, it was my fault. I knew Rilla was unhappy. I should have watched over her."

"Maybe so," said Reive. "But this isn't a matter of right and wrong."

Nisha blinked. She saw that it was stupid to keep imagining that there could be justice here.

"Uwa was Worr's sister," Reive went on. "Have you forgotten that?"

Nisha sighed. "Of course." Now it made sense: Grep would use any excuse to remove Uwa from her position of power, in case she might try to take revenge against him for killing Worr. "But what will happen to her?"

Reive turned and glanced at Ellel and Innaw. As usual, the two of them were sitting quietly, deferring to her.

"She will be stoned, I think," said Ellel.

Innaw shook her head. "Cast out," she said.

Reive turned back to Nisha. "I think Innaw is right. Grep will cast her out." She glanced across at Rilla's body. "This was a convenient thing for Grep."

Nisha felt sick at the thought. At the same time, though, she noticed the edge in Reive's voice. "You speak more freely than usual," she said.

"Perhaps." Reive eyed Nisha. "But we are all the wives of the chieftain, now, aren't we? Perhaps that allows us some privileges. And look, we have you to thank, Nisha."

Nisha moved uneasily. The edge in Reive's voice was making her nervous.

"I don't understand," Nisha whispered.

"Three men and a woman are already dead because of you." It was Innaw speaking. "Worr, Kron, Plorngah, and his wife Jees. Now there will be Uwa, too. What are we to think, Nisha? You come to our tribe, and in less than a month, half a dozen of our people are gone."

"And now we are ruled by Grep," Ellel said. She grimaced as she spoke his name. *They all fear and hate him,* Nisha thought to herself. *They feared Worr, too—but not as much. They don't want Grep to have more power.*

Nisha found herself feeling threatened by the women she had hoped would be her friends. "You forget," she said, "how many of *my* people have died. Not just Rilla, there, and Orlu and Lazonah, who were crushed to death. All the people of my tribe who lived in peace and harmed no one; they were all slaughtered by your warriors." Her voice was rising as she spoke. It was impossible for her to remain calm when she thought of what had happened.

"So you are taking your revenge?" Reive said the words so quietly, Nisha barely heard them. But they chilled her. If Reive could see that it was so, who else had realized?

"I've done nothing to any of your people," Nisha told her. She looked directly into Reive's eyes. "All I want is to live happily here. I would like to be your friend, Reive. Yours too, Ellel. And Innaw. We have no reason to distrust each other. We are all wives together. We all serve the same master and endure the same cruelties. There's no way I can leave here. I must make the best of things."

Reive grunted and said nothing. The other two women gave Nisha brooding, doubting looks.

Before Nisha could speak again, the door of the house opened and Grep strode in with two of his guards behind him. All the women fell silent. Grep was carrying something over his arm—an ornamented robe. It was Uwa's robe, Nisha realized. She felt an awful foreboding.

"Let everyone be aware," said Grep, "Uwa has been cast out. The men of the tribe decided, and it is so."

His voice was loud in the house. There was no reply. No one spoke. The silence was absolute. None of the wives even looked at one another.

The two guards stayed flanking the door while Grep paced slowly through the house, past all the women, and past the fire that burned in the center. "Now that I am your new chieftain," he went on, "there will be some changes. I never liked the way Uwa ran this house. She was a stupid woman."

Still there was silence. But the silence seemed to be

growing more apprehensive. Grep smiled, and his teeth gleamed in the dimness. "This will come as a surprise to you," he said, "but I've decided that my new wife, Nisha, will manage this house." He stopped in front of her and threw down Uwa's robe. Dumbly, Nisha caught it.

All around her, there were gasps of disbelief. The women started murmuring to one another, and the murmuring grew louder. Some of them seemed outraged. Suddenly, one of Worr's former wives stood up. It was Yan, Nisha realized. "This is not our way!" she blurted out.

Grep walked over to her, taking his time. He paused facing her.

Yan lowered her head. She dropped to her knees. "I'm sorry," she whispered.

Grep kicked her, sending her flying backward. She slammed against the wall and slumped down with a cry.

"My warriors are loyal to me," Grep said. "And I am the undisputed chieftain of this tribe. Remember that, or you too will be cast out." He eyed Yan and Worr's other wives as they huddled together—afraid, now, to meet his eyes. "Later today," he said to the cowering women, "we'll see if any of my warriors want you as their mates, now that Worr is gone." He turned to his two guards, who were still standing by the door. "Take this one away." He pointed to Rilla's lifeless body. "Throw her over the cliff."

He waited while his men stepped forward, took hold of Rilla, picked her up between them, and carried her out.

"As for you," he turned to Nisha, "this house is now yours." He reached down, curled his fingers under her jaw, and tilted her head up. She found herself looking directly into his face. His thin lips widened in a prurient smile, and then he gave her cheek a little slap.

Still taking his time, he walked out of the house.

In the evening, after everyone had eaten, a guard came to the Wives' House and told Nisha that Grep wanted her to go to him. She wished she could refuse, because all she wanted was to lie in Uwa's bed, which was now her bed, and close her eyes and try not to think about the things that had happened. But it would be impossible to disobey Grep's command.

So she went to Worr's house, which was now Grep's house. The guards eyed her warily as she walked in, and she saw the same expression on their faces that she had seen when the drunken man had found her in the night, near the gate. They looked at her as if she was tainted.

She went to the room at the end of the house and found Grep lounging on the bed where Worr had lain. Unlike Worr, though, he had a spear close beside him, and she saw the handle of a flint knife tucked almost out of sight beneath one of the straw pillows. He was not as confident of his power, yet, as he might like to seem.

"Sit," he said, pointing to the end of the bed.

She glanced at the earth floor and noticed blood stains as she climbed up onto the bed. Her memory of Worr battling his guards was still fresh in her mind. This was the corner where Worr had stood with a spear pointed at his face, and there was the fireplace where Grep had seized a stone and felled the big man. Nelik had died there; Toron had bled there.

Nisha tried to wipe the memories from her mind. She sat cross-legged on the corner of the bed. She looked at Grep, and she waited.

"You realize," he said, "that my men all fear and hate you." He picked up a splinter of wood and frowned as he scored it under one of his fingernails, cleaning away a speck of dirt. He flicked it aside.

"Yes," said Nisha.

"Rightly or wrongly," Grep went on, "they blame you for the death of Kron, and Plorngah, and Worr." He looked up at her through half-closed eyes. "Of course, since you're my wife, they won't interfere with you." He put his hands behind his head and stared idly up at the roof. "But suppose I weren't here," he went on. "Suppose something happened to me. Why, they'd kill you, or cast you out, or worse." He gave her a meaningful look. "You understand?"

It was something that she hadn't thought of, but she saw immediately that he was right. With a sick feeling, she realized that she depended on Grep, now, for her own survival. If he died, she would die. In which case, how could she ever kill him?

"I will serve you well," she said quickly.

He gave her a snake smile. "I'm sure you will." He reached inside his robe and let his hand fall down to his crotch while he continued staring at her. "The women hate you, too," he said, more softly. "Especially now that I've put you in charge of the Wives' House."

She frowned. "Was that why—"

"Quiet." He didn't raise his voice, but the command was absolute.

Nisha suppressed her desire to speak. She sat in silence, trying to quell her anger at being treated like a child.

"I gave the house to you for several reasons," he said, after waiting a moment to make sure that she was remaining silent. "Yes, I want them to hate you. If the women became your friends, you could teach them to be willful and disobedient, like you. But if they are your enemies, you will teach them nothing."

Once again, she felt shaken—by his deviousness, and by the way he saw into her. For a moment she wondered if she could ever outwit him. He was watching her carefully even now, noting all her responses.

"You will keep order in the Wives' House," he told her, "and you'll punish the women cruelly if they disobey you. If you fail to do so, then naturally I will have to punish you."

She felt a moment of despair as she tried to imagine how she could ever inflict pain on women who were already so downtrodden and abused.

He saw the look on her face, and he nodded slowly.

"I'll know if you fail me," he said, "because my three other wives will tell me everything."

Nisha understood it all now. She was in control of nothing; she had no real power at all. Grep would give her orders, and the other women would spy on her to see that she did as she was told. The whole thing was another of his little games.

If he really wanted to keep her from spreading discontent among the other women, it would be easy enough. He could shut her away somewhere on her own and keep her isolated for his private enjoyment. But that wasn't what he wanted. It amused him much more to toy with her, display her in public, punish her if he chose, and perhaps run a slight risk—like a warrior teasing a wounded prairie dog, jabbing it with a stick but staying just out of reach of its dangerous jaws. If the dog was too docile and posed no danger, there would be no fun in the game.

"Perhaps you understand, now, how things will be between us," he said.

She sighed. "Yes," she said. "I do."

"You will serve and obey me, Nisha." He looked at her, waiting for her to respond.

"Yes," she said. "I will." The words almost stuck in her throat; but somehow she spoke them.

He opened his robe. "So serve me now," he commanded her.

Chapter Twenty-Two

Many days passed, and she saw no way to defy Grep or win the trust of the women of the tribe. He had planned carefully, he had planned well, and she found herself forced to obey him—even though, at the same time, her power to please him and enthrall him seemed to grow greater all the time.

Almost every night he ignored his other wives and summoned her to his room. He watched her with a strange, avid intensity when she took off her robe and lay beside him on his bed. Just the way she moved seemed to fascinate him, and then, when she gave him pleasure, he would shout with the intensity of his climax.

A few times he took her roughly, penetrating her as if she was any one of his wives. She hated those times, because she was forced to lie motionless under him, and she was horrified by the idea that he might make her pregnant. But he soon lost interest in taking her that way, and she found with relief that all he really wanted was to watch her while she touched him. Even during the day, as she moved around outside and supervised the women in their chores, she often noticed him staring at her, studying her with brooding intensity.

After a while, she felt sure that it wasn't just the sex that was obsessing him. He had made her a prisoner of his world, continually threatened with punishment while, at the same time, she depended on him to protect her from the rest of the men. Yet somehow her spirit was still not broken. When she spoke to him, she often forgot to make herself humble and timid like the other women of the tribe. When she walked, she wasn't furtive like them; she naturally moved with grace and pride. The spark in her, whatever it was, continued to tantalize and fascinate him.

Meanwhile, she made a point of managing the Wives' House far better than Uwa ever had. She organized a work party to caulk gaps in the log walls with mud, and she had the women make more mattresses. Now they slept more warmly and comfortably at night, and consequently they worked harder and more willingly during the day. There was less need for them to be punished, and they pleased their husbands more willingly. They were still afraid of the men, of course, and they still viewed Nisha with deep suspicion, but the stink of fear in the house was gone. Sometimes, in the evening, the women even sang while they did their chores.

In Grep's little room, the sound of singing from the Wives' House was faintly audible, and after a few days he warned Nisha that it must stop. When she asked him why, he slapped her for being insolent, but she already knew the answer. If women were happy enough to sing, it meant they were no longer full of fear. And if that were so, it was an insult to his power over them.

"The next woman who sings," he told her, "will be beaten." He picked up a pine branch. "You'll hit them with this," Grep told her. "Forty strokes on the back, the buttocks, and the thighs." He held out the branch to her, waited to see if she would refuse.

She knew better than that, so she took it from him and promised to obey his wishes. Then she went to the women and warned them of the new rule and the penalty for breaking it. They bowed their heads, and there was a grim silence in the Wives' House that night.

But the next night, one of them forgot.

It was Reive who absentmindedly raised her voice while she worked to weave a beargrass basket. For just a few moments she sang one of her tribe's traditional work songs—and then froze, realizing her mistake. She looked up and saw all the other women staring at her, and she fell into silence. Then she looked at Nisha.

Nisha knew that if she did nothing, Grep would hear of it. Ellel would tell him, or Innaw, or even Reive herself. They would be too scared not to. In any case, they still resented her position of authority and would take some satisfaction in betraying her, even after the improvements that she had made in their lives.

And so, with a feeling of futility, she picked up the branch which Grep had given her. Without a word, she went to Reive. She took her arm, stood her up, and walked her to the wall at the far end of the house, while all the other wives sat and stared.

Nisha found herself wishing it could have been any other woman who had broken the rule. Still, it had to be done. Nisha turned Reive to face the wall, then stripped her bare. Feeling disgusted by the task and furious at Grep for forcing her to carry it out, Nisha lashed the girl with the branch—but so lightly, the skin wasn't even broken. At the end of it, the other wives in the house were exchanging amused looks as if they disrespected Nisha for her kindness.

The next night, when Grep called for Nisha, he told her that what she had done was unacceptable. "I'm going to show you," he said, "what should have been done. I'm going to give you the punishment that you should have given to Reive. And this is how it will be for you, every time, till you learn."

By the time Nisha returned to the Wives' House, she was barely able to walk. Reive came to her with compassion in her eyes, which Nisha had never seen before. Reive said she had known it would happen, and she'd already begged some salve from the shaman. With care and gentleness, she spread it into Nisha's wounds.

"Won't Grep punish you, now, for tending to me?" Nisha asked.

Reive shook her head. "Grep won't hear of this." She paused for a moment and looked around the house at all the other women. None of them said anything. They continued with their chores and pretended that nothing was happening.

So Reive became the first of the women who overcame her suspicion and resentment of Nisha, and after that, the two of them spoke more openly together. Nisha found herself describing the old ways of her own tribe and the life she had led on the mesa. In turn, Reive talked about her childhood in the Warrior Tribe and the three years she had spent, so far, as one of Grep's wives. She was still careful never to say anything that was directly critical of the village or its men, but she somehow managed to give Nisha the impression that she shared her hatred for the men. The only difference was that Reive saw no hope of ever seeking vengeance.

Nisha, of course, still dreamed of it constantly. It was the only thing that made it possible for her to tolerate her life.

Her subtle game of power with Grep continued through the next few weeks. And then, finally, Nisha saw her opportunity.

The stores of food were beginning to run low. Obviously, they would have to be replenished before the winter came. Grep sent out his warriors twice to raid other tribes, but both times, the men came back saying that the tribes had gone, leaving their food caches empty.

"Isn't it possible to feed your people just by growing corn and grains and hunting in the forest on the plateau?" Nisha asked. She was sitting in her place at the foot of Grep's bed while he reclined against his pillows, squinting in the flickering light of a fat lamp as he reflaked one of his spears, tapping a wedge of soft limestone against the flint to expose a new razor-sharp edge.

"My men are warriors," he said, without looking at her. "They are too proud to till the land. And if they hunted enough game to feed us, there would soon be no more animals on the plateau." He tested the flint with his thumb, then laid the spear beside him. "Also, our territory here is limited. It's unsafe to the east."

"Why is that?"

He eyed her for a moment. Over the past few weeks, he had gradually become more willing to tolerate her questions. So long as she showed respect, she could ask him almost anything—because he had learned that she was sometimes useful to him. Her mind was agile, and because she came from outside his tribe, she came up with ideas that were new to him. Grep was wise enough to understand that a leader should use any information that he found, regardless of its source—although, of course, he never allowed her any credit for her suggestions.

"There is a hostile tribe," he told her, "living to the east."

"You mean the Cave People?" she asked. "Aren't they the ones who were the fathers of your tribe?"

He grunted irritably. She had known it would anger him if she implied that his people were merely the children of a greater tribe. And of course, that was why she had chosen to say it.

"The Cave People are like animals," he said. He made a little sound of disgust. "They live like mole rats in their holes in the ground." Once again, he ran his thumb over the flint of his spear. "Still," he said, "they're fierce fighters. It would be foolish to fight with them. So, we let them keep their land."

"You mean you're afraid of them?" She made herself sound honestly surprised.

He looked at her sharply, and his face showed a little grimace of anger. "You know better than that." His voice was a warning.

She saw her mistake. She had been too obvious, trying to provoke him. "I'm sorry," she said quickly, and bowed her head.

He hesitated for a moment, then waved his hand as if

the matter was too trivial to worry about. "My men are not afraid to fight any tribe," he said. "But fear has nothing to do with it. It's a practical matter. I'd be a fool to choose to fight a strong enemy when there are weaker ones who have what I need."

It sounded as if he was being honest. He truly was a fearless fighter, which was the main reason his men respected him and were intimidated by him. At the same time, though, he was a practical man.

She suddenly saw an opportunity. "Didn't you just tell me," she said to him, "that your weaker enemies have been killed, or they've abandoned their homes and fled?"

"Some of them." He sighed. "Old Worr was a fool," he said, half to himself. "Instead of sending us out to kill all those tribes, he should have told us to spare their lives and make them our slaves."

She repressed her angry impulse to remind him that her tribe had been one of the ones that had been slaughtered. She told herself to think in the way he thought, from a cruel, cold perspective. There was no other way she could ever lead him on the path that she saw ahead.

"Maybe," she said tentatively, "there are still some tribes that you could enslave."

"That could be so." He hesitated. "In the flatlands far to the west—"

"But it would be simplest, wouldn't it," she interrupted him, "if it could be done here on the plateau." She paused for just a moment. "If you could defeat the Cave People—even if you lost many men in the battle—you would end up with more people serving you. The plateau would all be yours, and you could live off the labor of the people you conquered."

She had laid out a plan for him as plainly as she could. She felt herself growing tense with expectation, and she had to force herself to seem unconcerned. From the corner of her eye she saw him giving her a sudden speculative look, but he didn't speak. He swung his legs off the bed and stood up. He took two paces, then paused and swung around. "No," he said. "No, that's stupid women's talk. It's not as simple as you make it sound. You know nothing about fighting."

For a moment she felt defeated. She had had a chance—perhaps her only chance—and she had failed.

Yet there was something odd about the way he was looking at her now. And when she glanced at him—still trying to seem casual and unconcerned—he was more tense than he had been before.

"I'm sorry," she said quickly. "You're right, I know nothing about fighting."

She saw him relax slightly. Taking his time, he sat back on the bed. "I'll send a party out to the north," he said. "The land's rugged but it's fertile there. New tribes may have settled it by now. We'll see if they have what we need."

She nodded silently.

He waved his arm. "Go back to the Wives' House."

"Of course." She got up quickly, hiding her surprise. He never normally dismissed her so early, and almost always, he wanted sex before she left him. She hesitated in case he had some final command or instruction, but he wasn't even looking at her. He was staring at the opposite wall while once again he held his spear in his right hand and ran his thumb over the edge of the flint.

Nisha turned and ducked out of the door. Her feeling of defeat had vanished as quickly as it had come. There was no doubt in her mind, now, that Grep was considering her plan—though it was a concept that he would share with no one, least of all a woman.

Alone in the darkness, she walked slowly around the compound. One of the few advantages of her position in the Wives' House was that she could step outside as often as she liked now. The guards on the stockade had become accustomed to seeing her taking walks at odd times of the day and night, and they no longer even questioned it. They were happy to leave her alone.

She tried to imagine what Grep would do if he were really going to act on her plan. He was habitually cautious, and it did sound as if the Cave People would be well defended, fierce, and difficult to attack. Obviously, he would want to take them by surprise, and he would need to know the precise features of the land. She knew what she would do under those conditions: She would send scouts to study the area.

For the first time in many days, she found herself feeling some hope. All the abuse that she had endured, and the humiliation of serving Grep, might yet be worthwhile.

She paced slowly beside one of the long houses. The night air was a sweet caress on her bare neck and arms. In the distance, she heard an owl cry, and for a moment she listened, remembering when Winnor had made that sound to guide her to the gate. But Winnor was far away now. She hoped he would be proud of her if he could see how brave she was and how truly she was honoring her vow.

But this was no time to be thinking of Winnor. She had to think ahead. Whatever her exact plan was going to be, it couldn't work unless she found a way to slip out of the compound when she needed to.

She reached the far end. This was where Grep had sneaked in on the night he had caught her in Worr's room. He had used a rope to scale the stockade, and the guard who had been on duty that night had turned a blind eye, because he was loyal to Grep. Nisha grimaced. There was no way she could hope to achieve such a thing. It would be far too dangerous to try to seduce one of the guards, even if she could overcome their suspicion of her.

She stood for a moment, looking up at the crude wooden walkway that ran around the edge of the stockade near the tops of the tall logs that were firmly embedded in the ground. There was a man pacing to and fro up there, making the wood creak under him. Without a doubt, if she ever tried to scale the wall he would hear her or see her.

A ladder stood in the corner of the compound, leaning up against the walkway where the guard stood. He could get down that ladder to the ground in just a couple of moments, shouting an alarm as he ran. Or for that matter, the walkway wasn't much higher than a man's head. The guard could leap straight down to the ground. Or if she somehow actually made it over the stockade to the cleared area beyond, he could hurl his spear and bring her down without even moving from his guard post. And if he missed and she somehow made it to the woods, it would still be hard for her to move silently through the dry undergrowth.

The owl cried again, and she saw the guard turn toward the sound. He was silhouetted against the moonlit sky. She saw him shift his grip on his spear. He stood motionless for a moment, listening. Then he grew bored and resumed his pacing.

He was like a predator, she thought to herself; and if she tried to escape, she would become his prey. What could she do to deceive or divert him? Or could she somehow change from being prey to predator herself?

Chapter Twenty-Three

Two days later, Nisha was outside with Innaw and Ellel, teaching them to make marrow butter. It was hot, heavy work, and she paused often to rest. As she wiped sweat out of her eyes and sipped water from a leather pouch that she kept close by, she saw men gathering outside the Warriors' House, shouldering their packs and checking their weapons.

"Grep is sending them out again," she murmured to herself.

"Is this the way it should be done, Nisha?" Innaw asked.

Nisha looked down. The woman had been breaking animal bones into pieces by pounding them between two rocks. "The pieces should be smaller," Nisha said, finding it hard to concentrate on the menial task, or even care about it. She hesitated, then decided what she should do.

"Ellel," she called.

The other woman had been pouring water onto a wide, dish-shaped stone that had been placed over a fire. The water bubbled and steamed as it touched the hot rock.

"Yes, Nisha?" Ellel looked at her cautiously. Nisha felt a little moment of irritation. No matter how many times the women worked with her, they never seemed to trust her. No matter how hard she tried to fit in with them, they always treated her as an outsider.

Nisha went and looked at the water. "When all of it starts boiling—not just at the edges—put the pieces of bone in it. That will leach the marrow out. You'll see the water turn yellow. Understand?"

Ellel nodded.

"Later, we'll throw the bones away, and when the rock cools, the marrow butter collects at the bottom." It was strange to her that this tribe didn't know how to make things that had once been part of her everyday life. And yet, perhaps it was not so mysterious. The women here were taught to be fearful and to follow orders, which meant they were unlikely to think of things for themselves.

Well, that just gave Nisha more opportunities to make herself useful. She wiped her hands on a scrap of sheepskin, picked up an empty leather pouch, then walked across the compound on a path that would take her past the men who were gathering by the Warriors' House.

She slowed her pace as she came close to them, and she tried to pick up snatches of conversation. Some of the men were complaining because they were still footsore from their last trek. Some were hefting their packs, muttering about the weight that they would be carrying.

"It'll take more than two days," someone said.

"But Grep said—"

"You've never been that far north. The path down is treacherous."

"We need Lorg and Ulm with us. Should have been obvious."

Quickly, Nisha moved on. A couple of the men had already noticed her and were looking at her. She didn't want to risk any of them telling Grep that she had been loitering close by.

She went to the cistern, filled her leather pouch, then went back to the cooking fire. From other fragments of conversation that she'd heard in the past, she knew that Lorg and Ulm were the best scouts in the tribe. So, Grep had chosen not to send them north with the rest of his raiding party. She wondered if he was planning to send them east instead.

She took her place beside Innaw and Ellel again, and she set down the bag.

"Do we need more water?" Ellel asked.

Maybe it was an innocent question, but Nisha could never be sure. "We may need to add some, if too much boils away," she said, looking straight back at the woman.

Ellel nodded. She seemed to have no further interest.

Nisha watched the pieces of shattered bone as they boiled over the hot fire. The yellow marrow was melting and flowing out, mixing with the water. By the evening, the stone slab would be cool and the butter would be ready. She would scrape it into a pouch for storage—and she would keep a little for herself. It was dangerous to hoard food, and she knew she would be severely punished if she was found out. But if her hunch was correct, within a couple of weeks she would need all the rations she could get.

"I hope this time they'll bring back some supplies for us," said Ellel.

Nisha looked up. She realized that the raiding party had started marching out of the compound. Ellel and Innaw had paused in their work and were watching the men leave. It was common knowledge, now, that the tribe's food reserves were running relatively low.

Nisha waited till the men had left and the gate was secured behind them. *I hope they fail,* she thought to herself. She hated the thought of another tribe being attacked and slaughtered. More than that, though, she wanted Grep to feel pressured. The more desperate he became, the more likely he would be to do what she wanted.

The next day, she found another excuse to spend time out in the compound. She watched carefully as men came and went from the Warriors' House. The ones who had been left out of the raiding party sat cleaning and sharpening their weapons. A few others went outside to train a group of young warriors. But throughout the whole day, Lorg and Ulm were nowhere to be seen.

Nisha allowed herself a secret smile. Lorg and Ulm had not gone north with the rest of the men; but they had gone, just the same.

Two days later, she made a point of seeking out Reive when it was the woman's turn to grind seeds and corn. This was heavy, monotonous work that everyone hated, but Nisha kneeled down and offered to help.

Reive couldn't hide her surprise. She gave Nisha a quick, searching look.

"I had an easy day yesterday," Nisha said. "And besides, I still owe you a favor for what you did."

Reive shuffled to one side so that Nisha could take her place in front of the grinding box. "Are your wounds healed now?" Reive asked.

"Yes, they are." Nisha picked up the grinding stone. It was a rough rectangle with one straight, rounded edge. She leaned forward, scraping the stone across the seeds and corn in the grinding box, which was a big, flat stone with smaller slabs tied around it.

Nisha dug in her toes and took a firmer grip on the grinding stone. She worked hard for a few moments, reducing the grains to powder. Then she paused and glanced at Reive. "You know," she said, "some of these grains were probably taken from the stores of my own tribe. Some of this corn, here, I probably cultivated myself."

Reive frowned as if the concept seemed strange to her. So far as she was concerned, anything that the warrior tribe had in their village belonged to them. "I suppose you may be right," she said. She sounded cautious, but then, she always did.

"I still miss my people," Nisha said, as she went back to work. "But I miss the land even more. The desert is very beautiful, Reive."

"So you say, Nisha. I wouldn't know."

Nisha nodded. "I suppose not." Reive had never been allowed outside this village in her life—and she probably never would, till she grew old and was cast out.

Nisha lowered her voice. "Sometimes I imagine escaping, just go back to the land that I love."

Reive tensed, and her eyes moved cautiously. "I've warned you, before, not to say such things."

Nisha paused in her labor. "Would it be such a crime if I ran away? Do you think the men would come after me?"

Reive grunted dismissively. She obviously thought the question was hardly worth answering. "Grep calls for you almost every night," she said. "You think he wouldn't be angry if you took yourself away from him?"

"I suppose you're right." Nisha looked down at the grinding box. The grains were almost fine enough, now, to be used for flour. But there was still a lot more to be processed. She worked with the stone for a while longer, then started scooping the yellow-gray powder into a leather sack which Reive held up for her.

"I wish Grep would leave the village sometime," Nisha went on. "Didn't he always lead the raiding parties while Worr was chieftain?"

"Yes." Reive blinked. "Nisha, you are my friend now, but I wish you wouldn't talk—"

"I suppose Grep's afraid of what might happen if his back was turned," Nisha persisted. "I tell you, if he was away, and if someone left the gate open, and if the guards weren't looking—I'd be running out into the night, back down the trail to the west. I'd run all the way back to the desert lands where I came from."

Reive folded the neck of the sack and tied a thong around it. She didn't speak.

Nisha shrugged. "Well, I'm sure it'll never happen. I have to see to the evening meal." She stood up.

"You should be glad, Nisha, that life is so good for you here," Reive told her, squinting up and shading her eyes against the bright summer sun. "Think what happened to the other women from your tribe who came here."

"I am glad, Reive," Nisha said. "And I'm glad, too, that we're friends now."

Reive nodded. "Thank you for helping me." She gave

Nisha an odd look, then returned to her place in front of the grinding box.

Five days later the two scouts returned. Nisha noticed them arrive through the main gate, looking travel worn and weary. A little later, she saw them go to Grep's house, and they seemed to stay there for most of the afternoon. In the evening, she noticed them sitting together outside the Warriors' House exchanging brief greetings with some of the younger men, but saying nothing more than that. Wherever they'd been, they acted as if it wasn't worth talking about.

The next day, the raiding party made its way in through the village gates. They carried with them the carcasses of four deer and a couple of prairie dogs that they had speared along the way, but they brought no sacks of grain, no dried fruits, no flour, no pemmican.

The fresh meat was butchered and a feast was called for that evening. But there was no singing, no corn wine, and the portions were small. Grep was in a grim frame of mind as he told the leader of the raiding party to describe what he had found.

The man stood up and told a brief, simple story. The lands to the north were empty of human life. There were a few villages, but they were silent and barren, holding nothing but the bones of the people who had been killed by Grep's own raiding party two years before.

Kneeling at Grep's feet with his other wives, Nisha looked around at the people as they listened to this sad story. Many of them were fidgeting and frowning. The news, of course, was bad, but that wasn't the only cause of their discomfort. Usually, the warriors made important decisions on their own, in their house or in the Chieftain's House. It was unusual for the tribe to be gathered together like this, with all the women as well as the men. The strangeness of it was disconcerting, and people kept glancing uneasily at Grep, trying to understand what was happening.

Finally, Grep stood up. "People," he said, "you're all concerned about the winter that will be on us three months from now. You know that our food supplies are running low. And you see that we've been so fierce, so brave, so strong, we've driven away the tribes that used to live close by."

There was an uneasy silence. The only sound was the crackling of the fire and the sizzling and spitting of the deer carcasses slung over the flames.

"For five years, I've led our warriors," Grep went on. "I've never failed this tribe, and I never will. I pledge to you, you'll not be hungry this winter. If I fail in this pledge, I tell you now: I'll step down as your chieftain."

Nisha saw people blinking, looking disconcerted. This wasn't the domineering man they had grown to know and fear. He was speaking calmly, almost humbly.

Personally, she knew Grep too well to imagine that he would ever surrender his power. He was deliberately doing something, here, to set a precedent.

But why? Some of the men had been concerned about the food supplies, and Nisha had even overheard talk about putting the raiding parties to work as hunters on the grasslands to the south. But none of the men had seemed worried, yet, about the winter. It was too far away. And the women never seemed to worry about anything. They just trusted the men to know what was best.

So, Grep must be preparing his people for something that still lay in the future. It was very clear to her, now, what he had in mind. And for her, it meant that her greatest challenge was about to begin.

Chapter Twenty-Four

Once again, she was woken in the middle of the night, but this time, it wasn't Yan shaking her shoulder. Nisha looked up and found a man standing over her. For a moment she felt confused and frightened, because she had been dreaming of the night when the warriors came to her people in their homes on the mesa. But then she realized she was in the Wives' House, and she felt a new uneasiness. Men didn't normally come here, least of all during the hours of darkness. "Who are you?" she whispered.

"Grep wants you."

It was one of Grep's guards, she realized. Her uneasiness deepened. "He needs me to come to him *now*?"

"Yes. Quickly." He stood waiting.

Nisha reached for her furs and pulled them over the caribou skin that she wore when she slept. "Is something wrong?" she asked.

"Bring your things," he told her. "You won't be back here for several days."

Now she felt seriously alarmed. Her mind was suddenly full of questions—but there was no point in asking them.

"Quickly," the guard told her again.

She picked up a bag that contained many of her personal possessions—a spare set of moccasins, a wooden comb, some thongs and stones that she had been using to make herself a necklace, a pair of firesticks, and a dozen other small items. She hesitated, thinking about the illicit supply of food that she'd been hoarding. It was hidden in pouches under her straw mattress. If she was going to be away from the house for several days, would someone else take over her role supervising the Wives' House, and would that women use her bed here by the door? If anyone found the food, would they report her?

"Will I be coming back here tonight?" she asked.

"No. Come!"

She made her decision: She would leave the food. This guard might get suspicious if he saw her rummaging under her mattress, and he might even smell the pemmican or the marrow butter. She glanced around in the dimness, trying to tell if any of the women had woken up. The house was silent, but that meant nothing.

"All right," she said, "I'm ready."

She followed the man out of the house, into the night. In the moonlight, she recognized him: he was Tarak, a youngster. He was tall for his age, and he tried to make his voice sound deep and powerful, but in fact he was only fourteen. She felt annoyed that he had disturbed her sleep, and even more annoyed that he had frightened her. "What is this all about?" she asked, as he led her to Grep's house. And then, before he answered, she noticed men moving in and out of the Warriors' House, stacking packs and weapons outside in the darkness. Now she understood, and the realization filled her with a new dread. If Grep was preparing to lead his men out of the village and she was being taken to his house, it could only mean that he planned to keep her under some kind of strict supervision while he was gone. And that would destroy all her plans.

Inside Grep's house, another boy named Yuwul was standing by the door. The house was normally guarded by senior warriors, not youngsters like this.

Together, Tarak and Yuwul marched her to the far end of the house. They gestured her to enter Grep's room while they waited outside the doorway.

She found him wearing his bearskin and his heaviest moccasins, and he was tying his leggings, making himself ready for a long journey. He had colored his face with black and green stripes, the same war paint he had worn when he had fought and killed Worr out in the meeting place. There was a fierceness to him, a brisk determination that made her hesitate in the doorway.

He turned and saw her. "You will stay here," he said, "while I'm gone."

"You mean—in this room?" This was even worse than she'd feared.

"Tarak and Yuwul will guard you. You will not leave this room, for any reason, till I return."

The news jolted her physically. She looked at Grep and wondered if he had known, somehow, what she was planning to do. No, in that case he would have punished her and confined her before now. He was simply being cautious—as she should have expected.

"Where are you going?" she asked.

He went to the corner where he kept his spears. He gathered all of them together, tied the bundle with a thong, and slung it under his arm. "That's no business of yours."

"But how long will you be gone?"

He paused in front of her. He hated her questioning him if any other men were listening, and Tarak and Yuwul were only just outside. Grep suddenly took hold of Nisha's hair, shifted his weight, and threw her onto the bed. "Quiet, woman!" he shouted at her. "Otherwise I will tie you there, and leave you to lie in your own mess for the whole time that I'm gone."

He turned away from her and ducked through the doorway. "Be careful with her," she heard him say to the two warrior-boys. "Keep her well fed and safe from harm, but don't talk to her, and don't listen to her. If I find that you allowed her to leave this room for any reason, you will be punished." He paused. "If she causes trouble, don't try to discipline her. I'll deal with that when I return. Just keep her in this room. You understand?"

The two boys murmured their assent.

Nisha heard his footsteps, quick and purposeful, as he walked away through the house and out of its main door. She turned and pressed herself against the wall of the room, peering through a crack between the logs. In a moment she saw Grep joining his men outside in the moonlight. It seemed to her that almost every man in the village was out there. Grep moved among them, checking their weapons and their supplies. It took him a long while; he was very methodical.

Nisha felt overwhelmed with frustration. If Grep was leaving to attack the Cave People, and if his plan was good and his attack was successful, she would have failed a second time to defeat him. Worse: She had given him the idea for this plan, so it would be her own fault if the man who had led the slaughter of her people increased his power.

She pressed her forehead against the rough wooden logs, and she tried to think what she could do. Outside, Grep was finally completing his inspection. He shouted a command, and the men followed him toward the main gate. Nisha counted almost a hundred warriors—a far larger fighting force than the one that had attacked her tribe. There was no doubt in her mind, now, that Grep was going to attack the Cave People.

The noise of the men's footsteps died away, and very faintly, she heard the main gate being dragged shut. The men had gone.

Nisha threw herself on the bed. She lay there staring at the wooden roof of the house, trying desperately to decide what to do. She hadn't expected any of this—and of course, she hadn't been meant to. He had deliberately brought her here at the last moment, so that she couldn't make any preparations.

For some reason, she'd assumed that Grep would tell the people of his tribe about his plan before he actually set out. She should have known better: He was a secretive man. If his mission was a success, then he would boast about it. If it failed, he would say as little as possible.

She had to do something. "Tarak!" she called. She jumped up off the bed. "Tarak, come here!" She tried to make her voice sharp and commanding.

"What is it?" He was still standing right outside her door. He ducked his head through the flap and glared at her. He seemed annoyed—and not just because she was disturbing him. She realized that he felt insulted by being left behind. The older warriors were marching out to battle, while he was here guarding a troublesome woman. That was no pleasure for a boy who desperately wanted to be a man.

"There's a rat in here," she told him. "I just saw it. It ran around the bed."

"He'll do you no harm." Tarak turned away.

"But Grep said you were supposed to protect me."

Tarak ducked back out through the doorway. He didn't bother to reply.

She paced to and fro, feeling unbearably impatient. "Tarak! You must do something about this!" She made her voice sound sharper. Surely, it would annoy him to be bossed around by a woman.

"Be quiet," he told her. "Yuwul wants to get some sleep."

"But if there are rats in here," she persisted, "they could be a danger to me. You'll be punished if Grep comes back and finds I've been scarred by them. I'll tell him that you allowed it to happen, even though it would have been easy for you to do something."

Once again, there was no reply.

"I'd kill it myself," she went on, in a softer tone. "But I have no weapon. Nothing. Not even a club. You're a strong hunter; it would be easy enough for you, wouldn't it?"

Tarak swore. He came back into the room. "You should be punished, woman, for making such a noise!"

"But Grep would never allow you to do that." She gave him a disdainful look. "In any case, all I'm asking is for you to do your duty. You're a hunter, aren't you? It should be easy enough for you to kill this thing."

He clenched his hand on his spear. "All right! Where is it?"

Nisha felt like laughing at him. He was just a boy, so simple to deal with compared with Grep. He wanted to kill the rat now to vent his anger—and to prove himself to her. And he was so arrogant, he would never imagine that a mere woman could be dangerous to him.

"It went down there," she said, pointing to the corner between the bed and the wooden wall. "Be careful, Tarak."

He gave her an angry look. She was insulting his manhood, telling him what to do. Now it would be even more important for him to show off his ability to hunt and kill. He peered where she pointed. It was a dark, shadowy corner. He bent down for a closer look.

Nisha glanced quickly at the doorway. Through the crack around the flap she saw Yuwul sitting on the floor, facing away, ignoring the situation.

Nisha stooped and seized a large, round stone from the hearth. If one of them had felled Worr, it should certainly work on this boy.

"There's nothing here," he said. He started to straighten up and turn toward her.

She held the rock in both hands, raised it above her head, then hurled it forward with all her strength. The rock hit Tarak on the side of his head and bounced off, landing on the bed. He grunted with shock and dropped his spear. He fell to his knees, clutching his head and groaning.

Nisha grabbed the stone where it had fallen. "Yuwul!" she cried. "Come quickly! Tarak's hurt!"

She heard Yuwul getting up onto his feet, muttering a curse. Meanwhile, Tarak was slumping down onto the floor, dazed and confused.

Yuwul came in through the door. He glanced questioningly at Nisha. She pointed wordlessly at Tarak, widening her eyes as if she was horrified by what she saw.

Yuwul took two steps toward his wounded comrade. He stopped short. Then he turned back to Nisha and started to raise his spear.

She hurled the rock. Her aim was accurate, but he saw it coming. Instinctively, he reached out his hand. The rock hit his knuckles. He cursed and stepped back, raising his spear higher, as if he was ready to hurl it at her.

Nisha hesitated. She suddenly threw herself onto the bed, rolled across it, and dropped down on the floor beside Tarak. He was trying to stand up, now, but he couldn't keep his balance. She seized the spear that he'd dropped and she jumped to her feet, whirling to confront Yuwul.

The boy-warrior stared at her in disbelief. Never in his life had he seen a woman brandishing a spear. Also, he was facing his chieftain's wife. Nisha saw the uncertainty in his eyes.

His hesitation gave her time to aim carefully. It had been months since the last time she went hunting with her people, but she was so close to Yuwul, it would be impossible to miss. She cast the spear as hard as she could, aiming for the center of his chest.

Yuwul fell backward with a scream. He staggered and dropped down onto his knees, almost in the same spot where Nelik had fallen after Worr speared him. Yuwul clutched the shaft and struggled to pull it out of his body, but it had gone deep, and there was no way he could drag it free.

Nisha found herself breathing fast, trembling all over. She had seen men die, but she had never cast a spear at any person before. It violated her deepest taboos to inflict death this way, especially on a young man who hadn't done her any harm.

But, she told herself, she had had no choice. If she was ever going to fulfill her vow, and if she was ever going to escape from this terrible place, this was the only way.

"I'm sorry, Yuwul," she said, standing over him. "You shouldn't have defied me."

He coughed up blood. He looked frightened. "Help me!" he gasped.

Nisha heard a faint sound. She spun around just in time to see Tarak on his feet, lurching toward her. Quickly, she kicked out. Her foot hit him in the crotch and he gasped with pain and collapsed, clutching himself. "Stay there," she shouted at him. "Unless you want to die like Yuwul."

There was no more time for feelings of guilt. She seized the spear that she had cast at Yuwul, placed her foot on his chest, and wrenched the shaft free. He screamed and clutched himself where blood started pouring from the wound. "Perhaps it's best you die quickly," Nisha said.

Wordlessly, he stared up at her.

She wondered if she had the stomach to do this. But, she told herself, she had to. She tried to harden herself inside as she took aim, then thrust the spear down into his heart.

He made a terrible gurgling sound and arched his back. All his muscles seemed to go rigid. Then his eyes fell shut, and he stopped breathing.

Nisha was shaking so badly, now, she had trouble gripping the spear and pulling it free again. She turned back to Tarak. "Get on the bed," she told him.

He gaped at her.

"On the bed!" she screamed. "Else I'll kill you too!"

He looked at her as if he was seeing an apparition. Without a doubt, he would have been braver if she had been a man. Cautiously, watching her with wide eyes, he moved up onto the bed.

Nisha found herself shaking again, worse than before, and she tried to calm herself. "Lie face down," she told him.

He turned over.

She went to her bag of possessions and pulled out some thongs. Quickly, she tied his ankles. There was some ironic pleasure in doing to him what had been done to her. But that wasn't her real concern. The most important thing was to get out of the village, now, as quickly as possible.

She tested the bonds. They seemed secure. She went to the fireplace, found a small round stone, and forced it into his mouth, imitating the way that she had seen Worr gagged when he stood in front of his people. Then she groped around in Tarak's belt, found his flint knife, and used it to cut a strip off his robe, so she could bind it around his face and hold the gag in place.

She took one last look at him. He was staring at her in disbelief, as if an evil spirit had come to punish him. Well, maybe she was. She turned, then, seized her bag of possessions, dropped Tarak's knife into it, picked up his spear, and then seized Yuwul's as well. This was more than she'd hoped for: to have two good spears and a knife to take with her.

She stepped over Yuwul's dead body, thinking to herself that yet another man had died because of her. Well, so be it. If she could make her way east, now, there would soon be more.

Chapter Twenty-Five

Nisha hesitated before leaving Grep's house. Outside, the night seemed quiet. She peered around at the stockade and saw a couple of figures up there, leaning on their spears. Evidently, they had heard nothing. Probably they were youngsters like Tarak and Yuwul who had been left out of Grep's war party because they were not yet of age.

Nisha forced herself to walk calmly back to the Wives' House. If she ran, it could attract their attention and rouse suspicion. She left her spears leaning against the outside of the house, opened the door, and crept inside. For a long moment, she paused and listened.

Her own pulse was beating so fast and so loudly in her ears, it was hard for her to concentrate. Well, if some of the women were awake, there was nothing she could do about it. She slid her hands under her mattress, found the food that she had hidden there, and dragged it out. She added it to her bag of supplies, then picked up a sheepskin from her bed and draped it around her shoulders. Lastly, she grabbed a braided leather rope—the same rope that poor Rilla had used to hang herself and find freedom from the pain of her life in the Warrior Tribe. Nisha, too, was going to use it to free herself, but in a very different way.

She crept out of the Wives' House and closed the door. She paused a moment. This was the most dangerous part. She waited till she saw that the guards on the walkway around the stockade were moving away from her.

She picked up her spears and ran silently between two

of the long houses, all the way to the far end of the stockade.

She paused in the shadows and tried to slow her breathing. There was another guard here, just as there had been on the night when she had come to survey the possibilities for escape. Quietly, she set down her pack, reached inside it, and took out a long, supple strip of leather that she had prepared for this purpose. She hunted around on the ground and found several stones, each slightly smaller than her fist. She placed one of them in the center of the leather strip, folded the strip around the stone, then picked it up, holding its two ends together. She whirled the improvised slingshot around her head, then let the stone fly. It hit the stockade forty paces away.

The guard turned quickly toward the noise. He paused, listening. He took a couple of steps.

Nisha placed another stone in her slingshot, whirled it, and cast the stone as hard as she could, farther toward the opposite end of the stockade.

This time the guard didn't hesitate. He started along the walkway with his spear in his hand.

Nisha debated whether to throw one more stone. There had to be enough of a noise to attract the guards, but not so much commotion that it would make them sound an alarm. She was sure that Grep wouldn't have taken every single man out of the village; there were bound to be a few sleeping in the Warriors' House.

She waited till the guard up on the walkway had moved halfway to the opposite end of the compound. Then she ran across the meeting place, past the spot where Worr had died, past the pillar where Worr had been tied and Grep had been stoned. She reached the corner of the stockade and paused, breathing quickly. The guard who had gone looking for the source of the noise was being joined by the other two men who were on duty near the main gate.

Quickly, Nisha fired one more stone. This time she aimed beyond them, at a point near the gate itself.

She wasn't strong enough to make the stone hit the end wall of the stockade, but when it hit the ground nearby it made enough noise to attract attention. Two of the men turned and hurried in that direction. The third leaped down from the walkway and went to investigate at ground level.

She tied her two spears to her back, shouldered her sack of possessions, and quickly scaled the ladder that led up to the walkway. She looped her rope around one of the posts of the stockade and let the two ends of it fall down the outside of the wall. Then she threw her piece of sheepskin over the top of the stockade, where the logs were sharpened. She glanced behind her. The guards were still distracted. Quickly, she rolled over the top of the stockade, using the sheepskin to protect her from the sharpened logs. She seized the doubled rope in one hand, dragged the sheepskin off and threw it down, then started lowering herself hand over hand, with her feet braced against the outside of the wooden wall.

Moments later, she was on the ground. She tugged on one end of the rope and hauled the other end up and around till it fell down to her. With trembling hands, she gathered everything up and ran as fast as she could across the open space till she reached the safety of the forest.

She threw herself down and lay there for a long moment, gasping. Her pulse was racing. *Be calm,* she told herself. *You're safe now. Be calm.*

She waited, watching the dark shape of the stockade. She had left no trace of her escape, but she still wanted to be sure that no one was going to come out after her.

Very faintly, she heard a man shout something. Perhaps it was one of the guards telling the others to forget about the sounds they'd heard.

But then, distinctly, she heard the main gate opening.

Nisha froze. She held her breath. Should she run? No; even from that distance, they might hear her. The ground under the trees was covered with dry underbrush. There was no way to move through it quietly. She edged backward into some tall grass and waited.

Even though she was lying opposite the back wall of the compound, she was far enough to one side to see along the south side wall. Faintly, in the distance, she heard footsteps, then another shout. Two men were walking out from the compound—she saw their tiny silhouettes in the moonlight. Then a third one joined them. He raised his arm and pointed.

At first she couldn't be sure what was happening, because the men were too far away. But then two of them started off toward the forest—and she saw that they were heading away from her, to the west.

She let out her pent-up breath and lay on her stomach, feeling as if all the strength had gone out of her. They weren't going to find her. They were heading in exactly the wrong direction.

With angry satisfaction, she thought of Reive. *My friend,* she muttered bitterly. Yes, Reive was the smartest of the women—smart enough to understand exactly how the system in the village operated, and seemingly smart enough to rebel against it. But intelligence was not the same thing as bravery. Reive was no different from any of the women in that she doubted her own strength and depended on the men to lay down the rules that she lived by. She had never believed for a moment that there was any real chance of rebellion or escape.

Nisha had become suspicious on the night when Reive broke the rule against singing. It seemed to Nisha that Reive was too shrewd and cautious to forget such a simple thing. That must mean that Grep had told her to do it, so that Nisha would be obliged to punish her. And Grep must have known that Nisha could never beat any of the women fiercely. As a result Nisha herself had been disciplined—and then Reive had been waiting, conveniently, with the healing salve.

It had been a perfect way to establish trust between the women. Reive had been seemingly grateful to Nisha for not punishing her severely, and Nisha should have been grateful to Reive for easing the pain of her wounds.

Nisha had gone out of her way to confide in Reive after that—though she only told her things that would be harmless to her if Grep ever heard of them. Finally, she had made her little speech to Reive about longing to return to her homeland in the west.

And that was where the guards were going now. Nisha guessed that when she was in the Wives' House a little earlier, collecting her secret supply of food, Reive must have heard her. Perhaps Reive had lain there for a while, unsure of what to do. And then she had gone to Grep's room, where she found Tarak tied to the bed and Yuwul dead on the floor. At that point, Reive had run to the chief guard on watch—just moments after Nisha had escaped over the wall at the back of the compound.

They had probably checked the main gate and found it still secure. They'd probably wasted some more time searching the compound for Nisha before deciding that she must have climbed over the stockade somehow. And now, based on what Reive thought she knew about Nisha's deep desire to return to the land of her people, two guards were running out toward the west on a fool's errand.

Nisha shivered. It was fortunate, indeed, that she'd made up her story for Reive. Otherwise, they might have caught her—and she couldn't imagine what they would have done. Tarak had seen her kill Yuwul. She wouldn't have been able to deny that. Probably, the men would have kept her prisoner till Grep returned, and then she would have been tortured or crushed to death, or worse.

Still, she was free now. She told herself to think only about what had actually happened, not what might have happened. Her plan had succeeded. She was out of the village.

She picked herself up and used the rope to tie the sheepskin across her back. She tucked one of the spears behind her and carried the other. She slung her bag over her shoulder. Quickly, then, she started into the forest.

She had to bend forward to avoid snagging the low tree branches with the spear that she carried behind her, and she had to move cautiously to avoid tripping over the gnarled, dry roots of juniper and spruce that protruded from the gravelly soil. Clumps of sawgrass tore at her leggings. Strands of a spider web clung to her cheeks. And then, blessedly, she found a trail.

She paused and scanned the sky. The pole star lay to her left. The trail led due east. Probably it wouldn't take her very far, bearing in mind what Grep had said about his men preferring to avoid the territory of the Cave People. But surely, this was the way that Grep had set out tonight. He would never lead a hundred men through dense woodland if there was such an easy alternative.

She started along the trail and felt more confident now. She had built up her strength over the past few weeks, stealing more than her share of food, hiding some and eating the rest. Grep had enjoyed the game of putting her in charge of the Wives' House, setting her against the rest of the women, but he had underestimated her. And how could it be otherwise? He had lived his life surrounded by women who were docile and afraid.

She set herself a fast pace. At night, the land on the plateau quickly lost the heat that it had absorbed during the day. The air was cool and fresh. She could take long, quick strides without even breaking out into a sweat.

Here and there along the trail, she heard small animals diving into the undergrowth. Once, she heard the descending twittering song an elf owl. But for the most part she felt totally alone under the moon, and it was a good, pure feeling after so many weeks holding herself in check for fear of doing or saying anything that would anger Grep or cause one of the women to report her.

And then, as the moon was sinking behind her, she noticed a faint smell on the cool night air.

She stopped and breathed deeply. The smell was gone

as quickly as it had come—but then she caught it again. It was the smell of men.

Stealthily, now, Nisha moved off the trail, circling a little way to the north, where there was a slight rise in the land. Every once in a while she paused and strained her ears, and finally she heard them. They were making a camp no more than five hundred paces away.

She moistened her finger and held it above her head. She turned it, moistened it again, turned it again, until she was sure of the wind. The air was hardly moving, but there was a faint breeze from the general direction of the warriors. Good; her own smell, and any small noises she made, would be harder for them to detect.

She moved into some stunted pines and found a dry, springy carpet of pine needles that would make a perfect bed. Bushes screened her on all sides; she was well hidden.

She paused and listened again, and she heard the faint sound of water. Of course; Grep's scouts would have mapped the streams along the way east and would have chosen camp sites in advance. Nisha smiled to herself. The men were making her journey easy for her.

She dumped the robe, the sheepskin, and one of her spears, pulled a leather bag out of her pack, and slipped through the undergrowth in the direction of the running water. She already had a couple of pouches of water with her, but it wouldn't hurt to have more.

She emerged in a tiny clearing where a thin stream of water flowed out of a fissure in a face of limestone. She filled her pouch, then drank directly from the flow and let it splash over her face.

After she had refreshed herself, she looked around more carefully. She saw that the tiny stream ran from here toward the place where the men had camped. They were far enough away that there was no danger of her being seen or heard. Her only fear was that when they continued their journey the next day, she might not hear them leave and would be left behind. Still, it seemed likely they were planning to travel entirely at night. Certainly when they came closer to the Cave People, they would have to move as stealthily as possible.

She turned to go back to her hiding place—and then she felt a wicked impulse. Downstream, Grep and his men might be filling their water bags at this very moment. Nisha opened her robe, backed toward the stream, and squatted over it. She vented herself, laughing inside herself at the idea of Grep unwittingly consuming some of her waste.

Then she returned to her bed on the pine needles. She settled herself under the sheepskin, made a pillow from her pack, and lay listening to the tiny sounds of the night till they lulled her to sleep.

Chapter Twenty-Six

She woke at dawn but dozed on and off through the morning. Around noon, still lying in her hiding place, she ate some of her rations: corn bread, pemmican, and marrow butter. After that, she risked another visit to the stream to quench her thirst.

Later in the day, she heard the faint sound of voices from the warriors' camp, and she imagined the men sitting around telling stories, waiting for night to fall so that they could push ahead into the Cave People's territory.

Nisha whiled away her time daydreaming, relishing the freedom to do nothing, with no fear of being punished for it. She thought a lot of Jorlor, and hoped that his spirit would look kindly on her for her bravery and determination. She thought of all the other people she had known in her tribe, and she felt melancholy in the knowledge that all of them were gone. But then she thought of Winnor, somewhere out in the southlands, and she made a new vow: that after she had taken revenge on Grep, she would find the shaman.

As the heat of the day lessened, she ate some more and wove little finger-rings and tiny baskets out of the beargrass that grew close by. She found herself slipping into a childlike state where she no longer even thought about the danger she might face in the near future.

But then she heard faint sounds of someone shouting commands. Grep, she realized, was rousing the men and organizing his war party. Quickly, Nisha stowed her belongings and shouldered her bag. She crouched in her refuge, waiting and listening.

After a while, she heard nothing.

She hesitated. She didn't want to lag so far behind the men that she might lose track of them. She had no way of finding the Cave People on her own. All she had been told was that they were somewhere to the east; she hadn't dared to question Grep about their specific location.

On the other hand, she didn't want to risk blundering out too soon. So she waited, and she waited, until finally her patience ran out.

She crept back toward the trail, found it, and continued along it, moving with the utmost caution. But the smell of the men was fainter, and there was no sound ahead. Finally she emerged where they had made their camp and found only a heap of ashes and a wide area of flattened grass. She smiled with satisfaction, resettled her sack across her shoulder, and started striding confidently along the trail.

The sun set a little later, and for a while, there was no moon. But it seemed that fortune was on her side, because just as the trail narrowed and finally disappeared, the moon came up, shedding just enough light for her to find her way.

The ground was stonier, here, and the trees were sparse. She found herself following a low ridge that lay slightly higher than the plateau either side. Finally she came to a place where the ridge ended and she had to climb down over some boulders. Away in the distance, threading a path among the stunted pines, she saw tiny figures, black specks moving across the moonlit landscape.

She looked farther ahead—and she saw a pinpoint of yellow light that had to be a distant camp fire. It flickered in the waves of heat rising from the plateau, and it was so far away, and so faint, she could only see it clearly if she looked slightly to one side. But she felt no doubt now that she had sighted the home of the Cave People.

She judged that she had no hope of reaching it before dawn, and she wondered what Grep was planning to do. Probably he would camp when he was halfway there, hide his men again during the day, then make the last part of the journey during the next night. Would he launch his attack then, or would he hide and wait through one more day? That extra day would enable him to take his time, watch the Cave People coming and going in their daily lives, and decide on the best way to attack. It would also give his men time to rest before they went into battle. At the same time, though, it would mean a greater risk of a lookout or a wanderer stumbling upon the warriors, no matter how well they were hidden.

Nisha reminded herself that Grep had already sent his scouts to reconnoiter the land. He must have decided with them the best way of reaching the Cave People. Also, even though he was a cautious man, he was direct and aggressive in a fight. The more she thought about it, the more she felt sure that he would attack the tribe the very next night, just before dawn.

That gave her less time than she had hoped for. Still, her task was easier than Grep's. She didn't have to hide herself from the Cave People. In fact, the sooner they found her, the easier it would be.

Also, now that she had seen the distant fire, she no longer needed to follow Grep's men. She took a careful sighting and found that the point of flickering yellow light was almost directly east—perhaps just a fraction toward the south. Many times, out in the desert, she had had to find her way through a land where there were few distinctive features. She was confident that she wouldn't get lost out here, so long as she could see the stars.

She clambered swiftly over the remaining boulders, down onto the lower section of the plateau. She struck off slightly to the south, so that she would run no risk of encountering the warriors. She was moving with new purpose, now, as she strode swiftly among the low, dry, wiry trees.

* * *

By dawn, she was exhausted. She threw herself down, drank an entire bag of water, and ate all the rest of the marrow butter, since that was the richest, most satisfying food and was also the quickest to consume. She told herself that she must sleep no later than noon at the outside. Then she crawled under some bushes, dragged her sheepskin over her head and shoulders, and fell into an exhausted slumber.

She was woken by a strange prickling sensation all over her body. She rolled over, slid her hand inside her tunic, and found that she was covered with ants.

Nisha cursed herself for being so weary that she hadn't taken proper care to inspect her sleeping place. She threw off her clothes, shook them, and slapped the ants out of them. The anthill was close by, and she had accidentally kicked it in her sleep. Still, they were black ants, and small ones, not the kind that stung severely. And only a couple of them had found their way to the food in her pack. As she cleaned the last of them out of her robe, she decided that the ants were a good portent. The sun was directly overhead. If the ants hadn't roused her, she could have easily overslept.

Also, a colony of black ants meant that there was almost certainly water close by. She tried to see the contours of the land under the scattered trees and bushes. She sniffed the air. Yes, she detected the sweet freshness that could only come from a stream. She moved forward tentatively—and found herself almost tripping over a tiny furrow, no wider than her hand. It was sandy at the bottom, but the water that trickled through it looked clear enough. She stretched out on her stomach and pressed her lips to the water, so she could suck it directly into her mouth. Then she refilled the bladder that she'd drained. And then she looked ahead.

In this lattitude, even in the summer the sun never quite reached the zenith. It followed an arc that took it to the south on its journey from east to west. She squinted up, trying to judge if it had reached its highest point. She realized that it had actually moved a little lower in the sky since she first woke up. So, it was actually past noon.

She found a small, flat slab of rock, set down her spear, and balanced it on end so that she could be sure it stood vertically upright. She studied the shadow. If the sun was just past its noontime position, the shadow would be pointing a little east of north. If she imagined a right-angle to the shadow, that was precisely the direction that she wanted to take.

Nisha was starting to feel that her journey was favored, somehow, by the spirits. That was a dangerous feeling; she couldn't allow herself to become complacent. Still, as she started walking, she was buoyed up by a growing sense of confidence. Her plan had seemed wild and impossibly daring when she had thought about it back at the village, on nights when she lay awake in the Wives' House, with the docile women sleeping all around her. But now she found herself believing that the odds were on her side.

She still had to avoid being seen by Grep's men, but she felt sure she had overtaken them some time before dawn. There was no reason for them to exhaust themselves by pressing ahead as fast as she had. And now they would be lying low. They would post lookouts close by the camping place, but the scouts certainly wouldn't dare to explore the area while the sun was still in the sky.

As Nisha walked ahead, she felt the last of Grep's power over her slip away. Her body literally seemed to feel lighter now. She wanted to run through the woodland, and only the heat of the afternoon sun stopped her from doing so.

Then she came to the cliff edge.

There was hardly any warning. One moment, she was among the dry, twisted trees with their sunbleached limbs and dark green leaves reaching barely higher than her head. And then, abruptly, the trees ended. There was a narrow band of bare gray rock followed by a breathtaking chasm.

She stopped at the edge and stared at the vastness of the rift in the land. The plateau where she stood was so high above the surrounding terrain, when she looked over the edge, the trees that grew at the bottom looked like fragments of moss. An eagle was circling down there, far below her—yet it was still well above the land at the bottom. She watched for a moment as the great bird rode a current of air, twitching just the white tips of its wings to maintain its balance as it searched for prey below.

To her right, the cleft in the land opened into a flat, green vista that stretched into distant haze. To her left, the chasm gradually narrowed. It was as if a giant wedge had been taken out of the plateau. As her eyes followed the rim of it around, she found herself looking at the far side—and that was when she saw the village.

In the cliffs opposite, up near the plateau, was a wide, crescent-shaped cave. It was so wide, dozens of little square stone houses had been built inside it—tiny buildings made of stone, just like the houses that her tribe had built on top of their mesa.

Nisha found herself gaping at the beauty of it. There in the great gash of the cave, people had made an ultimate refuge, safe from the weather and from hostile tribes. It faced west, so that it would collect the warmth of the afternoon sun in the winter. Yet most of the buildings were recessed inside the cave, so they would be protected from the weather. Nisha had never imagined that such a perfect dwelling place could exist. She couldn't see how Grep could ever hope to invade and conquer such a place. It was a fortress.

But there was no time to stand here wondering about it. The sun had sunk halfway between the zenith and the horizon, and now she had to follow the edge of the chasm all the way in before she could circle around to the village on the far side.

She realized, now, why Grep and his men had followed

a path that took them slightly to the north. They had known about this chasm and had planned to avoid it. She eyed the distance carefully. Distances were deceptive in the clear air, but she decided that she could still reach her goal before sunset.

Fortunately, there were hardly any trees close to the edge of the cliff, and the rock was mostly flat. She strode quickly on her way, and the only sound in this special, wondrous place was of her breathing and the whisper of her moccasins on the flat, dry rock.

She reached the narrowest point of the cleft in the land and found a wide stream here, hurling itself down in a glorious white tail of spray. Quickly, Nisha kneeled and drank. She was dehydrated from walking so fast in the heat of the day. For a moment she looked over the edge at the waterfall, and she saw how it became a river again at the bottom of the cleft, broadening into a slow, dark snake of water as it found its way to the valley beyond. It was almost as if the water had carved this rift to flow in. Yet that seemed impossible. How could something as gentle as water cut a huge path through a substance as hard as rock?

She stood up and continued walking. Now that she was circling around to the east side of the cleft, she felt a renewed sense of purpose—and apprehension. Was it possible that the Cave People might be so cautious or so warlike, they would kill a stranger before even challenging her? It seemed unlikely, because any tribe—even a tribe of warriors—would want to know where the stranger was from, why she was here, and whether there were others with her. It would be in their own interests to capture her rather than kill her. Indeed, that was what she was counting on.

Still, this place was so far outside her experience, she felt her confidence weakening.

She came to a thicket of trees that grew almost to the edge of the cliffs. The rocks at the very edge looked unsafe here. There were big fissures among them, and they leaned out as if they were about to fall.

Nisha hesitated, then decided to circle a little way inland. She pushed through some brambles and saw a little nest of poison ivy just in time to avoid it. She ducked under a low branch—then stopped. There was a path ahead of her, winding through the trees. And once again, she picked up the scent of men.

Cautiously, now, she moved forward. For some reason, her skin prickled. Surely it was impossible that Grep and his warriors could be close by. She was certain that she had outdistanced them. They must be hiding somewhere far behind her, waiting for the safety of darkness.

She took a few more steps. She noticed a sapling ahead of her bending in the breeze—and realized that there was no breeze. She stopped and brought up her spear, just as a figure stepped out onto the path ahead of her.

He was not from Grep's tribe. She felt a wave of relief, and just as quickly, a renewed sense of caution. His bare chest was zigzagged with brown and black paint. He wore a necklace of bear teeth, and he carried a tall spear. His face was fierce and proud, marred by a scar that ran from the side of his forehead down to his jaw.

Slowly, Nisha lowered the point of her spear to indicate that she had no intention of threatening him. She saw his eyes move quickly, studying her.

"I am a friend," she said.

His expression didn't change. Had he understood her? Surely, he must speak the same language as Grep's tribe. It had only been three generations since Grep's people had split away from the Cave People.

"Friend," she said again. "I have a message. I must see your chieftain."

"Put down your spear," he told her. "Put it down on the ground."

She hesitated.

"Put it down!" He raised his own spear as if he was ready to cast it at her.

His accent was strange, but the words were clear enough. Quickly, Nisha dropped her spear. She extended her hands, palms up.

The man stepped cautiously toward her. She saw his eyes moving quickly again, checking the vegetation either side of her. "Turn around," he told her.

She told herself it was natural for him to be cautious. With a great effort of will, she turned her back.

She heard him picking up her spear behind her. Then she felt him pulling her other spear out from the thong that tied it to her back. There was a faint sound of wood on wood as the two shafts knocked together.

He circled her, keeping his own spear ready. Once again, she found herself face to face with him. "Who are you?" he demanded.

"I am from the west lands," she told him. "From the desert. Most of my people were killed by Worr's people. I was captured by the Warrior Tribe. But I escaped. I've come to you as a friend."

He took a long moment to consider this. Finally, he nodded. "Turn," he told her.

She turned her back to him again, so she ended up facing the same way as she had been originally.

"You will go to my people," he told her. She felt the flint tip of his spear pricking her neck. "Walk now."

"I *want* to go to your people," she said. "I have a warning for them. It's very urgent."

The spear tip pricked her again, a little harder than before, and Nisha realized it was useless trying to talk to this man. Obediently, she continued along the path in front of her.

Chapter Twenty-Seven

She emerged back into the sunlight and found herself at the edge of an area of land that had been cleared for two hundred paces in each direction. But this wasn't a barren, wasted space like the area around the stockade of the Warrior Tribe. There were neat rows of corn plants here, and rice grass, and jojoba bushes, and other species that she had never even seen before. A grid of shallow channels had been dug into the stony soil, bringing water to the crops, and people were working in the fields, using bison shoulder bones to dig new furrows for summer plantings—probably more rice grass, Nisha guessed.

For a moment, Nisha felt filled with nostalgia. She remembered all the times she had worked beside her own people in the summer plantings, while Winnor moved among them shaking his rattle, chanting, and calling on the spirits to bring rain to nourish the new seeds. Nisha felt excited that she was entering a village where that kind of communal life seemed to exist.

But then, as she continued along the path that led around the edge of the fields, she saw something that quenched her excitement. All the figures toiling to cultivate the land were women. Standing among them, watching over them, were warriors like the man who had found her. Nisha heard one of them shout something—a few curt words that sounded like an order, or a threat. He was holding a length of leather rope in his right hand, brandishing it as if he were ready to strike her with it.

"Stop," said the man behind her. "We go down here."

He pointed between two great slabs of rock near the cliff edge.

She gave him a quick, nervous glance. His accent was strange, and she wasn't sure if she'd understood him. "Down?" she said.

He gestured impatiently with his spear. "Between the rocks, there."

She felt a new wave of apprehension. Foolishly, even though Grep had said that the Cave People were fierce warriors, Nisha had imagined that they might be fair and decent to their own people. It seemed impossible to her that another tribe could be as cruel to its women folk as Grep's people had been. And when she'd seen their village from the opposite side of the chasm, the beauty of it had made her feel certain that it belonged to enlightened people.

But she saw no kindness in the face of the man who stood behind her, and she heard no warmth in the voice of the man out on the fields. The awful thought came to her that she might have moved from one brutal tribe to another that might be even worse. Why had she assumed that she'd be well treated here? She had imagined that they'd be grateful to her for warning them about an impending attack. And perhaps, yes, they would thank her. But what would happen after that?

She told herself to be stoic. She still needed to proceed with her plan—even though she felt as if she were returning to captivity as she moved toward the gap between the slabs of rock.

She found herself entering a narrow V-shaped cleft. Loose stones had been thrown down into the bottom of it, forming a crude pathway that descended at a sharp angle. She had to turn sideways to slip between the stone faces, and as she followed the path, the rocks blotted out most of the sky. Her captor, as she thought of him now, followed closely with his spear still ready.

She reached the end of the sloping cleft and found that the path doubled around between two more slabs of rock.

The small stones were loose underfoot, and she had to keep her palms pressed against the rock face in front of her in order to keep her balance.

The path doubled back again, and this time there was bright sunlight at the end. Nisha felt her way along, then hesitated as she reached the end of the cleft. She found herself looking out and down into the gulf where she had seen the eagle soaring. The cliff face fell away vertically below her.

But to her left, there was a narrow ledge. "This way?" she asked the man with the spear, hoping he would say no. But he just gave a curt nod.

Nisha carefully positioned her bag at the center of her back. She tried not to look at the sickening drop as she stepped out onto the ledge. She watched her feet carefully as she took each step.

Finally she reached a place where the ledge widened. And then she moved around an outcropping of rock and found herself on a path that opened out into the enormous cavern where the village had been built.

She stared in awe. The roof of rock was so high above, there was room in the center of the cave for buildings that were three stories high. Every dwelling seemed to have grown out of a previous one, creating a wonderful jumbled mosaic of rectangular shapes in the warm sandstone colors that she knew so well. And every house had a window facing the vista of the valley below.

Water was running somewhere. She noticed a little stream that had been carefully channeled between flat pieces of stone. The water seemed to come down out of a fissure in the roof of the cave; it flowed between the buildings and escaped out over the edge of the cliff. So the people here didn't even have to go up onto the plateau to quench their thirst.

Some women were working, building new homes deeper in the cave. She heard the clink of tools and the knocking of stone against stone. Women were using big rounded cobbles of granite as hammerstones to shape rough chunks of sandstone. Other women were using chippings and gravel to fill gaps in the new walls, and a third team was pressing a muddy paste into the filling. The workmanship was painstaking: The finished walls of the buildings looked so smooth, they could have been formed from single slabs of rock.

But here again, the teams of women were being supervised by tough, unsmiling males. One of them turned and eyed Nisha as she walked past, and his eyes narrowed with interest.

Nisha turned to her captor. "I told you before, I've come here as a friend," she said, as authoritatively as she could. "The tribe to the west—Worr's tribe—is planning to attack your people. I must talk to your chieftain." She gestured irritably at his spear. "Why do you keep threatening me? You think I can escape back up that path that we followed? Or are you afraid I will attack you with my bare hands?"

For a moment, they stared at each other. She forced herself to meet his eyes. Perhaps, she hoped, if she seemed confident enough, he wouldn't treat her like a slave.

But her words had angered him. He was glaring at her, and his eyes were fierce. "You have no right," he said, "to speak that way to a warrior and a hunter."

"But I am a hunter, too, in the tribe where I used to live." She continued to return his stare, even though it made her feel queasy inside. Her biggest fear, now, was that they would pay no attention to her. They might shut her away, or allow this savage to keep her as his mate, or put her in one of the work teams—anything rather than listen to her. "I tell you," she said yet again, "your tribe will be attacked, perhaps tonight. I risked my own life to bring you this news. Now, will you take me to your chieftain?"

He gestured irritably with his spear. "This way!" he snapped at her, pointing up a smooth stone path that had been laid between the buildings.

Nisha tried to tell what he was thinking, and what his intentions were, but all she saw in his face was anger. He could be granting her request, or he could be directing her toward a prison cell.

She turned and eyed the path that he wanted her to follow. It led to a tower in the center of the cluster of little houses. She took a reluctant step—then stopped as she saw a man emerge from the doorway in the base of the tower. He was so old that he could no longer stand straight, and his face was a crinkled mass of fine, dry wrinkles. But he moved with dignity, and his robe was beautifully ornamented with pictures of men and animals. Nisha sensed immediately that this might be the chieftain of the tribe.

The warrior with the scarred face moved ahead of her, stopped in front of the old man, and bowed his head respectfully. "Gogorah, the woman has asked to speak with you," he said. "I found her up on the cliffs. She says she is from Worr's people. She claims they plan to attack our village, Gogorah." The warrior hesitated. "I think she lies."

The old chieftain squinted past the warrior. He shaded his eyes from the bright sun that was slanting in through the mouth of the cave. Nisha moved forward so that the chieftain could see her more clearly. "I have no reason to lie," she said. "Why should I tell a story like that, if it wasn't true?"

"Be silent!" The warrior turned and half raised his spear. "You'll be told when you can speak."

"Bring her in." The old man's voice was as dry as dead grass, and barely audible. But there was no mistaking his authority. The warrior bowed again, then stepped over to Nisha, seized her arm, and hustled her forward. "Inside!" he barked at her.

She tried to wrench herself free from him as she ducked through the low doorway into the tower, but he kept his painful grip and forced her down onto the stone floor. She found herself looking up at the chieftain, who perched himself on a chair of logs that looked like a smaller version of the one that Worr used to sit in. The warrior, meanwhile, stood over her with the point of his spear touching her neck.

The room at the base of the tower was circular, just three paces wide. A ladder at one side led up through a hole in the ceiling to another floor above. Faint light filtered through the open doorway.

The old chieftain eyed Nisha's pack. "Have you searched her bag?"

The warrior moved uneasily. "Not yet."

"Give it to me."

The warrior wrestled the sack off Nisha's shoulders, then placed it diffidently on the old man's knees. With hands so bony that they looked skeletal, the chieftain pulled out Nisha's remaining food, her spare moccasins, and everything else that she had stowed for her journey. He inspected the items with casual interest, then tossed them onto the floor. Finally, at the bottom of the bag, he found the flint knife that she had taken from Tarak, after she had killed Yuwul.

The chieftain threw the empty pack aside and weighed the knife in his hand. His pale, watery eyes studied Nisha. "Worr's tribe has never allowed its women to carry weapons," he said, in a voice that was little more than a whisper.

"I stole it," she said, "when I escaped."

The old man gave her a thin smile, as if she had amused him by telling a particularly implausible lie.

"But I stole two spears, also." She gestured at the warrior standing beside her. "These spears, here."

The chieftain squinted at the spear in the warrior's hands, and the second spear that he had slung behind him. He beckoned.

The warrior stepped forward showed them to him.

Slowly, the chieftain's smile faded. "These are made and bound in the custom of Worr's tribe." He turned back to Nisha and studied her more carefully. "How is it possible for a woman to steal weapons from the Warrior Tribe?"

"Most of the men had already left the village," she told him. "They're on their way here, and I think they will attack your people tonight." She spoke with more certainty than she felt. It seemed the only way to convince him to take her seriously. "I had planned my escape for several weeks. I was not born in Worr's tribe; I was captured by his warriors three months ago." She hesitated. "You should understand, also, that Worr is dead."

The chieftain had been following her words closely. He frowned. "Dead?"

"Yes." Should she say how it had happened? Perhaps it would be a good way to prove herself. And since Grep's people were enemies of this tribe, it might encourage them to trust her. "I tricked Worr into breaking a taboo," she went on. "I was the wife of a man named Grep. Grep found Worr molesting me, so he killed him. Grep is now chieftain of the Warrior Tribe."

There was a long silence. Nisha began to feel uneasy. The man beside her had pulled back from her as if he were physically repelled by what she had said. And the old man's eyes were little more than slits now.

Finally, he spoke. "Worr was my great-grandson," he said.

Nisha felt trapped in a frozen moment. A tremor ran through her. "I'm—sorry," she whispered. "I thought—I thought the Warrior Tribe were your enemies. In any case, my plan was for Grep to die, not Worr. Grep is a tyrant. He's the one who wants to come here, and—"

The chieftain held up his hand. "Quiet," he said.

Nisha lapsed into silence. She quickly averted her eyes and stared at the floor. She found herself shivering. Would they kill her? They obviously had little respect for women in the first place, and now that they knew she had killed this man's kin—

"Many years ago," the old man said, "my son Yov left this tribe because I refused to step aside. He was angry and foolish. He would rather steal from others than cultivate the land himself. He was the founder of your tribe, till he died in an accident and his three sons came to power. Worr was the child of one of them—I forget which. He was an evil child. Years ago, a man who passed this way claimed that Worr had killed his father and his uncles in order to become chieftain. I wouldn't be surprised." The old man was ignoring Nisha and staring at the opposite wall now. He seemed to be looking beyond it at pictures from his memories.

He sighed. "Perhaps it's a good thing that Worr is dead. And perhaps it's good, too, if his people come here now and attack us. This has not been a good thing, our two tribes sharing the plateau. So we can resolve the matter once and for all." He grunted to himself. Then he looked down at Nisha again. "The fact remains, though," he said, "Worr was my kin."

"I'm sorry," Nisha said again. "It was truly an accident."

He gestured for her to be quiet. "There are always accidents, always trouble when women meddle." He coughed, then wiped his mouth on the sleeve of his robe. "You'll stay in this tribe until I have learned everything that I need to know from you. Then I will decide whether you should be put to work with the other women."

Nisha said nothing.

"Now," said the old chieftain, "begin by telling me everything you know about this man Grep, and how you think he plans to attack us."

Nisha sighed. There was no point in holding anything back. Her survival, now, depended on this tribe. And she still wanted them to clash. Maybe, she thought grimly, all the men on both sides would kill one another. Then the women would be free.

She told the chieftain her story, fully and frankly, although she took care to make it seem that the idea for the attack had come entirely from Grep. She tried to portray herself as an innocent spectator—a victim of Grep's cruelties—though she doubted whether the old man in front of her would care.

Finally, her story was done. The chieftain nodded slowly. "There is only one more thing," he said. "And that is, your reason for coming here to warn us."

Nisha hesitated for a long moment. Should she say that she had hoped to find a new home among people who were kinder than the Warrior Tribe? Or should she tell the whole truth—that she wanted to use this tribe to kill the men who had destroyed her own people?

"I thought that if I came to you," she said, "and I warned you of this threat, you might accept me into your people. I hoped you might thank me, and—"

The old chieftain grunted in disgust. He pointed toward the door. "Put her in one of the pit houses," he said, "and then call a meeting of the elders. We must make preparations. There may not be much time."

"Yes, Gogorah." The warrior nodded. He coughed respectfully to show that he wanted to speak further.

The old man frowned at him. He waited.

"Do you think the woman speaks truly, Gogorah?"

The chieftain slowly inclined his head. "She is a meddler and a liar, but I believe there will be an attack."

The warrior shifted uneasily. "What will we do?"

The chieftain grinned. All his teeth had rotted away, and his cracked lips widened to show a thin black slit of a mouth. "When the warriors come here"—he gave a little shrug—"we will kill them all."

Chapter Twenty-Eight

Outside, in the wide mouth of the cave near the cliff edge, the scar-faced warrior squatted down and took hold of a boulder lying on top of a flat slab of stone. Using all his strength, he rolled the boulder away. Then he grabbed the circular slab and managed to slide it to one side. Beneath it was a dark hole.

Nisha had thought she was standing on the floor of the cave. Now she realized her mistake. The floor here was artificial, constructed from sections of sandstone. When she looked more closely, she saw the individual pieces of it. There was another level down below.

There were pit houses, as the chief had said. And this one, evidently, was used as a prison.

"Down." The man pointed to the dark hole that he had uncovered.

There was no point in resisting. She certainly couldn't run away; the only exit seemed to be back along the narrow ledge to the twisting V-shaped cleft in the cliff face. Feeling a terrible sense of dread, Nisha crouched down. She saw that there was a ladder just below the rim of the hole in front of her. She lowered one leg, then the other, and found a wooden rung under her moccasins.

"Down!" the warrior ordered her again.

Reluctantly, Nisha lowered herself down the ladder, into total darkness. Before she had even reached the bottom, the warrior slid the stone back over the access hole, shutting out the sun.

Nisha's feet found an uneven floor of dusty sandstone.

She stood, clutching the ladder, feeling dizzy in the blackness. But there was a faint source of light. A small channel no broader than her arm seemed to lead through the rock to the face of the cliff outside. Nisha let go of the ladder, blundered through the darkness, and pressed her face to the channel. If she positioned herself correctly, she could even see a fragment of blue sky.

She turned, blinking. Now that her eyes were growing accustomed to the gloom, she saw that she was in a circular room, just like the chieftain's room in his stone tower. The floor was gritty and littered with bones. The place smelled dank and musty.

"Hello," said a woman's voice. "My name is Sookim. Who are you?"

Nisha gave a little cry. The voice had seemed to come from right beside her. She peered into the semidarkness. Was there really someone in here with her? "I'm Nisha," she said, when she managed to calm herself a little. "Where are you? I can't see."

"I'm sorry," the woman said. "I didn't mean to scare you."

"No. No. I'm glad there's someone here," said Nisha. She reached out, groping for the other woman. Her hand touched empty air.

"Where are you from, Nisha?" Sookim asked. "I've never heard your voice before."

"I come from—from another tribe," Nisha said. "Why are you in here? Are you being punished?"

"Yes," Sookim said. "For stealing food."

Nisha squatted down. Finally, in the darkness, she managed to see the woman. Once again she reached out, and this time their fingers touched and twined. Nisha felt tears at the corners of her eyes. She didn't know this stranger, but it was good just to touch a person who might not be an enemy.

Haltingly, Nisha started telling her story. She kept it as brief as she could, and she tried not to say anything that could be used against her. She had already learned from

Reive that a woman might seem friendly but could not be trusted if she served a man. Still, there might be a chance to make an alliance with this stranger. And talking helped to take her mind off the terrible situation that she was in.

"You must be a strong person," Sookim said, when Nisha had said her piece. "And what a pleasant tribe that you used to live in, where men give women so much freedom."

"But freedom isn't something that one person gives to another," Nisha said. "Freedom is something that everyone has, like air or sunlight. Someone can take freedom away, but no one has the power to create it."

Sookim laughed softly. "You won't be very happy here, Nisha. Perhaps it's not as bad as Worr's tribe, where women are cast out if no man wants them anymore. Here, we are allowed to live to an old age, so long as we can still work in the field. But still, the life is very hard."

"I don't understand why it has to be that way," said Nisha.

Sookim shifted. She stood up and stretched the stiffness out of her limbs, then squatted back down facing Nisha, less than an arm's length away. "I'll tell you the history of this tribe," she said. "It's said that the first houses were built by a wanderer named Mino, who just wanted to have a place where he could live in solitude. A woman found him and started living with him, and then they had children. But Gogorah's tribe was living up on the plateau, and they learned the secret path down here to the cave, and one night, they slaughtered Mino and his family in their sleep, and they've been living here ever since."

"Gogorah seems old," said Nisha, "I'm surprised he hasn't been forced aside—or killed, even—by his sons or by one of the warriors of the tribe."

"Gogorah only had one child," said Sookim. "A son named Yov who tried to take his father's power but was forced out—"

"I've heard that story," Nisha interrupted.

"Yes, I suppose you would have encountered it before. It was Yov who founded the Warrior Tribe. But my point was this: The warriors of the Cave People are fanatically loyal to Gogorah. They believe he is immortal because he drank from an enchanted stream somewhere up on the plateau. They believe that he talks to the Thunder Spirit, and if he ever dies, our home, here, will be destroyed in a flash of lightning."

Nisha shook her head. To her, Gogorah looked like a little old man, nothing more. She had certainly sensed nothing magical about him. "Do you believe that story?" she asked.

Sookim weighed her words carefully. "If I said to you that I don't believe it, and if you told any of the men, I would be punished."

Nisha sensed more spirit, more rebellion in Sookim than in any of the women she had known in the Warrior Tribe. She hoped that she wasn't deluding herself yet again. "Are there any other women like you here?" she asked. "I mean, do they disobey the men, or dream of fighting back?"

Sookim laughed. She reached out and patted Nisha's shoulder. "I'm the only one who still thinks of rebellion," she said. "I grew up in a tribe down on the lowlands to the southeast, Nisha. There wasn't as much freedom as you had among your people, but still, women were allowed to hunt."

"So how did you find yourself here?" Nisha asked.

"When I came of age, I started going on long journeys into the wilderness, all alone. I've always been a solitary person; I don't know why. I found a way up onto the plateau, and then I found the Cave People, and they captured me, and I've been here ever since. For five years now."

Five years. Nisha wondered if she could ever live here as a servant of the warriors for as long as that without throwing herself off the cliff or running wild and turning against her captors. "You must miss your old tribe," she said. It sounded inadequate, but it was all she could think of saying.

"Not so much anymore." She sighed. "I hope the evening comes soon. I hate it when they shut me in here."

Nisha stood up and peered through the channel that led through to the outside world. The sky was a darker blue, but still quite bright. "The sun hasn't set yet," she said. "Will they let us out when it gets dark?"

"My punishment this time is supposed to last for just one day," said Sookim. "So they'll release me after sunset. But for you, Nisha, I can't say. Are you sure that the Warrior Tribe will attack tonight?"

"Almost certain."

"And you think Gogorah believed you?"

"Yes. Definitely."

Sookim paused to mull it over. "I wonder what Gogorah will do. I suppose he could keep you down here for just a few moments more—or for a few days. I just don't know."

At sunset, the stone lid was pulled aside and dim light filtered into the pit house. "Both of you," said a voice. "Out."

Nisha felt a wave of relief. She seized hold of the ladder and scrambled up it. The open air felt fresh on her face. She took quick, deep breaths. She glanced at the man who had released her and saw that he was a young warrior who looked as if he had only just come of age. Then she turned as Sookim climbed up the ladder, and the two women stared at each other.

Sookim was a small woman—far smaller than Nisha had realized while they had been trapped in the darkness of their prison. She looked as if she was a little over twenty years old. She had a birthmark on the left side of her forehead: a purple swatch that reached up beyond her hair line.

"You see, now," Sookim said shyly, "I am not as beautiful as you."

Impulsively, Nisha reached out and took the woman's hand. "Don't speak so foolishly," she said.

"Gogorah needs you to help evacuate the village," the young warrior interrupted them. "Both of you." He kneeled down, and Nisha felt his hand on her leg. She looked in surprise and saw him tying a stout leather thong between her ankles. It was just long enough to allow her to move in small steps, but it would prevent her from running if she was foolish enough to try to escape.

"Now your wrists," he said, standing up in front of her.

Mutely, she held out her hands. He bound her wrists with another thong that was shorter than the one linking her ankles.

"What's happening?" Sookim asked. She was peering into the dim recesses of the great cave. "Everyone is leaving? All the houses are being emptied?"

"Gogorah will deceive our enemies," said the young warrior. He moved to Sookim and started tying her, just as he had tied Nisha. "We're taking everything up to the plateau. All the food, all the weapons. If the warriors come down here, we'll starve them till they surrender. If they try to escape back up to the plateau, we'll kill them all." His young voice sounded full of pride and anticipation.

"But how will they ever find the way down into the cave?" said Sookim. "It's not easy to see, especially at night."

The young warrior hesitated. "Gogorah seems to think they may know the way." He drew himself up. "Are you questioning his wisdom?"

"Of course not, boy-child," said Sookim.

He gave her a threatening look. "I'm no longer a boy. You know better than that."

"Forgive me." She bowed her head. "I forgot."

"Get to work!" a voice shouted. A man was standing a dozen paces away, glaring at them.

The young warrior grabbed the two women by their arms and hustled them forward. "Enough talking," he snapped at them. "It causes trouble when women talk. Come on, there's work to do."

He hustled them in among the stone buildings. In each house, men were gathering up possessions, scooping them into big leather sacks. Everything of value was being removed.

Nisha and Sookim were put to work in a house where there were deep food caches recessed in the floor. A warrior stood over them, supervising while they transferred seeds, nuts, dried fruits, and berries into separate sacks. With her hands tied in front of her, Nisha found that it was easy enough to cup her palms and scoop up the food. Meanwhile, all around her, the cave echoed with the sounds of footsteps and terse commands.

When Nisha and Sookim had gathered up all the food, each of them was given a sack to carry, and they were led out of the village. Nisha felt unsteady with the heavy burden across her shoulders, and she was afraid to walk out onto the narrow ledge that was the only way back up to the plateau. Below her, the valley was totally dark, a vast gulf filled with shadow. When she looked up, she saw that the last rays of the setting sun were touching the tops of the trees above the cliffs opposite. The evacuation had been well planned: If anyone was watching the village, it would be hard for them to see what was happening now, in the twilight. At the same time, there was just enough light for the people to see what they were doing.

"Move along!" someone commanded her.

She steadied herself as well as she could, turned her back to the sheer drop, and stepped up onto the ledge. She told herself that if she started to lose her balance, she would simply let the sack drop behind her. The men would be furious at losing the food, but at least she would live. Bit by bit, facing the rough sandstone cliff, she sidestepped along the ledge until she finally reached the cleft that led inward and up to the plateau.

The thong tying her ankles made it hard to ascend the slope, and the bag on her shoulders kept getting itself wedged between the slabs of rock either side of her. Eventually, though, she managed to get to the top.

A warrior saw her, grabbed her arm, and pointed. She saw another figure a dozen paces ahead of her, crossing the cultivated fields, and still another figure ahead of that. The villagers were hiding themselves and their possessions in a line of trees and bushes fifty paces away. Nisha went to join them, and she dumped her burden amid a huge pile of other sacks.

"You!" a man called to her. "You're the one from the Warrior Tribe."

"Yes," said Nisha.

"Come over here," said the warrior. "Gogorah wants you close by him."

"Then I should come with her," said a voice.

Nisha turned and saw that Sookim had come up beside her.

The warrior hesitated, then seemed to decide that there was no time to ask questions. "All right, both of you," he said.

They were taken to the thickest clump of vegetation. Warriors were climbing the stunted trees, and other men were passing handfuls of spears up to them. Gogorah himself was sitting in his chair, which had been moved up here from his place in the cave.

The chieftain peered at Nisha in the vanishing light. "Good," he said. He gestured to a guard. "Tie her hands behind her, then tie a leash around her neck and secure it to that tree." He noticed Sookim and grunted with annoyance. "The food thief," he said. "Tie her as well. Watch both of these women."

Quickly, two warriors carried out the commands. A few moments later, Nisha found herself immobilized, with her wrists lashed behind her and a short thong preventing her from moving more than half a pace from the trunk of the tree.

She glanced at Sookim, who had been similarly tied. "Why did you want to be with me?" she whispered.

Sookim turned away. She said nothing.

Nisha looked around, peering into the gathering darkness. The rest of the women seemed to have been grouped farther back in some long grass. She could barely make out the pale shapes of their faces here and there, and she heard them murmuring nervously to one another. Then a man moved among them, warning them to lie down out of sight and be silent.

A few more men came running up from the cave, bringing the last of the weapons. More spears were passed to the warriors in the trees. Nisha heard a muttered curse from above her, and a spear tumbled down, almost striking her. She tried to jump backward, and the thong around her neck snapped tight. "It's not right that I should be tied this way," she complained. "I risked my life to come here and bring you my warning. If the men from the Warrior Tribe find me, they'll torture me and kill me. You should give me weapons so I can defend myself."

Gogorah was seated half a dozen paces away. She saw him mutter something to one of the men who stood around him like a personal honor guard.

The man strode across to Nisha, his moccasins swishing through the tall grass. "Gogorah has told me to kill you if you make more noise," he said. "Do you understand?"

She tried to see his face in the darkness. His voice sounded casual, as if it wouldn't bother him in the slightest to sink his spear into her and walk away.

"I came here to help your tribe," she whispered.

He eyed her for just a moment more. "I've given you Gogorah's warning," he said. "I won't warn you a second time."

Nisha saw Sookim watching her. The woman gave a quick little shake of her head.

"I'm sorry," Nisha whispered, though it hurt her to say the words.

The warrior turned and strode back to his chieftain. He didn't even bother to look at Nisha after that.

She told herself to make the best of it. At least the chieftain had believed her and had taken action. As a result, it seemed quite likely, now, that her plan would succeed. Grep and his people would be trapped and killed—but was this what she really wanted? Yes, she still craved revenge against him for his crime against her people. Yes, if she held a spear in her own hands, she would cast it against him without hesitation.

But after Grep was dead, her own people would still be gone, and his violent acts against them and against her would still live on in her memory.

Also, there were young men in Grep's army who hadn't been in the raiding party that massacred her people. Did they really deserve to die?

She wondered why she was suddenly thinking this way. While she had been a prisoner of the Warrior Tribe, no punishment had seemed too extreme for its men. But now, she found herself feeling guilty at the thought of so much blood that was going to be shed because of her.

She tried to banish the feeling as well as she could. She leaned against the tree and she waited among the men of the Cave People, peering into the darkness, and listening for the slightest sound.

Chapter Twenty-Nine

The heat of the day evaporated quickly from the land. The stars shone down with a cold, hard light, and Nisha shivered as she stood in the darkness. Time dragged by with terrible slowness, and she heard the warriors moving restlessly, rubbing and slapping themselves in an effort to keep warm.

The vigil dragged on. "If he is going to attack, it will happen before the moon comes up," said a faint, dry, whispered voice. It was Gogorah, she realized, conferring with his guards.

Nisha tried to remember when the moon had risen the previous night while she had been hurrying across the plateau. She had no clear recollection; she had been too impatient to reach her goal.

She turned and looked back toward the east where the trees on the plateau formed a ragged silhouette against the starlit sky. As she strained her eyes, she thought she saw a faint, pale glow heralding the moon.

She shivered some more, feeling a deepening sense of dread. Standing out here, tethered to a tree, with the warriors growing impatient all around her, she had a terrible premonition that something had gone wrong. Grep had changed his plan and he was retreating, even now, back to his village, or he had decided to wait till the next night to make his attack. The Cave People would blame her—

"Ssst!" The sound came from directly above.

She looked up quickly, and all the men around her did

the same. The warrior who had placed himself in the tree was pointing with his spear.

Nisha tried to see what he had seen. Then she heard the faintest sound of a distant footstep rustling through grass. Black silhouettes came into view close to the edge of the cliffs.

She stopped shivering. She wasn't even aware of the cold anymore. She found herself tensing, staring with wide eyes, breathing quickly through parted lips. Instinctively, she strained forward till her bonds held her back. Which one was Grep? She couldn't tell. But he was there, she felt sure of it, and her vague feelings of guilt were suddenly gone. The sight of his warriors brought back all her anger, all her outrage.

But what were they doing? They didn't seem to be looking for the path down to the cave. They were ranging out along the cliff, pausing here and there and peering over the edge. Then a couple of them squatted down. One man threw something to another, and she heard a faint sound as the second man dropped it on the rocks. A rope, Nisha realized. Suddenly she understood. Grep and his men were searching the ground for tree roots or boulders. They would use them to anchor ropes, then lower themselves over the edge.

She turned to the warriors around her, wondering if they understood. She saw Gogorah muttering something directly into the ear of the man beside him, and then that warrior passed the message to the next, on down the line. Yes, they seemed to understand. But—they were doing nothing. Would they wait and starve out their enemies, as the young warrior had predicted?

Gogorah still gave no command as Grep's men secured half a dozen ropes and tossed them over the side. Silhouettes clustered around each rope, and Nisha thought she saw some men cautiously starting to lower themselves. She shifted in an agony of frustration. Why didn't Gogorah act?

"Cast your spears." It was the faintest whisper, but she heard it clearly. The chief raised his hand and pointed.

Up in the trees and all around Nisha, the warriors of the Cave People threw their first volley. She couldn't see the shafts flying through the night, but she heard the men grunt with the effort of flinging their weapons, and the tree beside her swayed and shook.

There were sudden cries from the men at the cliff edge. Some of the silhouettes fell, clutching themselves. Others turned in confusion.

"Attack." The chieftain pulled himself up and out of his chair. "Kill them all!"

His warriors sprang forward with terrible screams that echoed across the darkened landscape, and they went crashing forward through the tall grass. The men who had hidden themselves in the trees leaped down, hurling more spears as they ran. There were new shouts from Grep's men—shouts of panic.

"Destroy them!" Old Gogorah started hobbling forward, following his men. "Throw them into the gorge. Shed their blood. Show no mercy!"

"I spoke truly!" Nisha shouted to him. "I saved your people!"

He stopped and glanced back at her as if her voice were an annoying distraction, like the buzzing of an insect. He barely seemed aware of her. He waved his arm dismissively, then turned away from her and continued toward the battle. "Kill them!" he cried.

Nisha felt another wave of frustration. Gogorah's warriors would kill Grep's men—and then, she knew with sudden clarity, they would give themselves the glory. They would never share the credit with a mere woman. In fact, they might even feel angry with her if she reminded them of the part she had played. They would want to keep her quiet or get rid of her, one way or another.

"Be calm," said a voice. It was Sookim, close by.

"But there's no justice!" Nisha cried.

"Of course not. Be still now."

Nisha felt a tugging on the thong that bound her to the tree. "Leave me be," she muttered.

All along the cliff edge, Gogorah's warriors were doing their terrible work. Wounded men were being forced over the edge, and their screams echoed between the cliffs as they fell to their doom. There was no way for Grep to retreat, and no time for him to regroup his men and launch a counterattack. A small cluster of figures tried to escape by running farther along the the cliffs, but warriors of the Cave People intercepted them, and there were more war cries and death screams in the darkness.

Some of Grep's men started fighting back—fighting with terrible ferocity, knowing that they were trapped and facing imminent death. But they were hopelessly outnumbered now, and Gogorah's men kept pushing them back toward the cliff edge. One by one, Grep's people faced the terrible choice of throwing themselves onto their enemies' spears, or jumping to their destruction.

Nisha couldn't feel any sympathy for them. This was how it had been on the mesa when her people had been massacred. There was a terrible justice in what was happening now. She wondered if Grep understood. She hoped so. She hoped someone would throw him over the side, just as he had thrown her boy-child.

Nisha felt another jerk on the thong tying her neck. She turned in irritation—and found herself moving freely. She stopped in astonishment. "I chewed through it," Sookim whispered. "I started on it when we were first tied. You never noticed."

It was true, Nisha realized. The chewed end of the thong was dangling from her neck. "But—you are still tied," Nisha said. "And we're hobbled—"

"There's a spear on the ground. It fell from the tree. Remember?"

Nisha stared at the other woman in amazement. She had spent so many days among the women of the Warrior Tribe, she had given up hope of ever finding someone as determined and resourceful as herself. "Thank you," she whispered to Sookim.

And yet—she wished there was more time to think. Was it best to escape? The men might hunt her down. But suppose they did, and they dragged her back to their village; would it be any worse than if she stayed here voluntarily? Gogorah was a suspicious man. He would reason that if Nisha had been clever enough to betray Grep, she could betray him, too. There was no life, no future for her here. He might even have her killed.

Nisha made her decision. She slipped off a moccasin and felt around with her bare foot till she touched the wooden shaft of the spear. Quickly, she squatted over it. She leaned backward till her knuckles touched the ground, and she edged along till her fingers found the flint head of the spear. Quickly, she sawed her leather bonds across it.

In a moment, her hands were free. She seized the spear, dragged it out from under her, cut the thongs binding her ankles, then cut the last of the thong away from her neck. She moved to Sookim. "Do you want to come with me?" she whispered.

"Of course!"

She cut the woman's bonds.

Unexpectedly, Sookim seized her and hugged her. There was a brief shock of warm, physical contact. Then the woman ducked away into the darkness. Nisha grabbed her moccasin, put it back on, and ran after her. "Wait!" she hissed.

Sookim paused and turned. Nisha looked quickly around to make sure there were no men left here who would see her. All the warriors were still at the cliff edge, wielding their spears, slashing and thrusting at Grep's party. Screams and war cries still echoed in the night, though they were becoming less frequent.

Nisha searched in the darkness and found the huge pile of sacks that had been stacked under the trees. She started groping among them, clambering over them and feeling each one. Finally she found one that seemed to contain food. She sliced open its neck with her spear. Yes, it was full of powdered corn. She dumped most of it on the ground, then threw the bag over her shoulder. "Which way?" she hissed to Sookim.

"The way I came here originally," she whispered back. "Unless you know a better way."

Nisha thought of the long journey back to the village of the Warrior Tribe, and then the trail that led from there down to the lowlands, where she had once lived with her people. She wasn't even sure if she could find the village, and the trail had been difficult and dangerous when the warriors had brought her up it three months ago. In any case, there might still be men searching for her there.

"I'll follow you," she whispered.

"Good. Come!" Sookim seized her hand.

Nisha held back for a moment more. A few warriors were still fighting near the cliff edge, but the battle was almost over. Then she heard a cry—a man's voice echoing across the landscape. "Surrender! Surrender!"

For a moment, she couldn't be sure if it was one of Grep's people begging for mercy, or one of Gogorah's men warning the invaders to submit. The she realized, it couldn't be one of Gogorah's men. Gogorah had told them to kill everyone. He had no interest in telling Grep's people to surrender.

"Surrender!" the voice cried again, and the hair rose on the back of Nisha's neck.

"Grep," she muttered. It was his voice. She was suddenly sure of it.

"Come on!" Sookim called to her.

"But he lives!" Nisha cried out, feeling a wave of pure, unreasoning rage. She clenched her hand on her spear till her muscles hurt.

"Whoever he is, they'll kill him," said Sookim.

Nisha knew that the woman spoke truly. Yet she felt a desperate urge to go there to the cliff edge to see for herself, and use her own spear if she had to. She wanted to see Grep's face. She wanted to force him off the edge and watch him fall.

She stood trembling, immobilized by her fury.

"We must go!" Sookim called to her again.

Nisha closed her eyes, trying to control herself. There was really no choice. She had to leave. Slowly, with an immense effort, she forced herself to turn her back on the scene of the massacre—even though she felt as if she was betraying her vow.

There were no more shouts in the darkness—no more cries for mercy. That could only mean one thing, she told herself. Grep was now dead, and all his men were dead. The deed had been done. She was free. So why did she still find it hard to move away from the battle?

Sookim was running ahead across the fields. Nisha forced herself to follow. She almost lost her footing on the uneven, cultivated soil, and she splashed through a couple of the irrigation channels. Her bag of food banged against her shoulder, and her spear shaft snagged itself in a clump of berry bushes.

She found herself close to the patch of tall grass where the other women had been hiding. "Should we free them?" Nisha called out.

"No," Sookim called back. "They can't be trusted. And if some of them come with us, the men will follow."

Nisha peered into the night and saw figures huddled in the grass. All of them seemed to be tied as she had been, and she sensed their helpless fear. Her urge to free them was almost as strong as her need to go back and check that Grep had died. But she had to trust Sookim. The woman knew the Cave People; Nisha did not.

Nisha turned away from the women with tears in her eyes. Sookim had laughed at her for complaining there was no justice, and of course, Sookim was right. Still, it was unbearable to run like this.

She found Sookim waiting for her at the edge of the field, under the trees. "What's the matter with you?" the woman hissed at her. "I thought you were courageous. I thought you wanted to escape. Why else do you think I stayed with you over there? Why else would I chew through your bonds?"

"I know," said Nisha. Tears were running freely down her cheeks now. "You saved me, Sookim. I'm grateful. But it hurts me to have to run away. It tears me apart inside."

"Go back if you want," Sookim said. Her voice was suddenly cold. "But leave me the food and the spear."

Nisha shook her head hopelessly. "No," she said. "I'll stay with you. It's for the best."

"You're sure?" Sookim's voice was still unfriendly. "I don't want you with me if you have any doubts. I need a strong person."

"Yes." Nisha wiped her wet cheeks. Behind her, there were just a few shouts now, as the warriors of the Cave People called to each other. She imagined them walking up and down, looking for any of their comrades who had been killed or wounded. She imagined some of Grep's men lying on the ground, still alive but pretending to be dead. Gogorah's warriors would be spearing each one and rolling them all over the cliff. And Grep would be among them.

"The man I told you about," said Nisha, "who killed my husband and my child and took me as his wife. He was back there. He was the one I heard shouting."

"What of it?" Sookim said.

"I wanted to go back," said Nisha. "I wanted to kill him myself. For so many weeks I endured everything for the sake of avenging my kin by taking his life. And now I've missed my only chance."

Sookim stepped forward. She placed her hand on Nisha's shoulder. "I'm sorry," she said. Her voice was suddenly soft. "I thought you were afraid to come with me. Or—I thought, perhaps, you wanted to be away from me."

"No," said Nisha. "No, of course not. And I'm not

afraid; I have far less to fear now than before. I trust you, Sookim. I don't know why, but I do."

"Because I can take care of myself, and I don't depend on other people, and I know the way down from this plateau," Sookim said. The compassion had gone from her voice as quickly as it had appeared. She was brisk and businesslike. "We will survive, you and I. But only if we are clear headed and sensible. If you go back there they will kill you, because they always kill women who try to escape."

"It was the same in the Warrior Tribe," Nisha said.

"Yes. So, are you ready?"

"I'm ready. And thank you, Sookim."

"We don't need to thank each other. If one of us is threatened, the other will protect her—isn't that so?"

"Yes," Nisha agreed.

"So, follow. Believe me, the man you wanted to kill is already dead by now." Sookim turned and started moving quickly among the trees. The moon had risen, and faint light penetrated the branches above, showing the way.

Chapter Thirty

Sookim moved through the forest at a steady trot, dodging among the trees and around boulders. She never looked back, never paused to ask if the pace was too slow or too fast, and Nisha found herself resenting the way that the woman had taken command. Still, she reminded herself, it was Sookim who'd made this possible. Maybe the real problem was that Nisha had never known a woman who was as strong willed as she was.

They ran and ran, until running became an almost unbearable effort. Nisha felt so weary, she didn't understand how her legs still managed to move under her. Her chest ached, her muscles felt rubbery, but still Sookim kept on, and Nisha forced herself to follow. She made a private vow that she would not be the one to call a halt.

Finally, when the moon was high in the sky, they reached a swift-flowing stream. Without a word, Sookim threw herself forward. She lay prostrate on the ground, plunged her face into the stream, and took great mouthfuls of water, pausing after each one to gulp more air.

Nisha dropped her spear and the bag of food and stood for a moment, gasping. Finally she slumped forward beside Sookim and drank deeply from the cold, fresh stream.

They lay in total silence for a long while. There was no sound in the forest, only a light wind rustling through the trees. Finally, Sookim spoke. "I think we are free," she said. She turned toward Nisha, and she smiled. Suddenly she laughed out loud. "We are free," she said again. Impulsively, she seized Nisha and hugged her.

Nisha found it hard to share Sookim's joy. Even though she understood the reasons for running from the Cave People, she still felt as if she had betrayed her own principles somehow.

"Is something wrong?" Sookim asked.

Nisha sighed. "I wanted vengeance. And I think my wish has been granted." She looked up at the black web of branches and wondered whether Jorlor's spirit could see her, and if he approved. "I just wish," she went on, "that there could be an easier way."

Sookim stood up. She grabbed the sack of food and reached down to Nisha with her other hand. "Come," she said. "Bring the spear."

Nisha stood up without speaking. She followed Sookim into a deep thicket of bushes.

"If I were you," said Sookim, "I would be proud." She turned to face Nisha and ran her fingers over the contours of Nisha's face. "You are a brave woman. A fine woman. I wish you'd come to the Cave People five years ago, Nisha. Then I could have had a friend."

"We should rest," Nisha said. She kneeled down and found that the ground was carpeted with old, dry oak leaves from the previous winter. "We'll be cold, Sookim. I can feel the chill already, now that we're not running anymore."

"If we lie close together, we'll be warm enough." She hung the food bag from a nearby branch so that it would be safe from rodents and insects, then kneeled behind Nisha and pulled her close. "Just lie on your side like this," she whispered, with her lips close to Nisha's ear.

They nestled together. Sookim was right, Nisha realized: it was good to be close, and not just for the physical warmth. It had been such a long time since she had trusted anyone enough to enjoy being touched or held. "Thank you," she murmured, as she felt the weariness sweeping over her. "I owe you my freedom. You're a brave woman." And she put her hand over the hand that held her.

Nisha felt something cold on her neck. She woke with a start, reached back, and found a trickle of water. Strange; it hadn't rained during the night. The forest was alive with birdsong, thin sunbeams were slanting among the trees—and Nisha's robe was covered in dew. That was where the moisture had come from.

She sat up, shrugged out of her robe, and shook it.

Sookim yawned and rolled over. Suddenly Nisha felt the woman grabbing her from behind, laughing as she pulled Nisha back down into the leaves. Nisha rolled onto her back and Sookim's face was above hers, hidden in shadow so that not even the purple birthmark was visible. "I feel happy," Sookim said. Her breath was a light caress on Nisha's face. "And it's been so long since the last time I felt happy."

Impulsively, Sookim kissed her. She kissed Nisha's forehead at first, then her cheeks, and then—while she held Nisha's face between her hands—she kissed Nisha on the mouth.

It was a sweet, gentle kiss—and Nisha felt strange emotions flurrying inside her. Sookim was kissing her the way that a lover would, which was wrong—deeply taboo. Yet it was done so impulsively, so gently, it felt natural. But it was still taboo, even so. And why did Nisha feel her pulse speeding up? Why were her cheeks turning red?

Sookim opened her own robe, slid her arms around Nisha's naked body, and pressed herself close. Her skin was so soft and warm, it gave Nisha a physical shock that made her jump. "I want you," Sookim whispered. And her hand reached down to Nisha's thighs.

"But this is wrong!" Nisha cried.

"It is?" Sookim pulled away just a little. "Among the Cave People, this happens all the time. Most of the women find comfort with each other. The men know, but they turned a blind eye."

Nisha swallowed hard. She wanted to pull free—yet she didn't want to. "Not in my tribe," she said. "And in the Warrior Tribe, I think the women would have been too scared to think of doing such a thing."

"You mean," said Sookim, "you've never—"

Nisha quickly shook her head. "Never."

Sookim didn't seem disconcerted. In fact, she looked more intent, more eager than before. "Tell me, Nisha," she said, "where's the wrongness in it? And tell me, who knows more about a woman's body: a man, or another woman?"

Nisha was silent for a long moment. "This is very confusing," she whispered.

"Well, there's one easy way for it to be less confusing," she said, "and that's if you try it." Once again, Sookim pressed close, with her small, high breasts against Nisha's and her legs twined among hers. Sookim moved her hand boldly, now, across Nisha's belly, down between her legs.

Instinctively, Nisha gripped the woman's wrist, trying to restrain her.

"You want it, don't you?" Sookim whispered.

And Nisha realized that she did. During all her time among the Warrior Tribe, sex had been a weapon, nothing more than that. She had gone for months, now, without even thinking that someone might give her sweet, gentle pleasure. She felt her resistance weakening. And then, with a little cry of surrender, she closed her eyes and lay back in the leaves.

It was over soon enough. Sookim's touch was accurate, and she sensed each tiny nuance of Nisha's responses. She brought Nisha to a climax swiftly, and Nisha found herself clutching the other woman, shuddering with the simple pleasure, then slumping back with relief. There had been so much emotion pent up inside her. She hadn't even realized it. She felt as if a huge weight had been extracted from her, leaving her body warm, tingling, and as light as one of the leaves that she lay on.

Slowly, Sookim pulled away. She reached for Nisha's

robe, turned it with the dew facing outward, and pulled it over Nisha's naked body. "You're very beautiful," she said, looking at Nisha's face.

Nisha felt embarrassed. "Thank you," she muttered.

"I've never been beautiful," Sookim said. "Not even when I was younger." She reached up absentmindedly and touched her birthmark. "How does it feel, Nisha, knowing that almost any man would want you?"

"But I like your face," Nisha said. "You have a kind, wise face, Sookim."

"Not a beautiful one, though." She picked up her own robe and put it on. "Tell me, Nisha. Tell me how it feels."

"Well, I've never thought about it." She thought back over the past few months—and over the years before that. She had tempted Jorlor, no doubt about it. Really, she could have had almost any man in her village. And after that, among the Warrior Tribe, she had used her beauty and her sexuality quite shamelessly.

But then, as she thought some more, she saw the penalty that she also paid for being beautiful. "It's good," she said, "to feel that men want me. But it's bad, because I'm always afraid that they won't want me tomorrow. Men get tired of beauty, once they have it. Perhaps that's why I chose an older man for my husband. I wanted to feel sure that he wouldn't get bored with me."

Sookim shook her head slowly. "Strange. To think you would feel unsure of yourself." She shook her hair, then combed her fingers through it, pulling leaves out and tossing them aside. "Well, I suppose we should move on. It's a long journey to my old village."

"Is that where we're going?" Nisha asked, sitting up.

"That's where I'm going," said Sookim. "Don't you want to come with me?" There was a sudden note of caution in her voice.

Nisha hesitated for a moment. "I have a friend," she said, "from my tribe. The only other person who survived. He said he would wait for me with the Green Canyon people."

"Oh." Sookim stood up. She belted her robe with quick, jerky movements.

"But I'll come with you to your village first," said Nisha. "I don't even know the way to Green Canyon." She stood up and touched Sookim's shoulder. "It was—very lovely, what you did to me just now. I feel I should do something in return."

Gradually, the sternness in Sookim's face softened. She gave Nisha a quick, shy glance. "Perhaps there'll be time for that later," she said.

They ate greedy handfuls of the dry corn flour together, and washed it down with more fresh water. Then Sookim led the way along the bank of the stream, and Nisha realized they were walking south now. The water cut through a narrow gap in the rocks at the edge of the plateau, and after she followed Sookim through this little gully, she found herself at the head of a huge rock slide where an entire section of the cliffs had collapsed. The great torrent of boulders fanned out from where she stood, making a treacherous, tumbled path down to the plains far below.

Nisha started climbing laboriously from one boulder to the next, testing each one before she dared to put her weight on it. Her muscles were still weak and sore from the long run last night, and she felt muzzy headed from insufficient sleep. But Sookim was setting the pace once again, and Nisha was determined to keep up.

They spent the entire morning picking their way among the tumble of rocks. Finally, they found themselves stepping into lush vegetation—far more luxuriant than the dry, stunted trees on top of the plateau. Here on the plain were tall pines and spruce, and the air smelled richer.

They ate some more of the corn flour, and neither of them spoke very much. Both of them kept glancing back up at the plateau, half expecting to see warriors from the Cave People up there, searching for them. But the day was serene and silent, and Nisha told herself that the tribe had no real reason to pursue her and Sookim. If Grep was dead—and surely the Cave People must have killed him—there was no one left, now, with a grudge against her. She truly was free.

And yet, as she resumed walking with Sookim, she still didn't feel secure. "I think you know what I'm thinking," she said finally. "I fear the men will come after us. And I think you fear the same thing."

Sookim said nothing. She maintained her steady pace, walking beside the river bank as it snaked across the plain.

"I don't know how to get rid of my fear," Nisha went on. "I don't know how far I have to go before I feel safe from the men back at the cliffs."

"There's nothing we can do," Sookim said, "about those men."

Nisha frowned. "If there's nothing you can do about something, you simply don't worry about it?"

"I try not to," said Sookim.

Nisha laughed. "And you told me that I'm strong. I think you're far stronger than I can ever be."

Sookim glanced back at her. "Thank you," she said. "But I'm only strong if I have someone to be strong with me. I don't do so well, Nisha, when I'm alone."

Nisha gave her a puzzled look. She was thinking back to her first conversation with Sookim, in the pit house. "I thought you said you used to spend a lot of time in solitude. I thought that was how you found the Cave People."

"Did I say that?" Sookim laughed. "I suppose I did. Let's talk about it some other time, Nisha." The words sounded casual, but Nisha heard a hardness in them that discouraged her from asking any more questions.

Late in the afternoon, they came to a place where the water divided itself around a small rise in the land. The stream had become a river, by this time, and its water was slow and dark. Sookim stopped and pointed to some small shapes on top of the island ahead of them. "My people live there," she said. "I grew up in this place. I used to go hunting in the forests all around."

"You must feel excited," said Nisha. "To be home again after so long—"

"Yes," Sookim said. She sounded distracted, and her face was grim as she shaded her eyes against the sun and scanned the island. "Come on." And she started forward without waiting for Nisha to answer.

They crossed the river at a point where the water was so shallow, it barely came up over their ankles. Sookim cupped her hand to her mouth and gave a strange cry, once, twice, and a third time. Then, quickly, she climbed the steep slope where stubbly dry grass grew. At the top was a cluster of little wooden houses thatched with reeds from beside the river—perhaps twenty houses altogether. But most of them were falling down, and grass was growing inside them. The place seemed abandoned, and it was totally deserted.

Nisha looked at Sookim's face. She was grim but not surprised. She made her cry once again—and there was a rustling sound in the thick vegetation that lay just beyond the circle of houses.

A man with a spear came out from under the trees. He was thin, and his robe was ragged and dirty. He stared at the women with wide eyes and stood motionless for a long moment. Then, without a word, he dropped his spear and strode forward. He seized hold of Sookim, hugged her to him, and held her tightly.

There were more rustlings from behind him, and Nisha saw a boy emerging, followed by a woman who looked as if she was in the last month of pregnancy.

Finally the man relaxed his hold on Sookim. He looked at her and blinked, and Nisha saw that he had tears in his eyes. "You still live," he said. Then he grinned. He threw his head back and let out a shout of happy laughter. "You live!"

"Nisha," Sookim said, turning toward her, "this is my cousin Barem." She turned back to the man. "Barem,

Nisha helped me to escape—" She stopped as she saw the boy moving forward. "Is this Jep?"

Barem nodded eagerly. "He hid with me, and our lives were spared. And this is my new wife, Eena. She was a wanderer; she came here a year ago."

"Your wife Ullara—" Sookim began.

"Killed." Barem shrugged. It seemed he was describing something that had happened years ago.

"What happened here?" Nisha asked.

Barem frowned at Sookim. "You didn't tell your friend?"

Sookim looked away. She said nothing.

"What happened?" Nisha asked again.

Sookim turned to her with a look of anguish. "The Cave People came here five years ago. They captured me and two other women, and they killed everyone else—so I thought. The women who were taken with me both tried to escape, and they were killed. It seems that Barem, here, and Jep, are the only ones I have left now."

"But why didn't you tell me?" said Nisha.

"Because—" Sookim looked deeply unhappy. "The only way I managed to keep myself alive among the Cave People was by pretending. I made a story for myself, Nisha. I kept telling myself that all my people were still alive. And I made believe that I was so brave, I had never needed anyone else." She shrugged helplessly. "You see, in some ways, I am not so strong after all."

Barem built a fire, and his wife Eena cleaned some fish that Barem and his son had caught in the river. Nisha and Sookim made flat, simple corn cakes by mixing the last of their flour with water and baking it over the fire. It seemed a meager dinner, yet from the way Eena looked at the corn cakes, it must have been a long time since they had had even this much to eat.

Barem told them that after the Cave People had attacked, he and his son had managed to feed themselves on fish and small game that they trapped in the forest.

They had deliberately allowed the village to become over-
grown and had moved under the trees so that any people
passing by would never realize that anyone lived there.
And this is how they had survived for the past five years.

"But you could have moved farther south, or west,"
Nisha said. "There must be other tribes that would have
taken you in."

"Maybe so," said Barem. "But after what happened—I
was reluctant to trust anyone. And I thought, all this time,
there was just a chance that the women who had been
taken by the raiding party would find a way, somehow, to
return." His gaunt face was deeply shadowed in the flickering firelight.

Looking at him, Nisha decided he was a good person,
a decent man, but just like Sookim, he had been unable to
face the reality of what had happened to his people. Loyalty and hope had kept him here—but this had not been a
wise decision.

"I was telling Sookim there's a tribe called the Green
Canyon people," Nisha said. "A friend of mine, from my
own people, said he would wait for me there. He said
they are friendly and good."

"I've heard of them," said Eena. She had hardly spoken,
and she seemed to have been lost in her own thoughts for
much of the time. She hadn't said anything about her own
life and how she happened to have wandered here. "In
fact," she went on, "I saw the Green Canyon once. It's
wide and long, and there was a large settlement, even then.
I can tell you how to find it, I think."

Nisha felt a little surge of hope as she heard those
words. But she also felt frustration. "You should all come
with me," she said. She looked from Barem, to Eena, to
Jep, and Sookim. "It's not safe here. The Cave People
could easily come back this way if they decide to search
for me or Sookim. And there's barely enough food to
keep you alive."

Eena glanced uneasily at Barem. She said nothing.

Barem shook his head emphatically. "This is our home," he said.

Nisha decided there was no point in humoring the man. It would serve him far better if he could let go of his fantasy and face the truth. "Your home has been destroyed," she said. "There is nothing for you here anymore. There is no one else left from your people, now that Sookim has returned. There's no good reason to stay here."

He gave her a fierce look—but she saw the pain in his eyes. "This is our home!" he said again, with a tremor in his voice. "In any case," he went on, "Eena will give birth soon. She can't travel."

"But how can she raise a young baby here, hiding in the woods?" Nisha objected.

"All right, maybe when the baby is born, we will think about moving." Barem turned away from her. He poked the fire with a stick. "It is not good, Nisha, for you to tell me what's best for my people. That's for me to decide."

Nisha saw the futility of it. "I'm sorry," she said. "But if the Cave People come—"

"I'll hide from them with Barem," said Sookim, "just as Barem hid from us when we arrived. We'll be safe enough."

Nisha looked at her sadly. "So you, too, are staying here."

Sookim shrugged. "Of course. Barem is my cousin, and this is my home."

Later, Nisha lay close beside Sookim on a bed of dry ferns, in a simple shelter created by bending living saplings into an arch and tying them in place with vines. This little hideaway was where Barem normally slept with his wife, but he had insisted that Nisha and Sookim should have it.

Nisha realized that Barem was ashamed that he wasn't able to offer proper hospitality. It would have hurt his pride if she refused his offer, so she accepted it, and was glad to do so. Her limbs still ached from her long journey, and she was eager for a good night of rest.

The river made faint sounds close by, and owls screamed in the forest. It was much warmer here than it had been on the plateau, but still Nisha found herself cuddling close to the woman beside her. "I wish you would come with me," she whispered.

"And I wish you would stay here," Sookim said, without looking at Nisha.

"But you see why it's sensible—"

"Yes, I see." Sookim sounded weary. "All I know, Nisha, is that people always leave. I've never really had anyone, you know, as a mate. They never want to stay with me."

Nisha made a little impatient sound. "Turn over," she said.

"Not so loud. I don't want my kin to hear us talking."

"Turn over!" Nisha said again, lowering her voice but making it more insistent.

Reluctantly, Sookim turned to face her. There was very little light, but Nisha thought she saw tears glistening on Sookim's face.

"I'm not leaving you," Nisha whispered. "You're choosing to stay. Don't you see?"

Sookim avoided her eyes.

"When the baby is born," said Nisha, "I want you to try to make the journey to Green Canyon with your cousin and his son and his wife, and their new child." She gave Sookim a little shake. "You know that it's the sensible choice. You know it! You see how thin they are. They can't cultivate the land for fear of someone seeing that there are people living here. They have no food cache. Winter will be here in three months. How will you survive?"

"You want me to follow you?" Sookim whispered.

"Of course. You're a good person, and you can be a brave person. I was looking forward to getting to know you better. And—" She hesitated. "No woman has ever done—what you did with me."

Sookim clutched Nisha, then kissed her. "I was afraid you must be disgusted with me," she whispered. "After I lied to you about what had happened to my people, and you saw how weak I really am."

Nisha stroked her hair. "You just need to believe in yourself a little more," she said. "It's strange that you have so little confidence in yourself."

"Because I'm marked," Sookim said, turning her face as if she was afraid that Nisha could see the birthmark even in the dark. "They used to say such bad things. They said that when I was a baby, a bear who ate purple berries had spat on my face—"

"You're being foolish." Nisha deliberately took Sookim's face in her hands, turned it toward her, and kissed the spot where she knew the birth mark lay.

Sookim relaxed in Nisha's arms. "You're very kind to me," she said.

"Well, I owe you a lot," Nisha said. "I might be a prisoner back in that terrible pit house if it weren't for you." She slid her hand inside Sookim's robe. A part of her was surprised at being so bold, once again breaking a taboo that she had never even questioned until that morning. But Sookim had unlocked something inside her, and the woman's shyness, now, just made Nisha feel more confident.

"I want to repay your kindness in any way I can," she whispered, as her fingers touched Sookim's side, then her belly, and moved lower.

Sookim's breathing quickened, but she didn't resist. She lay passively as Nisha touched her. It was strange, Nisha thought—like touching her own body, except she felt nothing. It was like stepping outside of her own skin, seeing herself in the other woman.

Sookim gasped and pressed her knuckles to her mouth for fear of making too much noise. She stiffened. She made a faint sound at the back of her throat. Then she reached her climax, and then she lay limp.

Nisha watched as the woman slowly drifted into sleep. She stroked Sookim's face. "You are a strange person," Nisha whispered. "And I hardly know you. But I will miss you, all the same."

An owl in the forest screeched again. The moon crept above the horizon, mice and voles scurried amid the vegetation on the forest floor, and on either side of the village on the island, the river flowed on.

PART FOUR

Justice

Chapter Thirty-One

Nisha stood staring across a vista that was unlike anything she had ever seen before. She had been striding through tall, dry grass under the noontime sun, with her spear slung across her shoulder and a water bag that was almost empty slapping against her hip. She had been wondering if she would ever find Green Canyon, and thinking that perhaps Eena's directions had been wrong. Then she had noticed a ragged line dividing the plain ahead of her, and then, as she came closer, she realized that there was a great gulf, a gap in the land as if a giant hand had reached down and torn away all the rocks and soil.

The canyon was so wide, the bottom of it was an entire self-contained world of its own. There were little houses scattered down there and scores of cultivated fields. A river snaked through the center, and the land looked impossibly lush and green. Nisha saw tiny figures moving in the fields, and in the far distance, a great cluster of houses like a dozen villages put together.

The only question was how she could ever find her way down to the floor of the canyon. She scanned the rim in both directions. Then, in the distance, she saw someone toiling up a tiny path. She followed the line of the path in the canyon wall and realized that it emerged at a point no more than five hundred paces away. If she set off now, she might reach the top of the trail just before the person who was climbing up it.

Nisha made her decision. She moved purposefully,

taking long strides, feeling the grass brushing her knees and thighs. She wondered if it was safe to approach someone this way—but she trusted Winnor, and Winnor had seemed sure that the people here were friendly. In any case, Nisha told herself, she had her spear. And she could see clearly that there were no other strangers close by. It would just be her and the person on the path.

Still, she felt nervous as she hurried across the grassland.

When she came to the head of the trail, she looked down it and saw that the traveler was now within hailing distance. He was a man in his middle years but still moving with a spring in his step despite the long climb. He was using his spear as a staff to steady himself as he followed the narrow, rocky path. He saw Nisha, but he didn't pause and he didn't seem concerned. He came closer, till he was just a dozen paces away.

"Greetings," she called to him. She held her own spear by her side, where she could raise it in a moment if she had to, and she stayed a couple of paces back from the top of the narrow pathway, so she could run away across the plain, through the tall grass, if she had to.

The man stopped. He pulled something out from under his robe that looked like a scrap of hide but seemed thinner and more supple, so it actually rippled in the breeze. He wiped his forehead with it, then tucked it away again. "Greetings," he said to Nisha. The word sounded odd, the way he said it, but it was still recognizable. He took another couple of paces, then stopped again. He was squinting up at her with clear blue eyes. His face had been tanned a dark brown, reminding Nisha of the people of her own tribe who spent most of their lives exposed to the desert sun.

"Stranger, eh?" he said.

He was still leaning on his spear, but she saw him shift some of his weight off it, so that he could use it if he had to. She tensed—then realized that he might have just as much to fear from visitors as she had to fear from him. "I come in peace," she said.

He nodded slowly. "That's good," he said. "We're peaceful people." Still, his eyes were watchful. "Where are you from?"

Nisha hesitated. "If you have a little time, and if you don't mind speaking to a stranger, perhaps we could talk for a little while?" She noticed there were a couple of boulders a little way back from the edge of the canyon. It would make her feel more confident if he was sitting instead of standing opposite her, ready to raise his spear.

He shrugged. "I'll talk," he said. "I have nothing against strangers, so long as they're friendly."

Nisha moved back toward the boulders. She lowered herself onto one of them, still keeping hold of her spear in her right hand. She wanted to trust this man, even though she had learned, in the past few months, that most men could not be trusted.

Cautiously, the man sat opposite her. "Perhaps you should put down your weapon," he said.

"If you will do the same," she said, trying to sound more confident than she felt.

He laughed, showing teeth that were surprisingly white for a man his age. "A fair trade," he said.

Together, they lowered their spears into the grass—then dropped them. He raised both hands and held them out toward Nisha, palms up. She did the same. He grinned and took her palms and held them for a moment, and as she clasped his hands in turn, she felt the weight of her suspicions and anxiety lifting from her. She hadn't realized quite how nervous she had been.

"You've learned to be cautious, eh?" the man said.

Nisha nodded. Her smile faded as she thought of everything she had been through. "Most of my tribe were killed by invaders," she said. "My husband, my child—" She looked away.

"So what brings you here?" he asked.

"A friend of mine. A man from my people. His name is Winnor, and he told me to follow him here."

The man nodded. He said nothing.

"Have you heard of him?" Nisha asked. "He's a shaman; he has powerful magic."

"Winnor." He frowned, then shook his head. "I tend my fields down there, with my family. I don't pay much attention to strangers unless I run across them." He rubbed the side of his jaw. "You should go to the town of many houses, there." He pointed to the great cluster of little dwellings in the far distance, down on the canyon floor. "If your friend is in Green Canyon, someone there will have heard of him. Everyone goes to the town of many houses sooner or later, to trade."

Nisha gazed at the land below. "This is so strange," she said. "Life looks so easy, with so much water and so much land to till. I should think you'd be overrun by strangers coming here. And surely there must be tribes near here who would try to kill your people and seize your land for themselves."

The man chuckled. "The Sun God protects us, girl. See how he smiles down on us? We offer him gifts, and he treats us as his children."

Nisha laughed bitterly. "My people believed that Sun Spirit protected them," she said. "But still, we were overrun, and almost everyone was killed."

The man opposite her was silent for a moment. The easy smile left his face, and his eyes narrowed as he looked past Nisha, into the distance. "I shouldn't give you the wrong idea," he said. She saw that his good humor was like a robe that clothed an inner self that was not so gentle, but was hard and shrewd. "We worship the Sun God," he said, "but we also take care of ourselves. There are warriors down there who patrol the canyon. And each little village has a covenant with all the others. If one is ever threatened, all the others will defend it. All of them." He paused, waiting to see that she grasped what he was saying.

"I understand," she said.

"There are hundreds of people living in Green Canyon," he went on. "Hundreds, girl. Years ago, there were a couple of tribes near here who tried to steal from us—but we outnumbered them four to one. We defended ourselves, and we fought the men who were too stubborn or foolish to leave us alone. And now, no one interferes with us."

Nisha tried to imagine being part of such a strong community, where she would never again have to fear for her life. It had seemed to be like that on the mesa where she lived with her people, till the raiding party from the Warrior Tribe had come. Her people had thought they were invulnerable, living on top of the mesa in the big, wide valley. Perhaps this man in front of her was being over-confident, and yet his people had established themselves on a far larger scale.

She looked down at the lush fields. "It must be good to live here," she said.

He heard the wistfulness in her voice. "There's still some room for newcomers," he said. "So long as you respect our ways and don't take anything that belongs to someone else. You understand?"

"Would it be safe for me to go to the—the town of many houses?" She turned again toward the distant cluster of buildings.

He shrugged. "Of course. If you don't interfere with anyone, no one will interfere with you. Go there. But go in peace." He slapped his hands on his knees. "I have things to do. There are some herbs that grow up here on the plain, and they don't grow down in the canyon because the soil is too moist. So, I have to gather them." He picked up his spear, then stood up. "Good fortune, young woman." He nodded to her.

"Thank you," she said. She watched as he moved away among the tall grass. He walked calmly, with confidence, knowing that he had no enemies here.

She realized suddenly that he hadn't told her his name.

That was strange for a man who seemed so friendly. But then she reconsidered. Perhaps he had not really been as friendly as he seemed. He hadn't offered her any food or water, even though he was carrying ample supplies, and she must look travel weary after walking for so many days. He had told her she could go down into the canyon, and no one would interfere with her—but he had warned her not to take anything that belonged to other people. And from up here, it looked as if every piece of land had been claimed.

Really, Nisha thought, he hadn't been friendly at all. He had been polite, which was very different. Still, she thought, that was far better than she had feared. She picked up her spear and got to her feet. She was hungry; it had been a long journey from the island where she had left Sookim, Barem, Eena, and Jep, and she had only managed to spear a few rabbits and a couple of squirrels along the way. Those, and some berries, were all she'd eaten. Still, there must be food to spare down in Green Canyon. And surely, if she asked for help, someone would share a little of their supplies, at least till she found Winnor.

Her own people had always been generous and hospitable, on the rare occasions when strangers passed by, even though the land around the mesa had been far less bountiful than the land here in the canyon. If the people here had so much more, wouldn't they be willing to spare a little of it?

The path down into the canyon was long, narrow, and treacherous. Many times, loose pebbles and gravel slid under her moccasins, and she had to steady herself with her spear, like the man she had found climbing the path.

By the time she reached the canyon floor, it was past noon, and she was hungrier than ever. She drained the last of her water, then started along a trail that seemed to lead toward the town of many houses. Now that she was at the bottom of the canyon, her view of the town was blocked by nearby trees. Still, it would be hard to get lost down here, with the canyon walls to guide her.

The path was wide and straight—as straight as a sunbeam striking across the land. Nisha marveled at it. The surface was slightly rounded so that rain would run off to either side, and stone chips had been strewn over the packed earth. She couldn't begin to imagine the labor that it had taken to build such a thing.

Then she looked more closely at the fields, and she marveled again. The corn plants were bigger than she had ever seen—at least twice the size of the plants that she had cultivated with such desperate care out in the desert. But corn was not the only crop here. She saw agave plants in neat rows, and barley, and lima beans, squash, and amaranth. All the fields were lush, fed by irrigation ditches that had been dug just as straight and true as the path that she was walking on.

Back on the plateau, when she'd seen the Cave People's fields there for the first time, she'd been impressed by the scale of them. But that had been a tiny enterprise compared with the vista down here.

She walked past a cluster of little houses. They were constructed in a style she'd never seen before, using stone up to waist height and wood above that. She heard women talking together and laughing as they worked out in the sun. They were sitting in front of some frames of thin wood, and at first Nisha thought they must be stretching animal hide—but the frames didn't look strong enough for that. A web of fine strands had been stretched across them, and Nisha realized that the women were somehow interlacing the strands, creating large woven squares that flapped in the wind like the small fragment that the man on the cliff path had used to mop his forehead. The craft was like basket weaving, but with strands so fine, the result was more flexible than animal hide.

One of the women noticed Nisha staring at her. She paused, scrutinized her, then nodded a polite greeting before she continued her work.

Nisha moved on along the path. She was beginning to feel intimidated by these people. Could there really be a place for her here? She had none of their skills. She knew how to hunt—but she doubted there was much game in the canyon. There were few places where even a prairie dog could hide, let alone a mule deer.

She saw a man walking toward her, carrying a sack on his shoulder. The wind blew his scent to her, and she smelled the intoxicating aroma of fresh-baked corn bread. She made up her mind. She had to do something. "Greetings!" she called out to him.

He stopped in front of her. He was tall and heavily muscled. His hair was long, clasped behind his head and hanging below his waist. It was so clean, it shimmered in the sun. He was carrying a fine spear and wearing a robe that had been beautifully decorated with red and black zigzag patterns and pictures of scorpions and snakes. Nisha looked more closely and realized that the robe had been made from thousands of thin strands woven together, just like the squares that the women had been working on with their wooden frames. And the pictures weren't drawn or painted on the robe, they had been woven into it with amazing skill.

He saw her staring, and he smiled. "Stranger," he said.

"Yes." She looked down, feeling embarrassed by her torn, dirty deerskin and her moccasins, which were ragged from her long journey. Her face, she knew, must be lined with grime, and her hair was dull with dust. "I'm looking for a man named Winnor," she said. "He's a shaman. A healer. If he's here, he would have arrived in the last two or three months. Do you know—"

"There's a new healer in the town of many houses," said the man facing her. "That may be him." He nodded to her and started to walk on by.

"Please!" Nisha called to him.

He stopped.

"Please, I wonder—I'm so hungry. Do you have food in your sack?"

He paused for a moment. "You have something to trade?"

Surely, he could see how poor she was? She spread her hands helplessly. "My people were killed, and I was captured, and I escaped—I have nothing."

He glanced down at her hand. "What do you have there on your finger?"

"This?" She slipped off the little circle of woven beargrass that she had made—when? She thought back for a moment. She had been lying by the stream on the day after she had escaped from the Warrior Tribe. Somehow, this little woven ring had survived all the days since then.

"Here," he said. He reached into his sack and pulled out a big piece of freshly baked corn bread. He held it out on his open palm.

She placed the little woven ring of grass on his hand, and took the bread.

He nodded. "Good fortune to you, stranger."

"But—" She shook her head in confusion. "You have such fine clothes. Why would you want a little ring made of grass?"

He looked down at her. He seemed so strong and sure of himself, she wondered why he was even bothering to talk to her. "All things have value," he said. "Perhaps I'll meet someone who wants this." He tossed the little ring and caught it. "A child may want to play with it. Or I may keep it to remind me of this hungry young woman I saw on the road." He tucked the ring away and hung the bag of bread over his shoulder again. "If you learn to live in Green Canyon," he went on, "you'll learn to trade. That's the way of our people. Everyone has a skill— something he can make or do, which his neighbor may want more than he does."

She found herself staring at him, even forgetting her own hunger as she saw the real meaning of his words. The people here in the canyon hadn't cultivated the fields and learned their skills because someone had told them to, and they hadn't done it as a gift to one another. They had done it because they wanted to exchange things with one another. "What is *your* skill?" she said—and then wondered if it was rude to ask.

"I am a warrior," he said. "I walk the canyon and I protect the people from danger." He eyed her again, sternly but not in a way that made her feel scared of him. "And sometimes," he went on, "I may help strangers along the way." He gave her a curt nod. "Go to the town of many houses. Ask for the new healer. He may be the man you seek."

"Thank you," she said. She watched him in wonder as he walked past her, away down the path.

Chapter Thirty-Two

As she walked farther, she found more and more people on the path. Many were carrying heavy bags or bundles that looked as if they contained food harvested from the fields. Men and women greeted one another, and some of them nodded politely to Nisha, though no one actually stopped to ask her who she was or where she had come from.

She passed among an outlying group of stone houses, and then she found herself facing the town itself. She stopped and stared at it in wonder. The village built by the Cave People had been a clutter of dwellings that were attached to one another in a haphazard fashion. Here, she saw that the town had been created by people who had known what they wanted to build long before they actually started shaping and placing the stones. The dwellings were all in the same style, and they joined onto each other seamlessly, forming a great circle. She walked in through the main entrance, and she found another, smaller circle of homes inside. In the pathway between the two circles was a marketplace, with vendors sitting on the paved stone offering food, trinkets, blankets, robes, and clay pots beautifully ornamented with the same zigzag patterns that she had seen on the robe of the man who had given her the corn bread.

Nisha forgot, for a moment, the reason for her quest. She wandered among the people, staring at the vast variety of handmade objects and the great quantities of food. The traders were shouting out their wares and calling to passersby, but Nisha noticed that none of them called to her. They could see that she had nothing to offer in return.

It was all so strange compared with her old tribe. On the mesa, there had never been a surplus of anything, but all of it had belonged to everybody—except for a few special, personal objects and the home that a person lived in. If she had been short of food, she had gone to anyone else's home and taken whatever she wanted. If she had needed water, she had taken it from the cistern in the sure knowledge that sooner or later she would do her part, helping her neighbors to refill it.

Here in the town of many houses, she realized that there was no communal property. Everything belonged to someone. And nothing belonged to her.

She was so distracted by the market, she found herself bumping into a man who had been walking in the opposite direction. "I'm sorry," she said, stepping back—and she found herself looking at a figure unlike any she had ever seen before. He was plump, as if he had spent his whole life feasting. His skin was strangely smooth, and there was no trace of hair on his jaw. His face looked almost like the face of a woman.

"What are you looking for?" he asked her. His voice was higher pitched than normal; it hardly sounded like a man's voice.

"I'm looking for a shaman," she said. "A healer named Winnor. He came here—"

"His house is down there," the man said, pointing through a gap in the inner circle of buildings, toward some smaller houses nearer the center. "You'll find it easily enough. He has the skin of a mountain cat outside it." He nodded to Nisha, then moved on.

Nisha struggled to absorb this news. Winnor was here. Her journey was over. The strange, plump man hadn't needed to think twice about it.

Nisha broke into a run. Her moccasins slapped on the stone paving and she dodged among people as she hurried into the very center of the town. The houses here were jumbled together, and they looked more weather worn, as if this part of the town had been built first and the rest had come later. But Nisha hardly noticed. She ran among the buildings until, suddenly, she found herself looking at the skin of a mountain lion with its head dangling down over a doorway and its jaws gaping wide.

The open doorway stood in front of her. Nisha hesitated. Could this really be Winnor's house? She was afraid to hope for too much. She took a tentative step forward, and then another, and then she ducked inside.

The air smelled of smoke and herbs. A figure was bent over a wooden table, using a rounded stone to crush some wildflowers. A small fire burned amid a circle of stones. A big clay pot hung over it, emitting lazy wisps of steam. There were charms and amulets hanging around the walls, and another catskin, this one patterned with circles and spirals and mountain shapes. Nisha stared at the drawings, and now she knew she had come to the right house, because the art was in the style of her tribe. She had seen Winnor wearing that skin many times: at feasts and festivals, and when he used his magic to cure illnesses.

"Winnor," she called softly.

The man paused in his work and looked up at her. He stopped and stared. "Nisha?" he said. Then he dropped the rounded stone, and it thumped down onto the table. He stood up and strode toward her. "Nisha!" he shouted, and threw his arms around her.

Suddenly she felt as if no time at all had passed since she'd said goodbye to him outside the village of the Warrior Tribe. The tension and the expectation flowed out of her in a rush, and her legs almost collapsed under her.

"Here, sit!" he said, holding her arm, steadying her, leading her to a big stone with a flat top located near the fire. "Sit, warm yourself—would you like some soup?"

She was staring at him, still hardly able to believe that she had found him.

"You're thin," he said. "Are you all right? You must have

traveled far. Eat, girl!" He picked up a ladle that someone had painstakingly carved out of wood, and he spooned broth and large chunks of meat into a clay bowl. He picked up another piece of wood—then hesitated. "You've never used a spoon before," he said. "But here, I'll show you. I'll do it for you. Rest! Are you well? Are you unhurt?"

She was still staring at him. She had never seen him this way before. In fact, he had changed. In her tribe, he had always seemed so fierce and stern. She had been frightened, sometimes, of the magic that she sensed around him. And now here he was acting like her father—or her husband, even.

She took the bowl from him. "I'll manage," she said. And she took the spoon. It was simple enough, after all, to use it to push the food into her mouth. She suddenly found herself eating with ferocious hunger, and the smell of the cooked meat made her feel dizzy.

He saw her need, and he was wise enough not to ask any more questions. When she emptied the bowl, he filled it again, and then again.

Finally, when she had eaten so much that her stomach pained her, she set the bowl aside. "Winnor, I've been through so much," she said, "and I have so much to tell you. I didn't really believe I'd ever see you again. And I'm so happy to be here." Despite herself, she found that she was crying.

He went to her, stood her up, and took her to a separate room at the back of the house. Ignoring her protests, he made her lie down on a springy bed of branches covered in bison skin. It was just like the bed that she had slept on with Jorlor, back at the mesa, and she found herself crying some more. "Please don't look at me," she muttered, trying to hide her face from him. "I've been so strong and brave, Winnor, you wouldn't believe the things I've done, and the things that have happened to me. Please don't watch me now." She didn't want him to lose any respect for her. It was terrible to feel weak like this.

"There's no sin in showing your emotions, Nisha," he told her. "Just rest now. We can talk afterward."

"No, I'm not tired," she said. But even as she spoke, she felt a great wave of weariness sweeping over her, and she felt her mind becoming overwhelmed by fuzzy warmth from the stew that she'd eaten.

"Sleep," he said again, and he spread a sheepskin over her. She felt its gentle touch against her shoulder—and that was the last she knew before her eyes fell shut.

When she woke, she saw the sky through a square window in the opposite wall, and it was a deep purple. She had slept right through the afternoon.

She stirred, and the branches creaked under her. "Winnor?" she called.

"I'm here." His voice came from the shadows on the opposite side of the room.

Nisha blinked, feeling startled. He was wearing the ornamented catskin that she had noticed before. His face was composed, deeply serious. She marveled at the change in him.

"Cat Spirit has been speaking to me," he said. "I asked for his power, to restore your strength." He stood up and slowly took off the skin, handling it with deep respect. "It's good that you came here, Nisha. I was sure you would die among the Warrior Tribe. But you'll be safe here now. There's no doubt of that." He came and squatted down on the floor beside her bed. "How do you feel now?"

"Stronger," she said. "Although—this place confuses me, Winnor. The town of many houses. It's so different from everything I know. It scares me."

He smiled. "It scares you, and the Warrior Tribe did not?"

She smiled with embarrassment. "The Warrior Tribe scared me in a different way. What I mean is—these people here seem to know so much. And they have so much. And I have nothing."

He nodded gravely. "When I came here myself, two months ago, I wondered if there was a place for me," he said. "But a healer had died, and they needed someone to take his place. With so many people living in the canyon, Nisha, they need three healers. Well, it was easy enough for me to prove myself. One of the chieftain's sons had the coughing sickness, which was simple for me to cure. The Green Canyon people are hard workers, and great builders, and you see how much they've achieved. But there are things they have forgotten, which I still know— the ways of the spirits, and the healing powers of plants. These people have a need for me, Nisha. So they have given me a lot in return." He gestured around him at the stone house. "All this is mine now."

"I see." She nodded slowly. "So you give them your skill, and they give you a home, and food—it's another kind of trade."

"That's right. Everything here is based on trade."

"But what happens to people who have no skill?" she said. She wanted to add—people like her. But she felt scared to talk that way.

"People who have no skill must work in the fields," he said. "They receive food and clothes and shelter, but not much more. In this tribe—which is really a group of tribes—some people are richer than others, and no one objects, because that is the custom."

"It sounds cruel," she said. And it sounded a little grim, too. She tried to imagine working out there in the canyon, tilling the land, doing the same thing every day. It wasn't so different from the life of the women up on the plateau, working in the fields for the men of the Cave People. And yet, there was a difference, because it seemed that anyone who lived in Green Canyon was free to come and go as he pleased.

Still, it was a dull existence when she compared it to her life on the mesa, where she could spend whole days ranging out across the prairie with Jorlor if she chose, and if the hunting was bad and they came home empty handed, there was still a warm welcome for them and food that they could share.

"The customs here can seem selfish," Winnor said. "But you see how the people profit from the arrangement. Even the simple laborers here eat better than we ever did, Nisha. And they are safe here. No other tribe would dare to attack them." He shifted restlessly. "So tell me now, speaking of other tribes—what happened after I left you with the Warrior Tribe?"

She forced herself to think back. Even though it had been less than three weeks ago, it seemed like another lifetime. Haltingly at first, she told Winnor how she had used his suggestion of pitting one tribe against the other. She told him how she had planted the idea in Grep's mind, and how she had escaped from the village and warned the chieftain of the Cave People. Finally, she told him how she had freed herself with Sookim.

"So your task is done," he said, at the end of her long story. He stood up, went into the other room, and returned with a lamp that he had lit from the fire. Nisha saw that the lamp was a bowl made of clay, and it was filled with oil. The flame somehow clung to some twisted strands that stood in the center of the oil. She stared at it in fascination.

Winnor placed the lamp on a shelf. "Your task is done," he said again, "and yet—I see that your spirit is still not at peace, Nisha."

She felt disconcerted. She thought she felt happy to be with Winnor, in the security of this house, and yet, she knew from experience that he had an unerring skill at seeing into her. "I suppose I'm worried about finding a place in this tribe," she said, "but I don't think—"

"You are not at peace," he said again, with calm certainty. "Are you sure you truly finished the task that you set yourself?"

She felt a sudden pang. She'd driven out of her mind the idea that Grep might still be alive. But perhaps this was what Winnor had sensed in her. Haltingly, she told him about the cry for mercy that she had heard out on the edge of the cliffs, when the fighting had been almost over.

Winnor was silent for a long time—so silent, she felt he was no longer even aware of her. "So your enemy may have somehow evaded you," he murmured. He reached out his hand to her. "Come with me into the other room."

Obediently, she followed him. The town was quiet now; all the people who had been outside in the street seemed to have gone into their houses now that night had come. A cool wind whispered in through the open doorway.

Winnor picked something up, and Nisha saw it was a large, heavy panel of the woven stuff, folded into quarters. "What is that?" she asked.

"This is a blanket made of cloth," he said. "A plant—the cotton plant—grows well here, because there is so much water. Feel." He held the cloth out to her.

Nisha ran her fingers over the texture of it. It was unlike anything she had ever touched or seen before. "I wonder if I could learn how to weave cotton like this, one day," she said.

He grunted dismissively. "There are much more important skills for you." He unfolded the blanket and hung it over the doorway. Then he took another blanket and hung it over the door to the other room. "Now, the spirits will stay here with us," he said.

She sat on the stone near the fire and watched him as he went to his table and opened some small catskin pouches. "What are you doing?" she asked.

"There is a part of you which I cannot quite see—which even you cannot see," he said. "The spirits may show it to you, if we help them." He put together some herbs from the pouches, ground them into a powder with his stone pestle, then tipped the powder into a clay cup. He went to the cooking pot and used the ladle to add hot broth to the cup. "This man Grep may still live," Winnor said, "but even so, you have still avenged your tribe, Nisha. You've been so brave and resourceful, you've done more than any young woman could hope to do. You should feel proud."

"I do feel proud," she said. But even as she spoke, she heard the words ringing false. She lowered her eyes.

He nodded slowly. "There is something stopping you from taking the satisfaction and the peace of mind that should be yours," he said. "Drink, now." He held out the cup.

She took it. The strange smell of the herbs mixed unpleasantly with the familiar aroma of the broth. She forced herself to drain the cup quickly, in one gulp.

When she looked up, Winnor was wearing his lionskin again. He slowly crouched down, and the fire threw his huge flickering shadow onto the stone wall behind him. He poured water onto the stones around the flames, and steam billowed up. Suddenly he raised his hands, and they were like claws. He made a low growling sound, and Nisha wanted to leap up and run from him, because at that moment it seemed as if he was not just possessed by Cat Spirit, he had actually turned into a mountain lion. But something about the look of him made her feel as if she couldn't move. The flickering walls seemed to draw closer around her as Winnor started chanting, then stood and danced a leaping cat dance around the fire.

Nisha's body hardly seemed to belong to her anymore. She seemed to be drifting away, and her mind was suspended in space. She could no longer tell whether her eyes were open or closed.

There was a strange, metallic taste in her mouth, and distantly she felt herself doubling forward. There was a hand on her shoulder, and something in front of her—a clay bowl. Her stomach churned; she vomited.

But these things were in a world that no longer concerned her. Here in the darkness was the real world, and she realized with a shock that she was back on the mesa, lying in bed with Jorlor, listening to the terrible sounds of strange men making their way stealthily into the village.

Fear displaced her serenity. She was in the village—yet

she was outside herself, watching herself, at the same time. She saw the look of fear on her face. And she saw something else: the look of guilt.

Her people were asleep and unarmed. They were helpless. They would be killed—because they had been unprepared. And she herself was to blame. She had seen the footprint when she had been out with Jorlor the previous afternoon. She had known that strangers must be nearby. Yet she had done nothing. She could have warned her people—but she had failed.

"Wake up!" she screamed. "People, wake up!"

But it was too late, and the blackness was suddenly red with blood. Nisha found herself clutching herself, dizzy and gasping, with Winnor standing over her, kneading the back of her neck. She was in his house again. Only moments had passed, though it seemed like a whole night.

Nisha shuddered. She let out a despairing sob.

"Speak," Winnor murmured to her. "Say what you have learned."

She was crying uncontrollably now. Her face was wet with tears.

"Tell me," Winnor prompted her again. "You must say it, else you will never be free."

Despairingly, she turned to him. "It was my fault," she gasped. "All the people dead. My husband and my own child. I could have warned everyone, but I didn't. I'm to blame, Winnor, for the death of my people."

Chapter Thirty-Three

From outside the window, she heard the cries of traders in the market. There were footsteps and the murmur of people talking in the street. Nisha lay staring up at the square of blue sky, feeling a burden of despair that she hadn't known before—because she had refused to allow it into her mind.

She thought of Sookim, who wouldn't believe that her tribe had been massacred. Nisha had wondered how the woman could deceive herself so completely. But now she saw that Sookim had not been the only one who needed to lie to herself in order to live her life. It was a fact that Nisha had seen a footprint of a stranger on the day before her people died. It was a fact that she could have warned them to be alert for danger.

Of course, she could blame Jorlor, too. He had known about the footprint, and had done nothing. But Jorlor was gone now. She was the only one left to shoulder the responsibility.

She could tell herself that there were good reasons for not having worried about the possibility of strangers being nearby. The few people who traveled across the desert always seemed friendly. Her tribe had lived so long without fear, it was natural to assume that outsiders were friendly.

But still the fact remained: She could have done something, and she didn't.

She heard a faint noise and saw Winnor standing in the doorway. He had insisted, last night, that she should sleep in his bed while he slept in the other room. "So you are awake," he said, looking down at her.

She stared up at his face. In her days on the mesa, she had seen only the stern wisdom in him. But here, she saw the kindness. Suddenly she realized why: In her village, he had been a leader second only to the chieftain. Here in the town of many houses, he didn't have that responsibility anymore; he was just a healer.

"You still blame yourself?" he said, looking at her face.

She gave a little shrug. "Of course. How can it be otherwise?"

"You know that even if you had warned everyone, they might have paid no attention," he told her. "We were a trusting people, a peaceful people, and we were unprepared to defend ourselves. That was our fault, Nisha, not yours. The real responsibility for that lay with our chieftain—and with me, too, perhaps."

She smiled at him sadly. "Thank you, Winnor. But your words can't change the way I feel inside."

He sighed. "I feared you would feel that way." His face became solemn, and he seemed to draw back into himself. The kindness that she'd seen a moment ago was suddenly gone. "A person moved by guilt," he went on, "may find it hard to blame herself—and will blame others instead. She may want to punish herself—but again, she punishes others. Do you think, Nisha, that this is what happened to you, after they took you from the mesa? Was part of your vengeance against the warrior tribe driven by your own guilt, because you felt you had failed your people?"

She thought back. Certainly, she hadn't blamed herself then; the idea that she was partly responsible for the death of her people had been so awful, she had refused to think about it. Yet, she decided, Winnor was right: She had wanted to punish the Warrior Tribe in order to free herself from her own pain.

"You are very wise, Winnor," she said, looking up at him with deep respect.

The shaman eyed her solemnly. "Your real need was to

atone for your guilt," he said. "You can never find peace otherwise. I think atonement is still what you need, even now. You have not yet suffered for the sin that you feel you committed."

His words chilled her. "But I've gone through so much," she said. "I made my vow to the spirits of my loved ones, and I honored it. I suffered terribly. I still have the marks on my back from the beatings Grep gave me. It was awful, living in that village." She looked up at him, searching for the kindness that had been there before. "Please, Winnor, I need to heal my wounds, not endure new ones."

He rested his hand on her forehead for a moment, and his palm was dry and cool. The touch of it seemed magical; it calmed her churning emotions. "I will never hurt you, Nisha," he said softly. "It is up to you, now, to do whatever needs to be done." He turned away. "First you must eat, because you are still undernourished. Then you must bathe. And then you will offer yourself to Sun Spirit, and he will do what needs to be done."

Without explaining himself any further, he turned and left the room.

She dressed in her same ragged robe, because she had no other clothes. Winnor didn't offer her any, and she sensed that it wasn't her place to ask.

He served her fresh rabbit and bread made from rice grass and amaranth seeds. The rice grass was sweet, while the amaranth added a touch of tartness. The mixture was good, but it couldn't distract her from the feeling of apprehension that gripped her.

After she ate, he packed some things into a heavy bundle, keeping his back turned toward her so that she couldn't see. Then he took her out into the street. She wanted to know what he had planned for her, but he still wore a stern, forbidding expression, and once again she decided it was best to remain silent. She kept reminding herself of what he had said: that he would never hurt her.

She could trust him. He was a wise man—and the kindness that she had seen in him must still be there.

The river that snaked through Green Canyon passed directly through the center of the town of many houses. In fact, the people had lined the river bank with slabs of stone, and they had built two wooden bridges across the water. This was another piece of construction that amazed Nisha. The logs that had been used to build the bridges were so heavy, it must have taken a dozen men to carry each one. And there were no pine forests nearby. The wood must have been dragged for many thousands of paces.

Winnor saw her looking at the bridges. "You see what people can achieve if they have the will," he said.

Nisha nodded. She noticed a large man walking over one of the bridges toward them, and at first she thought he was the same plump, effeminate figure that she'd seen in the street yesterday. Then he came closer and she saw that although he looked superficially the same, he was a different person altogether.

"Why does he look that way?" she whispered to Winnor. "I saw someone else yesterday, who—"

"There are at least a dozen of them," he murmured to her, turning his back so that the man wouldn't see or hear him talking. "They were once proud warriors, Nisha. They attacked this tribe, and even after they were captured, they showed no remorse. The chieftains of the Green Canyon people decided that if these warriors were set free, they would probably return to attack again. They would always be a danger to the people here. So the chieftains gelded the warriors. You understand?"

"They cut off their—male parts?" Her eyes widened.

"Yes, they took away the scrotum of each man. They are eunuchs now. They no longer have the urge to kill. They would rather eat than fight."

Nisha surreptitiously watched the plump man as he walked past. He walked like a warrior; he had the straight back, the proud tilt of his head, and the confident stride. Yet his face was not fierce; it was soft and gentle.

"That seems barbaric," Nisha whispered.

"Would it be better to kill them?" Winnor asked. "They were offered the choice: to lose their lives, or lose their manhood. Remember, they had killed people in this tribe. What else could be done with them?" He took Nisha's arm. "Come, now. You must bathe yourself." And he led her to a long, rectangular building that stood beside the river.

He waited outside while she went in. She found that most of the floor of the building was made of water. In fact, she realized, there was a stone-walled pit with a narrow path around it, and the river had been allowed to fill this pit. Several women were bathing here, laughing and splashing each other, their voices echoing off the brown sandstone walls.

Shyly, Nisha joined them. In her own tribe all the people had bathed together, because they had no secrets, and there was nothing shameful in nakedness. But here in this tribe where there were so many people, she could never get to know them all. She found she was glad that there were walls around the bathing area to keep strangers from staring at her.

After she had cleaned away the dust and grime of her travels, she found Winnor still waiting patiently outside. "I wish I didn't have to wear this old robe," she said. "It's so ragged—"

"This will be the last day that you wear it," he told her. "Come, now. Follow me." And he led her on through the town till they emerged from the houses on the north side. Yesterday she had come into the town from the south, so this part of the canyon was new to her. It looked much the same as the rest, though. There were more fields and more clusters of little homes beneath the imposing red rocks of the north wall of the canyon. The sun was still too low in the sky to reach down into the canyon itself, but the tops of the cliffs were now glowing brilliant red and gold.

Winnor led her along a small path that branched off the main road. The path was sandy and rutted, and she guessed that it must be a stream bed that turned into a small river during the rainy season. It led directly toward the cliffs, where it disappeared into a thin gully.

Nisha couldn't contain her curiosity any longer. "Please tell me where we're going," she said to Winnor.

"A holy place. Up there, see?" He pointed. Nisha looked up and she saw tiny footholds that had been chipped into the sandstone cliffs. They led to a natural table of rock that jutted out above the canyon floor. Above and behind the table, a chunk of rock had fractured away, creating a very shallow cave.

"But why must we go there?" she asked.

"Trust me, Nisha." He laid his hand on her shoulder—and once again his touch somehow quelled her anxieties.

They reached the cliffs, and Winnor started climbing. The footholds and handholds were well worn, making it hard for Nisha to keep a firm grip. But they were spaced close together, and she managed to make her way up without too much difficulty. Soon she found herself stepping out onto the table of rock. She stopped for a moment, staring out over the floor of the canyon, which was still filled with shadow. As she looked at the rim of the canyon opposite, she saw the disk of the sun just creeping into view.

"Here," said Winnor. He pointed to a boulder that had somehow been dragged to the exact center of the table of rock. One side of it was almost entirely flat, and it was angled up toward the sky. "People come here to worship Sun Spirit," Winnor said, "just as our tribe once did, out on the mesa. If you show yourself to him, he may take away the darkness that still lies inside you. Shed your robe, now, and your moccasins."

She felt concerned. To expose her nakedness all day to the heat of the sun was a punishing ordeal, especially in late summer. This was the test that her child had endured; the same test that all children of her tribe had been subjected to, to prove their strength.

But then she looked up at Winnor and he seemed so calm and confident, it gave her faith. Quickly, she stripped her clothes off and kicked her moccasins aside.

"Lean against the altar rock," he told her.

Obediently, she went to the slanting face of stone and rested her back against it. The rock was still cool from the night air, but soon enough, she knew, the sun would change that.

"This will help," said Winnor. "Open your mouth."

She did as he said, and he placed on her tongue a small, dark object the size of her thumb.

"Blood root," he said. "Chew it well."

The root had been cooked, so it was tender. Its taste was sweet, and it dissolved quickly in her mouth.

Winnor was still holding the package that he had brought with him. He pulled something out of it and handed it to Nisha. She found herself holding dozens of thin wooden splinters, each of them about as long as her forefinger. They had been bundled together and tied with a piece of cotton.

"There are fifty-three splinters," Winnor told her. "One for each person in our tribe who was killed by the Warrior Tribe. If you want to shed your guilt, Nisha, you will offer yourself to Sun Spirit now, and you will think of each person who died at the hands of our enemies. And as you think of each person, you will take one splinter and press the tip of it into your skin." He paused, watching her gravely. "Of course, if you prefer not to do this thing, that will be your choice. No other person can take your guilt away from you. It has to be you alone."

She held the little bundle and stared out across the canyon, watching the sun creep up. Her nakedness made her feel vulnerable up here where she had only the birds and the insects for company. Still, she was willing to do as Winnor said. She realized now that she had been foolish, thinking she could atone for her own guilt by killing the men who had killed her loved ones. Winnor was right: The only path to atonement lay inside herself.

"I will do it, Winnor," she said calmly.

"Good." He turned. "I will wait down at the bottom of the cliffs. If anyone passes this way, I'll tell them this is a holy ceremony, and you must not be disturbed."

She heard his careful footsteps as he moved to the far end of the rock table, and then she heard him lowering himself back to the ground. After that, there was nothing: just a faint ringing in her ears, and the humming of flies, and the cry of a red-tailed hawk circling somewhere above.

She was totally alone with herself. And so, as the sun crept up and touched her with its heat, she forced herself to remember. She began with the one who had died last: Rilla, who had taken her own life in the Wives' House on the night after Grep had been made chieftain of the Warrior Tribe. Nisha closed her eyes and saw Rilla's face. Rilla had chosen to die, and yet in a way the death was Nisha's burden. Nisha took a splinter and pressed its sharp tip a little way into her forearm. Really, it didn't hurt so much. There was a warmth to the pain that merged with the warmth from the sun.

"Forgive me, Rilla," Nisha murmured to herself.

Next she thought of Orlu and Lazonah, who had tried to escape from the village of the Warrior Tribe and had been crushed by Worr. For each of them, she took another splinter and offered her pain in atonement.

The sun rose higher and the air itself seemed warm, now, against her nakedness. She breathed deeply, knowing that she would soon be stricken with thirst—yet the prospect no longer worried her. Her own son had passed though this ritual, and of course she herself had endured it when she had been an infant, too young to remember.

She thought of her boy-child, and she felt an almost overwhelming pang. "Forgive me," she gasped, as she took another of the splinters. This one she pushed into her skin near her heart, just beside her left breast. There was a thin trickle of blood, and the pain washed out across her body while the sun breathed its hot breath upon her.

And so she continued to stand alone against the slanting rock, as the time crawled by, the shadows shortened, and she gave herself to the ritual of redemption.

In the afternoon, when she had placed every last one of the wooden splinters, she experienced a vision. Her skin felt as if it were on fire, her mouth was so dry that she couldn't swallow or even move her tongue, and she was dizzy from the heat. But it seemed to her that her consciousness flew out and away from her like a bird, leaving her physical pain behind. She looked down and saw herself as a tiny figure amid the huge red cliffs, and the land below had a strange swollen perspective, hazy at the edges, as if her eyes were no longer focusing in their usual way. Directly below, even though the land was far away, it seemed that she could detect each individual blade of grass, and when a lizard scuttled from one rock to the next, she saw it as clearly as if she had been beside it on the ground.

She felt a strange desire to swoop down and claim the little scuttling thing—yet she resisted. She found herself circling, coasting through the rippling air, returning to her own self. But she did not reenter her body. Her viewpoint hovered less than an arm's length away. She could see every one of the little splinters, and her own skin reddened by the sun, and her face turned to one side, with her eyes closed and her forehead wet with perspiration.

Something made Nisha turn her head, even though it seemed a terrible effort. She opened her eyes and flinched in surprise. She tried to cry out, but the sound died in her parched throat. A bird was sitting on her outstretched arm. It was a big bird, a red-tailed hawk with brown wing feathers and a spotted breast. Its gleaming black eye seemed to be staring at her. For a moment she feared that it had come to her because she was dying, and it might devour her. But the hawk sat on her arm without moving, and its talons didn't pierce her flesh. She stared at it, and once again her vision seemed to shift, although this time she saw the two views superimposed—its view of her, and her view of it.

This was how it had been when Winnor had sent her his vision from the eyes of the mountain cat. Was Winnor responsible for this, too? Somehow she didn't think so. She felt a strange instinctive understanding of the hawk. It had been a solitary creature like her, soaring across the landscape. And now, for some reason, it had chosen her. She felt her spirit join with it.

The hawk gave a high-pitched cry. It eyed Nisha a moment longer, and then, without warning, it launched itself away from her. She watched as it circled, found a column of rising air, and soared upward, disappearing into the void of the sky.

Later, Winnor came to her as she had known he would. The redness of her closed eyelids faded away as the sun sank behind the opposite rim of the canyon, and she heard him close by. His moistened finger touched her parched lips. He sprinkled water on her face, then gave her a small sip from a leather pouch. The water was a balm to her throat and tongue. She let out a deep sigh of gratitude as it soothed her.

He plucked the wooden splinters from her and cast them into the wind. He sat her down and gave her more to drink. "Now," he said, "you are free. Your penance is done."

And it was true: she felt a peace that she hadn't known before. Her guilt had flown away from her as freely as the hawk. "Thank you," she whispered.

"You needn't thank me," he said. "You did it yourself, Nisha."

"I saw a bird," she whispered—but her throat was still so dry, and her tongue was so swollen, she could barely speak. "A red-tailed hawk."

"Later," he said. "Tell me later. Drink more now, and then I will carry you back to the village."

She heard a rustling sound and she opened her eyes. He was unfolding the bundle that he had carried up here originally. She saw that it was a robe: a fine, new woven robe in the style of the Green Canyon people. Carefully, he drew it across her nakedness. "You are reborn, Nisha," he said, "any you need suffer no more."

Chapter Thirty-Four

By the morning of the next day, she was feeling better.
Her skin still burned and throbbed, and she still had a persistent thirst that no amount of water seemed to quench.
But her mind was alert. In fact, her thoughts seemed
clearer than they had ever been since that terrible night on
the mesa. She felt as if all her uncertainty and confusion
had been peeled away.

Winnor had stayed up late with her, giving her water
and little scraps of food. He had rubbed oil into the dried
skin on her face to stop it from peeling, and he had given
her a herbal drink to reduce the swelling of her lips and
tongue. She had been too weak to talk to him very much.
He was sleeping in the front room, now, while once again
she lay in his bed in the room at the back.

Nisha heard a sudden, strange sound, as if someone had
suddenly taken a robe and shaken it. The morning light
darkened—and she realized the sound was of beating
wings. She gave a little cry of surprise as she looked up
and saw a bulky silhouette on the ledge of the window.
The bird sitting there had a large, rounded body, and its
dangerous hooked beak was silhouetted against the morning sky as it turned its head one way, then the other, peering down into the room.

Nisha stared at it in amazement. She had thought that
her vision of the red-tailed hawk had been a hallucination,
yet here it was. Was it a good omen, or a bad one? And
why had it chosen her?

She gave a little bird cry. The hawk leaned forward and

cocked its head. Then its beak opened and it screamed its reply—"Keearrrh?"

Nisha felt her skin tingle. "What do you want from me, Hawk Spirit?" she whispered. Slowly, taking care not to startle the bird, she reached for a slab of wood where Winnor had left some scraps of rabbit meat. She picked it up and leaned forward to place it at the foot of her bed. Then she sat back.

The hawk bobbed its head, eyeing the meat. Without warning, it jumped into the room, beating its wing furiously as it landed on the edge of the board. It started pecking at the morsels, devouring them greedily. She glimpsed its black tongue as it finished eating, raised its head, and stared at her with its beak still partly open. Its fierceness frightened her—yet it fascinated her, too.

Nisha looked into its eyes. She felt a wave of dizziness. She saw herself and she saw the hawk, both at the same time.

Then, as quickly as it had happened, the vision ended. The hawk leaped into the air. It flew around the room with a thunder of wings, and one of its feathers brushed her face. Then it landed on the window ledge again, and then it was gone, hurling itself out into the sky.

Nisha jumped out of the bed and ran to the window. She peered out and saw a tiny speck spiralling up into the blue.

"Keearrrh!" she said softly. She listened for an answer, but there was none.

Something fluttered down. It was one of the hawk's feathers, which had lodged in her hair. She caressed its silky brown sheen, then placed it solemnly on the windowsill to show the hawk that it was welcome to return.

Marveling at the changes that had occurred in her life, she pulled on her new robe. Her skin was still sensitive from the sun, but the cotton felt cool and soft.

"Nisha!" Winnor pushed aside the door flap and ducked in. "Did I hear you talking?"

She opened her mouth to tell him about the hawk—

then changed her mind. Perhaps this was something so magical and private, she shouldn't share it even with Winnor. "I was yawning," she said, "that's all."

He glanced at the wooden slab at the foot of the bed. "I see you ate well."

"But I'm still hungry," she said, with a shy smile.

"Good. Come into the front room. It's time for us to talk seriously now."

Later, after they had both eaten, Winnor built a fire. One of the villagers came in with a sprained knee that he wanted Winnor to look at, and Nisha sat in the corner, watching as Winnor examined the man, then fashioned a crutch for him and gave him a salve to put on the injury. Once again, Nisha saw the kindness in Winnor that lived behind his stern face. The villager was grateful, and he offered a large bag of mixed grains. Winnor took only half of it. "I have no use for more," he said.

"You could trade what you don't need to someone else," the man pointed out.

Winnor smiled. "I am a healer, not a trader. Go, my friend, and be well." He sent the visitor on his way.

Then he turned to Nisha. "Come and join me here," he said, gesturing to his table.

She sat opposite him, and he pulled out a pouch that she recognized from her life on the mesa. It was his traveling pouch, full of powdered medicines. He had always taken it with him when the tribe had gone on its rabbit hunts in the late summer. Quietly, now, he started telling Nisha the purpose of each little bag of dried herbs. This one would ease pain if a person drank it in hot water; this would form a paste to put on a wound to stop it from bleeding so freely; this would stop a wound from becoming infected; and on and on.

She felt disconcerted to be sitting with him like this, hearing him describe all his secrets. She felt as if he were taking off his robes, showing himself to her as a mere man instead of a shaman. "I don't quite understand," she said, when he had finished his explanations, "why you are telling me all these things."

Methodically, he placed the little potions back in his bag. "It is time to show you that the healer's trade is not so mysterious after all," he said. "It can be learned, just like hunting or farming." He set the bag aside and clasped his hands on the table. He looked at her frankly. "Nisha, now that you've put the past behind you, it's time for you to think of the future. I want you to stay here in this town of many houses. I want you to think of becoming a healer yourself. And I will be happy to teach you."

She stared at him in shock. "Me?" she whispered.

He nodded. "You are a strong, clever woman. It would be easy for you to learn."

"But—there's more to it than knowledge," she said. "You have a special *gift,* Winnor. The spirits speak through you."

He spread his hands. "You too have that gift. How else did you sense my presence outside the village of the Warrior Tribe? How else did Cat Spirit show you his visions? Didn't you wonder why you saw them while the other women saw nothing?"

Nisha sat for a long time, staring at the table in front of her, not knowing what to think. Winnor spoke truly; she could see that now, especially since she had melded with Hawk Spirit. But it was still a hard idea for her to accept. She had to change the way she thought of herself—the way she had always thought of herself. She was no longer just a young woman with simple desires for peace and security and perhaps a new family, one day, with a new husband. She was a woman of unusual talents and powers.

But Winnor didn't know, yet, what she had decided while she had been lying awake that morning, before the hawk came to her room. She wondered how to tell him. "This would be more than I'd ever hoped for," she said, "to learn your skills, Winnor."

He nodded, but he waited, because he could sense that she was leading up to something.

"I want to learn," she went on. "Of course I want to."

He frowned. "What could prevent it?"

Now she felt embarrassed, and she had a little stab of anxiety. If she refused his offer, or postponed it, would he change his mind? Would she never again have such a chance to learn from him? Still, she had made her decision. "This morning," she said, "I spent a long time thinking. You freed me from my guilt, Winnor. My need for vengeance is over. But there is still another need, which is real and must be satisfied. I ran from the Cave People, in fear of my life, because another woman helped me to escape. But I think, now, it was wrong for me to leave them. I need to achieve final justice."

He gave her a thoughtful look. "Are you still thinking about this man Grep, who may still be alive?"

"Yes," she said. "It bothers me that I don't even know whether he was made to pay for all his crimes. But I have other worries, too. Among the Cave People, the women are still enslaved, in the same way that the women of the Warrior Tribe were enslaved. This is wrong, Winnor. It offends me. And it offends me that I abandoned the women of the Warrior Tribe, without ever helping them to be free. I feel as if—as if my job is only half done."

He made an impatient noise and stood up. He paced across the little room, then back again.

A woman stopped outside the house and tentatively pulled the door flap aside. "Healer," she said, "I have a pain—"

"I'm busy now!" Winnor's voice was sharp. Then he got control of himself and went to the doorway. "I'm sorry," he said, more calmly. "You will have to come back this afternoon. I am speaking with the spirits. I can't be disturbed."

He waited till the woman turned reluctantly and left. Then he fixed the flap over the door again and turned back to Nisha. "This is foolish," he told her, and she saw that he was feeling impatient with her. "You have no obligation to these other tribes. It's time to begin your own new life here, Nisha."

She wondered if he were right. He was wise, far wiser than she thought she could ever be. And yet, the feeling inside her was pure and strong, and if she tried to fight it, she feared she wouldn't find happiness. "There's another thing to think about," she said. "Suppose Grep does still live. He may try to find me, or he may send other people to find me. I was the one who caused almost all his warriors to be slaughtered, remember that." She saw that he was starting to speak, and she held up her hand. "Yes, I know I'm safe here in the Green Canyon. But what if I want to wander up on the plain? I'll always be looking over my shoulder in fear. I don't want to live like that—like a rabbit afraid to leave its burrow."

He grunted, but said nothing.

"So I have to know whether Grep lives," she said. "And I want to see if I can help the people who were suffering so much. Then, after that, I will be free to return here and start again—" She lowered her eyes. "If you will still teach me."

He stood for a long time with his arms folded, a motionless figure, brooding silently. He closed his eyes, and she thought he must be speaking with the spirits. And then, unexpectedly, he threw his head back and laughed. The little room rang to the sound of his voice.

She felt hurt and confused. Was he laughing at her?

His laughter gradually died as he saw her expression. "I should have known," he said, smiling at her now. "You were always the willful one. You defied the elders when you married Jorlor. You have the free spirit of a bird, Nisha. I thought I could show you the right path to follow. That was my mistake. You are your own person now. You must find your own way. And if this is your way, so be it."

"Really?" The change in him had come so suddenly,

she still felt disconcerted. "But Winnor—if I go on my own path, and I do what I want to do, and then I return here weeks or months from now—"

"Yes, of course I will still help you. You are my kin, Nisha. The last of my tribe. Nothing can change that." He stepped toward her and took her hands in his. He squeezed them tightly and looked into her eyes, and for a moment she thought she saw something that had been concealed before, if it had been there at all. He was not just a shaman, not just a healer. He was also a man, about the same age as Jorlor, and he was looking at her in the same way that Jorlor had often looked at her. In her tribe on the mesa Winnor had never married, and people believed he might lose some of his powers if he coupled with a woman. But she had already noticed the changes in him since he had joined the Green Canyon people. Now she saw the biggest change of all: He desired her.

But then he turned away and the moment was gone as if it had never been. "I will help you prepare for your journey," he said brusquely. "I won't come with you, because this is your quest, and it would not be right if I tried to interfere. But I will do what I can to see that you are properly prepared."

"Thank you," she said. She felt confused. For a moment, she had almost felt that he wanted to embrace her. But now he had retreated from her again, and he was calm and controlled. At the same time, though, he was being very kind, helping her to do what she wanted to do, even though it might seem foolish to him.

Without knowing quite why, she suddenly found herself crying—with gratitude, she realized.

He placed his hand on her shoulder. "Be strong," he said.

"I am strong." She smiled through her tears. "At least, I'm strong when a man is evil. It's only when a man is good to me that I lose my strength."

* * *

That afternoon, he took her to a special place—a narrow gulch that branched away from the south side of Green Canyon. A stream ran down the center of the gulch, and there were some bushes and stunted trees trying to find a foothold on the rocky bottom.

"The people of Green Canyon have no use for this place," Winnor said, "because there's no way the land can be cultivated. So we won't be disturbed." He glanced around, then moved to a patch of sandy soil among the boulders. "Join me here," he said.

She walked over to him. Each of them was carrying a spear, but Winnor had brought something else as well—an object that he had refused to reveal to her. It was wrapped in a cotton bag that was long and narrow, almost as tall as Nisha herself. Carefully, Winnor set this package down against a boulder. She watched his movements and noticed how precise he was.

He stepped back. "How far can a strong man throw his spear?" he asked her.

"Perhaps three hundred paces," she said. "Six hundred, if he uses a bison bone as a throwing stick."

He pointed to the far end of the gulch, where the cliffs leaned in and the stream was fed by a tall, slender waterfall. "You see the stone there, where the water strikes it?"

She squinted into the distance. There was a rounded boulder directly under the flow of white water. "I see it," she said.

"Could you hit it with your spear?"

She laughed. "Of course not. It's much too far."

"And with a throwing stick?"

She judged the distance. "Perhaps—but with a stick, my throw wouldn't be accurate enough."

"Quite so," he said with a curt nod. He picked up the cotton bag and opened a flap at one end. He pulled out a piece of wood that was thick in the middle, tapering at each end, and gently curved. A heavy length of gut dangled from it.

"Whatever is that?" she asked.

"I will show you." He planted one end of the wood in the ground and pushed down on it with all his strength, bending it so much that Nisha was afraid it would break in half. Quickly, he fixed the gut so that it spanned the distance between the ends of the wood. He twanged the gut, and she heard it make a low, mellow tone.

He reached into the bag again and this time drew out a straight, slender wooden rod with bird feathers at one end and a small flint at the other. Nisha laughed as she saw it. "Is that a spear for very young children?" she said.

He didn't smile. "Watch," he said.

He picked up the wooden bow, notched the arrow in the gut, and drew the arrow back to his jaw. Nisha watched his muscles bunch, and she sensed the tension in the wood and the gut, poised and yearning for release. Winnor angled the bow up slightly, took careful aim—and let go of the bowstring.

Nisha watched in amazement as the arrow fled from the bow and soared across the sky. It moved so fast, she had trouble following it. And then, faintly, in the far distance, there was the sound of the flint arrowhead clinking against the boulder beneath the waterfall.

"Let me see!" Nisha cried with excitement, reaching for the bow.

Now Winnor smiled. He handed it to her. "It's a secret of the Green Canyon people," he said. "One of their chieftains gave it to me when I cured his wife's fever. He told me I had saved her life. Perhaps I did; I don't know. But I've been coming here and practicing since that day." He opened the cotton bag again and took out another arrow. "Try it," he said.

Cautiously, she slotted the arrow in the gut. The tension in it scared her. She imagined the gut snapping or the wood of the bow splintering—yet when she pulled the gut toward her, the bow bent smoothly, and it seemed safe enough.

"See how far you can shoot your arrow," Winnor said.

She sighted on the boulder under the waterfall. Then she remembered that he tilted the bow up, so she did the same. And as she did so, she noticed a movement in one of the little trees along the stream. A squirrel, she realized. Quickly, almost without thinking, she swung the bow and aimed it up into the tree. She waited. There was a long pause. The wind blew, raising the curtain of leaves, and she saw the squirrel clearly, clinging to a branch.

Nisha loosed the arrow. It flew away, and once again she was amazed by its speed. There was a tiny sound and she saw the squirrel dropping from the tree, speared by the arrow.

Nisha gave a shout of amazement. She was sure it had been mostly a matter of luck, hitting such a tiny target. But still, she felt a new power, a new sense of possibilities.

"Very good, Nisha," Winnor was saying. She grinned up at him—and her vision blurred for a moment.

She felt her perceptions dividing. Winnor was looking at her, and his smile was turning to a look of concern. She faintly heard him asking her if she was all right. At the same time, she saw the two of them as tiny figures among the boulders.

Impulsively, she started running. Her vision cleared as she blundered forward, splashing into the stream. She zigzagged among the rocks on the opposite shore, saw the squirrel lying dead on the ground, and pulled the arrow out of its lifeless body. She picked it up, then, and carried it out into the sun. While Winnor made his way toward her, looking puzzled, Nisha placed the squirrel on a flat-topped rock. She stepped back and closed her eyes. *Come,* she said inside her mind.

There was a long pause, and for a moment she thought that nothing was going to happen. But then there was a flurry of wings as the hawk dropped out of the sky. It landed on the stone, stared at Nisha, and quickly started tearing at the prey.

Silently, Winnor joined her. "What is this?" he whispered.

"It came to me when I was giving myself to Sun Spirit," Nisha murmured to him. "And again, this morning."

"But—how did you sense that it was with us now?"

Nisha shifted uncomfortably. She was still reluctant to talk about her strange melding with Hawk Spirit. "I just had a feeling," she said in a low voice.

"This is powerful magic," said Winnor, with wonder in his voice.

She felt a little jump of pride. At the same time, she saw that the hawk had finished feeding. It looked up at her from its feast, then curled its head around and wiped its beak to and fro under its wing.

Nisha extended her arm. *Come,* she said.

The hawk stood on the rock, eyeing her. It gathered itself up and leaped into the air. She saw it coming toward her, and she wanted to run from its terrible talons as they reached down—but she forced herself to remain motionless. The hawk clutched her arm, gently but firmly, and it furled its wings. "Keearrrh," it screamed.

She stood like that for a long moment, feeling the closeness of the bird and trying to reach out to it with her mind. She sensed its speed and its power, and its freedom. It turned its head to and fro—and then suddenly it was launching itself up into the air and beating its great brown wings. It circled the narrow gulch, then turned toward Green Canyon and was gone.

There was a long moment in which the only sound was of the water chuckling against the rocks in the stream bed. Winnor let out a slow sigh. "I was right," he said. "You have the free spirit of a bird." He touched Nisha's arm where the talons had encircled it. Then he drew back. "We will make more bows and arrows for you, Nisha," he said. "You can practice till you feel sure of your skills.

Then, you will be properly prepared for your journey." He looked up at the sky. "And with Hawk Spirit to give you his speed and strength, it seems to me that you will prevail."

Chapter Thirty-Five

It took her many days to master all the subtleties of the bow and arrow, and during that same time, she worked with Winnor to make copies of it. Each morning, she sat with him and painstakingly cleaned and prepared lengths of hardwood. Together they shaped flints into arrowheads, bound the flints to arrow shafts, and tested the balance of the arrows.

Now that he knew she would be leaving Green Canyon, he seemed careful not to show or share too much of his emotions. He was kind, helpful, and good to her, but as a friend only. She realized that this was because he wanted nothing to interfere with her decision to leave. But still, she found herself thinking about the look that she'd seen in his eyes in that one moment when he had shown his desire for her. She found herself wishing, in a way, he would reveal that side of himself again.

In the afternoons, they practiced together in the rocky gulch. Nisha soon discovered that her first shot at the squirrel had been a lucky one. The bow was much harder to master than she had first thought. Just the way in which she released the arrow was crucial—keeping her left arm rock steady as she held the bow, and moving the fingers of her right hand so carefully that when they surrendered their grip on the bowstring, they didn't move it even a fraction left or right.

Three weeks passed before she felt truly confident in her skills. By now it was autumn, and the days were shorter. She realized she was putting off her departure, because life was comfortable here in Green Canyon, and her journey was going to be hard and dangerous. But if she waited much longer, the fall rains would come, and it would be a poor time to travel.

And so, with a mixture of sadness and determination, a day came when she said goodbye to Winnor and set out alone, retracing her path back toward the north.

She journeyed for six days before she came to the island—and as she finally saw it ahead, she noticed a strange smell in the forest.

Nisha paused for a moment beside the river and took deep, slow breaths, parting her lips so that she could taste the air. It was a scorched smell, but something told her that it wasn't the smell of a cooking fire. Instinctively, she sensed that something was wrong.

She shifted the heavy pack on her back, took a fresh grip on her spear, and moved slowly forward with all her senses alert. She remembered this place; there was no doubt in her mind of that. As the island came fully into view, she saw on top of it the ruins of the little thatched houses.

She paused carefully. *Hawk Spirit,* she called.

There was no reply, no sudden flurry of wings.

The hawk had followed her for the first day of her journey, when she walked across the grassy plain above Green Canyon. But as soon as she had entered the woodlands, it had abandoned her. She still felt a sense of loss. During the long days in the canyon when she had practiced endlessly with her bow and arrows, she had fed the hawk many small pieces of game and it had come to her often. Still, she had learned that it could not be counted on; there were some days when she saw no sign of it at all. It truly was a free spirit, liable to disappear whenever it felt the urge to ride the columns of warm air that rose from the canyon floor.

Well, Nisha thought to herself, she could manage on her own. She stepped into the river at the shallow place where Sookim had crossed it, when they had first come here. Nisha still remembered the cry that Sookim had made. She raised her hand beside her mouth and tried to imitate it now.

There was no response. Cautiously, Nisha climbed the slope to the summit where the ruined houses stood. And here she found the source of the smell that had been carried to her on the breeze. She squatted down beside the remains of a huge fire. There was a great pile of blackened branches, and some embers still glowing amid heaps of ash.

Still Nisha sensed something wrong. She turned her spear and used the end of it to stir the ashes—and a bone rolled into view. At first she thought it was a leg bone from a deer; but then, as she peered more closely, she saw that it was human.

She straightened up and quickly glanced around. The forest was silent, but the silence was ominous, now. "Sookim!" she called. "Barem!"

She had seen no sign of warriors—no footprints, no broken blades of grass. During the past days of her journey, she had never once detected the smell of man. But she was only two days away from the Cave People now. They could be here.

A twig snapped, and some foliage rustled. Nisha quickly raised her spear—and she saw three figures coming out from where they had been hiding under the trees. "Sookim!" Nisha cried again. She threw down her spear and ran forward. "Sookim, it's me!"

The woman was thinner, and her face was pale and weary. Still, she smiled as she saw Nisha, and she hugged her tightly while Barem and his son stood to one side.

"I came back," Nisha said. "I had to find you, Sookim." She turned to Barem. "Greetings!" she said with a warm smile. "And to you, Jep—greetings!"

They clustered around her and smiled and hugged her, and they seemed pleased enough to see her. But there was a strange sadness behind their smiles.

"I have food for us all," she said. She hesitated. "Is there something wrong here?"

"My wife died giving birth," Barem said. He was no longer even trying to smile now. Nisha saw pain in his eyes. "The fire, there, was her funeral pyre."

Nisha stood for a moment, absorbing the news. "And the baby too?"

"Yes," Barem nodded. "She bled—we couldn't stop it. And the baby never opened his eyes."

Nisha turned and looked again at the remains of the fire. "So you burn your dead," she said. She had never heard of such a thing. It seemed—wrong.

"That's how the spirit is released," said Barem.

She turned back to him, reached for his hand, and clutched it in hers. "I feel for you, Barem. I would like to help in some way. Can I stay with you here for a little while? Can I share my food with you?"

"Of course." He gestured resignedly. "Stay, Nisha, for as long as you want."

As the light faded, they ate the breads, dried fruits, and fresh game that Nisha had brought. It must have been a feast compared with their usual meals in this lonely little place, but Barem was barely interested in eating, and Sookim and Jep seemed to be holding their appetites in check out of respect for him.

Bit by bit, Nisha told them of her travels. Then she turned to Sookim. "Has it been peaceful here?" she asked. "Did any warriors—"

"They came twice," said Sookim. For some reason, she seemed embarrassed and uncomfortable. "We hid among the trees and waited, and they moved on. I think—I hope—they've given up looking for us, Nisha."

"Did you actually see the faces of the men?" Nisha asked. It was impossible to hide the eagerness in her voice.

"Yes, I saw them." Sookim looked up at Nisha. "Why do you ask?"

"Did you recognize all of them?" said Nisha.

Sookim nodded. "They were warriors of the Cave People."

"All of them? Every one?"

Sookim frowned. "Yes. Why?"

Nisha told herself to relax. She was not going to learn the answer to her unspoken question—at least, not tonight. "I'm still thinking that one man from the Warrior Tribe might have lived," she said. "And he would be the one who is most likely to be searching for me."

Sookim shook her head. "I think I was the one they were looking for."

"Perhaps. Probably." She shrugged. The hopelessness and despondency of this place was beginning to close in around her. And she didn't understand why Sookim seemed so withdrawn. Nisha had come here full of new determination. She felt her spirit was gradually seeping away, now, like water being absorbed in dry sand.

"I must sleep now," Barem said abruptly. He stood up. "Come, Jep." Without another word, he walked back to his refuge under the trees, and his son followed him.

Nisha watched them go. She said nothing.

"Well," said Sookim, "I think perhaps I—"

Nisha reached out quickly and seized her hand. "Not yet. You must stay and talk to me for a while."

Sookim made a tentative movement as if she was going to pull her hand free, but then seemed to think better of it. "What do you want to talk about?" she said.

"Sookim! I came back here to see you!" Nisha shook her head in puzzlement. "Why are you being so unfriendly?"

The woman stared at the ground in front of her. Her hair fell forward, hiding the purple mark on her forehead. "I missed you, Nisha." Her voice was low. "It's been very hard here. I hated it when you left." She sniffed, and Nisha realized she was crying. "I told you, I hate it when people leave."

Nisha grunted in annoyance, then reached for the

woman and hugged her close. "Sookim, I told you that you could come with me. You decided to stay. That's not my fault."

"Things are so much simpler for you," Sookim muttered. "I had to stay with my cousin. They needed my help."

Wearily, Nisha stroked Sookim's head. "Well, this can't go on," she said. "I have a bad feeling about this place. It stole your cousin's spirit, and his wife died here, and now I see that it's stolen your spirit too. You have to leave, Sookim. That's why I came back here—to take you away from this place."

"But what about Barem and Jep?" Sookim said. "I can't abandon them."

"They will join us," said Nisha. "Believe me, Sookim. It has to be so." She heard her own voice, so full of certainty, and she hesitated for a moment, wondering if she really had the right to interfere in these people's lives—especially since the quest that she had in mind would be arduous and dangerous. But then she looked again at the miserable little camp here, and she knew with sudden certainty that if these people were going to survive, sooner or later they would have to leave. And it seemed to her they would never leave unless someone forced them to.

She stood up. "Come and lie with me now," she said, feeling a little touch of desire, despite the grimness of the evening and the sadness of her friend. "Let me comfort you, Sookim. And maybe we can give each other a little pleasure. Eena has died, but we still live. We should enjoy our lives while we can."

The next day, in the bright light of morning, Nisha opened her pack. There were five bows inside, and scores of arrows. The bows were smaller than the one that Winnor had first shown her, because she had known she would have to carry them a long distance. Still, they were almost as powerful.

She set out the bows while Sookim, Jep, and Barem sat

watching her. She saw their expressions of puzzlement and doubt.

"See," said Nisha. She picked up one of the bows, notched an arrow, and raised it in one swift motion. She sighted on a narrow birch tree on the opposite side of the clearing where the ruined huts stood. She loosed the arrow, and an instant later there was a solid thump as the flint embedded itself in the trunk of the tree.

Nisha turned to her three companions. "Would you like to try it for yourselves?" she said.

For a moment, no one moved. They stared at the arrow in the tree, then at Nisha, then at the bows and arrows on the ground in front of them.

Suddenly Jep reached out. "Let me!" he cried.

"Be sure you fetch all the arrows you shoot," Nisha warned him. "It's difficult to make them. It takes a long time, and they have to be balanced just so."

"What are these for?" said Sookim, touching the feathers on one of the arrows.

"To make them fly true," said Nisha. "And to give them the speed of a bird."

"They look like hawk feathers," said Sookim.

"Yes," said Nisha, with a secret smile. "They are."

The magic of the bows and arrows lightened Barem's spirits, as Nisha had hoped it would. It distracted him from his tragedy and gave him something to occupy himself. Nisha sat and watched as all three of her companions practiced throughout the morning. She gave a word of advice now and then, but most of the time, she left them to themselves. All of them were skilled hunters, even Jep, so they soon learned how to steady the bow, how to sight along the arrow, and how to set it free cleanly.

They ate a quick lunch, then practiced some more. Finally, when the day was almost over, Barem came to Nisha. "I want to thank you," he said, "for what you have brought us. With these weapons, we shall eat much better, here. I was concerned about surviving the winter, but now—"

"Barem, sit," she said.

He blinked, disconcerted by her peremptory tone. She pretended not to notice; it was clear to her that someone needed to be forceful with Barem, and if it had to be her, well, so be it. "Sookim! Jep!" she called. "Come over here!"

She waited until they had all gathered around her. As she looked at their faces, she sensed that she would only have one chance to get them to see her point of view. If she failed the first time, it would be harder the second time. It seemed that Barem had not been an adventurous man even before his tribe had been massacred, and Sookim and Jep took their cues from him.

"I didn't bring you bows and arrows so that you could stay here," Nisha said bluntly. "Yes, you might survive the winter—but not easily, even with these new weapons. And if the warriors have come here twice, they will probably come again. Next time, you may not be lucky enough to hide under the trees. You could be bathing in the river, or out in the woods setting snares—anything could happen."

Barem was frowning. "This is my home, Nisha. It is my choice to live here, not yours."

"These are my bows and arrows," said Nisha. She had learned the lesson of ownership from the Green Canyon people, and learned it well. "I made them. It is my choice who uses them, and how they should be used."

Barem wasn't the only one looking indignant now. All three of them were staring at Nisha as if she had tricked them. "You gave them to us!" said Jep.

"No," said Nisha. "I let you use them. I wanted you to see their power. Listen, now: I lost my tribe, as you lost yours. While I was in Green Canyon, I learned that I had been pretending to myself—as you once pretended to me, Sookim. You remember how you couldn't bear to admit that your people had gone, until we actually came here to- gether?"

Sookim blinked, looking unhappy. "Why do you men- tion that now?" she complained.

"I freed myself," Nisha said. "Now it is time to free yourselves, too. It's wrong for you to hide here, afraid of each stranger who passes by. It's wrong! I want you to shake off your fears and rise up and seek justice against the warriors who killed your people. Do you understand?"

There was a short silence. Barem laughed uneasily. "The four of us, against the warriors of the Cave Peo- ple?" He laughed again, louder this time. "What foolish talk is this?"

Nisha allowed herself a little hope. She had challenged him, and now he was responding. If he had simply turned away, she would have been ready to admit defeat. But he was ready to argue with her. That was an encouraging sign—a first step.

"Sookim knows the land up there," Nisha said, nodding toward the north. "Remember, once before I did some- thing that no one would have believed a woman could do. Scores of men from the Warrior Tribe lost their lives be- cause of me. And that was when I was all on my own."

She paused a moment, looking at each of them in turn.

"In fact," she went on, "I think it will be easier to con- front the Cave People than you imagine. I have these weapons now. I can hide in the forest, where the trees are too dense to allow enough room to throw a spear—but I can easily shoot an arrow from that dense cover. My en- emy will think he's safe because I'm so far away—but the arrows travel so far and so fast, he'll be an easy target. And I will be safe from his spear, because even if he uses a throwing stick, I can stay out of range."

She paused again. They were listening carefully, but she couldn't guess what they were thinking.

"All I need now is your help," she said. "And if we are successful, then you, too, will be free. You will have your confidence and your pride, and you won't have to hide anymore like mice in the forest."

Barem shifted uneasily. He had started to look worried. And that, too, was a good sign—it meant that he was taking Nisha seriously, wondering if he could ever do what she described. He hadn't just assumed that it was impossible.

"You really think we can do it?" It was Jep speaking. He was looking at Nisha as if he wanted to believe her.

"Yes," said Nisha. "Otherwise, I would never ask you to take such a risk."

"How?" Sookim asked flatly. "It's easy to speak like this, Nisha. But tell us how the four of us can hope to face the Cave People. How can we possibly defeat them, even if we use these bows and arrows of yours? You've seen for yourself how fierce they are, and how well protected they are."

Nisha smiled. It was good to hear the spirit in Sookim's voice again. This was the woman who had moved with such determination, when they had run through the forest on the plateau. If she had been strong then, she could be strong now.

"I will tell you exactly how it can be done," said Nisha. "All I ask is that you should listen with open minds, and hear everything before you decide."

Chapter Thirty-Six

The discussion and the arguing lasted late into the night. Jep was the first to take Nisha's side, though he was afraid to speak too strongly while his father still disagreed. Nisha could see, though, that Jep was eager to strike out away from this hiding place by the river; he was eager for adventure, and too young to care very much about the risk.

Sookim was cautious, doubtful, and stubborn, but she was willing to argue logically. And logically, Nisha had the advantage. She had had weeks to consider every possibility, every detail of what she had in mind. Point by point, she proved to Sookim that the deed could be done. She had an answer ready for each of Sookim's objections. And finally, Sookim agreed.

Barem was the last one to be convinced, and even when he finally gave his consent, Nisha felt that she would not be able to count on him as much as the other two.

Once the decision had been made, though, everyone's mood changed. Fatalism gave way to cautious hope, and Nisha saw that she had done a good thing, forcing them to change their lives. They hadn't been content, hiding here in the wilderness. They had been anxious about their future and ashamed of their past. Now that she had given them something to hope for, she saw their spirits lift.

The only question was whether she had given them real hope or false hope. In the past she had taken risks in the knowledge that if she was wrong, she would be the only one to suffer. Now she had three people whom she cared for, relying on her judgment. That was a new sensation, and it troubled her more than she liked to admit.

Two days later, they paused at the northern edge of the forest. From this point on, the land sloped up to the huge rockfall which Nisha and Sookim had descended during their escape from the Cave People. That rocky slope was frighteningly exposed. Nisha had decided that the only safe way to tackle it would be at night.

They sat, now, waiting for the sun to set. Nisha saw the nervousness in Barem's face, and it confirmed her feeling that she couldn't count on him—at least, not until he proved his strength to himself. Jep had the recklessness of a young boy, which meant that he would probably cause trouble for all of them unless she kept him strictly under control. Sookim was the only one who seemed calm and stable. But she was prone to such mood swings, Nisha wasn't sure she could even rely on her.

She suddenly felt she had to be on her own for a moment, to look inside herself and restore her own confidence. "Eat well," Nisha said, as they shared their rations. "I'm going to watch the plateau. I don't see any special reason why warriors from the village should be out here, but still, I want to be sure."

She moved away through the forest till she reached the last of the trees. Here, she ducked down and started crawling through the tall grass that covered the land ahead. She stopped when she reached a low ridge. From this vantage point she could see without being seen.

The rockfall receded into the far distance, curving up to the top of the cliffs. The tumbled stone caught the oblique rays of the afternoon sun, turning it into a mosaic of orange rock and purple shadow.

The cliffs either side of the rockfall looked timeless; she imagined they must have always been here, enduring while the vegetation and the creatures lived and died. She closed her eyes, trying to open her mind to the enduring strength of the land.

For a moment she saw only the sun-warmed redness of the inside of her eyelids. But then she found herself circling, soaring, looking down at a vision of grassland rippling in the wind. *Hawk Spirit!* she thought, with a burst of excitement. *Have you returned to me?*

The view shifted, and she saw herself as a tiny shape amid the tall grass.

Suddenly she understood. The hawk hadn't followed her into the forest because it distrusted the clutter of branches and leaves. Hawks were seldom seen in woodland; they always chose to soar over open country where they could scan a wide, empty sweep of land for their prey. The hawk hadn't abandoned her when she had walked into the woods. She had abandoned it.

You were loyal to me after all, Nisha thought. *Thank you, Hawk Spirit.*

She waited, trying to sense a response. Sometimes the hawk's thoughts seemed to come to her, though they tended to be formless surges of emotion. Nisha had learned that the hawk found pleasure in riding the wind, it found excitement when it saw creatures moving furtively below, and it took an awful delight in killing them. Sometimes, when Nisha felt the hawk's mind touching hers, the fierceness of it scared her.

She had learned, though, that the hawk respected her, perhaps because she fed it and spoke to it, or perhaps because it sensed the relative power of her mind. Often, if she formed a clear picture in her imagination, it would respond as if she had given it a command.

She tried to do that now. She imagined the way up to the rim of the plateau, and then she imagined moving along it, following the line of the cliffs till she came to the great chasm where the Cave People made their home. *Go there, Hawk Spirit,* she thought, *before day fades into evening.*

At first, the hawk didn't respond. Nisha told herself to

be patient. Step by step, she visualized the journey again, and then she imagined it for a third time.

Finally, the hawk turned in the right direction. A gust of wind lifted it, then threw it forward with unexpected speed. *Yes!* Nisha thought. *That way!*

The treetops moved past below and the air rushed by. Nisha felt dizzy; she had never tried to share the hawk's vision for such a long spell. The perspective was strange and distorted, but more than that, the mind itself was alien. The more she melded with it, the more her own personality gradually slipped away, and her drives and desires simplified until all she was aware of was the basic need to fly, dive, kill, and devour.

Somehow, though, she held onto her human motive. The hawk came to the great break in the cliffs, and she guided it in, then visualized the village in the cave as she remembered it. The hawk turned—and yes, there was the cave embracing the cluster of little buildings.

Closer, she thought.

The hawk hesitated. It tended to avoid places where many people lived. But Nisha willed it to dive down, and finally it obeyed her. She saw the buildings rushing up toward her. There was a dizzying moment as the world turned dark, but then the hawk's eyes adjusted to the dimmer light inside the cave and she found herself fluttering down, landing on the topmost ledge of the tower where she had first seen Gogorah, the old chieftain.

The hawk paused there, preened itself for a moment, then furled its wings and looked around at the little stone houses. Nisha saw people moving in and out of the buildings, and warriors bringing women down from the fields at the end of their working day. And then, as she looked through the hawk's eyes, she realized with a shock that she recognized one of the women. It was Ellel, one of Grep's wives, from the Warrior Tribe. It seemed impossible—yet as she looked at the woman's face, she was certain of it.

She realized then that the women from the Warrior

Tribe must have been brought here. The Cave People would have sent a raiding party, and with most of the warriors already killed and only a few young men left to guard the stockade, it would have been easy enough to seize all the women.

The hawk was uneasy. It shifted as if it wanted to soar back out into the safe, high, empty places. Its head turned—and Nisha saw a group of men talking together.

Her heart seemed to freeze inside her. *That one,* she thought. *Show me that one!*

The hawk launched itself from its perch. It swooped down, almost brushing the heads of the men with its talons. Nisha glimpsed startled faces looking up as the bird sped by. And indeed, it was just as she feared. There was no possible doubt. The face was Grep's, and even though it seemed impossible to her, he was standing openly with the other warriors, as a free man. Worse: He seemed to be giving them instructions.

The hawk swooped out of the cave and turned through the sky, looking for a place to roost for the night. *Thank you, Hawk Spirit,* Nisha thought, trying to hold back the wave of anger and bitterness she felt. *I will kill many small creatures for you. I will feed you well.*

There was no way the bird could respond. But Nisha felt something from it in return. A sense of companionship—pleasure, perhaps—and pride in what it had done for her.

She opened her eyes. It took her a long moment to focus on her surroundings, and then she felt horribly trapped within her human form. She moved her arm, and it was like trying to shift a heavy wooden log. She turned her head, and she felt as if she were wrestling with a boulder. She thought of herself as a strong person and a free person, but compared with the red-tailed hawk, she was a weak, clumsy prisoner.

Slowly, she crawled back toward the forest, then stood up as she reached the trees. Her mind was still full of the vistas that she had shared with the hawk. But the image she retained most vividly was of Grep's face.

It was a long, slow climb, as she'd known it would be. Now that Hawk Spirit was close to her again, she realized she could have tackled the rockfall safely during the day, using the bird to spy on the land ahead and make sure that no warriors from the village were watching. But it would have been hard to convince her companions of her power. They had enough trouble believing in her already.

They had to stop and rest a couple of times during the ascent, because Jep was still just a boy, and he tired easily, though he hated to admit it. Finally, though, they entered the forest up on the plateau.

Nisha thought she saw the thicket where she had lain with Sookim, although she couldn't be sure. She glanced at Sookim and found her looking back at her with a shy smile. Quickly, Nisha clasped the woman's hand, squeezed it tight, and released it. She turned to Barem and Jep. "Let's travel as far as we can now," she whispered. "I think we should be able to reach the fields by dawn."

And so they set out, picking their way through the forest. No one spoke, but she saw the anxiety still in Barem's eyes, and she sensed the mixture of excitement and fear in Jep. Even Sookim looked nervous now. "Courage," Nisha whispered to her. "Remember how bold you were, on the night we fled?"

"It's much easier to be bold," Sookim answered, "when you're running away from danger instead of seeking it out."

By the time they reached the end of the forest, Barem and Jep both looked ready to drop. They had lived on a starvation diet for the past few years, and they had no physical reserves. As the sky slowly brightened above the trees, Nisha sat them down and gave them most of the remaining rations. "We will eat, and then we will sleep," she said.

"But we're so close," whispered Jep, "it doesn't seem safe." He peered through the trees toward the open fields that were just visible ahead. From listening to Nisha's description, he knew that those fields would soon be full of women tilling the land while men stood guard.

Nisha turned to Sookim. "What do you think?"

"In all the days that I worked in the fields," said Sookim, "the men never walked into the forest. Their job is to watch over the women. Sometimes they stand at the edge of the fields where there's some shade from the sun, but they never leave the women unattended."

"What if they happen to send out a raiding party?" said Barem.

Nisha felt impatient with him. They had discussed all of these things three nights ago. But she told herself to let Sookim answer him. He was her cousin; he would listen to her.

"We're standing in the territory of the Cave People," Sookim said. "Why should one of their raiding parties go creeping through the woods on their own land, so close to their home? Even if they were out hunting, there's no game so close to the tribe. The men would walk along the rocks at the edge of the cliffs, where the going is easier."

Barem fell silent. He seemed grudgingly satisfied.

"It's still best to be cautious," said Nisha. "We'll find a spot farther back, if that will make everyone feel more secure."

Barem and Jep glanced at each other, but neither one said anything. It must be hard for them, Nisha thought, to be led by a pair of women. Still, there would be a chance for them to prove their male courage soon enough.

They found some dense underbrush and burrowed down into it. Jep complained that he wouldn't be able to sleep—but a few moments later, Nisha saw his eyes falling shut. He was so exhausted from the long journey, and so sedated by the food, his body gave him no choice.

Barem, too, dozed off. Nisha moved close to Sookim. "You're certain," she whispered, "that there's only one way down to the cave."

Sookim shifted restlessly. "I already told you, Nisha, the only way is through the cleft in the rocks and along the ledge."

Nisha realized she was behaving like Barem, wanting reassurance, finding it hard to accept someone else's judgment. But everything depended on Sookim being right. If there was any other way for the people to leave the cave, her plan would fail and they might all be killed.

Nisha thought it was ironic that the first time she saw the village, it had seemed such a safe haven. True, there was no easy way for warriors to attack it—which was why Grep and his men had devised their plan of lowering themselves on ropes. But the inaccessibility of the village was also its weakness. Since there was no easy way into it, there was no easy way out, either.

"Nisha," said Sookim, "suppose we're successful, as I think we will be. What then? What do you imagine, after the village is ours?"

Nisha didn't hesitate. "I'll stay here with you, of course," she said.

Sookim surreptitiously reached for her hand. "Thank you," she said.

Nisha had been afraid of that question. Truly, she wasn't sure what she would want to do. She felt drawn to this woman—but she also found herself thinking constantly about Winnor. Could he ever be her mate? And would he want to be? There had only been the one time when he had looked at her in that special way. And the idea of being paired with him was so strange and disturbing, she found it hard to imagine. At the same time, though, she had to admit that it excited her.

She could say nothing about this to Sookim, though—

at least, not yet. Maybe it was wrong to deceive her, but she couldn't risk damaging Sookim's confidence now. The woman's fighting spirit, and all their lives, might depend on it.

Chapter Thirty-Seven

Nisha dozed during the morning, though she kept starting awake at the slightest sound. She heard women singing as they worked in the fields, and once in a while there was a man shouting a command or scolding someone. The sound of their voices filled Nisha with anger. But soon, she told herself, she would have her chance to correct the injustice. Very soon.

In the late afternoon, she woke Barem and Jep. "We must take action before the women finish their work for the day," she whispered. "If you need to vent your bladder or your bowels, now is the best time. But please be careful. We mustn't make a sound."

Barem gave her an irritable look. "For years, I've lived by hunting in the forest," he whispered. "And Jep has hunted with me. We know how to move silently. We may even know better than you."

Nisha saw that in her anxiety to have everything under control, she'd been insulting his skills. "I'm sorry," she muttered.

He gave a curt nod. Then he and Jep slid out of the thicket.

Nisha felt a good, hard tension growing inside her. It was always easier for her to take action than to sit and wait. She glanced at Sookim and saw that her face was alert too, and her eyes were intent.

Barem and Jep rejoined them, and they all crept forward, moving slowly, placing their feet with infinite care. Finally, when there was only a thin layer of trees screening them from view, Nisha gestured for everyone to lie flat. They crawled forward a little farther, and stopped.

Silently, they opened their packs, pulled out their bows, and took out three arrows each. Nisha scanned the land ahead. There were eight men standing guard, just as Sookim had predicted. Nisha placed her hand on Jep's shoulder and wordlessly pointed to the two men who were nearest. She turned to Barem and pointed to the next two warriors. The two after that she assigned to Sookim. Since Nisha had had the most practice with a bow, she reserved the farthest targets for herself.

She turned on her side and held her bow in her left hand, parallel with the ground. It was awkward to notch and draw an arrow from this position, but they had practiced it before making their journey, and had been able to hit their targets with good accuracy. Beside her, Nisha heard Jep grunt with the effort of stretching his bowstring. She heard the faint rasp of the arrow shaft against the wooden bow.

One of the guards was pacing to and fro. He seemed restless, impatient to end his work day and return to the village in the cave below. Nisha waited, and she waited, till her left arm ached from holding the bowstring taut. Finally, the guard stopped moving. All eight of the men, now, were standing still. "Now," she whispered.

The bowstrings thrummed and there was a faint hiss as the arrows flew. Nisha was already notching her second arrow as her first one hit its target. She saw the distant figure stagger and drop to his knees, holding his chest and looking down as if he couldn't believe what he saw.

Three other men were falling, and there were some distant shouts of surprise and pain. All the first arrows had found their targets. Nisha glanced at Jep and saw him staring—in horror or surprise, she couldn't tell which. "Shoot again!" she reminded him.

Her own second arrow flew out, along with Sookim's, and then Barem's, and three more guards fell.

The last guard was looking around at his comrades. He

took a tentative step—then turned and started running toward the path that led down to the cave. Jep shot his arrow—but it fell short.

Nisha grabbed her last arrow. Beside her, she heard Sookim doing the same. She pulled the bowstring, aimed, and released it in one quick movement. Too quick; the arrow flew wide. With shaking hands, she started fumbling for more arrows in her pack. Sookim's arrow flew out—and it, too, missed its target.

There was a scuffling noise nearby. Barem was standing up, striding forward, raising his bow, steadying himself against a tree, drawing the string back with slow care. Finally he loosed his arrow—and it felled the man at the far edge of the field.

"No need to hide ourselves now," said Barem.

He was right, Nisha realized. And his training as a hunter had been worth more than her greater skill with the bow. He had remained calm while the rest of them had fallen victim to their own nervousness. She scrambled up and gripped him quickly on the shoulder. "Thank you, Barem," she said. Then the four of them ran out from under cover, into the field.

The women had paused in their toil and were staring around with confused, frightened eyes. Nisha ignored them. Her targets were at the far side; she had a long way to run. She raced across the tilled land while her companions scattered left and right. The first warrior that she'd hit was lying on his back, clutching his stomach and groaning. He seemed incapacitated, so she ignored him. The second man had been hit in the leg. He had dropped his spear and was limping toward the cleft which would take him back to the village. Nisha scooped up the man's spear as she ran, and she hurled it when she was only a dozen paces from him. He fell with a cry and lay on the ground, struggling feebly.

The warrior who had been hit by Barem's final arrow was also close by. But the shaft had struck him in the neck, and he was lying prostrate with his face in the earth, bleeding profusely from a severed artery.

Nisha turned, breathing hard, looking quickly around. She saw Sookim skewering one guard with his own spear. Another tried to stand up and fight back, but an arrow was lodged in his shoulder, and he was clumsy with pain and confusion. Sookim seized a heavy rock, turned, and hurled it against his head, felling him.

Barem had dealt with his man, and he was turning to Jep, who didn't seem to have the stomach or the strength to kill the warrior facing him. The hulking man had an arrow in his chest, and he was making an awful wet sound as he tried to breathe. Still he managed to raise his spear and was about to throw it at Jep when Barem picked up one of the arrows that had missed its target, notched it, and shot it into the warrior's heart.

Nisha stood for a moment with her ears ringing and her pulse racing. She saw Jep clutching his stomach, and for a moment she feared he had been injured. But then the boy leaned forward and vomited. He was scared, nothing more.

Barem seemed strong enough—in fact he was standing tall, with a confidence that Nisha hadn't seen in him before. And Sookim was seizing another rock, pounding it into the head of the man she had knocked down, just to be sure that she killed him.

"Sookim!" Nisha called to her. "The women!"

Sookim looked up. She seemed lost for a moment in her violent act of revenge. Gradually, her expression cleared. She gave a curt nod, remembering the plan.

Nisha turned to the men she had slain. Two of them had lost so much blood, they were no longer conscious. The third was the one she had shot at first. He was still lying on his back, still clutching the arrow in his stomach. "Get up," Nisha told him. "If you can get up, you may live."

He groaned, rolled over, and managed to rear up onto his knees. His hands were wet with blood. He stared at her incredulously. It was strange enough that he had been felled by a slim length of wood that had flown through the air out of nowhere. It was even harder for him to believe that his wound had been inflicted by a woman.

Nisha looked into his face. It was difficult for her to feel no sympathy for this man who had never done anything to her, but she couldn't afford to allow him any mercy. "Go down to the men in the cave," she told him, hardening her voice. "Tell them to bring Gogorah to me. Two of them can come with him, but only two. Do you understand?"

The wounded warrior nodded. Bending forward and clutching his stomach, he staggered to the cleft between the rocks and disappeared into it.

Behind her, Nisha heard Sookim shouting to the women, telling them to trust her, warning them not to run. All the women were hobbled with thongs, so it would be hard for them to go far. Still, there were so many of them, it was important to keep them in one group. And Nisha didn't trust them to act sensibly. They were so cowed by their lives as slaves, so trained to obey the men, there was no telling what they might do in this strange situation.

"Nisha!" It was Barem calling to her—a warning shout. "To your right!"

She whirled around and saw a man striding out from under the trees. He had been on sentry duty, she realized—like the one who had found her when she'd first come to the village. He stopped and stared at the fallen men, and then he turned toward Nisha.

She reached for the spear that was embedded in the body close to her on the ground. She wrenched it free, raised it, and hurled it. It hit the sentry just as he was raising his own spear. There was a terrible sound of flint on bone as Nisha's spear struck the man in the face, and then there was a crunching noise as he fell backward into thick vegetation. He started thrashing wildly and screaming.

Nisha winced. The noise of his agony was too much for her to bear. She ran to him, pulled the spear free, raised

it, then thrust it into his heart. Blessedly, then, his screaming stopped.

She found that she was shaking all over. This had been
far worse than she'd expected. She had lied to herself, she
realized, when she'd imagined how the attack would go.
She had told herself that the men would fall to their
knees, slightly wounded, ready to surrender. She should
have known that it wouldn't be that way.

Distantly, she heard questioning shouts. Either the
wounded man that she'd sent as a messenger had reached
the cave, or the people in the cave had heard some of the
noise from up here on the fields.

"Barem! Jep!" she called to them. "Bring all the arrows you can find!"

She took up a position opposite the exit from the cleft
in the rock, and she threw herself down in the grass. Once
again, she turned on her side. She reached in her pack,
pulled out a dozen more arrows, and notched one ready.
Behind her, she heard running footsteps. Then Barem and
Jep were beside her. She glanced at them, then stared
back at the cleft. Soon enough, a man came charging up
out of it. She shot him cleanly in the chest, and he fell.
But there was another one behind him, and another, holding their spears high. Jep and Barem loosed their own arrows, and the two warriors fell, blocking the exit.

"Bring me Gogorah!" Nisha shouted. She saw another
warrior running forward, leaping over his fallen comrades. She sighted on him and shot him in the stomach.
"Bring me Gogorah!" she shouted again.

Another pair of warriors tried to break out from the
cleft in the rocks—and both of them were killed. There
were five bodies, now, three of them still alive. The
wounded men called to their comrades, shouting for help.
One of them managed to pull himself out from under the
others, and he staggered forward, glaring at Nisha where
she lay in the grass. He raised his spear, and Barem shot
him in the leg. This time the warrior stayed down on the
ground where he fell.

There was a lull. The only sound was of the wounded men shouting and groaning.

"Pull your men back," she called out. "Then bring me Gogorah. Do you understand? We won't harm him. All we want is to talk to him."

There was another long pause, and she heard urgent, murmured conversation from deeper in the cleft. Furtively, a warrior peered over the fallen men, then seized one and hauled him into the crevice. One by one, the rest of the wounded warriors were dragged to safety.

Nisha felt just a little of her tension ebbing out of her. She glanced at Barem and saw that his face was flushed with pride and satisfaction at what had been accomplished. "We have them," he whispered.

"I think we do," she agreed. "But be cautious. You and Jep wait here while I check with Sookim."

Without waiting from him to answer, Nisha got onto her feet and ran back toward the forest. Sookim had herded the women into the far corner of the field, and now she was organizing them to tackle a different kind of work. A stream of water bubbled up out of the ground, here, and fed the irrigation channels that had been dug among the crops. The water also fed the cave below—through a fault in the rocky plateau that Sookim had described to Nisha three days ago.

Sookim was holding a spear, brandishing it at the women. "Push that boulder!" she cried, pointing to a rounded rock that was almost half Nisha's height. "All of you together, you can do it. Come on!"

Nisha walked closer—and when some of the women saw her, they cried out in surprise and alarm. They were from the Warrior Tribe. They recognized her, and they feared her.

"Listen to what she says!" Nisha shouted at them, pointing to Sookim. "That rock must move!"

The women gathered behind it, and they pushed with all their strength, spurred by their fear of these people who had emerged from nowhere, in the clear light of the

afternoon, with fearsome weapons that had felled more
than a dozen men. There was a wet sucking sound as the
boulder dragged free from the soil around it and started
rolling.

"This way!" Sookim shouted. "Here!" She pointed to
the place where the water disappeared into the ground.
The boulder rolled forward and there was a massive *thunk*
as it fell into place, plugging the stream.

Water began pooling around it and flowing away into
the irrigation system. Nisha squatted down, trying to see
if any at all was still escaping to the cave below. So far
as she could tell, there was none.

She glanced back toward the cliff edge. No more warriors were trying to charge out from the cleft there.

She turned to the women who had moved the boulder.
"All of you, back into the corner of the field," she said.
"Quickly, now! Sit there, close together."

She waited till they had done what she said. Then she
turned to Sookim. "The hard part is done," she said.
"Now, we wait."

Chapter Thirty-Eight

The afternoon was growing old, and Nisha was starting to feel worried. She didn't want to maintain a vigil here all night. Any one of the women might become rebellious, and it would only take a few to stir up the rest. More warriors could sneak up from the cave below, and they would be hard to see and harder to kill in the moonlight. She had been hoping that the Cave People would be so shocked and alarmed by the attack and by the loss of their water supply, they would either surrender or try to mount a counterattack right away. The longer the day dragged on, the weaker her position would be. She reminded herself that the warriors in the cave had no way of knowing how many people were up here. They probably imagined that an entire tribe had come to attack them. And surely they could see that without water, their position was hopeless.

She tried to be calm, and she shared none of her concerns with her companions. Jep spent some time walking around, staring at the guards who had been killed. Sookim stayed with the women in the corner of the field. Nisha and Barem remained by the cleft in the rocks with their bows ready, and they waited.

"I realize this man Gogorah is their chieftain," said Barem. "But do you really think we'll be able to reason with him? And do you think they'll surrender if he tells them to?"

"He's not just their chieftain, they worship him," Nisha said. She told him the legend that Sookim had told her:

that Gogorah was immortal, and he had the power of the Thunder God. "Of course, it's just a myth that he created to maintain his power over his people," Nisha said. "Really, he's just a cunning old man. I do believe he'll surrender if his own life is threatened."

Grep was the one who really worried her. Gogorah seemed the type who would rather collaborate with his enemy than lose his life. Grep, on the other hand, was proud—and he had powerful reasons for wanting Nisha to die no matter what it might cost.

"I hear something," Barem said suddenly. He drew his bow and waited, peering into the dark cleft in the rocks opposite them.

There was a scraping, bumping sound, and some unsteady footsteps.

"Who's there?" Barem shouted out.

"We bring you Gogorah," a man shouted back.

Nisha felt a surge of anticipation. She and Barem moved back a little, and Jep ran over to join them. Over by the women in the field, Sookim notched a fresh arrow in her own bow.

Two warriors came into view carrying a wooden chair supporting a frail, thin figure. As Nisha saw them, she realized that for all her show of confidence, a part of her had been reluctant to believe that this could really happen. But here he was, now, the chieftain of the Cave People, bowing to her will.

"Put him there!" Nisha shouted. Behind her, she heard the women muttering in surprise and alarm as they recognized their chieftain. She ignored them, just as she ignored the looks of hate on the faces of the warriors who had carried Gogorah up here.

"You two," said Barem, "over there." He pointed to the cleft.

Sullenly, they retreated.

Gogorah was turning his old head, blinking in the evening sunlight. He seemed to be looking for the many warriors that he had assumed were attacking his tribe. Finally he turned to Barem. "Are you the leader here?" he asked in his dry, frail voice.

"No," said Barem. He gestured to Nisha. "She is our leader." He hunkered down again with Jep, and he turned his attention back toward the cleft in the rocks.

Nisha stood in front of Gogorah. "Do you remember me?" she asked.

He stared at her without moving—without showing any expression at all.

"Are you sick?" she asked. He looked even thinner and weaker than she remembered.

"I am old," he said. His face was still expressionless, but now she saw the anger in his eyes. After so many decades ruling his tribe, he found his life threatened by two women, a skinny, underfed man, and a boy.

"First you must answer some questions," she said.

Gogorah stared at her. He said nothing.

"When the Warrior Tribe came to attack your people—were all of the invaders killed?"

Gogorah still stared at Nisha without speaking. His anger and his defiance burned silently in him. His lips were pressed tightly shut.

Nisha picked up a spear and turned it toward him. "I can easily kill you," she said. "I have already killed many men today."

Gogorah's nostrils flared. His face twitched. She saw his hands clench on the arms of his chair. "You are the one who will die," he whispered. "I will see to it—"

"Tell me!" She jabbed his throat with the tip of the spear.

He flinched, stiffened, then shuddered and closed his eyes. For a moment she was afraid that the shock had killed him. But then she saw his chest heaving, and once again he stared at her. "All the men from the Warrior Tribe were killed," he said, "except one."

So it was true, Nisha thought. Hawk Spirit had shown her the truth. "Why did you let him live?" she snapped, feeling her anger rise up.

Gogorah looked at her with disgust. "Woman, you have no right—"

"This gives me the right!" She jabbed him again, harder.

Gogorah squirmed in his chair and looked around as if he imagined that his guards might somehow come to protect him. But then he saw the fierce determination in Nisha's face. She might not kill him, but she would certainly hurt him.

Gogorah seemed to lose some of his strength. "I let a man live because he is my kin," he muttered.

"Grep is your *kin*?" Nisha's voice rose in disbelief.

"Yes. He is the half-brother of Worr, my great-grandson. The two of them shared the same father, though they were born from different wives."

"Grep told you that?" Nisha shook her head. "He lied. He must have lied."

"No." Gogorah raised his head. "He carries a spear that his father gave him, and that came from his father's father before him. I know the look of that spear, the way it is made, the way it is decorated—there's no doubt. When he surrendered and begged for mercy and showed that spear, I knew he was my kin."

"But he killed Worr," Nisha cried, "even though you say Worr was his half-brother."

"Yes," said the old man. "He hated Worr, because Worr had killed their father. That was how Worr seized power in the Warrior Tribe."

Nisha stepped back. Finally, she understood. Grep's constant anger, his alienation, his coldness—he was the younger brother, and his whole adult life had been consumed with a need for revenge.

"When I die," Gogorah whispered, so quietly that Nisha could barely hear him, "Grep will inherit this tribe. I have vowed this, and it shall be so."

Nisha laughed dismissively. "It shall *not* be so." She turned and looked across at Sookim. "Is there anything you want to say to this man?"

Sookim was watching Nisha curiously. She shook her head.

Nisha pointed her spear at Gogorah once again. This time, though, she turned and looked at the two men who had brought the chieftain up. "You!" she shouted at them. "Go back and tell your comrades, they must all come up here. One at a time. And if they don't obey, I'll kill Gogorah. The only men who can stay down in the cave are the ones who are too badly wounded to be moved. Do you understand?"

They glanced at each other. Then one of them turned back toward Nisha and took a step forward.

"Shoot him!" Nisha cried to Barem.

The bowstring whirred and an arrow was suddenly embedded in the man's shoulder. He stepped back with a startled shout.

"You see our power," Nisha called to the other man. "We have a weapon that you have never seen, with a power you can only dream of. Now go!"

The man glanced at his wounded comrade, then turned and hurried into the narrow fissure.

"Shall we kill them as they come up here?" Barem asked.

Nisha shook her head. "We have better things to do with them, after they surrender."

Gogorah grunted. "You will die, woman. You will all die. I will eat your flesh. The birds will peck the meat from your bones."

"Be quiet," Nisha said. She remembered how she had been afraid of his power, the first time they had met. And now he was just a frail old man making empty threats, while she literally held his life in her hands.

She heard the first of the warriors emerging from the cleft, and she looked around in time to see him raising his spear.

"Throw your weapon out here!" Nisha called. "Otherwise, your chieftain will die."

The warrior's eyes widened as he saw Gogorah sitting with her spear pressed to his throat.

"Do as the woman says," the old man called out. "She has already killed too many of our people."

Reluctantly, the warrior tossed his weapon out onto the ground.

One by one, then, all the men emerged. There were at least three score of them altogether. Standing in a group, staring at Nisha with rage and loathing, they were a frightening force. She wondered if she should have let Barem kill them after all—but she truly believed that it had to be done this way.

Still, it terrified her to think that the only thing holding them in check was her power over their chieftain. She felt a knot in her stomach as she contemplated her next action. She had thought that this would be the safest part of her plan, yet now she realized it was the most dangerous.

She scanned the faces of the warriors. "There's one who still isn't here," she called out. "Grep. The man named Grep. Where is he?"

There was a long silence. Some of the men glanced at each other, but no one spoke.

"Nisha, we have no time for this." It was Barem, speaking without looking at her. He was still lying with Jep, keeping his bow trained on the mob in front of him—but it was a puny weapon against so many men.

She saw he was right. She had to act. Well, they would find Grep down in the cave soon enough, and then she could deal with him.

She looked at Gogorah. "Tell them," she said, speaking slowly and clearly, "to lie down on their stomachs. Tell them to put their hands behind them. They are our prisoners now. They will be tied in the same way that the women, there, are tied. Do you understand?" She nudged him with the spear. "Tell them. Otherwise, I will kill you."

He raised his head and contemplated her for a moment. The tendons tightened in his neck. His mouth widened in a terrible smile. "I will tell them nothing," he said.

It took Nisha a moment to realize what he had said. She felt herself growing cold inside. "I'll kill you!" she warned him again, and her voice was shrill.

Gogorah looked at his men. "Attack!" he suddenly shouted, and his voice was far louder than Nisha would have thought possible. "There's only four of them, you fools! Attack! I cannot die; the Thunder God protects me. Attack!"

Nisha turned to face the men. Gogorah's words had roused them from their stupor. They were taking their first steps forward. She stared at them in horror.

Jep cried out in fear. Barem cursed. He suddenly sprang to his feet, threw down his bow, and grabbed a rock. He took two steps toward Gogorah, raised the rock in his two hands, and brought it down with all his strength on the chieftain's skull.

There was a terrible crunching thud. Gogorah screamed and fell back in his chair. Barem seized the spear out of Nisha's hands and plunged it deep into the chieftain's chest. He shifted his grip, braced himself, and lifted Gogorah into the air on the end of the spear like a piece of meat being plucked from a cooking fire on the end of a stick.

Barem turned and smashed the old man down on the ground in front of the warriors. "He's dead!" Barem screamed. "The Thunder God has forsaken him. The old man is dead. Do you see? Do you understand? Your tribe will be destroyed!"

The mob of warriors suddenly stood motionless. Every one of them stared at the crumpled figure lying in a spreading pool of blood. Some of them shouted in fear and disbelief.

The sun had almost set. As it sank beneath the horizon, the light grew dimmer.

"The Thunder God is your enemy now!" Barem shouted. "He curses your tribe. On your knees! Bow down before him! He has given us the power to kill your chieftain. We will kill you, too, if you don't obey."

Many of the men fell to their knees. Barem bent and seized his bow. Nisha understood immediately what had to be done. She ran to her own bow where she had left it in the grass. By the time she was notching her first arrow, Barem and Jep had already shot two of the men who were still standing. Nisha aimed at random at a warrior, loosed her arrow, seized another, and aimed again.

Sookim started using her bow, from where she still stood guarding the women. Arrows rained on the warriors. A couple of them tried to dive forward and reach the spears that they had tossed away, but they were quickly killed. One man tried to turn and run, but Nisha brought him down with an arrow in his back.

And then, it was done. About thirty of the warriors lay face down, obedient and unharmed, trembling in fear of lightning bolts from the heavens. The rest of the men were scattered about, clutching their wounds, screaming and dying.

"Sookim!" Nisha called. "We must free the women and tie the men!"

Nisha waited till Sookim answered with a shout. Then she turned to Barem. She took a step forward—and found herself suddenly stumbling. Her legs were weak. All the strength was ebbing out of her. She fell against Barem and tried to steady herself, throwing her arm around his shoulders. "I was wrong," she muttered, feeling sick with remorse. "Forgive me, Barem. If you hadn't acted, we would have all been killed."

"You were too decent," he said. "That was your only mistake." He smiled at Nisha. "It's lucky, though, you told me what these fools believe. Otherwise, I wouldn't have known what to say."

She breathed deeply and managed to recover some of

her strength. For a moment, she had truly thought that she was going to die. "Let's deal with them now," she said. "Let's make them safe. Then we can go down to the village in the cave."

Chapter Thirty-Nine

There was a big fire burning in the center of the cave, and Nisha heard voices echoing off the curved rock—Sookim's voice, and some of the women talking and arguing with her. But Nisha was sitting alone, out on the edge of the cliffs, staring into the darkness with her spear resting across her knees.

There was a lull in the voices behind her. Then a man shouted something, and women shouted back at him. This kind of interplay had been going on for a while, and Nisha was reluctant to give it her attention. She stared down into the dark depths of the valley, and she wondered where the red-tailed hawk was roosting tonight. And then she thought of Winnor, and she imagined him sleeping in his safe little home in the town of many houses.

There was a footstep behind her. Nisha turned quickly and jumped to her feet.

"It's only me," said Sookim. She paused, silhouetted against the dim red glow that lit the interior of the cave. "What are you doing out here, Nisha? Why won't you join the rest of us? I could use your help."

She sighed. "All right. I'll come."

Sookim glanced at the darkened landscape, then back at Nisha. "Do you imagine he's out there?" she said.

"No, of course not." She realized that she was sounding rude, and she tried to calm herself. "Sookim, there were three reasons why I wanted to do what we've done here," she said. "To bring justice to these people, to help you and your people, and to settle things between myself and this man Grep. For me, you know, the third reason was the most important—and yet I've failed. I'm sure he was here. But he's nowhere to be found."

"He could still be hiding," said Sookim. "Are you sure you've searched all the houses? Some of the women are ready to help us now. We can gather them together into a search party—"

Nisha shook her head. "I've already looked everywhere, twice over."

"Even the dark places, like the pit houses?" said Sookim.

"Yes. I had Barem hold a torch while I stabbed down into each pit with my spear. Grep's gone, Sookim." She turned again and stared across the darkened valley. "I don't know how it happened, but he's gone. And I think one of his wives is with him. The one named Reive. She's nowhere to be found, either."

Sookim stepped closer. She put her hand on Nisha's shoulder. "You said you'd put the past behind you," she reminded her. "You said you're free."

"Yes," said Nisha, "free from my guilt. But still that man is evil, Sookim, and he hurt me, and so long as he is out there, none of us can feel completely safe."

There were some shrill female shouts from inside the cave, and then a man bellowed in pain.

"Please come," Sookim said, tugging at Nisha's arm.

"If you want me to reason with the women from the Warrior Tribe," said Nisha, "you're wasting your time. I'm sure they still distrust me."

"Come anyway," said Sookim. "Just for me."

Reluctantly, Nisha went after her. They followed a path between the houses to an open meeting place halfway to the back of the cave. Scores of women were gathered here, with their children among them. About thirty men, some of them wounded, had been tied hand and foot.

The women had raided the stores and had been feasting. The smell of corn wine was in the air. One woman had jumped up and was standing over one of the men, jabbing him with her spear.

Sookim strode over and took hold of the woman's shoulder. "Stop this," she said.

The woman turned and glared at her. "Do you think you've taken the place of the men, now, Sookim?" She shook her head. "You have no right to tell me what to do."

Nisha stepped forward. She raised her hand and gently pushed the spear to one side. "I gave you your freedom," she said. "But not the freedom to hurt someone who can't defend himself. If you do that, then you're no better than the men who used to do it to you."

The woman's face was fierce in the flickering firelight. "I don't think you understand," she said. "This one used to call himself my husband. He beat me, and he forced me to serve him. I think it's his turn to suffer for a while."

Nisha looked at the man lying on his back. His robe had been ripped open, and there were half a dozen small wounds in his chest, some of them bleeding. He was breathing through clenched teeth, glowering up at the women, and wrestling with his bonds.

Nisha turned back to the woman with the spear. "I understand your need for revenge. And if you want to kill this man, I don't think anyone will stop you. But listen to me first, and then decide."

The woman eyed her doubtfully. "What do you have to say?"

"Come back beside the fire," Nisha said. "Let everyone hear this."

Grudgingly, the woman followed Nisha back to the group that was sitting around the flames.

Nisha stepped up onto a low wall that had been built around the edge of the meeting place. "Hear me!" she called out.

Her voice echoed under the roof of the cavern. As the echoes slowly dissipated into silence, the women stared up at her. Some of the children whimpered.

Nisha surveyed their faces. She saw all kinds of expressions—uncertainty, hope, anger, caution. She wondered how these women must feel to have spent all their lives under constant threat of punishment—and now to find they were free. For some of them, like the one who had been tormenting her husband, freedom was something to be seized and used to the full, even though she had never experienced it before. For others, the idea seemed frightening. They had suffered as servants, but as servants they had at least known the security of a set routine and a list of rules to follow. Now, everything that seemed fixed and certain had been overturned.

"Those of you from the Warrior Tribe already know me well," said Nisha. "And yet, perhaps you don't know me as well as you may imagine. It's true that I brought conflict to your tribe. I caused trouble, and men died because of me. You may feel I had no right to interfere in your lives. But remember, your warriors killed almost all the men and women of my tribe. I wanted vengeance, I wanted justice, and most of all, I wanted to be free."

She saw some of the women glancing at one another, but she couldn't read their expressions. No one was standing up in anger against her, though, and she was thankful for that.

"This place is yours now," Nisha went on. "This tribe will be your tribe. I think Sookim should be your chieftain—but that, too, is for you to decide. All I want to say is that you should take time and think carefully before you shed any more blood. Sooner or later, you will need your menfolk." She gave her audience an ironic smile. "You may even decide to put them to work for you in the fields."

Some women laughed—but the one who had tormented her husband stood up to confront Nisha. "This is all very easy for you to say," she said. "But how can we ever trust these men? They're warriors. Ever since they were children, they've been taught that they had a right to rule us. You know that if they have any chance at all, they'll take back what they've lost, and they may shed our blood in order to get it."

Nisha spread her hands. "Yes, I see that. Of course, you're right. But listen: two weeks ago, I visited the Green Canyon people. Men and women work side by side there, just as they did in my tribe. It can be done. Things can change—if not for this generation, then for the next one."

The woman wasn't satisfied. "You say we shouldn't shed any more blood. But if a man's so full of violence and anger that he'll always be a danger to us—what can we do?"

Nisha thought for a moment. "Perhaps," she said, "you should do what the people of the Green Canyon do to warriors who attack their tribe. They castrate them."

There were gasps from around the fire.

"I've seen it myself," Nisha said, raising her voice. "When a man loses his scrotum, he becomes as gentle and docile as a sheep. Believe me; this is so."

The women started murmuring among themselves. The one who had challenged Nisha was frowning at her. "You think this is right, and spilling blood is wrong?" she said.

"I think if a man threatens your life," said Nisha, "you have a right to defend yourself. And if you offer him a choice of death or losing his manhood—perhaps this is better than no choice at all."

Many of the women by the fire were talking so loudly, now, Nisha saw it was going to be hard to make herself heard. Well, she had said all that needed to be said. She suddenly felt so weary, just the idea of talking seemed too much of an effort.

She stepped down from the wall where she had been standing. "Thank you for hearing me," she called out, "and I wish you good fortune. But now I must rest."

She went to the tower that had been Gogorah's home. She paused for a moment in the little circular room, and she looked at the spot where the chieftain's chair had stood. She remembered how she had been forced to kneel in front of him. But now he was dead, and his power had gone as if it had never been. It seemed to her that there was an important lesson here: Tyrants were mortal, just like animals or children. It was simply a matter of finding the courage to confront them.

She went to the ladder and climbed it to the floor above. There were some tree stumps to sit on here, ranged around a fireplace, and she saw some ornaments in the faint firelight that came through the window. There was a white deerskin hanging on one wall, decorated with picture-stories showing hunters and their game out on the plateau, and the cave in the cliffs with only a couple of tiny houses inside it. A ceremonial spear stood in one corner; a massive stone axe lay on the window ledge.

Another ladder led to a third floor of the tower. Nisha climbed it and found herself in a tiny room. A bed of boughs and sheepskins stood against one wall. So this was where the old chieftain had slept. If it had served him well enough, it should serve her too. She lay down on the bed and pulled the sheepskins over herself.

Even though she was exhausted, she lay awake for a long time. Her mind was still haunted by all the sights she had seen—the woman tormenting the man who had been her prisoner, the warriors falling and clutching their wounds, Sookim crushing a man's skull with a stone in her hands, and Gogorah impaled upon Barem's spear. In her heart, she felt sure that what she had done was right. Still, it was an awesome thing to take so many lives and change the whole destiny of a tribe. She hoped she would never be in a position to make such a decision again. With Winnor's help, perhaps she could learn how to save lives instead of ending them.

Gradually she slipped into a restless sleep—but the images of blood and death still haunted her dreams, and now, instead of being the aggressor, she was the victim. Dark, silhouetted figures were creeping up on her, although every time she turned to confront one, it vanished.

Still she heard their stealthy footsteps behind her, and she sensed them raising their weapons, preparing to strike.

She started running—yet the world seemed fixed around her. Her arms and legs were churning in empty space. She tried to scream—but she couldn't breathe. Her lungs seemed paralyzed.

She felt herself panicking. The dark silhouettes were enveloping her like storm clouds sent by the Thunder God. They were going to suffocate her.

She felt a sharp stabbing sensation on the side of her neck, and she woke, gasping for breath. There was a dark figure leaning over her. Nisha gave a little cry of horror. Was she still asleep? No, she realized: someone was up here in the little room. It was a man, and he was holding a spear at her throat. She smelled his odor—and she recognized it. "Grep," she whispered.

"Quiet, or you'll die."

She could just make out his dark shape in the dark room as he lowered himself and sat down on her hips, pinning her to the bed. Behind him, Nisha glimpsed another figure—and she knew at once who it was. "Reive," she muttered. She saw the woman's eyes gleaming in the faint light that filtered through the window. It was almost dawn outside the cave.

Were they going to kill her? It would have been easy for them to do it while she was asleep. But instead, they had woken her. What did they want? And how had they hidden themselves? She'd felt sure that they were nowhere in the village. Her thoughts were chattering in her head. Were they going to try and take her away with them? And why was Reive collaborating with Grep like this, when she could have been free if she chose?

Nisha looked down and saw that the spear was the same one that Grep had used to kill Worr—the ceremonial spear, decorated with tufts of animal fur and dried squares of human scalp dangling on thongs. This was the spear that had belonged to Grep's father, and his father's father.

Carefully, Grep passed the spear into Reive's hands. He stood up, then, and started loosening the thongs that held his robe closed.

"What do you want?" Nisha whispered.

"This is not a time for you to ask questions," Grep told her.

Nisha squirmed in frustration. She couldn't bear the thought that after everything she had been through, she might die now, alone with this terrible man and his wife-slave. She looked at Reive. "Why are you following this man?" she whispered. "Why didn't you choose to be free?"

Reive glanced at Grep as if she needed permission before she could speak.

"Answer if you wish," Grep said.

"There is a natural way of things," said Reive. "There are people who lead, and people who follow. There are those who are strong, and those who are weak."

Grep had removed his robe and was stripping off his leggings. Nisha had an awful premonition about what was to follow.

She turned back to Reive. There was probably no hope at all of rousing this woman against her mate, but still, she had to try. "You are not weak," she said.

"Maybe so," Reive agreed, "but Grep is stronger than any woman or any man. He has chosen me, and he protects me, and that is the natural way of things." She spoke quietly, simply—and Nisha realized it was really the first time she had ever heard Reive voicing her real, secret thoughts.

"But he won't protect you a dozen years from now," Nisha said. "Have you forgotten how women were discarded in the Warrior Tribe?"

"Enough," said Grep. "Woman, move aside." He flicked his hand at Nisha.

Cautiously, she edged toward the far side of the bed, till her shoulder nudged the wall. The spear point followed her, maintaining its steady pressure.

Grep lay down beside her. She saw the black flint knife, the sacred object of her tribe, still hanging on a thong around his neck. She felt a wave of outrage that he should still possess it, and her anger helped to drive away some of her fear.

Grep leaned on his elbow and stared at Nisha. His body was tense, and she saw the way his thin lips pulled back from his teeth, like the mouth of a snarling dog. He hated her, she realized. He wanted to destroy her.

It was terrible to be forced to lie close to him like this, and be unable to move. Her eyes flicked toward Reive, then back to Grep. Surely, there must be some way to summon help. If she screamed, a dozen women would hear her, and probably they would capture Grep and kill him. But before that happened, Reive would sink her spear into Nisha's throat. Was it worth the sacrifice?

For a moment, she really thought it might be. But almost immediately she felt a renewed burst of anger. It was intolerable to sacrifice herself now. Surely, there had to be justice.

"Sit up," Grep said softly.

Nisha waited till the pressure of the spear point diminished a little. Slowly, she sat up on the bed.

"You are going to please me now," Grep said. "Just as you used to please me in my tribe. But this time, Reive will watch us. And this time, there will be no chance for you to disobey me."

His eyes were murderous. Nisha knew with absolute certainty that after she did what he wanted, he would kill her. Probably he had never hated anyone as much as he hated her—because she alone had robbed him of all the power that he used to own. First she had taken away his warriors, and now she had taken his women—except for one.

With a trembling hand, she reached out toward him. The spear jabbed the back of her neck as she moved. Nisha paused and glanced around. "I must be able to move a little," she whispered.

Grep nodded reluctantly. "Give her a little room," he said.

Reive sidestepped and repositioned herself alongside Nisha instead of behind her. But the spear was still carefully aimed at the side of Nisha's neck. Nisha remembered how Kron had bled when Grep had punctured his artery. She shuddered at the idea of her own blood gushing out like that.

"All right," said Grep. "Now you will do what I want you to do."

Chapter Forty

Nisha tried to suppress her loathing as she touched him. She had done it before, she told herself; she could do it now. She reminded herself that in this way, she still had some power over him. But that must be why he had come here now, risking his life in order to play this game with her. To him, power was everything. Before he killed her, he had to humiliate her; that was his way.

He stared at her steadily while she touched him. Out of the corner of her eye, Nisha saw Reive watching intently. But Nisha's main focus was on Grep. Her gaze locked with his, and the two of them glared at each other, each of them consumed with hatred.

It took a while for Nisha's skills to rouse him, but slowly she sensed his physical transformation. His breathing deepened. His nostrils flared. Little tremors rippled across his belly.

Nisha started touching him more slowly and more gently, delaying his climax. She watched as he arched his back, forcing his crotch up toward her. "Don't stop," he told her. His voice was a tight command.

She moved her hand tantalizingly, trying to think how she could summon help and save herself. The light outside was definitely getting stronger. Soon it would be daybreak. But even so, there was no reason why anyone should climb the ladders to the top floor of the tower. Nisha realized she was fooling herself if she imagined that someone else was going to rescue her. If she was going to live, it would have to be through her own will alone.

"Do it!" Grep hissed at her. He clenched his fists. "Satisfy me, woman, or you will die now."

She found herself trembling with a terrible mixture of fear and rage. She could bring him to his climax, and then be killed; or she could refuse, and be killed anyway.

Nisha reached her decision. She clenched her hand on him. She started touching him in long, swift strokes. She watched as his eyes widened. He gasped, and the cords of his neck stood out. His fingers clutched at the mattress under him. His mouth opened in a silent scream.

From the corner of her eye, Nisha saw Reive staring at Grep's face. The woman seemed transfixed. The spear point wavered.

Grep reached his climax. His body spasmed, and he thrashed on the bed. Nisha flung herself forward. She seized the flint dagger that hung around his neck, and she wrenched at it with all her strength. The thong snapped. She raised the dagger high in both hands, then smashed it down into Grep's chest.

Immediately, Nisha rolled off the bed. Reive's spear stabbed at her, and the point of it grazed Nisha's shoulder. But Nisha was now on the floor. She heard Reive cry out in fury, and the woman stood up and raised her spear, ready to bring it down where Nisha lay at her feet.

Nisha seized Reive around her legs, dragged her, and toppled her. Reive screamed and the spear clattered out of her hands.

Nisha grabbed it. She scrambled up and banged into the wall. Reive was on the floor now. Nisha had only an instant to take aim before she thrust the spear, but her aim was true. The point sank into Reive's chest.

Reive screamed. The noise was startlingly loud in the tiny room. Nisha dragged the spear back, and Reive clapped her hand over the wound. Blood started flowing out between her fingers. She screamed again.

Nisha turned to Grep. He was rearing up, staring at

Nisha in fury. The black knife was still embedded deep in his upper chest.

Nisha took aim. She gathered all her strength and stabbed at him with the spear.

He rolled forward at the same moment. The spear point cut a long, deep slash in his back and dug into the bed behind him.

Grep tumbled off the bed and threw himself head first into the hole in the corner of the room where the ladder stood. There was a crash and a thump as he fell to the floor below.

Nisha cursed silently. He had the reflexes of a warrior, while she had never hunted anything fiercer than a prairie dog. She glanced at Reive and saw her still lying on the floor and clutching herself. She was shuddering. She seemed to be going into shock.

Nisha strode to the ladder, peered down, and saw Grep jumping from the second floor down to the ground floor. She freed her spear from the bed and threw it down at him, but it landed behind him.

Nisha swung her legs through the hole in the floor, slid down the first ladder, then slid down the second one. Her bare heels hit the ground hard, sending a message of pain up her legs, but she barely noticed. She seized her spear and ran out of the tower. She was determined that he wouldn't hide from her again.

He was only a dozen paces ahead of her, clutching the dagger in his chest as he ran toward the mouth of the cave. She saw him glancing to one side, then the other. He was looking for a weapon, she realized. But there were none. Sookim had carefully gathered up all the spears the night before.

A female voice shouted something from close by—a sleepy question. "Wake up!" Nisha screamed. "Help me!" The sound of her shout resounded in the cave.

She pounded after Grep. He hesitated, and she saw him considering whether to try to escape along the ledge. But that would make him hopelessly vulnerable. She would kill him easily if he went that way. She could simply thrust at him with the spear and send him flying off the ledge to his death far below.

Grep made his decision. He ran to the edge of the cliffs. Nisha stopped uncertainly. Did he have a weapon hidden there? He seemed to be groping for something. But then she understood: The previous night, he had hidden himself using the same method as when he and his men had tried to attack the Cave People. There was a rope there that she hadn't seen in the darkness. He must have lowered Reive and himself to a hiding place below the rim of the cliffs. There must be a ledge farther down—a ledge like the one where Winnor had hidden on the mesa.

"Stop!" she screamed at him. She raised her spear, bracing herself with her legs spread wide apart.

He looked up at her. His eyes were wild, and he was panting. Blood was running from the wound in his chest. Nisha saw droplets falling onto the rocks. He bared his teeth at her, and she wondered if he would try to lunge at her anyway, regardless of the spear.

"Stand up," she told him. "Stand!"

There were more sleepy women's voices behind her, asking what was happening. Nisha ignored them. All her attention, now, was on Grep. The spear was heavy in her hands, but it seemed to possess its own terrible life. She couldn't guess how many men had been killed by this weapon over the years. All she wanted, now, was for it to claim one more.

Slowly, Grep got to his feet. His face was so full of fury, he was a wild beast. His skin was slick with sweat. "Give it to me!" he shouted. He held out his hand for the spear.

Nisha grunted in disgust. She kept herself well out of reach. "Give me the dagger," she said.

He looked at her as if he didn't understand.

"The knife!" she screamed at him. "The sacred object

of my tribe! You stole it. You defiled it. You have it in your chest now. Pull it free and give it to me!"

He blinked, groped for the knife, then dragged it free and flung it down onto the ground in front of her.

Behind Nisha, women were emerging from their houses, crying out in surprise and alarm as they saw her confronting the bleeding man on the edge of the cliffs. She paid no attention to them; she was focused totally on Grep. "Now," she said, trying to steady herself. "This is your choice, Grep. You can surrender to our tribe, and let us do whatever we choose to do. Or you can die."

Blood was running swiftly from the open knife wound. He pressed his palm over it, threw his head back, and let out a terrible sound—half growl, half shout. And then, without warning, he bent his knees, leaned forward, and hurled himself at Nisha.

She had only an instant to react—but her instincts were true. She brought the spear up as he charged at her. She clenched her hands on it with all her strength. She saw him reaching for the spear, trying to seize it and turn it aside. She pulled it back, then stabbed it forward. His grasping fingers missed the shaft. The point plunged deep into the center of his chest.

For a moment he was immobilized, impaled on the weapon, hanging there. His weight threatened to drag it out of her hands. But still he refused to give in. He somehow steadied himself on his feet. He grabbed the shaft and wrestled with it, while his blood spattered down.

Nisha saw that she had no choice. She braced herself, then pushed forward as hard as she could.

Grep staggered backward. He still struggled with her, but he was losing his strength. Nisha's bare feet dug into the fissured rock. She forced herself forward. "You murdered my husband!" she screamed at him. "You killed my child!"

He lost his footing and gave a little shout of rage. He held onto the spear as if he hoped it would save him. But she gave one last push, then released her grip on it.

Grep toppled backward, waving his arms. He gave a long, moaning yell that echoed up and down the valley as he tipped over the edge of the cliff and fell into the chasm.

Nisha ran forward and a dozen women joined her, all of them dropping down on their hands and knees so that they could peer over the edge. Far, far below, she saw Grep's broken body amid a great splash of blood. He had been literally torn apart by the impact.

Nisha kneeled there for a long time, staring at the remains of her enemy. There was a hissing in her ears, and for a moment she feared she might faint. Gradually, though, she regained her strength. She stood up and stepped back, still barely aware of her surroundings.

She noticed the black flint knife on the ground at her feet. She bent down to pick it up.

As she did so, she heard a faint sound: footsteps running toward her. Still dazed by the horror of Grep's death, she squinted into the dimness of the cave.

She saw Reive coming toward her in a stumbling run. The woman's robe was covered in blood. Her face was a white mask of pain. She was holding the stone axe that Nisha had seen lying on the window ledge of the room on the second floor in the tower.

Reive swung the axe—and Nisha threw herself flat. Reive was uncoordinated, barely able to run in a straight line. The axe cut only air. She tried to stop herself, then gave a little cry of dismay as she tripped over Nisha. Then she, too, was gone, turning in the air, falling, following her husband to the rocks far below.

Nisha felt the flint knife under her belly. She grabbed hold of it and rolled onto her back. She clutched the black blade between her breasts and stared up into the lightening sky, trying to calm herself. All her enemies were gone now. There was nothing she needed to fear anymore. She was safe here.

The women at the edge of the cliff were pulling back,

chattering to one another. A couple of them kneeled beside Nisha and asked if she was all right.

"Don't concern yourselves about me," she told them. "Just let me lie here in peace. I'll join you in a while, when I have my strength again."

Reluctantly, the women did as she said. She heard them still talking, moving into the cave. She stared up at the sky—and she saw a faint black speck. It circled, drifting lower.

The hawk came into plain view, and she saw its distinctive red tail. It eyed her for a moment, then pulled its wings in and dove down out of sight.

Nisha closed her eyes. *Feed yourself well, Hawk Spirit,* she thought. *With your help, I overcame my enemies. Now you have the reward that I promised you. You can feed on them where they lie on the rocks. Tear them open with your terrible beak, and eat their hearts.*

Epilogue

Nisha sat alone, staring out over the valley. The sun was beating down on her now, but she hardly felt it. There were sounds of women talking, arguing among themselves, but she hardly heard them.

"Are you unhappy?"

The voice seemed far away, but Nisha gradually realized it came from close beside her. She blinked and turned her head, and she saw Sookim looking at her with gentle concern.

Nisha drew a slow breath. She rubbed her face like a sleeper trying to wake. "No," she said softly. "No, I'm not unhappy. In fact, I feel truly content for the first time in many months."

Sookim smiled—but it wasn't an easy smile. "It seems you don't really need the rest of us anymore," she said.

Nisha reached for the woman and held her close. A gust of wind blew Sookim's hair across Nisha's face, and Nisha closed her eyes for a moment, surrendering herself to the smell of Sookim and the warmth of her body. "It's good to be with you," she whispered.

"Truly?" Sookim slowly pulled back.

"Truly."

"You—did promise to stay here," Sookim said. "You remember, while we were hiding in the woods, just before we attacked the guards in the fields? You said you would never leave."

Nisha reached out and stroked Sookim's hair. "I didn't

say I would never leave," she said. "Only a fool would promise her whole future. I said I would stay, but I can't tell you how long that will be. I can't imagine myself, or you, or this tribe, a year from now. Anything might happen."

Sookim blinked and pulled back, looking as if she had been slapped.

Nisha seized her hands. "I'm happy with you, Sookim. But you forced me to say what I said, before we attacked the men in the fields. Suppose I had refused; would you have still helped me to overthrow them? Would you have fought as fiercely?" She looked into the woman's eyes. "I had to say what I said, because without your loyalty and strength, we would have all been killed."

Sookim was looking distraught. "You mean you lied to me," she said. She tried to drag her hands free.

Nisha kept her grip. "No. Listen! I *will* stay here. I will stay—for a while."

Sookim shook her head. "This isn't right, Nisha. You tricked me."

Nisha sighed. She had been dreading this conversation, and it was just as hard, now, as she'd feared it would be. "Think with your mind, not with your heart," she said. "How much do you know me, Sookim? How much do you really need me? Think! Aren't you stronger now than before? This can be your tribe, now. You can be their chieftain if you choose. And it's a tribe where there are far more women than men." She paused a moment, waiting for her words to be understood. "You aren't powerless anymore. You don't need to depend on other people as you once did. You said yourself, many women in this tribe used to lie with each other secretly. There must be a lot of them who admire you and covet you now. Did you consider that?"

Nisha saw a faint blush on Sookim's cheeks. The woman turned away, hiding the purple swatch on the side of her forehead. "I'm only interested in you," she said. But her voice wasn't quite as strong as before.

"Well, we have each other for as long as we both wish it," said Nisha. "So we will see what happens, you and I. But this is no time to make predictions. We have all changed, and the village will change even more. You should go and tell people what needs to be done now, instead of worrying about the two of us. I'll still be here when it's time for you to rest, and I'll still be here tomorrow, and even the day after." She smiled faintly. "That I can promise you."

Sookim hesitated. "You will?"

Nisha shrugged. "Of course."

Sookim nodded. "All right," she said.

Nisha finally released the woman's hands and squeezed her shoulder. "Be bold!" she said. "Aren't you the woman who helped to take back this whole village from the men who used to rule it with pain and fear?"

Sookim smiled sadly. "Sometimes I wonder who I am. Sometimes none of it makes sense to me."

"Well, this is not the time to think of that," said Nisha. "Go back to your people now. Give them your advice. Help them. They need you."

Reluctantly, Sookim stepped away. "And what will you do?" she asked.

"I'll sit for a while longer," said Nisha. "And I'll look out across the land."

Sookim nodded. "Very well. I'll—be back later."

Nisha waited as the woman's footsteps receded. Then she sighed and closed her eyes.

Hawk Spirit, she called.

At first there was no answer. Then she sensed the hawk's mind. The sharpness of it had been dulled. It was dozing in the heat of the day. It had been sated by its bloody feast.

Come to me, Hawk Spirit, Nisha called.

Sluggishly, reluctantly, the hawk stirred. Nisha glimpsed treetops as the bird launched itself into the air. There was the familiar feeling of disorientation as the ground receded and turned, and then she saw herself from afar.

She opened her eyes. The hawk was coasting toward her. She held out her arm and then waited without moving as the hawk came close, spread its wings wide, thrust out its talons, and perched upon her.

Nisha looked at the hawk admiringly. *So strong,* she thought, *so fierce, and so free.*

She reached up to the object hanging around her neck. She had knotted the broken thong, and the flint knife was dangling like a pendant between her breasts. But she had decided, now, there was a better place for it to be.

Carefully, trying not to disturb the hawk, she used her free hand to pull the thong up and over her head. She took the thong between her teeth, bit through it, and let it fall away. Then she held out the knife.

Take this, she said in her mind. She conjured up a picture of Winnor's home in the town of many houses. *Give it to the man who taught me how to use a bow and arrow. He will recognize it, Hawk Spirit, because it was a sacred object in his tribe. It will show him that I overcame my enemy, and that I'm thinking of him now. And he'll be wise enough to see that next month or next year—when the time is right—I'll return to him.*

She didn't know how much the hawk understood. It cocked its head and eyed the flint knife, then looked at her face.

Take it, she repeated. She held the knife out in front of the bird's feet.

The hawk stepped off her arm and closed its talons around the flint blade.

Once again, Nisha imagined the town of many houses. She pictured Winnor's face. And suddenly the hawk threw up its wings and beat them furiously, soaring into the sky.

Nisha shaded her eyes. She watched the bird rise and circle around; then, decisively, it flew to the south.

Nisha smiled as she watched the hawk go on its way. She sat and stared until the bird was a tiny black speck. "Keearrrh!" she cried to it.

And then it was gone.

Author's Note

This book completes the trilogy that began with *Children of the Ice* and continued with *People of the Mesa*. Several thousand years have elapsed since the mesa was colonized in the second volume of this series. A great transformation has occurred—literally the end of one era and the beginning of a new one.

Thousands of primitive people entered the North American continent in paleolithic times. They multiplied and spread across the land, apparently wiping out entire animal species that had no fear of them. For a while, there seemed to be an unlimited supply of food for the killing, and humanity flourished. But then, as the easy supplies of game were exhausted, there was a population crash caused by mass starvation.

The few survivors had to develop a new way of life in harmony with their environment. They limited their population growth via various rituals (such as testing the strength of infants, as described in this novel). More importantly, instead of continuing to feed themselves by hunting and gathering, they developed agriculture.

There is ample evidence that by 1,000 years B.C., agriculture had become the primary means by which many tribes survived. And as they learned to cultivate the land, they had to give up their nomadic habits and make permanent homes close to their crops, so that they could tend them year round.

In the American West, two tribes built amazingly complex societies. The Anasazi created cliff dwellings such as the one described in this novel, which is loosely based on the famous ruins at Mesa Verde in Colorado (now a national park). Meanwhile, the Hohokam developed sophisticated agricultural systems in valleys farther west where there was a reliable supply of water that enabled them to irrigate a variety of crops. Hohokam ruins are less well preserved than the Anasazi sites, but are much larger in scale, and much more elaborate.

The Anasazi and Hohokam communities ultimately dispersed for reasons that are still unknown. Their beautiful, ambitious dwelling places were abandoned long before Europeans colonized the American West.

What is known, however, is that nomadic tribes were gradually replaced by firmly rooted, self-sustaining societies that enabled people to live in relative freedom from hunger and fear. Trade was developed, and arts such as pottery and weaving were perfected. And in this way, to a limited extent, savagery gave way to an early form of civilization.

⊘ SIGNET

FASCINATING SAGAS

☐ **THE MIDWIFE'S ADVICE by Gay Courter.** "A terrific read . . . Hannah Sokolow is back, cutting a vibrant path through New York in the early 1900s and teaching her patients that women deserve full-blown eroticism as much as men do."—Noah Gordon, author of *Shaman* (176928—$5.99)

☐ **SHAMAN by Noah Gordon.** Sweeping across decades of change and conflict, growth and loss, this majestic epic brims with medical authenticity and the tumult of America in the making. "Powerful, unflinching."—*The New York Times Book Review* (177010—$5.99)

☐ **A DANGEROUS TEMPTATION by Barbara Kyle.** This is the story of Honor Larke, lady-in-waiting to the first Queen of King Henry VIII of England. But the king wants to divorce his wife in favor of his sultry mistress, Anne Boleyn. Now Honor must takes sides, as she moves from being a pawn to being a player in a game of power, passion, and perfidy . . . a dangerous game in which a single mistake would mean certain and fiery death.
(179323—$4.99)

☐ **A DANGEROUS DEVOTION by Barbara Kyle.** Henry VIII of England was dead, with the blood of his wives on his hands. His vengeful daughter Mary took the throne, vowing to wipe his memory from the land. In the cruel carnage that swept the realm, no one who favored Henry was safe, not even the brave and honorable Robert Thornleigh. Only his dazzlingly beautiful daughter Isabel could rescue him from prison and brutal death.
(179331—$5.99)

*Prices slightly higher in Canada

THE FLAMES OF TREASON
AND TREACHERY ENGULF THE
PROSPERING COLONIES

RENNO—Born among white men, raised among the Seneca, he is the great chief who must unite two worlds.

JA-GONH—Renno's pride, every inch his father's son. First he would win honor, then be forced into exile, and, finally, return triumphant to avenge his grandfather's death.

AH-WEN-GA—The lovely daughter of an aged Seneca war chief, she must live like his daughter but fight like his son.

GOO-GA-RO-NO—Renno's daughter, who follows her passion for a Frenchman and pays a bitter price.

ROGER HARKNESS—An English soldier of fortune, he comes to the New World to fight at Renno's side.

GRAY FOX—A Huron, an agent of the French, he moves through the Indian nations like a serpent wreaking havoc, fanning the flames of war.